As she ascended to the dry foothills, she did not consider where such a meeting might lead. She only knew she had to see Tall Man again. She had never felt more completely alive as she followed the beaconing light above her. She lost it when she entered the pine-clad ridge above and experienced a moment of anxiety that she might not be able to find him, but he had followed her progress from his hiding place and appeared before her suddenly on his pinto pony.

She reined in for a moment, overwhelmed by her reaction to seeing him again. He was everything she remembered, and she gazed at him with awe, the forest surrounding them receding from her vision. His clear, handsome features had been engraved on her heart for so long that it responded by beating rapidly in her chest. He rode forward to take her reins without speaking and led her upward through the trees until they reached a spring feeding a small pond.

"We are safe here," he told her. . . .

WALK IN BEAUTY

Sabina Grant

FAWCETT GOLD MEDAL • NEW YORK

Part 1

Beauty above me,
Beauty behind me,
Beauty beneath me,
Beauty before me,
All about me is beauty.
I walk in beauty.

—NAVAJO SONG

Chapter 1

Elspeth breathed in the thin air and felt that earth and sky had never come together more harmoniously than in this place, on the final day of their journey on the Santa Fe Trail. The unfettered blue of the New Mexican sky was complemented by the dun-colored earth and the pine trees high in the Sangre de Cristo Mountains on their left, and she wished they could pause so she could paint it, though her watercolors were packed somewhere deep in their belongings in the back of the wagon. She knew she would see some Indians soon. Her blue-green eyes had been alert for them for many weeks. And the Spanish wonders of Santa Fe, which her brother-in-law had been expounding for nearly a year in Massachusetts and all the way across the plains, were only a few hours away, now. She clutched her long hands together in the lap of her wrinkled cotton skirt to conceal the surge of adventure she was feeling, but it was difficult to suppress her interest in everything around her. She did not dare ask her brother-in-law about Indians again. Captain Morrison did not have the same interest in them as she did. He viewed them as savage enemies, because he had fought them in the past, not as the noble children of nature that Elspeth and her sister had come to think of them in Boston. He sat beside her in the front of the only civilian wagon in the mule-drawn army supply train they had joined in Fort Leavenworth, and in spite of her efforts to please him, she could not hold her tongue altogether.

3

"Why are the mountains called Blood of Christ?" she asked. "Are the sunsets there more splendid than elsewhere?"

"I have no idea," he replied, without taking his concentration off the team. "Really, Elspeth, for a young lady of sixteen, you ask more questions than a child. Can't something have a name without your knowing how it got it?"

Thea's husband had to be different from other men, she thought. If he were not, there was very little to look forward to in life. Her only salvation from being a dependent in his household would be by marriage some day, and if other men were like the captain, marriage would not improve her situation. She thought of her sister, resting in the rear of the wagon; indeed, her thoughts were seldom far from Thea. Her health was the reason the captain had proposed and carried out their relocation to the Southwest, but the long, difficult journey had been hard for Thea. Like her mother and father, Thea had a weak chest, and her constitution had not been strong enough to endure the heat and dust and a suspense as long as the low-brushed plains when the soldiers were on constant alert for Comanche. Even Elspeth's high spirits had begun to flag on the plains. She would almost have welcomed an Indian attack to break the monotony. The captain should have kept his stories of Indian outrages to himself, instead of describing the Comanche Death Circle and leaving a loaded handgun beside Thea's cot with instructions for her to use it on Elspeth and herself if the Comanche overwhelmed the supply train. Thea's consumptive fever made her excitable enough without all that. Elspeth had spent hours reading to her sister in an attempt to calm her, and they practiced their Spanish together while she secretly scanned the low horizon between the ropes and canvas. If a war party was really about, she wanted to see it. It was not that she did not believe the possibility of attack; she was just too young to think that they would harm her or Thea. She could not take open exception to anything the captain said or did, though, even when his actions seemed ill-advised. The man in the family always knew best, or was supposed to. Even in her father's household, that had been the case. For many years, Elspeth had wished she had been born a boy; if she had, she would have gone to sea long before now.

"Thea should be up here with us when Santa Fe comes into

view," she said without thinking. "She hasn't seen very much. It would be good for her."

"She's ill, Elspeth," the captain said tersely. "I couldn't slow the wagon now anyway. My friends in the army were good enough to allow us to accompany them. We can't cause any delay. The wagon isn't balanced right because of that damned loom. It isn't easy to control."

The loom was something better not discussed. He had threatened to jettison it every morning since they left Fort Union, when he secured the ropes. There had been a terrible scene about the loom when they were packing, and he had complained about it ever since, almost as if he wanted to leave their entire life behind them: their house, their books, their music, their very Welshness. Thea finally had to beg to take their mother's loom on the grounds that it had more than sentimental value. Both she and Elspeth enjoyed weaving; the things they made on it were practical. She argued that she had already given up her piano and their servant; she would not give up the loom. The captain muttered something about "damned Welsh weavers," a remark Elspeth found difficult to forgive. He capitulated only when Elspeth showed him how easily the large vertical loom could be dismantled to conserve space. So the loom had traveled with them, its harnesses, beater, and treadles carefully wrapped in old quilts, while he continued to curse its presence.

Thea was infinitely patient, Elspeth thought. She had maintained her good humor throughout the ordeal of the trip; and, only this morning, when her husband was abusing the loom again, she was more amused than upset by his tirade.

"I suppose he must take his frustrations out on something," she said, with a faint smile. "All this can't be easy for him, either. His fate is to cart me around and care for both of us. We must remember that he has traveled this far for me, Elspeth."

"I'll stay back here with you today," Elspeth volunteered, adjusting Thea's handwoven shawl against the cool morning air, but her sister would not hear of it.

"On the day of our arrival? You'll do nothing of the sort. I want you to see everything, so you can describe it to me later. Aside from his displeasure over the loom, Robert hasn't been horrid, has he?"

Elspeth was silent for only a moment before she shook her head. "Of course not," she replied brightly. "He's been very good about teaching me Spanish. We wouldn't have learned much just with a textbook and dictionary, as we tried to do in Boston. He seems to speak it quite well.''

"You've learned more than I have," Thea said ruefully. "I've often dozed when you've tried to give me lessons. Aside from being my eyes and ears today, you'll probably have to interpret for me later. You're so clever, Elspeth. Father was right when he said you were the strongest one in the family. If anyone was spared this disease, I'm glad it was you.''

Thea spoke sincerely, and Elspeth experienced a feeling of guilt about her own robust health in the face of her sister's frailty. "I'm not clever," she said in an attempt not to discuss Thea's illness. "I just have this awful curiosity about everything. I'd rather be as beautiful as you than have such an inquiring mind." She did not tell her that the captain had referred to both of them as "bluestockings" the other day, because of their education and views. She should not have expressed their ideas about slavery to him, apparently. "I wish I were as musical as you, and that I could sing instead of painting and writing poetry," she said wistfully. "If I were an envious person, I'd envy your dark hair, too. It's so lovely, and mine is so colorless and drab."

Her hair was as thick and heavy as her sister's, but it was an indeterminate shade of brown and still braided like the school-girl she had so recently been—until the captain withdrew her from the Frobisher School for Young Ladies. Their fine-boned faces revealed their relationship, but Thea was the beauty of the family with her pale skin and blue eyes. Everything about Elspeth, except her active mind, was more subdued than in her sister. Her complexion was darker; her braided hair, which was medium to light brown, had never been exposed to full sunlight though it had a natural sheen; her eyes were neither blue nor green; and, when she lowered her lashes, as she had begun to do this past winter, her beauty was easily surpassed by her sister's. Not self-effacing by nature, her position in her brother-in-law's household, as she hovered on the brink of womanhood, made her quieter than usual. Only when the full force of her intelligent aquamarine eyes fell upon someone was her potential realized, though she was not aware of it yet.

At Thea's wedding three years before, there had been no cloud over Elspeth's life. Though her mother had not lived to see her eldest daughter married, their father, David Williams, had found prosperity in America after leaving his native Wales when the girls were small. The home he provided was happy and comfortable, and he allowed Elspeth the freedom to pursue her interests; she was able to read and dream and spend long hours at her mother's loom. At the time of the wedding, he was planning to open another fabric mill. His daughters were so precious to him that he encouraged Thea to remain at home when the captain was posted to the New Mexico Territory. Thea's constitution had always been frail; he feared the rugged life on the frontier might destroy her. Ironically, shortly after her husband returned to Boston, it was David Williams himself who had died. The captain resigned from the army almost immediately to devote all his time to his wife's financial affairs, and he began to speak of the healthful climate of New Mexico and of the people who had been cured of lung ailments there. Once he had made his decision, Elspeth's schooling was not considered. That was when she recognized her new position in life.

She had never been able to call him by his Christian name. If he had not been a captain, she would have called him Mr. Morrison. He constantly corrected the Welsh elements in their speech and grew stern if one of them used an expression like "in by there," but he had not been able to eradicate the lilting quality of their voices. Like many Welsh people who had not been able to adapt themselves to the Church of England, they were not overly religious, though they attended church so Thea could sing in the choir. The captain was proud of his wife's voice, as though it were an attribute he had acquired for himself, without realizing that music was another aspect of their Welshness, part of their very souls, which must have an outlet. He did not know about Elspeth's poetry, because it was so personal that she shared it only with her sister.

She had not written poetry for a long time, though lines lilted constantly through her head. She had not painted or drawn, either. Once the preparations for the journey began, she had little time for anything else. She had been too busy getting all the linens and their clothing laundered and packed into their trunks, and filling barrels with carefully wrapped china and glass, performing all of the tasks that would be too exerting for Thea. Sensing that her position was to undertake these tasks and care for her sister, she threw all of her energy into what was expected of her. She loved her sister, wanted nothing more than to see her better again. The realization that the captain considered her no more than a servant—instead of a young girl who missed her father and required at least minimal affection—embittered her slightly, but it did not deter her from hoping for a better life for all of them.

Beyond the fact that living in the Southwest would be good for her sister, Elspeth found herself becoming excited by the opportunity to see something of the world. The New Mexico Territory had come to the United States only twelve years before, after the war with Mexico, and it still retained its Spanish flavor. And, then, there were the Indians. She and Thea had been brought up to deplore unfairness and had espoused the cause of the American Indian for some time, just as they deplored slavery in the South, an issue very popular in Boston in 1860. The captain was not accurate in designating the Williams sisters "bluestocking"; they did not join groups of women for literary and social lectures. In the quiet of their home, they followed events that interested them and discussed them between themselves. They favored Mr. Lincoln in the upcoming presidential campaign solely on his platform that the country could not remain "half-slave and half-free." They had written a letter to Washington regarding the displacement and genocide of the Western Indians. Elspeth suspected that Thea did not express her opinions to her husband in private, and Elspeth knew instinctively that she must keep her own enthusiasms to herself. Her father had once remarked that Elspeth had inherited her mother's legendary intuition, which almost bordered on second sight. She did not understand such things, but she was aware of some things before they actually happened, and her misgivings about the captain bothered her. She had tried to like him, even rationalized that it was her position in his household that was really troubling her, but, no matter how hard she tried to bridge their differences, an invisible wall stood between them which she could not overcome.

She glanced at him as he sat beside her in the front of the wagon. He appeared more relaxed with the tension of the plains behind him, but she could not read his expression. Elspeth had thought him very handsome in his uniform when he married Thea, but, by some mysterious metamorphosis, he had shed most of his good looks when he resigned from the army. His eyes were the same shade as his tightly waving tan hair. His wide jaw and short nose combined to give him what she could only describe as a "piggy" appearance, though his physique was still as trim as it had been. A few times during the past weeks, he had been almost playful with her when she was practicing her Spanish; then, just as suddenly, his mood would change, making her search her mind for something she might have said to offend him. She almost preferred it when he was consistently stern, as he had been in Massachusetts.

"We aren't stopping in Santa Fe," he announced now, without looking at her. "I've decided to push on, so we can reach Don Diego's *estancia* before dark. Incidentally, Santa Fe means 'Sacred Faith,' the Catholic one, of course. You're so interested in place names."

She did not care about names as she struggled with his startling statement. Their destination had been Santa Fe from the beginning; there was a house awaiting them there. He had described it in detail many times during the winter; she felt as if a secure rug had been snatched from beneath her. Had they been following a mirage, which receded just when it was within reach, like those they had seen in the desert? She stared at him in bewilderment. He had never mentioned anyone named Don Diego. He had spoken only of their comfortable adobe house in Santa Fe and of the pleasant Mexican servants who would be awaiting their arrival. She tried to compose herself. Perhaps their house was near that of this Don Diego, whoever he was. Yes, that was the only reasonable answer. They were being welcomed by a friend, so they could rest for the night before all the confusion of moving into a new home. He had thought everything out carefully, considering only Thea, who had not rested in a comfortable bed for such a long time.

"Does Don Diego live near us?" she asked quietly as the first flat-roofed adobe houses of Santa Fe came into view through the dust in front of them. He urged the team forward nonchalantly, letting her question hang in the warm air for so long that she did not expect an answer. She would not antagonize him by repeating it.

"We'll be staying with him for a while," he finally told her. "He's a close friend of mine, an important man. I have business with him. I may even build my house near his at the foot of the mountains."

* * *

Her concern for her sister dimmed her first impression of Santa Fe, which appeared dusty and flat and drab, dwarfed in importance by the wide expanse of the sky and the mountains around it. Her initial reaction to what she saw around her was that it was a poor Mexican town, hardly a city at all, and not really Spanish, either, though the Americans did not seem to have made any changes in the decade they had been here, aside from building Fort Marcy, which flew the American flag on a rise behind the old Palace of the Governors. Someone had recently planted a few bedraggled cottonwoods and dug some irrigation ditches to sustain them at the edge of the Plaza. The somnolent population appeared to be mostly Mexican, though there were a few American traders in the garb of mountain men leaning against the mud-walled buildings surrounding the Plaza, nearly lost among the natives with colorful striped serapes over their shoulders. The white dresses worn by the Mexican women would have been indecent in Boston, but Elspeth envied them a little in the heat of the day. The army wagons were held up in their ascent to Fort Marcy, and the captain could not leave the train until the wagons in front of them moved, so Elspeth had about ten minutes to observe her surroundings.

"You've been harping about Indians," the captain said sarcastically. "There should be enough there in the Plaza to satisfy you."

Vendors stood or crouched beside their vegetables and fruits in the Plaza. There were some stockily built men and women who wore their hair differently, cut in bangs across their foreheads and bound into a tight chignon in back. Their clothing differed little from that of the Mexicans, except that they wore moccasins. The women bound their legs in broad white strips of leather, making them appear larger than normal. A few people wore blankets less colorful than the serapes as they sat impassively in the sunlight. They stared at the wagons without interest and disregarded her attempt to smile.

"They're peaceful enough," she remarked. "A handsome people . . . and they aren't red at all. It's difficult to distinguish them from the Mexicans."

The captain grunted. He had barely looked at them. "Indians are Indians. Don't let their looks deceive you. The Pueblos haven't given us any trouble for a while, but they went on a rampage and killed the American governor in Taos a few years back. When the Spanish were here, the red devils took over the Palace of the Governors for a period of about twelve years and used the chapel for their pagan rites. A Catholic chapel used as a kiva,'' he said, with a faint grin. "That would have been something to see. Never trust an Indian, Elspeth. You never know what he's thinking. He may be fancying your scalp."

He maneuvered their wagon onto a street at the far edge of the Plaza and waved the army wagon behind him on, shouting a few words of thanks and promising to see them at the fort in the near future. Elspeth waved at the soldiers, with whom they had spent so many weeks and miles, experiencing almost a sense of loss for the comrades who had treated them with kindness on the long journey. She was conscious of a feeling of emptiness as another wagon closed the space that their civilian one had left. She was completely alone with the captain now, dependent only upon him for everything. Perhaps it would not be so bad staying with someone else for a while. When he had male companions, he tended to ignore her. It would probably best for Thea, too, until she regained her strength, though she dreaded telling her that their house was not even built yet.

They passed a large adobe church, which looked as old as the Palace of the Governors, and she noticed that it was maintained better than the smaller church they had passed as they entered the city.

"Our Lady of the Assumption,'' the captain remarked. "Don Diego's family attend it when a priest can't come out to them. They dislike the bishop intensely, because he's a Frenchman."

"French?'' Her curiosity was stirred. "What's a French bishop doing in new Mexico?"

"Came to clean up the clergy after the war, as I understand it. Sent by the American Archdiocese. He was a missionary among the Indians in the Great Lakes region or something, with a good record of conversions. The Mexicans and Spaniards didn't make much headway with the Indians for some reason. That's something else you must watch out for here. The damned Catholics will try to get you under their wing."

She wondered why the Indians had to be converted at all; as she understood it, they had their own religions. Her father had professed to be a pagan Celt at heart; though no one had taken him entirely seriously, religion had not played as great a part in their lives as it had in the families of her friends. Her thoughts were interrupted when the captain drew up the wagon and tied his reins in place. "Crawl into the back and get our coffee cups," he said, brushing his forehead with his bandanna. "I can get some food at a little cantina I know, if it's still there. I could use a drink, and we'll need something to tide us over. The de la Cruzes don't dine until eight."

"Thea should have some milk," she reminded him as she disappeared into the back of the wagon, where her sister was sitting unsteadily on her cot. The tin cups were packed where Elspeth had put them this morning after making their breakfast, and she moved in the crowded area with difficulty to take them back to him. She remained with her sister when he walked away with them.

"Are you all right, Thea?" she asked in the hot, dusty canvas interior. "Would you like to get out for a while?"

Thea smiled wanly. "This 'beneficial' air's a little hard to breathe," she said, with a hand on her chest. "The elevation must be as high as Robert said it was. Did you see the Indians in the Plaza? I caught a glimpse of them by sitting up. Don't look so crestfallen, Elspeth dear. I did hear about our house. When I'm not dozing, I can hear most of what you're saying up front."

"I'm sorry," Elspeth sighed, putting her arm around her sister's shoulders. "But it may be all right, after all, Thea. You need a good, long rest. Has the captain ever mentioned this Don Diego to you?"

"Yes. They became friends when Robert was stationed here. Don Diego's from an old Spanish family that's been here for generations. I don't know what he had in common with Robert, who was only a lieutenant then. I'm sure Robert knows best, Elspeth, but I am disappointed about our house. I don't want to be a burden on someone else's hospitality."

"You're never a burden," Elspeth assured her, concerned about her sister's shallow breathing and hoping it was just the altitude. "If I can find your comb and brush, I'll tidy your hair while we're waiting. We should look as nice as possible when we arrive."

"I suppose it's too much to hope that any of the frocks in the trunks will be less wrinked than what we're wearing," Thea said while Elspeth brushed her long, black hair. "Sleeping on one's dress doesn't improve its appearance, and yours isn't much better than mine.''

"The de la Cruz family will understand," Elspeth consoled her. "We've just completed a rather grueling trip, Thea. I'll press some of our dresses when we get there.''

"Robert didn't actually tell us the house was built, did he?'' her sister asked quietly. "I really thought he had.''

Elspeth, who was certain that he had, wondered if he had been describing someone else's house, perhaps that of his friend, Don Diego, but she smiled reassuringly. "It's better this way. You can see the plans before it's built, and everything will be just as you want it. Thea, are you all right?''

Her sister smiled and removed her hand from her heaving chest. "We've lived at sea level all our lives," she said wryly. "Now we're at six thousand feet. Robert warned me I'd feel it at first. It'll be good for me when I become accustomed to it. My doctor did recommend a change of climate, you know.''

The doctor had recommended Italy, but Elspeth did not remind her sister of that as she pinned her hair neatly in place. The only assurance that this place would be good for Thea came from the captain's stories of all the people who had been cured. But the warm, dry air should help Thea, who had been growing worse in Massachusetts. She was tidying her own hair when the captain appeared at the rear of the wagon, and she had to relieve him of the steaming cups of coffee he was balancing on the end of a slatted wooden crate.

"No milk," he explained lightly, "but the food smells just as good as it did when I was here before. Tostadas with beans and chilies.'' He scooped one up and handed it to Thea, who hesitated, not knowing how to attack the delicacy without a knife and fork. "Just balance the tortilla like this . . . and eat," he instructed, illustrating the process, an expression of satisfaction on his face as he chewed.

While Thea hesitated, Elspeth bit into hers and the hot green chilies burned her mouth, nearly bringing tears to her eyes. The captain watched her with amusement, and she was determined not to back down, even if her throat was burned out. Actually, the food was rather good, what she could taste beyond the chilies. Preoccupied with her defiance of what could only have been meant as a rather unkind joke, she did not warn Thea, who was thrown into a coughing fit by her introduction to Mexican food.

Her sister's reaction made the joke too unkind, and she lowered her eyelids so the captain would not see the anger in her eyes.

"Perhaps you can find something more suitable for Thea," she suggested evenly. "She's been having some difficulty breathing at this height, Captain, and she's never eaten anything that hot before."

He regarded the two young women with displeasure as he backed away from the wagon. "All right, but she'll have to eat while we're moving. And you'll both have to adapt to new ways. You should have enough Spanish to speak to Don Diego's sisters. They don't speak English. I'm the only American they've met since we won the Territory."

Thea glanced at Elspeth with alarm, but Elspeth squeezed her arm encouragingly. "You've probably learned more than you think," she consoled her. "It'll be all right. You'll see."

Chapter 2

The loose, white clothing of the Mexican laborers working in their fields was more suitable than their own in the late afternoon heat. Thea fanned herself with her hand without taking her gaze from the dim purple mountains ahead of them. She had insisted upon riding in the front of the wagon, but she was already beginning to wilt and Elspeth supported most of her weight.

"I've never seen so many farms," Thea remarked. "Surely, we'll be reaching your friend's house soon, Robert. I didn't realize he lived so far from the city."

The captain laughed pleasantly. "It's all one farm, my dear. Don Diego's. The land's been in his family for generations. The legality of the Spanish land grants has been questioned recently, but no one's attempted to evict him yet. The peons, all those workers, live here year round."

Elspeth consulted the small Spanish dictionary she kept in her apron pocket and discovered that a peon was a person who worked to pay off a debt. It seemed impossible that so many Mexican workers were indebted to Don Diego. And, when the captain had referred to his friend's holdings as an *estancia*, a small farm, the word had certainly been a misnomer; this was a very large estate, a hacienda, or perhaps a rancho, if Don Diego also raised cattle.

The captain indicated a high adobe wall up ahead. "We're almost there. Everything is contained within those walls: the house, the stables and servants' quarters, even a well. The place was built to withstand a siege by marauding Indians, because it's only a few miles from the mountains.''

Thea attempted to smooth her wrinkled dress and sighed helplessly. ''We look dreadful. I don't know what your friend and his family will think of us. We really should have spent the night in Santa Fe, so we could make ourselves presentable, Robert.''

He did not reply, and Elspeth wondered what business he had with Don Diego that was so important he did not consider presenting his wife in the best light. When she had reassured Thea that their host would understand their appearance, she had not realized they would be staying in the home of an hidalgo, a member of the nobility.

A young Mexican wearing leather pants and carrying a rifle slipped through the heavy wooden gate as their rattling wagon approached. A smile of recognition crossed his dark face, and he issued a command. The gate was open when they reached it, several Mexicans already running toward it. Elspeth understood the greetings that passed between the captain and the guard, and the guard's subsequent orders to the Mexicans inside the wall. Her confidence in her Spanish was restored. After some difficulty maneuvering the team and wagon through the opening into the compound, the captain drove into a beaten earth courtyard that accommodated the wagon easily. He threw the wooden brake on the wheels and tied his reins in place before climbing down to assist Thea and herself. One of the servants was different from the others, Elspeth noticed; he did not look like the other Mexicans. His long, matted hair was full of straw, as if he slept in the stables, and he carried himself with an air of defeat in his dirty white garments. Their gazes met briefly, but she could read no expression in his dark eyes, and he turned to care for the mules as though he had not seen her. He was young, much younger than she, and she was struck by the absence of hope in his bearing. Her attention was diverted from him when the wagon suddenly began to move on without them.

''Wait!'' she cried in English. ''We must get our things. Our trunks . . .'' Before she could reshape the words into Spanish, the captain's hand tightened on her arm.

''For God's sake, Elspeth,'' he cautioned her. ''Your things will be brought to the house. There are servants to look after such things.''

She flushed with embarrassment and hoped the Mexicans had not understood her. The captain escorted Thea and herself across the courtyard toward the wooden verandah of a sprawling, one-storied adobe house. Sweet-smelling vines shaded the porch and trees clustered around it, providing the only shade Elspeth had seen in the compound. Two women dressed in crisp cotton frocks, with lace shawls over their hair and shoulders, awaited them in the coolness beneath the vines, but there was no sign of the master of the house. As the captain introduced the de la Cruz sisters, she observed that they were in their early thirties and wore golden crosses around their necks. Doña Elena, the younger of the two, had a serene oval face and soft dark eyes. She seemed delighted over the prospect of female companionship. Her older sister's face was more severe. Frown lines had already set between Doña Isabella's sharp black eyes. Her face was a stern mask. Elspeth found it easy to understand why she was a spinster, but she wondered about Doña Elena. The only thing alarming about the ladies was that she could hardly understand a word they spoke. Both sisters seemed to have a speech impediment, which made it impossible for them to pronounce many syllables without a lisp. Either that, or the captain had instructed her with the wrong accent. When he urged Elspeth to respond to their questions, she smiled dumbly, not certain what the questions were, and Doña Elena kindly placed her hand on Elspeth's shoulder as they entered the house.

"Don Diego won't be back until this evening," the captain told Thea. "The ladies have offered us refreshments, and you can bathe and rest until dinner. The servants are taking care of your wardrobe."

"I can't understand them," Thea admitted quietly. "Not a word, Robert."

"Castilian's slightly different," he conceded. "Not the lingua franca of New Mexico that I taught you. You'll learn to understand them. I do, though I speak to them in Mexican."

"It's wonderfully cool in here," Thea murmured as they entered a room that Elspeth thought must be the parlor. White walls and dark wooden beams encompassed the elegantly simple area, which contained several carved chests, some intricately doweled wooden chairs, and a leather sofa. A circular wrought-iron chandelier with half-burned candles hovered over them, an iron chain securing it to a hook on the wall, so it could be raised and lowered. A small, conical hearth, which swelled from the adobe wall, was, surprisingly, in one corner of the room, unlike any fireplace she had ever seen. She felt that she was actually in a foreign land, at last, as she appreciated these marvels.

The captain escorted Thea to the leather settee and indicated that Elspeth take the place beside her as the de la Cruz sisters sat down across from them on chairs that seemed to have been built to accommodate their full skirts. Elspeth was grateful that her position in the captain's household did not necessitate conversation as they awaited the refreshments that Doña Isabella had ordered as they entered.

"Doña Elena welcomes you with affection," the captain translated grudgingly. "We are invited to stay until we are settled, and she hopes it will be for a long time." Thea again mentioned the coolness of the house, and he interpreted their hostesses' reply. "The walls are nearly three feet thick—to keep out the heat of summer and the cold of winter. They're remarkably well-suited to the climate." He seemed slightly on edge, either uncomfortable in the position of interpreter, which had been thrust upon him, or because of the absence of the friend he had been so anxious to see. "The Spaniards were intelligent enough to adopt the architecture of the Indians," he explained on his own. "The vigas, the roof beams, are strictly Pueblo, the same as the fireplace. Most adobes have only one story, because second stories begin to sag."

He was interrupted by Doña Elena, who had caught the essence of his explanation. "She says their house is over a hundred years old and requires constant maintenance," he translated. "There are workmen of all types here. But the adobe brick floor is the original one." He tapped at the worn bricks with his toe and added, "The Spaniards added ox blood to their bricks to make them harder and deeper in color."

Thea reflexively raised the hem of her skirt from the floor with a shocked expression on her face. Elspeth managed to control herself better, though the vision of a slaughterhouse and bleeding, bellowing oxen filled her mind. She wondered if the captain got some morbid satisfaction when he succeeded in distressing them. "Customs differ," she heard herself telling him.

"I'm sure it was practical. The bricks have survived for so long, and they are still quite lovely."

"Yes," Thea agreed quickly, "their age alone makes them attractive." Then, smiling at her hostesses, she added for translation, "Your home is very beautiful."

Elspeth could have said as much in Spanish, but she felt self-conscious speaking the language to these high-born ladies. An uncomfortable silence descended upon them, which was broken only when a Mexican woman appeared bearing a tray heaped with fresh fruit around a blue glass pitcher and glasses. Doña Isabella solemnly poured cool lemonade for each of them, while her livelier sister passed the fruit to her guests. Elspeth tried not to consume a peach and some grapes too greedily. She had not realized how starved she was for fresh fruit, and she wondered if there would be garden vegetables for dinner. They ate in silence. Aside from their initial greeting to the captain and their use of him as an interpreter, the de la Cruz sisters had not addressed him directly, almost as if it were improper to do so.

Doña Elena offered to show Elspeth to her room, and Doña Isabella put Thea and the captain into the care of a servant, who led them all down a dim hallway. Elspeth was directed into her room first and immediately stopped thinking of the others. A hot bath awaited her, and the lace-trimmed white sheets had been turned back invitingly on the canopied bed. Doña Elena introduced her to a middle-aged Mexican woman who smiled pleasantly, indicating the bar of soap in her hand. The amenities were so welcome that Elspeth grasped Doña Elena's smooth hand impulsively.

"*Gracias,*" she said shyly. "*Gracias,* Doña Elena."

The gentle Spanish woman, who would have graced the home of any man, touched Elspeth's hair and smiled at her, but Elspeth understood only the words, "poor dear child" when she spoke. After Doña Elena departed, Elspeth found herself conversing almost without hesitation with her matronly Mexican maid, Concepcion.

She awoke late in the evening and took stock of her surroundings for the first time. Her room was larger and airier than her room in Massachusetts. Heavy brocade drapes covered the sides of her bed, drawn back with a gold fringe to reveal the room. When she sat up, she found herself facing a painting of a haloed saint with roses in her white hands and an expression of religious fervor on her face, the oil pigments darkened by age. The dark, intricately spiraled walnut furniture seemed to be old, too, though it was so highly polished that her finger left an imprint when she touched it. She wondered if it had been transported here from Spain by way of Mexico a century ago. The deep windowsill was too high to sit on comfortably, and she could only see part of the courtyard, which was illuminated by sconces protruding from the walls. The heavy gate was secured for the night, separating the inhabitants of the compound from the outside world. When she observed no movement in the growing darkness, she soon lost interest in the narrow view and returned to make her bed, though she suspected it was not her duty. On her attempt to replace the heavy lace spread that had been folded on a chest at the foot of the bed, she observed that it had been carefully mended in several places; perhaps it, too, was treasured because it had come all the way from Spain. A dusty aura pervaded the head of the bed, and she shook the brocade curtains cautiously. No dust appeared, but she realized that the fabric itself was thin enough to tear if she had shaken it harder. The Spanish fabrics in the Indian-styled house seemed to be wearing out, though they were carefully maintained. Since the family seemed affluent enough to replace both lace and brocade, Elspeth assumed that the de la Cruzes did not wish to alter any part of their old life. The Spaniards had lost the Territory to Mexico in 1822, but this house—with its uneven brick floors— had maintained its Spanish character during the Mexican rule and for thirteen years under the Americans, indicating a pride in heritage that Elspeth had not encountered before. She was considering what she had learned of Spanish history when there was a light tapping on the door and Concepcion entered without waiting for her to answer.

The jovial woman held one of Elspeth's nicest frocks across her arms, freshly pressed and ready to wear, the rose-sprigged white organdy billowing out as she walked. "You must dress for dinner," Concepcion told her. "The *padron* returned late and dinner was delayed for him. You were sleeping so soundly that I did not wish to awaken you."

Elspeth was not surprised to hear Don Diego referred to as a nobleman in this house. The room had revealed some of the house's secrets, and she had always been quick to sense the mood of her surroundings. She marveled that her dress had been discovered in her trunk, though, and pressed while she was sleeping. She slipped into the petticoat that accompanied it and allowed Concepcion to assist her with the dress.

"I've always done my own hair," she objected quickly when Concepcion picked up the hairbrush. "It's very simple, really. I'll just rebraid it."　　　•

"Not while I'm your maid," Concepcion said, leading her to the dressing table. She began to unbraid Elspeth's hair efficiently, and there was a pleasant pride in her voice when she exclaimed, "How thick it is! I would like to give you curls, but that would not be proper for a young girl. A young lady must be proper in every way if she wants a husband some day."

That sentiment appeared to cross cultural borders, Elspeth thought with amusement. The goal was always the same. She nearly asked why the de la Cruz sisters had not married, but she checked herself in time, realizing that would be impertinent. She wanted to point out that she was a well-brought-up girl, who did not have to stop to consider what was proper, but she refrained from saying that, too. She wondered if she would be confined to the house, almost cloistered as the de la Cruz sisters appeared to be. She did not like that prospect; there was too much she wanted to see.

"Is Don Diego nice?" she asked, considering the subject neutral enough to mention, and she was surprised by Concepcion's disparaging grunt.

"Diego de la Cruz is not for you," she said firmly as she braided her hair, ignoring Elspeth's protest that she was not interested in him in that way. "What can I say? He's a *rico*, and the rich make their own rules. His wife died when little Francisco was born. He went all the way to Spain to get her, but she faded away and died. The poor lady. He has never returned there for another wife, though he may have to make the trip if the Americans try to take his land."

The brief biography agreed with Elspeth's previous impressions of the ties to Spain, but she wondered why he had not purchased new fabric for the bed curtains when he went in search of a wife. "How old is his son?" she asked.

"Seven," Concepcion replied fondly, "a beautiful child. But too lively for his maiden aunts, believe me. There," she said, appraising Elspeth critically, "you look like an angel, senorita.

A ribbon would be nice, but it is not necessary. You might get ideas about the *padron*, and you deserve better. I'll take you to your sister, now."

Elspeth was relieved by the effect of the long rest on her sister, who had more color in her face than had been there for some time. Thea looked calm and lovely in her blue silk gown, her shining black hair dressed in the curls that Elspeth had been denied. "You're beautiful," Elspeth told her, bending to kiss her forehead as she sat before the mirror. "Isn't it wonderful the way they found our gowns and had them ready for us?"

"If we have to dress for dinner every night, we'll soon exhaust our wardrobe," Thea remarked, with a smile. "Robert should have allowed us to bring more clothing. You look lovely, darling, but why didn't you get curls, too?"

"I'm too young. It isn't proper," Elspeth told her with a straight face. "I'll never catch a husband if I'm not proper, Thea—didn't you know that? Concepcion's wonderful. I'll be spoiled in no time. And I can actually understand what she says."

"I can understand Rosa a little, too. Better than I can the de la Cruzes, unfortunately; but Robert assured me we won't be here long. He intends to build our house quickly, I think. He doesn't like me to ask about it. He thinks I'm being ungrateful, that I should enjoy being treated like a fine lady."

"Don't you enjoy it?" Elspeth asked. "I thought it was interesting."

"Being treated like a lady is very much like being treated like an invalid, Elspeth. You wouldn't understand that, thank goodness. At least, you'll have some time to yourself while we're here. I imagine I'll be in the company of Doña Elena and her sister most of the time." She turned serious blue eyes on Elspeth. "Do you think you'll like it in the Territory? You didn't have much choice in the matter, and that's troubled me."

"Oh, yes!" Elspeth responded quickly. "Even without seeing much, I'm glad I came. Everything's so new and different, and the country's beautiful in its starkness, isn't it? I'm anxious to explore more of it."

"Now that you're rested, you're ready for anything again," Thea said, gazing at her fondly. "Perhaps we can return to Santa Fe soon. I'd enjoy that, too. The Indians didn't seem ill-treated there, did they? From what I could see from the wagon, they were trading openly and unmolested in the square."

Elspeth thought of the ill-kempt boy she had seen upon her arrival here and the peons in the fields, but she did not mention them. She was too new here to make judgments. "It's like being in a foreign country," she told Thea, voicing what she had been thinking. "There are so many things besides the language that we'll have to learn . . ."

The captain entered without knocking and seemed surprised to find Elspeth there. He was wearing his best suit, and everything about him exuded satisfaction. "Don Diego's back," he informed them, without realizing how quickly servants communicated news. "I've just spent half an hour with him, and things are working out just fine." Elspeth thought they must have discussed their house, but he did not mention it. "You look very nice. Remember who you're dining with tonight, and don't discuss your views on everything. What's acceptable in Boston might not be well received here."

"We're too hungry for conversation," Elspeth remarked, "even if we were capable of it. We can hardly understand their Spanish. It's unlikely we'll say anything offensive."

She felt as if she had stepped into a foreign place in a another time when they entered the dimly lit parlor. The ladies wore dark taffeta gowns which closed at the neck, with gold crosses suspended on heavy chains their only accessory, and despite the richness of the fabric, the effect was pious and severe. Don Diego did not belie the impression in his black suit with the tight trousers slashed at the ankles and bolero-style jacket trimmed with matching braid. He was every inch the hidalgo, more handsome than Elspeth had expected, light-complexioned with strongly arched eyebrows over lazy dark eyes. His face was almost pretty in its perfection, an effect contradicted only by his aquiline nose and neatly trimmed mustache and sideburns.

"At last, we meet." He addressed them in English, pausing to appreciate Thea's appearance before lifting her hand to his lips. "You grace our house with your beauty, Mrs. Morrison. We shall never allow you to leave."

Unfamiliar with such gallantry, Thea blushed and said softly, "You are very kind, sir. My sister and I appreciate your hospitality."

His attention rested on Elspeth, who nearly backed away fearing he might kiss her hand as well; she had barely had time to repair her damaged fingernails.

"So this is the younger sister," he said, with a faint smile, observing her closely with his lazy, long-lashed eyes, "the scholar. Oh, yes, I know about you, senorita. We are twice blessed by the presence of your budding beauty in our household." Somehow he found her hand in the folds of her skirt and lifted it to his lips, apparently not noticing how chafed and rough it was. "My son is looking forward to meeting you. He has great plans for your amusement, while I cherish the hope that you can improve his English. There has been no need for my sisters to learn the language, but a man must take his place in the world, and one day Francisco will have to deal with the Americans as I do. But not too soon, I hope," he added quickly, drawing discreet laughs from the captain and Thea. "What fortunate men we are tonight, Robert, surrounded by so much beauty. We each have two lovely ladies to escort into dinner. It will be my pleasure to accompany those of your family."

He lifted both forearms, and Elspeth was forced to put her dry hand on the black faille of one sleeve while Thea graced the other. She hoped that her hand would not snag the fine fabric or that it did not perspire due to nervousness. The Spanish male was infinitely more colorful than the female, she decided, even in dark clothing, and she wondered suddenly why Concepcion had said this man was not good enough for her. Was he concealing some wickedness that the servants, if not his pious sisters, knew all about? Her intuition warned her that he was dangerous, a man to avoid as much as possible.

The candles on the refectory table illuminated its surface warmly, but the light barely extended to the faces of the diners, making her wonder why they bothered to dress for dinner. The dim light suited her very well at the moment, allowing her the anonymity to watch and listen without calling attention to herself. The china and crystal were placed directly on the polished table, without the use of a tablecloth, and the simplicity of this impressed her as much as the elegant effect. The men conversed only in English, which Elspeth thought discourteous to the Spanish ladies; but, after his lavish compliments to Thea and herself, Don Diego appeared to ignore them, too. The roast lamb and fresh vegetables cooked in olive oil were delicious, and Elspeth satisfied her hearty appetite unobserved as she listened to the man. She had feared more of the eye-watering hot food that the captain had obtained in Santa Fe, and she was grateful for the milder Spanish cuisine.

"We're fortunate to have lamb tonight," Don Diego told the captain, who was accepting a second helping. "The small ranchos have suffered much in the year you've been gone, Robert. Whole flocks of sheep stolen, and the Americans aren't handling the problem any better than the Mexicans did. They make treaties with the Navajo only to have them broken within a short time. Treaties with Indians are useless."

The last words were spat out as if he had a better solution, and Elspeth's fork stopped at her lips as she listened. The captain obviously did not want to become embroiled in a political discussion and he took a sip of wine before remarking, "Surely the Navajo aren't ranging this far from their stronghold?"

"I doubt that their impregnable canyon actually exists," Don Diego replied. "They are nomads with a thousand miles of the West to roam, apparently great land for sheep. They have not appeared here, but the ranchos on the Rio Grande have been raided."

"You haven't started keeping sheep, have you?" the captain asked. "If you don't keep sheep, you've nothing to worry about from the Navajo."

Don Diego smiled at the way his accusation against the Americans had been deflected and glanced at Thea and Elspeth. "Ordinarily, we try not to discuss the merits and faults of the American administration of the Territory," he said. "Robert's a clever man. He just reminded me." Then, to the captain, "Of course I don't keep sheep, my friend, except a few for the table. But the Navajo aren't beyond stealing horses as well, and that worries the *padrons*. We love our horses like our children."

Elspeth could remain silent no longer. "Who are the Navajo?" she asked, with interest. "I've never heard of them before. I thought there were only Pueblos and Apache here."

Don Diego studied her with his faint, almost arrogant smile. "They are the same, senorita, the Apache and the Navajo. They speak the same language. The designation depends on whether they live in the north or south. The early Spaniards referred to them as the 'Apaches de Nabahu'u', the enemies from farmed lands. There's a book in my library which might interest you.

It's in Spanish, but Robert assures me that you've studied my language."

"But not mastered it," Elspeth replied, reluctant to explain how her difficulty with Castilian had come about. "I have a dictionary, though, and I'd like to try to read the book, senor."

"My pleasure." He nodded, but she noticed that the captain was anything but pleased. He had cautioned her to hold her tongue about the things that interested her, and she had disobeyed him.

"My sister-in-law has a romantic notion about Indians that's purely Eastern," the captain said. "It's advocated by writers and speakers who've never been to the West. If they'd seen the carnage of an Apache raid, they'd be speaking out of the other side of their mouths—"

"Please," Don Diego objected, raising his hand to check the captain's words, "not at table, Robert. And never in the company of ladies. Their sensitivity is much greater than our own. Your lovely wife does not look well, as it is."

Elspeth glanced at Thea and reached out to touch her icy hand. The discussion of Indians had not brought on the chill. One of the vagaries of Thea's illness was a fluctuation in temperature. Her apparent normality earlier in the evening had misled Elspeth, who rose quickly to assist her from her chair, muttering an apology to those at the table. Don Diego gestured toward his sisters, who rose in a rustle of taffeta to help Elspeth. The captain remained scowling in his chair, and Elspeth wondered briefly if he had informed their host about his wife's illness. Perhaps he was remaining behind to do so now; otherwise, he should be assisting her with Thea, instead of the de la Cruz sisters, who might also be innocent of the nature of Thea's distress.

"I'm so sorry," Thea whispered as they helped her down the corridor. "I felt so well earlier. Now I've ruined everyone's evening."

"You've done no such thing," Elspeth assured her, opening the door to her sister's room. Doña Isabella wrapped a blanket around Thea's shoulders and forced her to sit down on the bed while Doña Elena ran to summon the maid. She returned to stand beside the group at the bed, staring at Thea with compassionate eyes.

"You will be warm in a minute," Doña Elena consoled Thea. "I have sent for our doctor."

Elspeth did not realize at first that she had understood Doña Elena. Perhaps it had taken a crisis to make her lose her awe of the de la Cruz sisters; or, perhaps, her ear had become attuned to their speech. Realizing that her accent was probably uncouth to them, she thanked them with the single word *"Gracias,"* as she had done before. She and the maid, Rosa, helped Thea out of her gown and put her to bed in her undergarments. Doña Isabella disappeared for a moment and returned with a servant bearing cloth-covered warm bricks to tuck under the covers. Elspeth was impressed by the efficiency and kindness of the sisters as she remained holding Thea's hand. When there was no more for them to do, they slipped quietly from the room to await the doctor.

Thea soon fell into a deep sleep, but Elspeth did not leave her bedside. The captain did not appear to inquire after his wife. Elspeth wondered about his connection with Don Diego, just as she had wondered about their business earlier. Don Diego had not mentioned their house this evening; indeed, he had actually expressed the wish that they remain with him for a long time and intimated that Elspeth might be his son's governess. She tried to overcome the uneasiness in her mind as she listened to Thea's labored breathing. She leaned over to feel her forehead, which was too warm now, and tears sprang to her eyes.

Whatever else was taking place, she must not lose Thea, as she had her parents, to this devastating illness. The captain's actions were always largely unexplainable. She was probably making something out of nothing because of her own distress, listening to her feelings instead of good common sense. But her feeling that the captain had betrayed them in some way was very strong.

Chapter 3

Dr. Felipe Ibanez did not arrive until well after midnight. When Elspeth saw him, she wondered if a man as old as he should have been called from his bed at all. He dismissed everyone from Thea's room and remained there for some time. If he knew English, he chose not to speak it, and Elspeth drew the captain aside in the parlor, where everyone had gathered to await the old man's verdict.

"Isn't there an American doctor in Santa Fe?" she asked in a whisper. "Thea can't even speak to him, and he looks as if he might topple over at any minute."

"He's their family physician," the captain said, without emotion. "He brought them all into the world, and they appear healthy enough under his care. We're guests in this house, not in a position to question their decisions. No, not another word, Elspeth," he cautioned her when she started to speak again. "Won't you ever learn to keep your place?"

"But they haven't had consumption," she persisted, ignoring his warning. "Thea needs a doctor who's familiar with her illness."

"No one's done much for her so far," he said, turning away. "The best physicians in Boston could only tell her to seek a better climate."

When Dr. Ibanez entered the room with his worn leather bag, a discussion arose between him and the de la Cruz sisters, who insisted that they nurse their guest with the assistance of her maid, Rosa. Elspeth did not understand everything that was said and stared at them in confusion until she heard Don Diego's voice at her side.

"Dr. Ibanez has decided you are too young to spend so much time with your sister, senorita, and he is right. My sisters are very good at that sort of thing. They consider it their duty. They are noted for their good works. Every servant who has ever fallen ill can attest to their Christian charity."

"But I've always cared for Thea," Elspeth protested, "just as she cared for our father . . ."

"You can see the result of her nursing your father," he told her. "We can't have that happen to you. Dr. Ibanez's opinion is that it is unsafe for you because of your youth. My sisters have nursed cases like this before and never contracted the illness. You must see the wisdom of this."

There was an undeniable note of authority in his voice that left Elspeth feeling helpless. She gazed at the old doctor's rheumy eyes and burst into tears. She had never been separated from Thea, but there was no way she could oppose everyone around her. Doña Elena was at her side at once, proffering her a lace handkerchief.

"It's all right, little one," she consoled her. "We'll take very good care of your sister. You must seek happier endeavors than the sickroom. You can spend your time with Francisco. And, I promise, you can visit your sister every day, for a short time."

The captain, who had been instructed to take a separate room—as he had done so often in Boston when Thea had to take to her bed—seemed more annoyed by his wife's condition than solicitous. "Perhaps we should make our trip, now," he told Don Diego in Spanish, convinced by now that Elspeth understood very little. "We could do it in two weeks' time."

Don Diego considered the matter for a moment before he replied. "Very well. I will make the arrangements." Then, more graciously, he told Elspeth in English, "Francisco will help dispel your anxiety about your sister, senorita. He speaks English, but he has little opportunity to use it. You'll enjoy my son's company, and he's looking forward to meeting you."

Elspeth was too stunned by the captain's intention to leave at this time to pay much attention to Don Diego. She nearly objected aloud to the captain's proposed trip, but she managed to control herself, though she was seething inside with helplessness and anger. She realized suddenly that the misconception about her comprehension of Spanish might be to her advantage in the company of the two men. The trip was possibly tied to the real reason the captain had brought them here. She no longer cherished the illusion that it was for Thea's health.

The house was built around a *placita*, a charming inner court-yard containing a garden and shade tree, an area so much like a cloister that it seemed an unlikely place to find a child, though she had been directed here to meet Francisco. A Mexican nurse sat on a wrought-iron bench in the shadow of the tree, but Elspeth saw no sign of the child until a ball rolled out of the covered walkway where he had concealed himself. As she moved toward the spot, he appeared before her, small for his age, with an expression of disappointment on his pretty face.

"Elspeth?" he asked, with a frown, the lisping sound of her name suiting his Castilian tongue well. She nodded and smiled at him encouragingly, but his large dark eyes revealed that he had expected someone quite different. "You are grown," he complained petulantly. "I thought you'd be a little girl. Some-one I could play with."

"I'm not that grown up," she consoled the lonely child. "In fact, no one thinks I'm grown up at all. I like to play, too, but I haven't had anyone to play with in ever so long."

His long-lashed eyes narrowed with suspicion. "You came to teach me English," he accused her. "You're only saying you like to play. Before Father left yesterday, he told me you were a *girl*, not a lady."

"I'm sixteen years old and not considered a lady," she told him, with a smile, though she sensed the extent to which the boy had been spoiled. "You can teach me your games. I'm all alone here, Francisco. I need a friend, too. You speak English too well for me to teach you much, but I'd appreciate it if you would teach me your language."

"Your sister's dying," he said. "They told me all about it."

"My sister's *ill*," Elspeth corrected him, but her heart sank over the information he had received. She recovered herself enough to manage another smile, though she was beginning to doubt that she could like the boy. She had come here because she had been told by Concepcion to come this morning, and because she looked upon her tutoring as a way to repay the de la Cruzes for their hospitality. "Of course, if you aren't interested in being my friend," she hazarded, "I can go back to the library. There's a good book I'd like to read there. I don't want to force myself on someone who doesn't want me for a friend."

Francisco weighed his options with solemn eyes. "Will you really join me in my riding lessons? Father said you would. I have a lesson in a short time."

The suggestion delighted Elspeth, who had always wanted to learn to ride, but it unnerved her slightly, too. "I've never been on a horse, but I'd like to try to ride." She indicated her freshly laundered cotton dress and he understood before she said more.

"Father said you could wear Doña Elena's old riding habit. My aunts do not ride," he said disparagingly. "They don't ride or play games, but they are fine ladies. If you fall from the horse, you mustn't blame me."

He called to his nurse to have the riding habit taken to Elspeth's room at once, his inborn arrogance evident when he spoke Castilian. He would grow up to be a proper *padron*, Elspeth considered, wondering if everyone sounded different speaking his native tongue. Certainly, it increased one's confidence if one was uncertain in a foreign language.

"In one hour," Francisco informed her, "at the stables, señorita."

"I don't know where they are. I haven't been out of the house since I arrived," she confessed.

"Permit me to accompany you then," he volunteered, his resemblance to his father more evident when he displayed gallantry. Then, in an almost conspiratorial whisper she would never have connected with Don Diego, "If you come sooner, I will show you everything."

"Less than half an hour," she assured him, raising the hem of her skirt to run toward her room. "I bet I can run faster than you can!"

The tight riding boots she had found in her room belied that statement as she hobbled across the packed earth toward the stables with Francisco a short time later. The gray riding habit fit pretty well, but the small boots pinched her toes and rubbed her heels excruciatingly, and she drew curious stares from the multitude of servants who worked away from the house. Elspeth had not realized how self-contained the compound actually was until she observed all the craftsmen and servants going about their individual tasks. She was curious about the colorful adobe kitchen building, which was garlanded with red chilies drying in the sun and strings of garlic and other herbs. So many white-clad women were working there that she was amazed that they did not get in one another's way.

"Is the kitchen always detached from the house?" she asked her small guide, who did not seem to notice all the industry within the building.

"No," he told her. "There was a bad fire in my grandfather's time. It burned part of the house. When he built the kitchen again, he built it away from the house."

"Doesn't the food get cold being carried so far?"

He shrugged to show his lack of interest in womanly concerns. "Has your dinner ever been cold? Clay pots hold the heat. The path with the wooden roof is for the servants when they carry food to the house in the winter. So they will not be cold. Father is good to the servants, though most of them are— what is the word?—they do not work hard."

"Lazy?" Elspeth said in disbelief. "They seem busy enough to me. It's like a beehive. What do all these people do?"

"Wash clothes, sew them. There is a *carpintero* . . . one who works with wood."

"A carpenter," Elspeth said, attempting to teach him English without his noticing, but Francisco did not repeat the word. He grew slightly moody. "What else?" she asked.

"The usual things servants do," he replied. "Some of the men work with iron and tin. Some of them make adobe and plaster the walls."

He is proud, Elspeth thought, too proud to accept her clarifications of the servants' positions. She decided not to correct him again, until he trusted her more, but at least she would identify the buildings in the compound for herself. "What is that long building, the one with all the doors?" she asked.

"The servants live there," he told her, without concern. "You ask stupid questions, Elspeth."

A Mexican woman was nursing her baby at the door of one of the cubicles composing the servants' quarters, and Elspeth had a glimpse inside of the small, windowless room. The buildings were all some distance from the high walls surrounding the compound, though a large tree with wide branches nearly brushed the wall in front. When her attention focused on an upright loom beneath the tree, a partially woven striped blanket at its base, she exclaimed, "One of the women weaves! I've never seen a loom like this. I weave, too, Francisco. Which of the women is the weaver?"

He did not understand everything she said in such a rush, but he was curious about her excitement. "She is making something," he said. "For the floor, I think."

"Yes, but who is she?"

"One of the Mexican women, I think. I have never seen her. I have never noticed this"—he indicated the loom helplessly—"this thing before. We must go. My riding master is waiting."

She saw the long-haired horse handler near the stables, the youth with the expressionless face, and asked, "Who is that boy, Francisco? I saw him the day I arrived."

"He is called Mateo. He probably has another name, but no one knows it. He's only an Indian slave."

"You mean servant," she said, thinking he had used the wrong word, but Francisco shook his head.

"No. Slave. Father buys them in Santa Fe sometimes. They are captured by other tribes and sold there."

Elspeth could not believe what she had heard. "Even with the Americans here?" she said numbly.

"No one likes Indians," he said impatiently; then, "What is it, Elspeth? You are not sick like your sister, are you?"

Elspeth did feel physically ill, but she attempted to conceal it. "No, I'm all right. How long has Mateo been here?"

"As long as I can remember. I don't give my attention to such things. He's only an Indian."

"What kind of Indian?" she asked, still studying the youth with the long, matted hair.

"I don't know. Jicarilla Apache, perhaps. Some of them are Apache."

"I didn't think Apache would work for anyone," she said, and the little boy laughed.

"You're thinking of the other Apache. The Mescalero and Chiricahua in the south. They kill people. They would not be good slaves."

"And the Apaches de Nabahu'u?" she asked, recalling the book she was reading with the aid of her dictionary.

"Some people have Navajo slaves," Francisco responded, "but I've never seen one. I hope I never do. They steal sheep and kill people. Are you talking about Indians because you're frightened of the horses, Elspeth?''

Her riding lessons would have been completely enjoyable if the presence of the Indian slaves had not troubled her so much. She recognized several others in the days that followed, and it was difficult to put them out of her mind. Their faces haunted her, especially during siesta, when she lay awake staring at the dark beams of the ceiling, unaccustomed to sleeping during the day. She tried to imagine what sort of life the Indians had been deprived of when they were kidnapped and sold by their enemies. One of complete freedom, certainly. She tried to see the hacienda through the eyes of a child of nature, unschooled and unfamiliar with the ways of white men. How frightened they must have been upon their arrival, how lonely they must have felt. Probably even lonelier than she was, though she was surrounded by more gracious living than she had known in Massachusetts, and she was grateful for her riding lessons every morning.

She did not trouble Thea with her discovery of the slaves on her short daily visits with her. The information would have upset her sister as much as it did her, and Thea needed complete rest and tranquility. There was little she could do but rest in the darkened room, which Dr. Ibanez had insisted upon, a room in which she was unable to benefit from the clean air and sunshine. Elspeth described the loom she saw every day without its weaver, though, in her attempt to describe something of the outside to her.

"Suspended from a piece of wood?" Thea asked, with surprise. "An *upright* loom?"

"Yes. And weighted with stones at the bottom. It's really very interesting, Thea. I can't imagine when the weaver works, unless it is late in the evening. The rug grows a little every day, but I've never seen her. She's working with natural wool, in gray and black and white, and it's handspun, I think. Wound around sticks, instead of in balls like ours.''

"I should like to see it," Thea said with a sigh. "There's so much I'd like to see. Not that I'm complaining," she hastened to add, "though it does get boring lying here. Doña Elena and Doña Isabella are angels, but we don't speak much. I'm trying to speak to them more. I really must learn, you know. You must tell me about everything you see. And, for goodness' sake, find out about that weaver! You simply must watch her at work.''

The next afternoon, Elspeth abandoned her uneasy siesta and crept out of the house while everyone else was sleeping. She felt better outside, though the sun was extremely hot and even the guard at the gate had pushed his sombrero over his face to sleep under the intensity of its rays. She felt like a prisoner within the confines of the walls and walked quietly in the direction of the stables, seeking the company of her *Plata*, the silver-gray horse she had been riding. Deprived of human companionship, she had grown very fond of the mare, but she had little time in Francisco's company to show her fondness by scratching the animal's nose and talking to her. The boy was so full of energy that he invariably wanted to play after their lessons, and he seemed to think she was his to command, which she probably was under the circumstances. Under the guise of play, she was determined to improve his English before his father returned.

When she passed the kitchen building, she was surprised to see someone working at the loom. A young girl sat on the ground with her legs tucked to one side beneath her faded cotton skirt, so intent upon her weaving that she was unaware that she was being watched at first. Even at a short distance, Elspeth recognized that she was not Mexican. Her shining black hair was looped into a loose chignon, tied in the middle with wool to secure it; and, unlike the Pueblos Elspeth had seen in Santa Fe, her hair was not cut around her face. She was obviously from another tribe. She did not react when Elspeth moved closer, though the motion had not gone unobserved. She was not going to run away and, heartened, Elspeth walked to her side and crouched down to watch her work. The girl glanced at her, her remarkably handsome face as impenetrable as those of the other Indians, though there was an almost oriental cast to her features, especially her dark eyes. Her complexion was lighter than most, smooth and almost poreless, and her dress fit poorly, as if it were a castoff like Elspeth's riding habit. She ran the long notched stick that acted as a shuttle through the warp several times without looking at Elspeth again, so calmly that she appeared to have dismissed her observer from her mind.

''Did you make your loom?'' Elspeth asked softly, but the girl seemed puzzled by the words and did not answer for a moment.

"Si," she replied doubtfully, touching the finely woven rug, "I make it."

Elspeth smiled and placed her hand on the upright post nearest her to indicate it was the loom she had inquired about, and the girl, who seemed younger than herself, understood and smiled in return.

"Si," she said. "I made it . . . with permission."

"I weave, too," Elspeth told her in a companionable way. "My name is Elspeth. I am new here."

"They call me Maria." The young weaver spoke the name heavily, as if she did not like it, and Elspeth realized that she was a slave like the others, though she was obviously better treated. Her dress must have come from Doña Elena's old chest, and her hair was clean and glossy.

Elspeth hesitated for a moment before asking her next question. She finally decided that, if it was in bad taste, her position as a newcomer might excuse it. "Are you an Apache like the young men?"

Maria's countenance had been only friendly until then, and though it was not actually less so now, she lifted her chin proudly. "I am *Dineh,*" she said, adding with faint derision, "I am not Apache."

" '*Dineh,*' " Elspeth repeated, bewildered by the designation, which was totally unfamiliar to her. "May I stay and watch you? My loom is different." She touched the post again, because Maria did not know the Spanish word for loom. "It is . . . flat."

"Flat?" Maria asked, with amusement, indicating the position with her hand extended, palm down, and shaking her head in disbelief, as if she could not imagine such a thing. "No one can work that way. I will teach you."

Elspeth felt completely welcome. Maria seemed to be as lonely as she; perhaps she had found a friend. An Indian friend. She would like nothing better. She accepted the lessons readily, and the girl smiled shyly.

"I come when the Mexicans are sleeping," she said. "Come at this time, and I will show you how to weave."

During the following afternoons, Elspeth and Maria established a pleasant, though hardly voluble friendship; the Indian girl had less Spanish than Elspeth, and sometimes they had to communicate with gestures. She discovered that her friend lived apart from the servants' quarters, in a decrepit one-room adobe building closer to the house, which must have once served for storage. She was unable to determine either her position here or her tribe. Whenever she asked, she received the same proud answer, spoken without moving the lips, "Dineh." She decided it must be a small tribe, perhaps a Pueblo clan designation she had not heard about, though nothing about Maria was Pueblo.

When she asked Francisco about it, he shrugged his inappropriate, grown-up shrug and replied, "I know the names of all the tribes. That is not one of them. Where did you hear it?"

Elspeth was silent for a moment. She had not revealed Maria's presence even to Thea, because of the explanation about the Indians at the hacienda that might ensue. Now, she dared not mention her to Francisco, because it would reveal that she did not spend siesta in her room. "In a book, I think" she said, feeling little guilt about the lie. "Yes, it was in a book."

"You should learn to speak Spanish, instead of reading books," he reprimanded her. "How can I learn English from you, when you don't speak Spanish properly? How can I respect you when you speak like a Mexican?"

"We aren't in Spain," she told him patiently. "My accent's all right here. There are more Mexicans in the Territory than high-born Spaniards like your father."

"The Mexicans are only servants," he responded. "You're supposed to be my friend. You're living in my hacienda, and you should speak like a lady."

Instead of arguing with the boy, Elspeth decided to speak only in English when she was with him in the future. She had hoped that she and Francisco could be friends, but every day he had revealed the stamp of his upbringing more clearly. He was not to blame. He had lived his entire life in the confined world of the fading aristocracy. She was in no position to do anything about that. She would carry out the duty that was expected of her, which was to make him more conversant in English. The de la Cruz sisters were extremely kind to Thea, and she still had to answer to the captain.

She brought the Welsh shawl she had woven to Maria one afternoon. The Indian girl studied its intricate pattern with interest, but she expressed disbelief when Elspeth told her that both of her parents had been weavers.

"Men wove once," she said, "but not anymore. The . . ." She groped for the word in Spanish and gave up with a sigh. "The woman on the rock said only women can weave. She taught us how to weave."

"The woman on the rock?" Elspeth inquired, and Maria murmured something in her native tongue.

"The woman with many legs?" she hazarded, and both girls dissolved into laughter, covering their mouths so they would not be heard during siesta. Maria had often smiled in Elspeth's company, but she had never laughed before, and her face was filled with sunlight as her dark eyes scanned the area around them purposefully.

"There!" she cried, pointing her shuttle into the branches of the tree. "The woman like that!"

Elspeth's gaze followed the shuttle, but all she could see was a spider waiting in its web among the leaves. Suddenly, instinctively, she understood. A spider had many legs and it wove. "Spider," she told Maria in English, not knowing the Spanish one herself. "In my language, it is called *spider*."

Maria repeated the word carefully. In the week they had known each other, her fluency in Spanish had increased, almost as if she had had little opportunity to use the language or, perhaps, had disdained to do so until now. "*Spider* woman gave us weaving," she explained. "She lives on a tall rock in *Tsegi*, where we live. If children are bad, they are told she will come down and eat them." She attempted to smile, but her eyes were clouded by the memory of her homeland.

Elspeth sensed Maria's pain. "You miss your family," she said, placing a hand on her friend's shoulder. "Do they live very far away?"

"*Sí,*" Maria said in a flat voice as she inserted her shuttle into the loom. "Very far away. I have been here for the time of the Winds and the Male and Female Rains. I have no hope. I will not see my family again."

The winds and the rains must be the seasons, and Elspeth calculated that Maria had been here for less than a year. She wanted to reassure her that she would see her family, but she had no way to insure it and she did not want to give her false hope in the place of that she had lost. She was in no position to become involved in the affairs of the hacienda, being no more than a dependent herself.

"Hasn't anyone ever tried to leave?" she asked before she could stop herself, but Maria continued weaving with an expressionless face.

"There is no way," she responded. "I must live among Spaniards and Mexicans, because there is no way to leave. I must live among Apache, though we cannot look into one another's faces."

"The Americans are in New Mexico," Elspeth said hopefully. "Things will change. I'm an American, Maria."

"The Americans are the same. But not you, Elspeth. You are different. You are from the land of the weavers."

"I wish there were such a land," Elspeth said, with a sad smile. "A peaceful place where bad things do not happen. If the Americans knew you were here, they would do something, Maria."

Maria's hands trembled on the taut warp of her loom. "You must not tell them," she entreated. "You must not tell anyone that you know me. Nothing would change, and I would not see you again. He would send you away if he knew. You make things better for me."

"You make things better for me," Elspeth said. "I won't tell anyone. I wouldn't know who to go to. But it's hard, knowing about such things and being unable to do anything about them."

"Do not think about it," Maria told her, rising to her feet and indicating her place before the loom. "Come. You have seen me weave. Now, I will teach you."

Dinner had become almost informal during the absence of the men, Elspeth and the de la Cruz sisters dining simply and almost in silence. When Doña Isabella knocked on Elspeth's door, she was brushing her hair for the usual early supper, her mind completely occupied with thoughts of some way to help Maria, and she started slightly, as if someone had read her mind.

"The gentlemen have returned," Doña Isabella informed her. "Do you understand me, Elspeth? Don Diego and your brother-in-law have just entered the gate." Then, without noticing Elspeth's stricken face, she added, "I've instructed Concepcion to dress you for dinner tonight. It will be later, so I've brought you an apple so you won't be hungry before then."

The two weeks had passed too quickly, Elspeth thought as she gazed at the apple in her hands. She wondered if she would be able to see Maria with them here. She still had not forgiven the captain for leaving when Thea was so ill; and, now, she was more conscious of Don Diego's Indian slaves than she had been before. She did not think she could face the men at the table.

"Concepcion," she said as her maid laid out her dress on the bed, "may I have dinner in my room tonight? I don't feel very well."

The Mexican woman turned to observe her and strode across the room to put her hand on her charge's forehead. "There's nothing wrong with you," she assured her. "You'd have to be bedridden like your sister to be excused from dinner. Your only problem is that you don't get outside enough. Except for your riding lessons, you're cooped up all the time reading books. The men would be offended by your absence. Let me do your hair. You've been sitting there brushing it for nearly an hour."

Elspeth submitted to the woman's attentions reluctantly, her thoughts still occupied by the Indian slaves. "Concepcion," she asked suddenly, "have you ever heard of an Indian tribe called Dineh? I saw the word in a book."

The woman shook her head, but her pleasant expression changed. "No. Why do you read about Indians? When you've been here awhile, you'll try to forget all about them. Only a few Pueblos pretend to be Christians."

"Is that your only objection to them?" Elspeth sensed that Concepcion's sudden tightness of expression hid something more personal. "You've been here all your life and know more about them than I."

Concepcion tugged at Elspeth's hair more roughly than usual. "I know about them," she said. "They killed my father and stole my sister when I was a little girl. All my life, I've lived in fear that they might strike again."

"Stole your sister? I'm sorry, Concepcion. I didn't know."

"We had a small farm on the Rio Grande. I was only a child, but I'll never forget that day. My mother hid with me in the brush beside the river, where we'd gone to get water. There was nothing she could do to help the others. We never saw Margarita again. She was eleven years old, three years older than I was. I still pray for her. If she's still alive, she's probably more Apache than Mexican, but she probably died in slavery."

Elspeth was deeply shaken. "I've heard of such things, but not from anyone who's witnessed it," she said, wondering what sort of madness had reigned in this Territory over the years, Indians capturing white children, and whites using Indians as slaves. "You said slavery. Is that why the Indians capture white women—and girls—to do their work?"

"And worse. The Apache must be half-Mexican by now, from stealing women here and across the border. For a long time, I prayed every night that my sister was dead. If you must think of Indians, think of them with dread, senorita. Have nothing to do with any of them, even in the Plaza. They might like the way you look. You're a strong, healthy girl and promise to be beautiful."

"The Ute steal girls from other tribes, too," Elspeth said, "and sell them to the Mexicans . . . so I've heard. Perhaps if one side stopped the practice, the other would, too."

"Perhaps, but I doubt it. They're animals, all of them."

Elspeth was tempted to ask about the slaves at the hacienda, but she remained silent. Maria had been right. No one must know that she had observed her, not for the time being, at least. She did not have a plan yet, but she wanted to help her friend return to her family. "Things are different here than I imagined," she said thoughtfully. "Much different, Concepcion. I'm so sorry about your sister . . ."

"Well, I have good news about yours," Concepcion told her, dismissing the subject. "She will be joining you at dinner tonight. It will be all right for this one evening, if she doesn't excite herself."

Elspeth's happiness about spending the evening with Thea overrode her reluctance to join the men. Though her sister was still pale and weak from being in bed for so long, she was in good spirits, and Elspeth watched her carefully from the shadows surrounding the candlelight at the table; she would not allow herself to be taken by surprise again regarding her sister's health. She wanted to be invisible at the table so she could pursue her other thoughts, too. Concepcion's story had put thoughts into her mind that she would have to sort out later; in the meantime, an amorphous idea was taking form her in her mind that she could not entirely dispel.

The captain spoke little, concentrating on the wine, but Don Diego was as gracious as he had been on the night of their arrival.

"It is a relief to find you looking so well, Mrs. Morrison," he told Thea. "Your husband and I have been discussing the construction of your house. If your improvement continues, we'll have to consider it seriously."

"I should like that," she assured him, with a wan smile, "though I can never thank you and your dear sisters enough for your hospitality and kindness. Every woman desires her own home, though, and I won't be completely settled until I'm in mine."

"We've decided on the site," the captain said between sips of wine. "It isn't far from here. If your doctor permits, I'll take you to see it. Don Diego's agreed to part with a small parcel of his land, enough acres to put into corn and beans and to keep us self-sufficient. I've already purchased it."

"Thank you, Robert," Thea told him, with an affection Elspeth found difficult to comprehend after his desertion of her in her illness. "And thank you, Don Diego. There seems no end to your kindness. Elspeth and I"—her eyes tried to penetrate the shadows to see her sister, who had been swallowed up in shadow—"will always be grateful."

"My son reports that you've developed into quite a horsewoman in a short time, Miss Williams," Don Diego said, directing his attention to her. "He says you're almost as good as he. This pleases me immeasurably."

"That's high praise from your son," Elspeth responded quietly. "I enjoy riding. Thank you, Don Diego."

"Perhaps you would like to ride with me in the morning? The captain will be accompanying us, of course. That would be agreeable to you, wouldn't it, Robert?"

The captain remained silent for a moment. "I suppose so," he answered at last. "One of the women should be able to ride well, and Elspeth's the logical choice at present."

Elspeth's feelings about the ride were mixed. She longed to see what was outside the walls, but if she had been given a choice, her riding companions would have been different. She always felt edgy in the captain's company and, since she had learned about Don Diego's Indian slaves, her opinion of Don Diego had plummeted. Even the argument that he lived in a different culture did not excuse him.

"You'll have to join us before breakfast," the captain told her, the matter having been decided without her consent. "I'd like to go over and look at that parcel of land."

Good Lord, she thought, did he buy it sight unseen? She knew nothing about conducting business, but his approach appeared relaxed, even for this part of the world.

"When Mrs. Morrison is stronger," Don Diego interjected as the fruit was served, "we must plan an excursion to Santa Fe. My sisters always enjoy a little shopping. And, after being confined so long, I suspect she would appreciate it, too."

Don Diego was solicitous, concerned about Elspeth's safety on their first ride, and he assisted her on small points of horsemanship that would make riding easier for her. She had not realized how claustrophobic she felt within the walls. When the gate was opened, it was all she could to do keep from galloping out, but she kept her horse at a nervous canter so she could control her better. Plata whinnied, her mane raised by the early morning breeze, as anxious to run freely as her mistress. They circled the wall by retracing the road the wagon had taken before, riding partially through cultivated fields in the direction of the captain's land. Even in her moment of freedom, Elspeth found herself studying the outside wall for some breach that would aid her in the plan she was formulating, but she found it impenetrable. Tall yuccas with swordlike leaves grew along the front wall as if they had been planted with a purpose. She could see the top of the tree near Maria's quarters over the wall, but it would be impossible to negotiate the barrier from the branches that nearly touched it. As they turned the corner and rode along the path in the fields, Elspeth was already trying to form another plan to breach the high wall.

The green, half-grown corn being attended by straw-hatted peons did not extend much deeper than the hacienda compound on the north, and they were soon riding through land that was either lying fallow or not utilized at all. Don Diego's cultivated fields all lay to the south of the hacienda and extended westward toward Santa Fe. She wondered where his cattle were, but she chose to ride in silence without making inquiries. The morning was fine and cool, the lavender and purple shadows just lifting from the mountains, and she felt glad to be alive. As the cultivated land receded behind them, along with the path, a wide expanse of brush-covered earth as wild and arid as it had been upon the arrival of the Spaniards stretched out before them as far as the mountains, and Elspeth had to restrain herself from loosening Plata's reins again under the wide, gently bluing sky. They appeared to be heading directly for the mountains, which had been high in the distance but gradually took on the form of semibarren foothills, the higher peaks still tantalizing them in the distance. Don Diego indicated a dark, lush gully that descended from them.

"That creek is always running," he explained. "It drains from the hills. You'll have no problem with irrigation. You'll be only an hour's ride from the hacienda. The only reason I haven't put this land into crops is because the rest of my property is under cultivation."

Elspeth gazed up at the mesquite-dotted slopes of the foothills and the pine fastnesses beyond. Their house would be almost at the foot of the mountains, and that pleased her; it would be a relief from the flatness of Don Diego's fields. The captain was the only person who appeared doubtful.

"We'll be too close to the Sangre de Cristos," he commented, studying their mysterious vastness. "We'll need a higher wall than yours, Diego. Our position will be more vulnerable."

Don Diego dismissed his concern with a laugh. "My dear friend, when my grandfather settled here, the walls were necessary. There's nothing to fear from the Indians there, now. The Pueblos are completely subdued. They'd never trouble you."

"No doubt. I'm more concerned about Apache and Comanche. Oh, I know there hasn't been any trouble for some time, but that doesn't mean it's over. I don't want any Indian slaves, either. I trust them less than you do. Has it ever occurred to you when you lock your gate in the evening that you're harboring a veritable Trojan horse within your walls? The peons you've offered will be sufficient. It's safe enough to arm them in an emergency."

Several thoughts crashed together in Elspeth's mind. She realized she should not be surprised that the captain knew about the Indian slaves; he had spent a good deal of time at the hacienda in the past. His only objection was that they were a potential menace in his military mind. At the same time, the Trojan horse theory had a certain appeal; she wondered if it could be incorporated into her forming plan.

"I'm not a fool," Don Diego proclaimed good-naturedly. "The mountains are full of Pueblos, who are enemies of all the

slaves I hold. They would never attempt to escape into the Sangre de Cristos." He had spoken in Spanish, but he continued in
English: "If you think you need a wall, you shall have one, of
course. I've only kept mine restored to preserve the hacienda as
it was in the time of my ancestors."

"That may be," the captain responded, "but I'll be away a
lot of the time, and the ladies must be secured in my absence."

"As you wish," Don Diego said, smiling at Elspeth, "but
I'd assumed the young ladies would accept my hospitality when
we're away. My house is yours, senorita."

Elspeth was too astonished by the captain's plans to respond
with even a smile. Surely, the captain did not expect Thea and
herself to manage the farm in his absence? Nothing was turning
out as expected. She wondered about the trips the men intended
to make, leaving them alone in a strange place. She said nothing, because she did not wish to reveal that she had understood.
Her decision to play dumb regarding Spanish had gleaned this
much information already, and she was determined to continue
the subterfuge until this feeling that nothing was what it appeared was resolved in her mind. To confirm the impression,
she asked innocently, "I'm sure I've seen these mountains before, but I'm all turned around from our travels in the wagon.
Are they really the Sangre de Cristos again?"

"Yes," Don Diego said quickly. "They are named for the
blood of Christ, senorita."

"What a peculiar name," she said, glancing at the captain,
with whom she had had a similar conversation. He was still
gazing at his plot of land without listening. "I suppose it has
some significance?"

"There are many stories about that, senorita. It is my opinion
that the mountains were so named because the *penitentes* took
refuge there. They came to the New World with the conquista-
dors and have thrived here for many years. They punish their
flesh for the sins of men, just as Christ did on the cross. In the
period when there weren't many priests here, they performed
the sacraments of Baptism and Marriage until more clergy arrived."

"Are they connected with the Church?" she asked, trying to
dispel an unexplainable shiver across her shoulders. "Why Blood
of Christ, Don Diego? How do they punish themselves?"

"The Brotherhood itself is not recognized by the Church,

though they perform many acts of charity.'' He fell silent a moment, as if he had already said too much, before answering her second question. "They flagellate themselves with whips and branches of cholla cactus, I believe. I know it must be difficult for you to understand . . ."

"They're damned fanatics," the captain interjected bluntly. "I saw them once during Holy Week in their black robes and peaked hats. You're right, Diego. One must have Spanish blood to understand that sort of thing."

"I didn't say I understood it," Don Diego replied, with an easy smile, turning his mount in the direction of the hacienda. "It's just a fact of life here." Then, anxious to change the subject, he directed his attention back to Elspeth. "You've wanted to give Plata her head since we began our ride, senorita. That's the mark of a true rider, but you must exercise in safety. I shan't challenge you to a race, but I'll ride beside you while you race home. Don't take the mare lightly. She has fire in her yet.''

Chapter 4

"I can't stay long, Maria. The men have returned, and I'm not sure if I can leave the house during siesta every day. I wanted to see you, so you'd understand."

"I thought I would not see you again," Maria told her, concentrating on her rug and avoiding Elspeth's eyes. "It will be sad without you."

"I'll come again. I have to find out how soundly my brother-in-law sleeps during siesta, if he sleeps at all. He'd be angry if he knew I left the house. I haven't told you about him. I don't like living with him, but I've nowhere else to go. I love my sister, but I really shouldn't be living with them. Until we came here, I was like a servant in my own house. I don't like him very much." She sighed deeply, feeling some relief at speaking the words aloud. "I shouldn't bother you with my troubles. I'm sorry. You have troubles of your own."

"We are the same, I think," the Indian girl said, reaching for Elspeth's hand. "I am sorry you aren't happy, Elspeth, but we have each other."

"You're my only friend. The only person I'd speak to about such things. They're taking me riding with them every morning, and I think I have a plan, Maria. At least, I'm finding out what's outside the walls. I think they'll be leaving again soon. I don't know where they go. It's all very strange."

"It doesn't matter where they go," Maria said bitterly, "as long as they do."

"Can you ride?"

Maria smiled faintly. "Of course I can ride. Why do you ask?"

"It's too soon to tell you. I haven't thought it out yet. I'll be back as soon as I'm sure it's safe."

"I'll be waiting, my friend," Maria said, releasing her hand. "The only person I wait for is you."

Elspeth rode in silence, trying to ignore the presence of the men so she could appreciate the scenery and the sky, the only soothing things she had found in New Mexico so far. She watched the heavy white clouds cast shadows on the raw land or delighted in the free flight of a hawk wheeling high above them. No matter where they rode, she was conscious of the wide, ever-changing sky, which gave her a sense of freedom that she had never known before. She felt as if she might leave the cares of the world behind and soar upward on wings into its vastness. Her sense of hopelessness returned only when they approached the hacienda. She could not overcome the obstacle of the walls in her plan, and the sight of them was depressing. A large yucca, decked with creamy flowers grew just beneath the spot where the tree limb almost touched the inside wall, still the only accessible place from the inside. The stiff, sharp-tipped leaves of the plant, which gave it the name Spanishdagger, would cut a person to ribbons if one dropped from the wall above it. The dirt road to Santa Fe began at the gate and negotiated its way through the cultivated fields full of peons; she knew that from riding here in the wagon. In the opposite direction, toward the mountains, there was only a riding path, overgrown and neglected, as if no horse had passed that way for some time. She estimated the mountains to be about three miles away at this point, and the covering growth gave her a feeling of satisfaction. A rider could disappear into it easily, be lost to any pursuer until the foothills gave some shelter.

They did not ride to the building site again; indeed, no more mention was made about their house. One evening, Don Diego was in a particularly expansive mood from the wine at dinner. He began to extol his ancestors and held forth at length about the early search of the Spaniards for the Seven Cities of Cíbola, the Cities of Gold of the seventeenth-century explorers. His account included the massacre of Indians in the pueblos along the route of those daring men.

"They searched for gold, and what did they find?" he said with a laugh. "Stone and mud pueblos! Many good Spaniards were killed by the Indians in the battles that followed, but they found no golden cities."

"They settled this country," Thea interjected quietly, "so their efforts weren't in vain. Even if there wasn't any gold, their civilization survives, Don Diego."

"Mm," he mused, "but the gold is still there. Perhaps not lost cities of it, but mines that have been discovered only to be lost again."

"How does one manage to lose a mine?" Thea asked, with a smile, and Elspeth noticed the sudden sharpness in her brother-in-law's eyes.

"Quite easily, my dear Mrs. Morrison," Don Diego replied amiably. "My great-great-grandfather, Don Miguel, did it. He made a rudimentary map before the Indians killed him, but for all intents and purposes the mine is lost . . ."

A motion from the captain made him desist in his account of the map, and he pushed his wineglass away. "But here I am, speaking of things unfit for the ears of ladies, and at table, too. Forgive me. I shouldn't like you to awake screaming over the massacres of history tonight."

"On the contrary," Thea said, "I found your account very interesting. The massacres of the past don't unnerve me. I'm only frightened when the threat is more immediate." She cast a meaningful glance at her husband. "The idea of Comanche attacking us on the plain was quite horrifying, but we're safe from all that now, thank goodness."

"Your wife's as brave as she is lovely," Don Diego complimented the captain. "You're certain to have brave sons if the quality is inherited in the female line as it is in the brave bulls of Spain. But I can see you don't encourage me to discuss the *toros*. We shall leave bullfighting for another evening."

"I'd like to hear about them," Elspeth said softly. "I'm interested in your culture."

Don Diego laughed. "The quiet one has spoken. What an amazing little creature she is. Not a word all evening, then she wants to hear about bullfighting."

"She's too inquisitive by far," the captain said. "It comes

from being brought up in Boston around too many books. If she ever saw a bullfight, she'd faint dead away.''

Don Diego regarded Elspeth seriously and shook his head. "No. You're wrong, Robert. She wouldn't faint at the sight of blood, or anything else, I think. You can't imagine how refreshing it is to converse with females who don't blush and hide behind their fans. I like American ladies.''

"Elspeth isn't a lady yet. She's just a child," the captain said, with a bored voice. "She may talk your ears off, but I don't think you'd like what she has to say. She's an opinionated child.''

"Not for long," Don Diego told him, with a smile. "Such children have a way of changing almost overnight into marvelous butterflies. I think young Elspeth won't have bad dreams about anything we've spoken of tonight.''

Though Elspeth did not dream of Indian massacres that night, her dreams were troubled and more vivid than usual. The theme connecting them was gold. Her father appeared several times during the night, more serious and grave than she remembered him, jingling gold coins in his pocket, with a large gold watch across his vest. She saw the captain more often, though, first in uniform at Thea's side at their wedding. When he bent to kiss his bride, his face revealed only narrow-eyed greed, an expression Elspeth had caught too fleetingly to register at dinner. Then, on his deathbed, her father was pouring gold coins into his son-in-law's tense, grasping hands from a small purse that seemed bottomless, so many coins that the captain had to excuse himself when he could not hold them all, saying, "I must look after our financial affairs.'' Instead of going to their banker in Boston, he was suddenly transported to the hacienda, where he counted the shining coins into Don Diego's hands over an ancient map lying between them on the library table. Both of the men laid their hands upon the edges of the map, and the old parchment began to bleed gold from the areas indicating land, which made them laugh together like the good friends they were. Her father's voice dragged her upward from the dream, almost as if he had been in the room. "Elspeth, nothing is as it seems. Remember what I'm saying so you can change things.''

She awoke with a start, expecting to see him beside her, the fabric of the dream still fresh in her mind. The morning sun struck the threadbare brocade curtains on her bed, and she sat up with her arms around her knees, curiously troubled. The revelation of the lost gold mine had set her off, of course, she reasoned, but suddenly everything had been put into a new perspective. Her father's words made her examine it, for it had surely been his voice she had heard in its every inflection. What was the business the captain had been so anxious to conduct with Don Diego? Where had they gone on their two-week trip, which they intended to take again? The map, incautiously spoken about, had provided the clue. Perhaps Don Diego was not as wealthy as it appeared. The captain had purchased their land from him. Had he also bought into the old Spanish treasure map? That would explain so much that had occurred since their arrival. His total lack of concern about Thea's health should have alerted her sooner. Perhaps she was just imagining things; but, if she was, why did it feel so right? And, if her father had wanted to warn her, why had he waited until now, when she could do so little about anything?

"I had a strange dream," she confided to Thea as she sat in the inner courtyard for the first time that morning, having prevailed upon Dr. Ibanez to allow her sister to breathe some fresh air. "I can't quite get it out of my head."

Thea remained silent for a moment. "No one died in it, I hope?" she finally asked.

"No. It wasn't anything like that," Elspeth reassured her. "It was the feelings that it evoked that troubled me. I saw Father clearly, Thea, and ho spoke to me." She laughed for her sister's benefit. "It's all nonsense, really. We all dream every night . . ."

"It isn't nonsense when *you* dream," Thea said, with a serious face, "any more than it was with Mother. She saw things in her dreams that actually happened later, just as you did when you were younger."

"They weren't important things."

"I've told you before, you have her gift, Elspeth."

"I'm not sure I believe in such things," Elspeth told her. "Intuition, perhaps, but that's very primitive. It can also reflect the way one feels personally about things . . . and people, though. I don't think I'm more intuitive than anyone else."

"Intuition's just the ability to know something without using rational thought," Thea said. "A kind of mental leap—like arriving at a mathematical answer without going through all the steps in between. It's stronger in some people than others. What did you dream that's upset you so much?''

Elspeth clasped her hands together tightly and concentrated on a bee winging around an open rose nearby. "I haven't sorted it out yet. It didn't portend disaster or anything like that. It's pretty complicated, really."

"Did you ride with the gentlemen this morning? You're a little pale, Elspeth. You're usually fresher and more relaxed after you've been riding."

"Yes," Elspeth said, "I rode with them." She had hardly been able to take her attention off them after the implications in the dream. They had not held any conversations in Spanish for her to eavesdrop on, and the ride had not been satisfactory from that viewpoint. She wondered again what her father expected of her, but the thought was interrupted by Thea's sudden, panicked scream. Her heart turned over in her chest before she saw what had alarmed her sister, who had not been outside before.

"It's only a lizard," Elspeth said, with a laugh, taking Thea's hand as she watched with repugnance the narrow little reptile pumping its body on the garden wall.

"Are they poisonous?" Thea asked, staring at the little creature with wide blue eyes.

"No," Elspeth assured her, "though Francisco thinks otherwise. He told me that the 'yellowbellies are all right, but the bluebellies are poisonous.' I looked it up. It's a common skink, none of which is poisonous. Francisco puts little thread harnesses on them and makes them pull wagons he makes out of matchsticks. I'm learning all about the insects and reptiles on my rides with the men. I know which ones to avoid."

"I shall avoid all of them," Thea said, relaxing under Elspeth's touch. "It did give me an awful start, Elspeth."

Elspeth smiled, relieved to be out of the world of her dreams. "I know. I felt the same way at first, but they're all over the place. One becomes accustomed to them, even begins to like them. I felt very bad when Francisco stepped on the tail of one of his, and the lizard ran away without it. The tail continued to move on the ground, as if it were still alive. Francisco says they grow new ones."

Thea shuddered. "Everything's so strange to me. Francisco must be good company for you, darling. You're fortunate to have him here."

Elspeth did not tell her that the boy had deliberately trodden on the lizard's tail. "He's a charming child," she commented wryly. "I suppose he isn't that much different from other little boys. I haven't had much experience with the monsters until now."

Maria turned her face away, instead of greeting Elspeth with her usual warmth. She was stung by the gesture, but she sat down beside her friend and watched her weave in silence for a while, thinking Maria must be cross with her for ignoring her so long. They had often sat together not feeling the need for words, but today the silence was uncomfortable. Maria's shoulders, usually so proud and straight, were slumped slightly, and Elspeth could feel her unhappiness.

"It's been difficult to get away," Elspeth explained at last. "Don Diego and the captain don't retire for siesta at the same time as everyone else."

"You ride with them every morning. I've seen you from my door," Maria said quietly as she tied a strand of gray wool onto her shuttle. "You ride well, now."

"I don't like to be with them, Maria, but I've found out what's beyond the wall. There's a large yucca where the branch nearly touches it, and the road ends at the gate with nothing beyond the hacienda to the mountains. It's overgrown . . . What have you done to your hand?"

A red welt had risen across Maria's hand, almost as if she had burned it against hot metal, but she dismissed it as unimportant, still not looking at Elspeth. "It will heal itself. It isn't important."

"I can bring some ointment from the house."

"No, please stay," Maria said quickly. "I like to be with you." She continued her work as though she did not grasp the significance of Elspeth's explorations beyond the wall. "I've missed you," she whispered tightly. "I felt all alone."

Elspeth did not pursue the subject of her explorations; something more personal seemed in order after their separation. "I had a dream last night," she confided. "A strange dream concerning gold. My father spoke to me in it, Maria. My sister says I see things other people don't." Maria turned to her with interest, and Elspeth cried out, "What happened to your face?"

A long welt, similar to the one on her hand, ran from her

hairline to her chin. She dropped her shuttle and covered the disfigurement with her hands. "It is nothing," she said, turning away again. "It will go away."

"It looks like you've been hit by a whip!" Elspeth cried angrily. "Who did this to you, Maria? I'll . . ."

"There's nothing you can do," Maria said with tears in her eyes. "I am a slave. You know that. Slaves are hurt when they don't do what is asked of them." Then, earnestly, as if pleading her case, "I cannot hurt anyone, Elspeth. My family laughed at me, because I couldn't even kill a sheep."

"You haven't hurt anyone. Someone's hurt you, and I want to know who it is. I'll go to Don Diego, so it won't happen again."

"No! You must not go to him. It would only make it worse. Please tell me you won't go to him. We would not see each other again."

Outraged by the abuse of her friend, Elspeth found her mind working quickly, the idea she had half concealed even from herself suddenly solidifying into a plan of action. "You must leave here, Maria. You must escape. I'll help you. I can get food and everything you'll need. I'll even give you Plata, though she's not mine to give. If you crawl along the top of the wall for a short distance, you can avoid the yucca and drop to the ground. It isn't far to the mountains." She had not considered how she would get the horse outside the wall at night, but she was certain that would come to her, too, now that she had to get Maria away from the hacienda. "We'd have to do it at night . . ."

"I can't go," Maria whispered, her expression revealing her helplessness. "Those are not the mountains of my people. I am far from my home. I don't know where I am."

Elspeth thought Indians could find their way anywhere, and Maria's admission seemed unrealistic to her. Her continued prompting produced no result, though. Maria told her that she had been captured by the Ute, who had traveled in many directions to the city where she was sold. She did not know where she was in relation to her own people. "If I saw one of the Four Sacred Mountains, I would be all right," she said, with misery in her eyes, "but we are far from there. I don't know where I am."

Elspeth was determined not to abandon her plan, not when someone was mistreating Maria. "First, I'll find out *who* your people are," she assured Maria. "Then, I'll find out *where* they are. I promise you that you shall return to them, no matter what I have to do.''

The invitation to the ball at the Governor's Palace arrived late the next morning and, though the event was three weeks away, Doña Elena and her older sister went into a flurry of preparation. They turned out the massive wooden chests in their bedrooms and heaped silks and satins upon the beds; some of the gowns were faded, but others were as crisp and colorful as when they had been stored away.

''Are they very out of fashion?'' Doña Elena consulted Thea, with concern. ''The last time I wore this,'' she said wistfully, holding a full-skirted rose taffeta gown against her and staring into the mirror, ''was at a fiesta three years ago. We haven't attended many events since then.''

''Your Spanish gowns are never out of fashion,'' Thea reassured her from the chair into which she had sunken, almost overcome by the excitement. ''Are you certain that we were invited, too? Our wardrobe will present a greater problem.''

''Oh, yes, senora,'' Doña Elena said, turning to her and Elspeth. ''I think you are the reason we were invited. The Americans have never invited us before. We haven't been inside the Palace of the Governors since the Americans came. You are welcome to anything here. I'll summon our dressmaker to make any gown over for you.''

''My mistress needs rest.'' Rosa grumbled, assisting Thea from the chair. ''Everything doesn't have to be done today. You're behaving like girls, just because the *Americanos* have finally noticed you.''

Elspeth had been only partially observing what was happening, her mind occupied with how she could help Maria escape, a problem that had kept her awake most of the night. As soon as Thea left with her maid, the attention of the de la Cruz sisters was focused entirely on her. They held one gown after another up to her and argued whether it was proper for a sixteen-year-old girl to wear anything but white, while Elspeth stood between them as unresponsive as a dressmaker's mannequin.

''She's American,'' Doña Elena said. ''Perhaps American girls don't have to wear white. This blue taffeta suits her so well. It brings out the blue in her eyes.''

''Sixteen requires white,'' Doña Isabella stated emphatically, replacing the blue gown with a white silk. "She's of marriageable age, but she's still a maiden. A maiden should wear white."

"She'll be seventeen at the time of the ball. Her sister was speaking of her birthday just the other morning. If all maidens must wear white, it should include us, too, Isabella. But we wear colors . . ."

"When one is past a certain age, it no longer matters. It's our responsibility to do the proper thing regarding Elspeth. Really, Elena, you are such a fool at times!"

I do not know where I am. The words echoed in Elspeth's mind and made her shiver as though they were a premonition. She found it difficult to conceive of the total helplessness of not knowing where one was, and she tried to understand what Maria must be feeling. She did not know why the statement affected her so deeply, but she shuddered and clasped her arms around her chest as if she were cold.

"You aren't going to be ill?" Doña Isabella asked, with alarm, touching her forehead. Elspeth shook her head and smiled faintly. What was it her mother used to say about such feelings? Something about a goose walking over one's grave. She wondered if the expression was from Celtic folklore. It had always made her shiver, too.

Though the preparations for the ball intruded upon her formation of plans on Maria's behalf, the long-awaited excursion into Santa Fe was a welcome diversion, which she thought might be helpful to her cause as well. If she could find only one Indian like Maria, she could gain the answers needed regarding her tribe and its location. Thea rode with the other ladies in a rather dilapidated carriage, which Elspeth had often noticed housed in a building near the stables. Don Diego went to great pains to insure her sister's comfort, even providing a velvet lap blanket, though the day was warm and fair. Elspeth rode with the men, though she had never ridden quite so far before, and she found doing so in a summer frock and wide-brimmed straw hat, instead of her riding habit, more difficult. Don Diego had instructed them to look their best, because he had a pleasant surprise for them, and her dusty, well-worn riding habit was anything but flattering.

The city was not as far as Elspeth remembered it from that last, weary journey in the wagon. The square adobe spires of its old churches came into view much sooner than she expected, and the town appeared to rise into cubicles that gradually became houses out of the earth itself. As they entered the fringe of the city, where small cornfields surrounded the unplastered adobes with red chilies drying over their doors, a horde of Mexican children who had been playing in the lanes surrounded the carriage and gazed with awe at the ladies in their finery. Don Diego drove them away with a few rough words, which surprised Elspeth, and he turned to her to explain.

"The poor are always with us, senorita. Unfortunately, they are always dirty and sometimes diseased. I couldn't allow those urchins near your delicate sister. But, they are our children, aren't they? As good Christians, we must look after them. I suspect it is no different in Boston."

Indeed, it was much better here, Elspeth considered. At least, these people had small plots of land and the sunshine, unlike the wretchedly poor Irish back home. They didn't seem to be working as peons in someone else's fields, either. She still had not clarified the real position of the peons in her mind. As they neared the Plaza, they passed larger houses, some of them devoid of windows facing the street, some encompassed by plastered walls not unlike those at the hacienda. What struck her most was the almost total absence of trees and gardens in the narrow streets. The Palace of the Governors was as neglected as she remembered it, marred even more by the weathered wooden portico over the worn brick sidewalk which defaced the entire front of the building. She wondered why an invitation to such an uninviting place had generated so much excitement at the hacienda, and she did not look forward to the ball. Her attention was distracted immediately, though, by the activity in the Plaza, and she began to search for someone with a hairstyle like Maria's, while Don Diego was still speaking of the palace like a genteel tour guide.

"It was built before the keel of your *Mayflower* was laid," he said loud enough for Thea to hear as well. "It has housed all the governors since the 1600s—Spanish, Mexican, and now American. . . ."

His voice was reduced to a hum in Elspeth's mind as she desperately searched for an Indian like Maria. She saw only the Pueblos, who had been in the Plaza when they passed before, selling their wares among Mexican vendors offering fruits and vegetables and finely woven Chimaya serapes. A few blue-clad soldiers from the fort circulated among the shoppers, along with some rough, unkempt American men, whom Elspeth took to be real frontiersmen.

"Pueblo pottery is excellent," Don Diego's voice intruded into her thoughts. "You must allow me to show it to you, se-norita."

The carriage drew up in front of Seligman's General Store, and he dismounted to assist the ladies from the carriage, while Elspeth secured Plata's reins at the hitching post and joined them. "My sisters wish to make some purchases for the ball," Don Diego told her. "Ribbons and scent and things like that. Mrs. Morrison wants to see what's available to ladies in the Far West. Unless that is your wish, too, we could see the Indian pottery now."

"In the Plaza?" Elspeth asked cautiously, for it was where she wanted to go. He nodded, and she accepted readily as Thea and the de la Cruz sisters disappeared into the store. She looked around for the captain, who always accompanied Don Diego, but they appeared to have lost him, though his horse was hitched beside theirs. Don Diego smiled at her consternation.

"The ladies come to the city to shop," he told her, "but gentlemen have other diversions. I suspect that your brother-in-law has joined some of his fellow Americans for a small drink in one of the saloons. Surely there's no impropriety in my es-corting you through the busy Plaza?"

"Of course not," she said quickly. "I'm grateful for your company, senor. I had no idea so many . . . unusual . . . men were in the city. Where are all the women?"

"At home where they should be, I imagine, avoiding the dis-reputable types that come here even this time of the day. The mountain men came first," he elaborated, "but that was before my time, of course. Then the traders from Missouri made their way here by the Santa Fe Trail and opened New Mexico to American enterprise. They were already firmly entrenched be-fore the Mexican War. Taking over the government was only a slight transition. The Americans seem more interested in gov-erning militarily than otherwise at the moment, but that's un-derstandable in view of the Indian problems in the Territory."

"Those men," Elspeth said, indicating some of the ill-kempt, unshaven men lounging nearby, "are neither traders nor soldiers. What brings them here?"

"It would please me to say that it's the fine climate, or even that they're settlers, senorita," he told her, offering his arm. "Unfortunately, it is neither. They're the same type that California brought west in the late forties. Unsuccessful in the gold fields there and in the silver claims in Nevada, many have drifted here. But they aren't worth talking about. You're interested in pottery, a much more pleasant subject on such a fine day."

Elspeth's interest in the Indians as they strolled through the Plaza was so intense that she ignored the possible impropriety. When she finally spotted an Indian who was obviously not a Pueblo, her excitement was so great that she made no attempt to conceal it, though the lank-haired, buckskin-clad young man was not much like Maria.

"A Ute," Don Diego remarked. "We see them here occasionally."

"Why do they come here?" she asked boldly, searching the vicinity for slaves the Ute might have brought with him, but Don Diego did not fall into the trap and made no mention of Indian slaves.

"Sometimes they appear when the Ute agent, Christopher Carson, comes down to report. They are relatively subdued and quite devoted to him."

"Kit Carson?" Even Elspeth had heard of the famous Indian scout, though she did not know he had settled down as an agent. "I've read about him in the newspaper back home."

Don Diego chuckled. "I daresay you must have, and most of the stories fabrications—like his daring escape from the Comanche Death Circle. Still, he's a character of sorts, the kind of man the Territory always has attracted. Do you see anything you like?"

Elspeth was so interested in the people that she had hardly looked at their wares. She picked up a small piece of pottery and turned it in her hands. "It's very lovely," she said to the Pueblo vendor, who exhibited no reaction. Then, unable to suppress her curiosity any longer, she asked Don Diego, "Have you ever heard of a tribe called Dineh, sir?"

"I can't say I have," he said, with the same lack of interest his son had shown. "Most tribal names simply mean the People, as if they were the only ones on earth. Allow me to make a gift of the small pot you fancy.''

''I couldn't do that,'' she said, quickly taking her coin purse from her bag. She hoped her small allowance would cover the purchase and was relieved when the vendor counted out some change into her hand. She stared into his face, attempting to read some sort of reaction there, either contempt or approval, but the Indian's face was inscrutable. After spending so much time with Maria, who laughed and wept in her presence, Elspeth realized the controlled expressions around her were curtains pulled down to hide feelings from the white man.

Before they rejoined the others, Don Diego paused in the scant shade of the young cottonwoods and regarded her seriously. ''It would have pleased me to present you with even so small a gift,'' he said, ''but young ladies aren't supposed to accept gifts from gentlemen, are they? Just as children shouldn't take sweets from strangers.''

She could not give him an honest answer so she remained silent. Her objection to the gift had nothing to do with propriety. She was carefully planning to free one of his slaves, which in itself was probably a breach of hospitality. She simply had not wanted to be personally indebted to him over the small gift. Now that her quest for Maria's people had ended in failure, she was anxious to join her sister and the other ladies. She was beginning to feel uneasy in Don Diego's company, slightly disturbed by the way he studied her.

''You're so lovely, Elspeth,'' he said softly. ''Your beauty will soon surpass that of your sister's, because it is of the mind and spirit as well as the flesh. I understand that you'll be seventeen by the time of the ball.''

She felt herself stiffening under his flattery, not knowing where it might lead. The tone of his voice was far too intimate. She glanced in the direction of the general store as if her salvation lay there, and he recovered his dignity quickly, as if he realized his compliments were unwelcome.

''We must seek out the rest of our party,'' he told her more heartily, ''for our day has just begun. I want to show you our old churches, which are much earlier than anything in the East. And, after that, I have a very pleasant surprise for all of you. I want you to see Santa Fe in it's best light.''

He proffered his arm once again, and she put her hand upon it reluctantly.

Thea immediately voiced her relief that so much was available in the store as she regained the carriage. "I'd imagined we'd be completely cut off from everything we'd need," she told Elspeth, "but those remarkable German merchants have brought the East to the Territory. What is it, Elspeth? You do look grim, my dear. It isn't the heat, is it? It has warmed up in just an hour."

The captain reappeared almost miraculously; it was not evident that he had not been with them all the time. Elspeth sensed that her stroll with Don Diego might have been prearranged. She heard him tell Don Diego in Spanish, "I've been listening to the prospectors. We have nothing to worry about. Most of them have been panning the upper Rio Grande without any luck."

She recalled her dream about gold and the map passing between the two men with a sense of unreality. She remained silent as they followed the carriage on horseback through the dusty, narrow streets. Surely, I'm not part of their deal, she considered, though Don Diego seems to think so. I have nothing to offer in worldly goods; besides, Concepcion had made it clear that she should avoid him. The coincidence between the dream and the stated interest in the gold prospectors troubled her more than Don Diego's admiration, though. Why had her father told her to remember his words? She couldn't even help Maria. How could she stand up to the captain with such an accusation regarding his motives and her father's finances? She would infuriate him, and even her spirit trembled over doing that.

Don Diego's surprise was luncheon in the home of his friend, Don Pedro Navarro, a middle-aged gentleman who occupied one of the houses that presented a face as blank as an Indian's to the outside world. When the carved doors admitted them, they found themselves surrounded by Spanish luxury on a scale far surpassing the hacienda. They were escorted through wrought-iron gates into the inner garden, where a table had been set surrounded by carefully nurtured yellow roses. Caged birds sang above them as they dined in the surprising setting. Don Diego had been true to his word about showing them the best of Santa Fe. Thea complimented their host on the beauty of his dwelling. The expressionless houses really were not what they appeared from the outside. If it had not been for the incident in the Plaza and what she subsequently heard, Elspeth would have been as totally charmed as her sister and the Spanish ladies by the unexpected luncheon. Fortunately, she was not called upon to express any opinions, and Don Diego ignored her in the presence of the others. Her mind would not dismiss what she had seen and heard, and her dream had settled in to haunt her.

If she had been as excited as the ladies, she might have missed what was perhaps the strangest occurrence of the day. As the two Spanish gentlemen parted, they crossed themselves surreptitiously over the heart and clasped hands in a most peculiar way, with their fingers pointing upward as if in prayer.

Chapter 5

Elspeth knew the area surrounding the hacienda for a few miles, except in the direction of the mountains, but without further information about Maria's people her plan was useless. When the men began to retire to the library after lunch, instead of taking their siesta, she was even more frustrated, because she did not dare leave the house to see Maria. If someone was abusing her friend, she was not even there to comfort her. In her exploration of the house, she had found the door through which the food was brought from the kitchen building, an exit much closer to Maria's loom than the front one that she had been using, which also eliminated the chance of being seen in the outside courtyard, but she had hesitated to use it because of the activity of the captain and Don Diego. What were they discussing in the library when they should have been resting like everyone else? she wondered as she tossed on her bed, unable to sleep in the afternoon. Surely, the old map and their prospecting did not take that much planning, and that they would remain here until after the ball was certain, since the event was less than a week away.

As she lay awake one afternoon, it suddenly occurred to her that she might have to go against Maria's wishes and report the mistreatment to Don Diego to protect the girl. She did not like the prospect of speaking with him alone again; indeed, she had found it even more difficult to speak to the men on their rides than before. She was not certain that what he had said to her in the Plaza was really improper, but she had not liked the expression in his eyes when he had studied her. At least, she knew where she stood with the captain and her reasons for disliking him. In her inexperience in such matters, she was not certain why she distrusted Don Diego. Except for his compliments when they were alone, there was no reason to assume that he was not a gentleman. And, if Maria was being beaten, it did not matter what she felt about him. Since escape was impossible, her friend must be protected, even if it meant that Elspeth would never be able to see her again.

She was still struggling with the problem when there was a light tapping on her door and Doña Elena entered, refreshed from her slumber, her whole face beaming with excitement.

"Get up, you slugabed," she said breathlessly. "My brother wants us all to come to the verandah. He was very mysterious, but I think it is a surprise. Slip into your dress and touch up your hair, Elspeth. Everyone else is there already."

Elspeth felt she could live without any more of Don Diego's surprises, but his sister's enthusiasm was touching. She was particularly fond of Doña Elena and felt a compassion for her that she did not entirely understand. A transformation had taken place in the younger de la Cruz sister since the invitation to the Governor's Palace. She was like a young girl going to her first ball. Elspeth did not understand the society of the true Spaniards here, but it almost seemed as though this warm, beautiful lady had little experience with such functions. She had too much to offer life to have it pass her by forever.

Thea and Doña Isabella were in the parlor with the men when they entered, and Don Diego smiled at Elspeth's consternation. "The sleeping beauty has arisen at last," he commented softly, gazing at her affectionately with his languid eyes. "Our little family is now complete. Only the very young sleep so long and peacefully. Come, my dear ladies. I can see that Elena can hardly wait. She was like that even as a child."

He led them through the entry hall and flung the door open like an artist revealing a masterpiece. A small table had been laid beneath the vines of the verandah with chairs set up around it. For a moment, Elspeth wondered if he had attempted to reproduce the magic of Don Pedro's *placita*. Strawberries blushed in crystal goblets beside a pitcher of cool, refreshing lemonade. He seated each lady separately, leaving Elspeth until last and placing her beside him. His sisters chirped with delight over the surprise, and even the captain, who had been disgruntled lately over having to remain at the house, smiled wryly as he took his place beside Thea. He caught Elspeth looking at him and held her gaze for a disconcerting moment, until she broke the communication by averting her eyes, realizing that she was always watching him in an attempt to anticipate his next move.

They were seated on one side of the table facing the courtyard, an arrangement not conducive to intimacy, and Elspeth nibbled at her strawberries, vaguely aware that something was different about the scene before her, but unable to decide what it was.

"How refreshing this is after siesta," Thea said, with appreciation. "There's even a breeze. It's a lovely surprise, Don Diego."

"I sent runners for the cool springwater while you slept," Don Diego said expansively. "But this, my dear ladies, is not the surprise."

He motioned with his hand, and a carriage appeared from the side of the house, shining brightly and accented with gold leaf, drawn by a matched team of black horses. His sisters could not contain themselves when they saw it, and Doña Elena rose from her chair. "It's our carriage! But it looks like new, Diego. You've had it completely restored, right down to the family crest!"

"How could I take such fine ladies to the ball in anything less?" he remarked, with a smile, glancing at Elspeth for approval. She forced a smile, but she felt it quiver on her lips.

"It's very grand," she acknowledged awkwardly. "The grandest carriage I've ever seen."

Don Diego motioned the coachman to circle the area before them before driving the carriage back toward the stables. His sisters stared after it, fanning themselves in the heat. The breeze had diminished and Thea, who had brought no fan, used her handkerchief to cool herself for a few moments before Don Diego noticed her distress. "If you've finished your refreshments, you should get out of the sun, now. We don't want it to damage your fair complexions."

The ladies rose to enter the house, with Elspeth following, but were stopped suddenly by Don Diego's exclamation. "*Madre de Dios!* How did he get beyond the gate?"

The force with which he spoke made them turn, and Elspeth's heart leaped in her chest. A tall young Indian was leading two horses toward them, his free hand held out from his side to indicate he was unarmed. Clad only in deerskin trousers and soft moccasins, his wide shoulders and bare chest bronze in the sunlight, he had left himself vulnerable in his attempt to prove he concealed no weapon. His hairstyle prompted Elspeth's initial reaction: it was styled like Maria's, except for the red headband around his forehead, which contrasted colorfully with the rough turquoise stones he wore in his ears. She had never seen a more beautiful man.

"Navajo," the captain commented. "He's got guts, I'll give him that. He seems to want a powwow, Diego. Under the circumstances, you'd better hear him out."

When she thought about it later, she realized the captain's advice probably saved the young man's life, though his intention had been to spare the ladies the violence that would surely have ensued. Don Diego's eyes flashed dangerously, but he remained silent after his initial outburst. A motion of his hand would have brought a rain of gunfire from the astonished guards who had left the gate open while admiring the carriage. Before Don Diego could determine another course of action, the young man stopped a few yards in front of them and removed some folded blankets from the back of one of the horses. He placed them on the ground like an offering.

"What do you want?" Don Diego demanded harshly.

The Navajo appraised him silently, his clear features revealing nothing, his dark eyes surveying the party on the verandah.

"What's your name?" the captain asked, and when no answer came, he grunted, "Probably doesn't speak Spanish, few of them do. We may be at an impasse. They don't use sign language like the Plains tribes. I doubt he's come here to sell his goods, though."

"My name is my own," the young man said at last in Spanish. "The Mexicans call me Valerio. I am here to ransom my sister." He indicated the two fine horses. "The coyote Ute who captured her told me she is here."

Maria's brother! Elspeth's relief would have been greater if she had not been so conscious of Don Diego's reaction to his demand. She noted the Spaniard's sudden pallor before the blood suffused his face and his eyes narrowed with anger again.

"There is no such person here," he snapped. Elspeth gazed at him in angry surprise, which was not lost on the Navajo. He did not meet their eyes, but he seemed to observe everything. "My guards will shoot if you don't leave at once. You have no business here."

The young man stared into the face of each person on the verandah individually, as if to imprint them permanently in his mind. He glanced briefly at the indignant Elspeth; she had to restrain herself from crying out the truth. Then, abandoning the blankets where he had left them, he turned and led the horses toward the gate. Don Diego drew in his breath to shout at the guards, but the captain put a tight hand on his arm.

"Don't," he cautioned. "You might live to regret it. We don't know how many others are out there. Secure the gate and post a heavy guard during the day. They never attack at night. The plundering Navaho and murderous Apache are afraid of the dark."

Elspeth remained staring at the closed gate when the others turned to enter the house, her emotions in complete confusion. Her indignation at Don Diego's lie vied with her admiration for Maria's brother, who had aroused a sweet, unfamiliar sensation in her. She was certain he would rescue Maria, and she could hardly wait to tell her friend the news.

"Elspeth!" the captain said shortly, jolting her back to the present. "For God's sake, get inside. No one's to leave this house until the danger has passed."

She bent over quickly to gather up the precious blankets and held them close as she entered the cool house, which had been shocked silent by the encounter. A feeling of peace exuded from the soft wool she clutched to her breast as she slowly followed the other ladies. She was far enough behind them to overhear the captain's remark to Don Diego when he thought they were alone.

"Since when do Ute speak to Navajo? They were dying words, I suspect. If that girl's worth more than two damned fine horses to you, I think you'd better lock her up."

She knew Maria would be frightened locked in her small cubicle without knowing the reason; somehow, she must acquire the key to her friend's room so she could speak with her. She lingered in the parlor with some embroidery for the remainder of the afternoon and watched Don Diego leave the library hastily and return a short time later. She wondered if he kept the key on his person or, hopefully, secreted it in the library, in his desk or the table. The captain had left earlier with several of the guards, his military blood stirred by the prospect of tracking the Indian. When Don Diego appeared again, he went directly to his quarters without noticing Elspeth on the settee in the parlor. She listened to his retreating footsteps with her heart in her throat. If she did not make use of the opportunity at once, she might not have another today, and Maria needed reassurance. She abandoned her embroidery hoop with trembling hands and crossed the hall to the library.

If she were interrupted in her search for the key, she could say she had come looking for a book, she thought to bolster her courage. The odor of cigar smoke permeated the room, pronouncing its almost exclusive male occupancy. She had always felt like an intruder here. The odor of smoldering tobacco grew stronger as she approached the table, and she saw that Don Diego had left his thin cigar in a brass ashtray there, so hastily snuffed that it had continued to burn. Perhaps he had been distracted enough to be really careless, she hoped as she opened the drawer. Her heart lurched at the sight of a small iron key resting on the charts enclosed there.

She was tempted to take it at once, but she hesitated. Someone would have to carry food to Maria this evening—the key would be missed. But surely Don Diego would not have the servants calling on him for the key, she reasoned; there must be a duplicate. Her fingers closed around the key, and she left the library cautiously, carrying a book in her sweating hand.

The house was unnaturally quiet, as if even the servants were speaking only in whispers about a possible Indian attack.

Elspeth did not look up from her plate during dinner, though she found it almost impossible to swallow. The others ate in silence, too, any conversation restrained by Don Diego's dark mood. The captain, who had arrived back only a short time ago, finally broke the tension by speaking aloud.

"He was alone. I only found the hoof marks of three horses, the two he brought with him and those of his own, which he left unfettered behind the eastern wall. I lost his trail in an overgrown area leading to the mountains. There was no point in pursuing him further. It was getting dark by then."

"Do you think he'll return with others?" Thea asked in a

small voice. "Perhaps there is a whole band hiding in the mountains."

The captain emptied his wineglass. "Why should he return? Don Diego assured him that the person he was looking for isn't here."

"He must be very angry," Thea considered, "even if he is mistaken. One can't really blame him if the Ute stole his sister. Why do you suppose they told him she was here?"

The captain did not respond as he allowed a servant to refill his glass. Don Diego glanced at him and finally answered the question himself. "The Ute lied to him, Mrs. Morrison. Indians aren't noted for truthfulness. You've had quite a fright. I'm sorry it happened under my protection. There is really nothing to fear. I've taken every precaution against further intrusion, and you can sleep peacefully tonight. The cowards never show themselves during the night anyway."

"The incident could have been prevented," Doña Isabella spoke up unexpectedly. "I'd like a word with you later, Diego."

She knows about Maria, Elspeth thought, with disbelief. How could someone like Doña Isabella know about the young Indian girl and not try to do something to help her? She was a pious, compassionate woman, but apparently her compassion did not extend to Indians any more than the rest of the white people here. And what did she hope to do about Maria, now? Dear God, don't let anything change until Valerio returns, she thought.

She was not prepared for the angry words that came from Doña Isabella's room later, though. The heavy walls and doors muffled the argument between Don Diego and his sister; she caught only a word or two from her own room as she lay in bed. Doña Isabella was objecting to something indignantly, though, and his response that it was not her concern came through clearly before the door slammed in the corridor. He had evidently left the room angrily. She listened for his footsteps, but she could not hear them. The banging of his own door further down the corridor finally revealed that he had retired for the night.

She remained awake until she could hear no sound in the house or in the courtyard outside her window. Her view from the window was limited, narrowed by the thick adobe walls into which it was built, but she saw several guards at the gate, some of them sleeping. Everyone was so certain that Indians would not trouble them at night. She wondered if Don Diego had posted additional guards along the inside wall; if he had, she risked being shot when she ventured out. But the universal complacency about the safety of night reassured her. With a pulse throbbing in her neck, she dug deeply into the winter garments which had been put away in the chest in her room and identified her dark hooded cloak by the texture of the fabric. She had not dared light a candle. After covering herself with the garment, she waited listening at the door for a long time before finally slipping silently through the corridor to the dining room, and the kitchen exit that lay beyond it. From here, she could conceal herself in the covered walkway without being seen, but her hand trembled as she lifted the latch and she took a deep breath to steady herself before she left the house.

The courtyard was patterned with dark shadows and some moonlight, as still as a chiaroscuro painting, when she opened the door enough to ease herself through. The moon was at its quarter, a dim, silvery cradle in the star-filled sky; its phase, at least, was with her. The kitchen building and Maria's dwelling, as well as the servants' quarters, were in deep shadow. She remained in the walkway for a moment, gazing at the darker shadow of Maria's locked door before she moved toward it and attempted to insert the key into the lock. A baby wailed in one of the dwellings along the adobe row, and her heart bounded; even normal sounds were magnified in the darkness. She searched for guards along the walls where the light reached, but Don Diego's confidence had been complete. Unless she woke someone by turning the key in the lock, she should be indistinguishable in her cloak.

The door opened inward into one small room dimly illuminated by a tiny window in the rear. Maria was cowering on the narrow bed with her back pressed to the wall, and Elspeth identified herself in a whisper as she dropped the hood of her heavy cloak. Maria nearly cried out with relief, but Elspeth beckoned silence until she closed the door behind her and sank down beside her friend.

"Your brother was here today," she said quietly. "He came to ransom you, but Don Diego denied that you were here."

The girl uttered a name in her own language and put her hands to her lips. "They did not kill him, did they?" She asked so quietly that Elspeth had to strain to hear her.

"No," Elspeth reassured her. "They were so astonished that

they let him leave. The captain lost his trail near the foothills. I'm sure he wasn't deceived by Don Diego. He'll be back. I had to tell you so you wouldn't be frightened."

Maria began to weep softly, and Elspeth embraced her sympathetically. Her eyes had adjusted to the darkness, now, and she could discern a small table and a stool, the only furniture besides the bed. The hastily dismantled loom lay in pieces against the wall.

"This is a bad life," Maria told her through her tears. "I feel shame when he lies with me. But what is not given freely isn't shameful, is it? Among my people, it would not be shame."

Elspeth was too shocked to respond for a moment. "Who lies with you?" she asked tightly. "What's been happening to you, Maria?"

"The senor . . . Don Diego. You will not like me now. That's why I'm here."

"Of course I like you, but it's shameful of him. Was it he who beat you, too?"

Maria nodded in the darkness. "He's bad, Elspeth. Something is wrong with him. He must feel shame, because he whips himself afterwards. Sometimes, he wants me to whip him, but I can't, though I hate him. I've never hurt anyone. When I don't obey him, he whips me as well."

Elspeth felt sick as the pieces came together in her mind. The Brotherhood whipped themselves, and Don Diego had spoken of them with pride. If he was not a member, he practiced their punishment, at least. *Blood of Christ,* she thought, feeling the warmth drain out her despite the heat of the room. "You must leave here," she said numbly. "Go to the mountains, where Valerio's probably waiting. You can't remain here, Maria."

"*Hastiin nééz* will come for me," her friend said proudly. "He knows I am here. He will come."

"Is that your brother's real name?" Elspeth asked, attempting to repeat the name of the young man who had occupied her mind since she saw him. "He said only the white men call him Valerio."

"He is Tall Man to us. He is very brave. He will return when the moon is thin. But how will he find me?"

"Night is the only time to come, but they say your people are afraid of the dark. Would he come at night?"

"Yes, he's very brave," Maria repeated. "And you are as brave as my brother, because you came out tonight."

"But not as beautiful," Elspeth responded, "and probably not as clever. How can we mark your dwelling so it won't be seen before he comes? We must do it tonight, because I may not be able to get the key to see you again before then."

Maria was silent for a moment. Then she rose from the mattress, which rustled softly from its filling of corn husks. "We must do it with what we have. He will know it is from me."

She knelt beside the pieces of the loom and detached the spools of natural wool with an effort, pulling at them to break the knots holding them to the crumpled warp. "We can draw the wool from my door to the wall beyond the tree. He will scout the walls, and the tree is the only place to climb over without being seen. You said so yourself when you were trying to help me."

"Yes," Elspeth said as she weighed the spools in her hands, calculating the amount of wool against the distance. "There isn't enough. It must go over the wall so he can see it."

Without discussing it further, they began to move the upright wooden posts to free the rug entwined in them and just barely visible in the dim light. "We don't want the white wool," Elspeth decided. "At least we can see that and avoid it. I'll tie the ends together tightly with small, firm knots, so it won't be detected on the ground. I hate to do this to your rug, Maria."

They unwove the rug steadily and wound the wool around a stick until Elspeth thought they had enough for their purpose. She also rejected the black wool, and it took them some time to attach the gray and beige strands, which could not be distinguished in the darkness, and wind them carefully around the stick. These shades would blend with the earth in the courtyard; within a few days, they would be completely invisible there. In the interim, she would have to patrol the area regularly to keep the strand concealed. The angle of light from the window had changed by the time they completed their task.

"It's close to daybreak," she said, with concern.

"No," Maria assured her, "it's only the false light before dawn. How can I ever thank you, my friend? After tonight, I may never see you again."

Elspeth embraced her. "You can thank me by being happy,

Maria. I wish I could go with you. You're everything that's good and beautiful. You . . . and your brother.''

The feeling that had been troubling her since she saw Valerio welled up again, and she did not speak again as she put on her cloak and crept out of the door with the large spool of yarn in her hand.

She arrived at the stables in her riding habit early the following morning to scrutinize her night's work and inconspicuously kick dust over a short length of gray wool that still lay exposed. The beige wool blended well with the stucco of the wall; unless one was looking for it, it was hidden from view. The strand she had run from the rough edge of Maria's wooden doorframe at the bottom worried her slightly, though it was not really noticeable. If someone saw it and picked it up the entire length of the yarn would rise from the ground. The "thin moon" Maria had spoken of as the time for Valerio to rescue her was still a week away.

The men were astonished to see her in her riding habit when she reached the stables. The captain frowned, and Don Diego did not speak for a moment.

"Senorita," he said at last, "I fear you can't accompany us this morning. It's far too dangerous with Navajo in the vicinity. We are still not certain he was unaccompanied.''

"Nothing could happen to me under your protection," she said quickly, "and the captain's an experienced Indian fighter. You aren't riding toward the mountains to flush the Indians out, are you?''

"Well . . . no," Don Diego admitted, "but we're going to look for any further sign of them.''

They seemed relatively certain that no one had accompanied Valerio, she thought; otherwise, they would have reported the incident to Santa Fe. "That silly Indian's probably gone by now," she told him, wondering if guile came naturally to every girl nearing seventeen. "Surely there can't be any reason for my not riding today. I enjoy the company of you gentlemen so much on our rides together.''

The remarkable thing was that her efforts at manipulation were successful. She was allowed to ride with them—with one man protectively on each side of her. The spool of wool had fallen in a good place, enmeshed in the sharp spikes of the yucca near the tree branch. Valerio would find it and know its significance when he scouted the walls. The purpose of her morning ride had been accomplished.

"I should report yesterday's incident at the fort," the captain said thoughtfully. "They'd know there if any Navajo raids are taking place in the vicinity."

Don Diego's objection was sharp and spoken in Spanish: "You'll do nothing of the sort, Robert. What happens at my hacienda isn't something to be discussed by the Americans. Not with the land grants as unpopular as they are."

The captain did not reply. After overhearing him in the hall the day before, Elspeth knew he was cognizant of the actual situation. He knew about Don Diego's relationship with Maria and understood that the presence of her as a slave was potentially volatile now. But Don Diego's statement was enough to make him abandon his projected action. She found that interesting. Perhaps Don Diego had a greater hold on her brother-in-law than she had suspected. The interaction between the two men baffled her.

She counted off the nights in her mind, verifying them by observing the changing moon from her window. The light in the courtyard grew dimmer every night under the waning moon, until there was finally only a faint sliver in the sky, as Maria had predicted. She knew she would not sleep that night. If the captain had not been so adamant in his belief that Indians never struck at night, the whole plan would have been in jeopardy. But he seemed to have put Valerio out of his mind after a week. He had even mentioned their house earlier at dinner.

"We'll be able to move in soon," he said, gazing thoughtfully at Elspeth, "as soon as the plaster dries on the walls. Directly after all this business about the ball is over, I reckon. I rode over there today, and the workmen have done a fine job."

Elspeth was relieved that they would be leaving the hacienda soon. She could not bear to be under the same roof as Don Diego, though she had to be civil to him until Maria was safely away. She had not seen her since the night they had worked together unraveling the rug. Even Elspeth had to look carefully to perceive the strand of wool running to the wall, now, because it had taken on the hues of the earth more successfully than she expected. What if Valerio did not come as Maria anticipated?

she wondered as she paced her room. Or, worse, what if Don
Diego was in Maria's quarters when he did come? She shivered
and pulled her shawl around her shoulders. Her first sight of
Valerio had not left her since she saw him standing tall and
beautiful in the sunlight. She realized sadly that she would never
see him again. She hoped he would not come unarmed tonight,
as he was on the day she saw him. The thought of that fine, sun-
drenched body deprived of life was unbearable. Suddenly, she
realized she could not wait in her room without knowing what
was happening outside.

She discarded her shawl and draped herself in the heavy cloak
she had worn the last time she visited Maria. She would have to
be very cautious so she would not ruin the escape. She decided
to go only as far as the kitchen building, where she could watch
Maria's locked door at a distance. If there were any trouble,
perhaps she could provide a diversion. She made her way on
bare feet through the dining room and stepped into the night
without incident, hardly daring to breathe as she moved to the
dark shadows beneath the overhanging kitchen roof. She stood
with her back against the rough adobe wall, barely able to discern the door of Maria's dwelling, which was enveloped in darkness, but she knew she was not alone in the courtyard. One of
the shadows near the door moved; she smothered an involuntary
gasp in the folds of her heavy cloak. Valerio had really come,
as Maria said he would. Elspeth realized that until this moment
she had acted with hope more than conviction. But he was actually here, and the blood began to pound in her ears with the
realization that an escape was really underway. She thought that
her intake of breath had been inaudible, but there were ears
more acute than her own and, suddenly, unexpectedly, she was
pressed hard against the wall with a hand over her mouth.

Her eyes widened with surprise, but the heavy beating of her
heart was not related to fear. She sensed Valerio's nearness at
once, knew that it was his hand pressed against her lips. Another
shadow detached itself from the darkness as silently as a ghost,
and she heard Maria whisper something faintly in her own
tongue. Valerio lessened his grip on Elspeth, and his fingers
moved lightly over her face like a blind man's, lingering on her
lips.

"*Gracias*, senorita," he whispered, his breath warm against her ear, and clasped her shoulder firmly in a gesture of appreciation before he and Maria dissolved into the night.

Elspeth remained long after they had gone, her legs too weak to negotiate the darkness in silence to return to the house. She should have felt exultation over the successful escape; instead, she experienced a terrible sense of loss. She did not understand it, because it concerned Valerio more than her dear friend Maria. She had been overwhelmed by his nearness; she would never feel his touch or hear his voice again. The realization pained her. He and Maria had gone to a wild, free place in the fastness of the Navajo stronghold, too far away for her ever to find them. She wished with all her heart that she had gone with them.

Chapter 6

Don Diego learned that Maria was missing at breakfast, and he had difficulty containing his rage. He rose so abruptly that he nearly overturned his chair, and Elspeth had never seen such a dangerous expression on his face. He left, still clutching his napkin, only to return a moment later with instructions for the captain.

"Ride to Santa Fe and report that a Mexican woman's been kidnapped by the Navajo. I'll mount some men and ride to overtake them before they disappear too deeply into the mountains. You must go directly to the commandant at the fort, Robert. This is an outrage."

The captain did not concern himself much. He seemed reluctant to involve the army in the incident. He did not leave for the fort. After a leisurely breakfast, he announced casually that he wanted to see how the abduction was carried out—and did not appear to notice when Elspeth accompanied him across the courtyard. He drew thoughtfully on his cigar until they reached Maria's door, where the Mexican servants parted to make way for him and gradually faded away to return to their own tasks, their faces as difficult to read as those of the Indians.

Elspeth was alert for any trace of the strand of wool as he knelt to examine the spot where the lock had been in the door. Small chips of wood lay on the jamb, but she saw no evidence of the yarn even when she kicked at the dust with her foot. She moved to the shade of the tree to observe the wall, but the strand

77

had disappeared as completely as Valerio and Maria, who must have rewound it on the other side of the wall to protect her. When she returned, the captain was rising from a crouch with some wooden chips in his hand.

"Very neat," he commented, with grudging admiration. "Old wood's easier to chip than flint arrowheads, but he must have been here for a while. He removed the entire lock without anyone hearing a thing."

"Why would the Navajo take a Mexican woman?" she inquired innocently. "He was looking for his sister, wasn't he? Perhaps he didn't do it at all."

"It's difficult to understand the way they think," he said, ducking inside to investigate Maria's small room. Elspeth's heart missed a beat, but he came out without noticing what was left of the rug among the pieces of the loom. Looms had never been his strong point. "I don't want the army bothered by this. He'll probably claim that several hundred sheep are missing, too. It's the usual procedure. American soldiers shouldn't waste their time searching for nonexistent sheep. It isn't as if an American woman had been taken captive."

That explained his indifference, Elspeth thought; he knew very well that the captive was not Mexican, but an Indian slave. He had been ready to report Valerio's presence in the area only when he feared there might be other Navajo in the mountains who might attack to get Maria back. Don Diego had prevented it then; now, the captain did not want to be an accomplice in his friend's follies.

"Do the Navajo ever capture American women?" she hazarded, wondering what it would be like to live among them, but the captain shook his head.

"That hasn't been laid at the door of their hogans, yet," he said as he studied the tree and the wall beyond it. "The Plains Indians have, of course, but there are more American settlers there."

"Have any of the captured women refused to return home?"

He gave a short laugh. "Not damned likely. One returned with her face tattooed, the custom of the tribe she lived with. She came back despite her disfigurement. You needn't worry about anything like that here, Elspeth. I'm pleased to see you're taking Indians more seriously, now that you've seen what they can do. That's a step in the right direction, at least. In this case,

I'm certain he won't come back. You can sleep easily. There's nothing to fear.''

Contrary to the captain's assurance, she did not sleep well during the following week. She tossed and turned until late into the night, attempting to dispel the fantasies that seemed to come of their own volition. She could not escape the image of Maria's brother, proud, half-naked in the sunlight, or the memory of his fingers pressed against her lips in the darkness. She knew what she felt was foolish and extravagantly romantic, but her sternest arguments against it did not abolish the emotion. Valerio and his sister were gone forever, probably halfway to their homeland by now; she would never see him again, and it was just as well. At the same time, she wanted desperately to see him, quickly assuring herself that another meeting would dispel what was troubling her, put it into perspective.

She was pale and abstracted during the last fitting of her ball gown, oblivious to the voices of the women around her. The slender moon had grown bright enough to illuminate the courtyard faintly and the vigilance had relaxed at the hacienda. Only two guards kept watch at the gate, now, and Elspeth had noticed them sleeping one night from her window. Doña Isabella had carried the dress to her room after dinner accompanied by her sister and Thea, and they chattered as happily as though nothing had happened such a short time ago. She found the sound of their voices as annoying as the constant rearrangement of the folds of her gown and regretted her own impatience and desire to be alone. She found herself rubbing her eyes, which burned from lack of sleep, and yawning openly. She excused herself with embarrassment, but Doña Elena was sympathetic.

"I am weary, too," she said gently. "The weather is so hot, and all the food and wine at dinner. The gown fits beautifully. Everything is ready, now. I think we should all retire."

Elspeth dismissed her maid as soon as she was in her nightgown and went to bed without having her hair brushed. Tonight, she would sleep, she told herself firmly; there would be no more of the wonderful foolishness that kept her awake as soon as she turned off the oil lamp beside her bed. She lay back with a sigh, but more than ever before, the sleep she sought eluded her. There was a tension in the air she could not explain and it drew her to the window several times before midnight. Her small view of the courtyard revealed nothing unusual. Half illuminated by the moon, it was more in shadow than in light. No torches were burning, and at least one guard was sleeping soundly, as she should be. She threw herself down on the bed with determination, but even the profound silence did not lessen the tension that made her strain to hear the sound she seemed to be awaiting.

She had just begun to doze, when a night bird cooed close to her window. She turned over, hazy with sleep, and the whisper she heard was unmistakable to her. She had reflected too long on its very tone. "Senorita."

She rose quickly. There was nothing outside the narrow window but the bougainvillea leaves blowing slightly in the night breeze. "Valerio?" she asked softly, gazing into the shadows. "Is it you?"

"Yes. Come outside, quietly. Put on your dark garment. I must speak to you."

"I can't see you."

"That's good. I'm a shadow. You must be the same. Meet me by the back wall, beneath the tree behind the house. It is safe there."

She threw the hooded cape over her nightdress with trembling hands and hastened to the meeting place. Though she strained her eyes, she still could not see him and began to wonder if she had been dreaming after all—until a shadow detached itself from the deeper shadows and beckoned her toward it. He had darkened his skin with something and discarded the buckskin trousers for a meager loincloth. He was nearly invisible, but the touch of his hand was unmistakable.

"This is dangerous," she whispered. "Where's Maria? You're risking your—"

"She's safe . . . with a friend. You must listen. She said you are unhappy here. We did not want to leave you behind. Do you want to come with us?"

Elspeth remained silent. Her dream had come to life, almost as if she had willed him here, but this was reality: she could not answer as in her dreams. "My sister needs me," she breathed at last. "I want to come, but she's been ill."

"I understand that feeling," he said. "Perhaps she will be better when I return."

"We won't be here long. The captain's building a house."

"I know the place. I've watched him riding there. I want to

help you as you helped us. I want you to come with us. The expression in your turquoise eyes confirmed that Maria was here that first day. There was goodness and compassion there. I want you to be happy. I want to see you again.''

"I want to see you, too." Unconsciously, she lapsed into the Spanish "thee" pronoun, the familiar form used only to those closest to one: family, children, lovers. His indrawn breath indicated that he had noted the endearment.

He took her hand in his and pressed something into it. "Turquoise brings good fortune. We will meet again. Nothing can prevent that.''

His cheek brushed briefly against her own, and he was gone. If he had come like a shadow, he left like a breeze, leaping the wall without effort. Elspeth remained there for a few minutes with her fingers closed over the object he had given her, the only physical assurance that the meeting had taken place.

Later, she considered Valerio's turquoise earring under the lamp in her room for some time and finally placed it against her lips. The pain in her chest had become so poignant that even she knew what it meant.

The night of the Governor's Ball came shortly after Valerio's visit. Elspeth should have enjoyed wearing the flounced white silk gown with its full skirt and having her hair in heavy curls on her neck for the first time, but her thoughts were far away. She went through the motions to please Thea and the de la Cruz sisters, who had been looking forward to the event with so much anticipation. The young officers from Fort Marcy did not interest her at all; she was distracted when she danced with them. Even in their full-dress uniforms, they did not compare with her vision of Valerio—proud, half-naked in the sunlight. They undoubtedly held the captain's opinions of Indians, and she felt like freeing herself from their arms, conscious of the irony of looking upon her own people as the enemy.

The Palace of the Governors was almost as decrepit within as its sagging portal on the Plaza had indicated. The wooden floor of the ballroom contrasted sharply with the worn, wandering bricks of the other floors and was obviously a new addition. American furniture and crystal chandeliers were equally anachronistic in the moody Spanish building which affected Elspeth's emotions strongly. She sensed that terrible things had taken place within the thick adobe walls. In addition to the governor and his lady, in fashionable evening dress, the guest of honor, Miguel Antonio Otero, the congressman from the New Mexico Territory, presided over the festivities. He and his lovely Southern wife had recently returned from Washington, and she was a vision in a billowing lawn skirt decked with pale yellow satin roses over a crinoline.

"What a beautiful fashion," Thea remarked as she fanned herself between dances. "I wish it had made its way North. One would have to learn to walk and sit in it, I suppose. She seems to drift above the ground." She lowered her voice and hid her face with the fan. "I know I shouldn't say it, but she seems rather flirtatious and syrupy, doesn't she?"

Thea was enjoying herself. Her color was high and her blue eyes sparkled. Elspeth did not want to inflict her mood on her sister, so she attempted to take an interest in the gown. "It's pretty," she admitted. "Crinolines wouldn't be practical in Boston, though. Not with all the snow and wet weather. The weather must be milder on a plantation in the South."

"She must have a lot of servants. Can you imagine pressing the fabric in that skirt? Do you suppose they keep slaves?"

"Probably. I wonder how she met her husband."

"In Washington, I imagine. Oh, dear, here comes Don Diego again. You really must dance with him, Elspeth. You can't plead fatigue all evening."

"Are you rested enough to grant me this dance, senorita?" he asked, with one hand grasping the braided trim on his short Spanish jacket.

Elspeth bit her lip. She could hardly bear the touch of his hand. She had tried to avoid him as much as possible since the incident with Maria, but it was growing increasingly difficult. He seemed to be there no matter where she went, his dark eyes intent on her. Their house would be ready for occupation later in the week, and she was looking forward to the move. Though Thea was ignorant of the reason for Elspeth's antipathy, she quietly came to her rescue.

She said. "If you aren't averse to dancing with an older woman, I'd be happy to oblige you, senor. I do love to dance."

He arched his dark eyebrows sardonically. "Older, senora? You're the most beautiful woman here. So popular with the

American officers, I hesitated to ask you. We shall leave our sisters sitting here against the wall, too timid or too disapproving to enjoy themselves.''

Doña Elena and Doña Isabella had not danced all evening; they seemed old-fashioned and out of place in the building constructed by their ancestors. Only a few Spaniards were present, and they were accompanied by their wives. Elspeth observed that they were not socializing much, either out of pride or discrimination, though the dispute over the land grants might figure in their aloofness. Under American rule, they had much to lose.

After the captain returned, a tall, fair-haired man in civilian dress clothes sauntered toward them. He had level gray eyes and appeared more relaxed than the other men in the room. Instead of asking her to dance directly, he put the question to her brother-in-law, standing nearby, who did not appear to like the gentleman and hesitated with his reply.

''I'd like to dance,'' she said, with a challenging glance at her brother-in-law, ''if the captain will introduce us, sir.''

''Dr. Stephen Cabot,'' the captain said, startled by her forwardness. ''My sister-in-law, Miss Williams, sir.''

She felt his gaze on her back when they moved to the dance floor. He would scold her for her forwardness later; in the meantime, she would discover why the doctor, who seemed exemplary in every way, was out of favor with the captain. If the captain did not like him, he must have something to recommend him.

''I didn't know there was an American doctor here,'' she said when he took her into his arms. ''I thought only Dr. Ibanez was available when my sister was ill. You must forgive my brother-in-law, sir. He's unusually protective this evening.''

He smiled. ''You needn't apologize. The feeling between us is mutual. He thinks I'm an Indian lover, and he's probably right. A number of citizens avoid my practice because of it.''

Elspeth lost step in the dance and paused for a moment. ''Forgive me,'' she said. ''I didn't think there were two of us in the entire Territory. Your admission surprised me.''

He studied her with amusement. ''Yours surprises me. I hope you aren't one of those Easterners who speak of noble savages and think they can do no wrong. I'm interested in who they really are and what can be done to help them.''

''I was one of those Easterners,'' she replied, ''but I've

changed, I think. The best friend I've made here was an Indian girl. She called herself Dineh, but I found out it means Navajo.''

"It means the People," he said. "Each tribe considers itself the only people, but Dineh is a Navajo-Apache word. They're cousins of sorts, though they follow different ways of life.''

Elspeth hung on to his every word. Her instinct about him had been right. He was the person she had been looking for to find out more about the Navajo. She parted from him when the dance ended, and the captain chastised her at once.

"He's the last person I want you to know," he said. "You've come to your senses regarding Indians. He has no sense at all. He rides out in the hills to provide medical care to the Pueblos, but I think he's actually studying them.''

"Please don't fuss," she said, emulating the Southern lady's use of the fan Doña Elena had provided for the occasion. "He's nice. An interesting gentleman. And he's every bit as proper as the young officers you've trotted out to dance with me.''

"I didn't have to trot anyone out," he told her more amiably. "If no one's mentioned before, you look very pretty tonight. You apparently don't fancy dancing with Diego, but how would you like to dance with me?''

She knew she would not like it at all, but she could not offend him if she wanted to spend more time with her newfound friend. "Very well," she agreed, closing her fan with decision. "We've never danced before, Captain. I was too young at your wedding.''

"You're all grown up, now," he said as he maneuvered her onto the floor, "and you've done it better than I'd have imagined.''

Only the fullness of her skirt prevented him from pressing her against his body, and she attempted to draw away, only to find herself held more tightly. She caught a disapproving glance from Doña Isabella, but she was helpless in his arms unless she caused a scene. She hoped no one besides Doña Isabella was observing his shameless behavior. His breath was hot against her cheek and smelled of alcohol, and she stiffened in his arms. The captain always maintained less control when he was drinking, and he must have taken a glass from every tray that was offered. The music never seemed to end. She was stifling and tried to make some space between them so she could breathe. He had never behaved like this toward her before, but she attributed it to his drinking. She glanced around, pulling her face away from his, to see if anyone was watching. Several officers, whom he had introduced earlier as friends, were observing the captain with mild alarm. As soon as the music finally ended, they approached him in a group.

"We're going out to the courtyard for a smoke," a captain said diplomatically. "Why don't you join us, Morrison? It's getting like a fishbowl in here. One can hardly breathe."

Always anxious for the camaraderie of his army friends, the captain joined them readily after taking another glass from the tray of a passing servant. As the men walked away together, Doña Isabella drew Elspeth to her side. "You must never allow any man to hold you so closely, my dear, especially your brother-in-law. Everyone must have noticed, and they're probably talking right now."

"I don't know what came over him, Doña Isabella," Elspeth told her, still shaken by the experience. "It must have been the wine."

The older woman's stern features relaxed into sympathy with Elspeth's innocence. "It probably was the wine," she agreed. "But you mustn't allow it to happen again under any circumstances. The correct thing would have been for you to leave the dance floor. *Madre de Dios*," she breathed wearily, "here comes Dr. Cabot again. I'll explain to him that you don't care to dance . . ."

"No," Elspeth said quickly. "He's a perfect gentleman, Doña Isabella. His behavior will dispel the impression that the captain left. For whatever reason people disapprove of him, it cannot be his manners."

"I haven't been here long," she confided when they were dancing. "I'm terribly ignorant about so many things. I'd like very much to speak to you, Doctor."

"I find your directness refreshing, Miss Williams," he said, with a faint smile. "I'd like to hear about your Navajo friend. We can sit over there." He indicated a red plush sofa slightly removed from the crowd. "You shall have a cup of punch and I'll enlighten you in any way I can."

She was not certain if sitting apart with a gentleman was entirely proper, but she did not care about its propriety. When he returned with the punch, he remarked, "Since we're both from the North, I think I can speak freely. I always do, in any case. Congressman Otero has just returned from Washington, where he tried to push through a bill to grant slave status to the territories of New Mexico and California. The colorful gentlemen hanging around him are high-born Spaniards and Mexicans who approve of his action.''

"That's *monstrous*," Elspeth said. "Surely the government wouldn't consider it. If Mr. Lincoln's elected, slavery will be abolished completely."

"The Otero bill wouldn't alter the status quo. New Mexico's been committed to slavery since the early Spanish days. You must have noticed at the de la Cruz hacienda."

"Yes," she said, and before she could stop herself, "I helped my friend escape, Doctor. Her brother came looking for her."

"You what?" he asked incredulously, with a glint of admiration in his eyes. "I must say, there's more to you than I expected. Not many people would back up their convictions that far."

"The whole thing was shameful, Dr. Cabot. Maria was being used in a most shameful way." She did not elaborate out of modesty, but she explained Valerio's visit and the way the escape was accomplished. Just mentioning Valerio made her want to speak at length about him; she controlled the urge with difficulty. "Don Diego wanted to say that sheep were stolen, too. There were no sheep, even my brother-in-law said so. He didn't want to report anything to Fort Marcy."

"The story got out anyway," he said. "I didn't believe the story of the Mexican woman for a moment. Most of the affluent Spanish and Mexican landowners have some Indian slaves. The Navajo don't abduct Mexicans as a rule, though they do raid sheep. They're relatively peaceful unless the Ute stir them up, or they feel they must retaliate against an army intrusion into their territory. They raid sheep because they have to survive, and the Mexicans have raided their flocks. The number has always been exaggerated. The Indians have never understood the Spanish or Mexicans. They can't comprehend how the devil outsiders managed to get control over their lands. They didn't lose a war with the United States, so how was the land transferred to us on a sheet of paper? One can hardly blame their thinking that way. This old palace is a testimony of sorts of what they suffered under the previous governments."

Elspeth gazed up at the large rafters supporting the ceiling, their wood dull with age and the smoke from torches. "It's a strangely depressing place," she whispered. "A feeling of darkness descended upon me when I entered its doors. Probably because it's older than any building I've been in before. I don't actually believe that buildings retain the residue of their past. My mother did, very strongly, but she was from Wales and believed in ghosts, too. I have to confess, though, that I've shivered several times this evening for no apparent reason."

"Oh, there's probably a reason," he said, without taking his gaze from her face, "if you're sensitive to that sort of thing. There's an entire wall here covered with shriveled human ears, probably going back to the Spanish—though some of them are more recent. You see, they took ears to prove how many Indians they'd killed. Narbona, the only person who's ever entered the Navajo stronghold, brought back the ears of eighty-four warriors in 1804. No one else has managed to find the canyon, but you can be sure the Navajo haven't forgotten. I'm sorry," he said, noting her expression. "I didn't mean to distress you, Miss Williams. You've already found enough to trouble you here. I don't want to discourage you more."

"It's foolish to live in ignorance," she said. "It's better that I know—"

"Good God," he said suddenly, "it's begun already. I hope my services aren't required tonight."

An argument between two young officers had been growing in intensity while they were talking. When Elspeth's attention was called to the dispute, she could not imagine what could have brought the officers to the point of forgetting themselves in public. As Dr. Cabot escorted her back to her family and away from the confrontation, she detected that one of the combatants had a faint Southern drawl. The captain had returned, considerably sobered by his excursion into the courtyard, and he was observing the impending duel with a clouded face.

"The damned fools," he muttered. "This is inexcusable. They're in the same army, after all."

"What are they arguing about?" Thea asked nervously, with the color high in her cheeks. "They won't strike each other, will they?"

"One of them is a Northerner, the other from the South," the captain said, with disgust. "You may be watching the face of things to come. If your precious Lincoln wins the election, there'll probably be a civil war.''

"Surely, it wouldn't come to that," Thea protested, fanning herself rapidly though it was not that warm. "Civil wars happen in other countries, not our own.''

"We'll be in a pretty pickle if there is one," the captain said as though he were thinking aloud. "Half of the soldiers here are Southerners. If they defected, the Indians would raise hell. Prospecting would become impossible.''

He had not mentioned the word aloud until now, and Elspeth looked at him quickly. His first thought had not been the protection of women and children, because his interest in gold was all-consuming. Dr. Cabot was also staring at him with disbelief, though he made no comment in the presence of the ladies.

The dispute between the young men was settled by the intervention of a senior officer. Elspeth was relieved that it had gone no further. Within a few hours, she had been confronted by the possibility of the Territory having slave status, a potential threat of war between the States, and the grim legacy of Indian ears displaced on a palace wall. The single incident between the young officers proved too much for Thea, who began to cough and shiver. When she hemorrhaged into her lace-trimmed handkerchief, Dr. Cabot immediately rose to the situation.

"It's all right," he assured Elspeth. "It isn't arterial bleeding. I was in the same condition when I came here, and I'm completely cured. Who's her physician?''

"Dr. Ibanez," Elspeth said, holding Thea's hand and attempting to calm her. "This has never happened before.''

"After being treated in the best tradition of medieval medicine, it was more or less inevitable," he said angrily. "Captain Morrison, do I have your permission to treat your wife? I won't share my patient with another physician.''

The white-faced captain agreed readily, forgetting their differences in the emergency. "She's never coughed blood before," he muttered. "There's never been anything like this . . .''

Dr. Cabot accompanied them back to the hacienda, where he remained for several days supervising Thea's treatment. Instead of lying in a darkened room with the shutters closed, he soon had her nearly living in the open air and sunshine of the enclosed garden. The diet he prescribed and insisted upon was more than

Elspeth could have eaten, but he forced the nourishment on Thea, cajoling at first, and finally telling her outright that she would be dead within six months if she did not do as he said. Elspeth and the de la Cruz sisters lingered on the sidelines, forbidden any contact with his patient, but he reassured them often in both English and Spanish.

"I'm cured and so shall she be. The climate here's ideal for lung conditions, but one must be out in it to benefit from it. Not just for a few hours as a special treat, but all day long. I'm treating her the way I treated myself when the physicians in New York gave up on me. I was cured within six months, and I was worse off than Mrs. Morrison."

"I should have been more aware," Elspeth fretted, "but she'd seemed so much better. I dismissed her high color and agitation when she was dancing. I should have recognized that she was overexerting herself . . ."

"How old are you, Elspeth?" he asked quietly.

"Seventeen. Today's my birthday, Dr. Cabot."

"You're all grown up then, aren't you? But hardly qualified as a diagnostician. You needn't reproach yourself, my dear. From what your sister's told me, you've been more loving and caring than would be expected of any girl your age. She told me about your parents, too. All of which brings up another important matter. I must examine you and everyone else who's been in close contact with her."

When Don Diego was informed of the medical examinations, he refused to have the women in his household submitted to what he considered an indignity. "Dr. Ibanez would never suggest such a thing," he said arrogantly. "I absolutely will not allow it."

"Perhaps you'd prefer to watch your sisters cough themselves into their graves," Dr. Cabot said bluntly. "My examinations won't be limited to the women, sir. Captain Morrison and yourself are also included. Tuberculosis is an insidious disease, which doesn't respect either class or sex. You may be infected yourself. Your son could be infected."

Don Diego, who had been ignorant of such possibilities, quickly reconsidered. "You must do what you think necessary, I suppose. But Dr. Ibanez—"

"—received his training from Arab manuscripts in Spain in the last century, Don Diego. The old gentleman can't help what he is, and he isn't that much different from colleagues back East regarding this illness—though even they would have examined everyone before now. My treatment isn't revolutionary, it's just common sense.''

The de la Cruz sisters and Rosa, Thea's maid, were horrified at the thought of submitting their modest bodies to the scrutiny of any man, even a physician, but Elspeth was as sensible as she was modest. "I'll go first," she volunteered. "If I consider anything that takes place indecent, I'll tell you so."

Actually, she was allowed to protect her modesty with a sheet while the doctor examined her chest by percussion and listening with his stethoscope. Aside from taking too many deep breaths in succession, which made her see small sparkles in the air, the examination did not bother her. She had felt some tension when Dr. Cabot reached under the sheet to listen in the area of her bare breasts, but his manner was so detached and scientific that she soon relaxed. He reminded her of an explorer so intent upon finding a bug that he was unaware of anything else.

"Well," he said, with relief, "you're as sound as a dollar, young lady. It's a miracle considering the length and closeness of your exposure, but it's a blessed miracle."

"My sister says I'm the strongest one in our family," she told him, looking over her shoulder at him as she buttoned her blouse. "I've never been ill in my life."

He smiled his warm smile. "For one so old, you're in a remarkable state of preservation. But you must take good care of yourself, Elspeth. I can see by your tanned skin and light hair that you enjoy being out-of-doors."

"Yes," she said brightly. "It's peculiar, the way my hair's gone all streaky and blond. I suppose it's the sun."

"Which you'll continue to get a lot of," he advised, considering her with his friendly gray eyes. "I only hope the others are as fit. If they are, I shall be leaving today. I'll ride out once a week to see your sister. If you need me, of course, you must send for me at once. I shall forego my trip to the Pueblos for a month or more, so I'll be available."

"I shan't be here," she said, "not at the hacienda. Our house is finished, and the captain wants us to move into it at once. I'll ride over to see Thea every day. I wish she were coming, too, but the de la Cruz sisters wish her to stay here. They're remarkably kind ladies. They still consider me a child where Thea's concerned, but at least the house will be in order when she's able to join us.''

"You'll be there alone with Morrison?" he asked as if he could not believe the arrangement, and Elspeth laughed.

"We don't get along very well, but we'll be too busy to aggravate one another, I think. Don Diego practically insisted that Concepcion come, too, but I'll hardly need a maid. I like Concepcion very much, but I don't like being fussed over."

"Perhaps Don Diego was thinking of her as a duenna," he suggested. "In that capacity, perhaps she should go with you."

"It's all been decided," she said carelessly. "I certainly won't need a duenna, either, Doctor. The captain will be there to chaperone me. If that's what Don Diego had in mind, he was just adhering to his own customs. You know the way the Spanish are."

"He seems to be taking a particular interest in you, nevertheless," he remarked casually as he washed his hands. "Or hadn't you noticed?"

The suggestion silenced Elspeth for a moment as she recalled Don Diego's remarks in the Plaza. "I hardly speak to him," she said at last. "His sisters are so nice, but I can't abide him. Not after what happened to my friend Maria. Actually, it'll be a relief to get away from here. I haven't had a chance to really enjoy this country without shadows being cast upon it. I don't want to be indebted for my riding lessons forever, so I shall still give Francisco his lessons. I ride very well, now, you know."

He had been observing her in silence with his friendly gray eyes and he smiled. "I'll bet you do. You seem to have everything figured out; at least, to the extent of your experience. I'd like to come to visit you at your new house, if I may. I could come by when I look in on your sister."

"I'd like that," she said sincerely. "You're the nicest gentleman I've met in New Mexico, Doctor. The moment I saw you, I knew we could be friends, even without knowing that our interests were so similar. I didn't realize that you were the one person who could cure Thea that night, either. Thank you so much for taking care of her. . . ."

He waved her gratitude aside with his hand, but his face was suddenly very serious. "You need a little care, too, I think, Elspeth—from someone whose experience with life is broader than your own. At the same time, it won't do any harm for everyone involved to know that you have another protector. Now, we must get on with the other examinations and hope they turn out to be as happy as yours.''

Chapter 7

Elspeth appreciated her strong constitution during the weeks that followed. The new house was smaller than the one the captain had described to them in Boston, and the adobe building material posed unexpected problems. The walls inside were plastered with dun-colored clay, which made the rooms seem smaller than they were. Elspeth sanded them vigorously until they were smooth and applied white calcimine wash to brighten them. While the captain supervised the peons Don Diego had given him in an effort to get in a late crop, she labored to make the house fit for habitation. Their furniture would barely fit into the four rooms, and its style did not suit the architecture, but she maneuvered it to get the most pleasing effect. She stitched curtains by hand and scoured their copper pots until they gleamed on the kitchen wall. She rose early in the morning to prepare the captain's breakfast and carried his midday meal to the fields. The peons cooked their own meals of beans and chilies in a lean-to they had constructed for themselves.

Late in the afternoon she rode to the hacienda to visit Thea, the captain sometimes accompanying her, with both of them riding his horse. They were always encouraged to remain for dinner, but the captain usually declined. Elspeth was grateful for this, though it left her with another meal to prepare. She did not like to be under the same roof as Don Diego. Thea's health was improving steadily under Dr. Cabot's care. She would be coming to her own home soon, and Elspeth wanted it to be warm and inviting when she saw it for the first time.

She had never been more conscious of the mountains. From the time the sun rose over the wooded peaks, until the nearby foothills were swathed in evening purple, she felt drawn to them as if Valerio were waiting there. He was never far from her mind, though she knew he was still far away. As the weeks wore on, she wondered if he would remember his promise to return and wondered what she would do if he did. The only thing of which she was certain was that her heart was full of him.

She looked forward to Dr. Cabot's frequent visits both for his pleasant company and their mutual interest in the Navajo. After his calls at the hacienda to see Thea, he often rode the additional distance to have coffee with Elspeth, and they invariably touched on her favorite topic. He did not question the existence of the canyon stronghold in the north, but he did not think all the tribe lived there.

"I'm certain the tribe's larger than people think," he told her. "No one's been in that area for over thirty years; their numbers surely must have increased. I don't think they're nomads as some writers have asserted, either. The Spanish name 'Apaches de Navajo' doesn't just link the tribes. It means 'Enemies from farmed lands.' They're shepherds, but they must farm, too. Shepherds change their residence to seek better pastures, according to the time of year, but the Navajo have probably maintained the farming the Spaniards observed early on. The Apache shun it and no longer tend flocks. They raid for beef, not for sheep. I think there is a canyon and the Navajo farm there, but they take their sheep to pasture farther afield."

"There must be danger if they don't stay in their stronghold," Elspeth said, with her chin resting on her hands. "How far away is it?"

He shrugged and shook his head. "Several hundred miles, perhaps. They must leave the stronghold, or the Ute wouldn't be able to capture them the way they did your friend. I suspect the brother was a slave at some period as well. You said his Spanish was good."

"Yes," she said shyly, knowing she must not mention Maria's brother too often. "I miss my friend. But she must be reunited with her family by now, and I'm happy about that."

"You were fond enough to let her go her own way," he said,

with an affectionate smile. "Not many people are so generous in their friendships, my dear. I've never asked. What did you have in common?"

"We both weave. Didn't I tell you? She even spoke of 'the land of the weavers,' as though it was a special place. We were both lonely for a special friend, I think. We were content when we were together. I miss her, but I'm glad she got away."

"With your help," he murmured. "I see your loom won't fit inside the house. May I help you assemble it out here for the time being?"

Elspeth brightened visibly. "Would you? It isn't as portable as a Navajo loom. The parts are too heavy for me to move."

"And your bother-in-law hasn't offered his assistance," he observed, as if it were what he might expect of him.

"I wouldn't dream of asking him," Elspeth admitted, and added quickly, "He has a particular dislike of the loom. It's rather a funny story. I'll tell you about it sometime."

"And what does he think of my calling to see you? He seems to make himself scarce when I arrive. I thought he was supposed to chaperone you. He doesn't even ask about his wife."

"I report what you tell me about Thea," she said, the color rising to her face at his keen perception of the captain's indifference. "I suspect he thinks we speak of nothing else. He disapproves of our interest in Indians."

"If that's his main objection, I propose to make myself less popular by putting your loom together."

She had been lost in thought for some time, staring wistfully at the mountains from her loom. She did not hear the captain's approach and started when he spoke, as if he could read her thoughts.

"The mountains might look like a good place to ride, but don't let me catch you doing it. If we have any trouble it will come from there. A party returning from Taos saw Indians only a few days ago. Apache, maybe, or Comanche. An excursion into the hills might be a death sentence, or worse, so don't get any ideas."

"Comanche?" she asked, with an interest he mistook for trepidation. "I didn't know they came this far west."

"They haven't for a while, but they've come frequently in the past. Even other Indians fear them. I should have built this outside wall higher and extended it around the property while the house was under construction. It'll have to wait until fall, now. There's too damned much work to do, and I practically have to drive those lazy peons every minute. Just don't complicate things by taking a ride into the foothills.''

She did not question the logic of his warning, but she continued to watch the shadows of the clouds over the mountains into which Valerio had disappeared. She tried to imagine what life would be like with him in the unexplored vastness of his homeland, realizing even as she dreamed that her attachment to him would bring emotions ranging from distress to fury to her family and friends. Her daily life was anything but easy; she needed a dream in which to escape. And knowing she would never see Valerio again made it safe to dream of him. He was the first person she thought of in the morning, and the last as she drifted off to sleep at night.

When she finally got her own horse, she found it even more difficult not to venture toward the foothills. If Plata had not come as a gift from Doña Elena and Doña Isabella, she would have found it necessary to refuse her. As soon as it was clear that Don Diego was not involved, Elspeth was filled with delight over the gift, without realizing at first what had prompted it.

Don Diego observed her happiness with his cynical dark eyes. ''The captain's horse was too lively for you when you rode to the hacienda alone,'' he commented. ''My sisters insisted that you have Plata, senorita, and Francisco endorsed the idea. Since your birthday was overshadowed by the ball, we've decided to celebrate it tonight. Of course, you must stay for the night, too. We couldn't allow you to ride back in the dark, even with Robert.''

She and the captain could not refuse. But, later, Doña Isabella came to Elspeth's room with a different explanation of the gift. ''It wasn't proper for you to ride double with the captain, holding on to him that way. Elena and I knew we must do something about it.''

''I'm so pleased that you did,'' Elspeth said, almost embracing her, but Doña Isabella was too severe in her manner to welcome overt affection. ''I can never thank you enough for everything you've done. Thea's much better, isn't she?''

''Dr. Cabot is amazed at her progress, but it will take more time, of course. Tell me, Elspeth, is everything all right between you and the captain? He isn't overly familiar, is he?''

"Goodness no. We don't see each other that much. Only over dinner at night and when we come here, really. There's so much to do.''

Doña Isabella gave a faint sigh of relief. "You really should have Concepcion there with you," she advised. "If you have any problems . . . any kind, at all , , , you must come to me. Do you understand?''

Elspeth could not imagine anything that would require her to do so, but she nodded, her face as serious as Doña Isabella's. "Dr. Cabot has been kind enough to come to see me every week. He thinks Thea should be home even sooner than he expected, Doña Isabella. I'm looking forward to that. It's so nice to have someone to discuss things with. He's such a nice man.''

"Yes," Doña Isabella agreed, "and only thirty. The age difference isn't too great. You're a young woman, now, my dear, and you must consider your future. Dr. Cabot may be just the man for you. I think he's rather handsome.''

Elspeth did not know which astounded her more, the suggestion of Dr. Cabot as a husband, or Doña Isabella appraising a man's looks. "I'm far too busy to think of such things," she stammered. "I appreciate all your kindnesses. I hope I can repay them some day.''

"You can do so only by being happy, Elspeth. You really must do something about your appearance, though. You're outside too much. Your complexion's too dark, and you have streaks in your hair. A lady's complexion should be as fair as possible. You really should carry a parasol.''

Elspeth smiled politely, trying to imagine herself carrying a parasol when she was drawing water at the well or riding horseback. No one was kinder than the de la Cruz sisters, but they had never had to come to grips with the realities of frontier living.

After he finished the planting, the captain spent more time around the house attending to the minor problems of its construction. He sat at the kitchen table when she prepared their meals, and she began to feel uncomfortable under his constant observation. He followed her every movement as if he were watching for something to criticize. To avoid friction, she anticipated his wishes, refilling his wineglass before it was empty at meals, passing dishes before she was asked, so tense in his presence that she found it difficult to eat.

"No wonder your waist's so small," he commented one evening. "You eat like a bird. I'd never noticed how light your hair is, either. Your coloring's the exact opposite from your sister's."

"It's the sun," she explained nervously, touching her hair. "Doña Isabella thinks I should carry a parasol to protect myself from it."

"Nonsense. I like you the way you are. I've always found blondes and dark-skinned women attractive. You're a happy combination of both."

She did not know how to respond to the inconsistency he was exhibiting. He did not begrudge the time her weaving took from her chores; indeed, he had made no mention of the loom, though he had cursed it across the country on their journey. Perhaps he was actually beginning to appreciate her contribution to his household; her position in the family might have changed slightly. Any change should have been a relief, but it made her feel uneasy, instead. She sensed a tension in her brother-in-law that she could not explain. When she rose to wash the dishes and finish her evening chores, she was aware that he was still watching her, and she rushed to finish so she could excuse herself. She latched her bedroom door behind her for the first time, as though she expected some threat from him. She wished he would start criticizing her again instead of looking at her that way. The expression on his face baffled her. If it had been anyone else, she might have taken it for affection, but the captain had never felt kindness toward her before.

He mounted his horse early the next morning and rode in the direction of the hacienda without asking her to accompany him. She drew a bucket of murky water from the well and began to make preparations for the noonday meal, though he had not said if he would be here for it. She had finished the ironing the day before, so she felt she had some free time to go to her loom.

She had been weaving for some time, lost in her own thoughts, when the sound of an approaching horse broke into her daydreams and made her think of the time. He's returning for his meal, after all, she thought, with annoyance, wondering where the time had gone. But it was Dr. Cabot who dismounted a few minutes later and flung his reins over the rail.

"What a pretty picture you make," he commented as he walked toward her with a smile. "No, don't stop. Continue with what you're doing."

"I thought it was the captain," she told him as he sat down beside her on the narrow bench. "He should be along in time for lunch."

"He's taking lunch with Don Diego. They're as thick as thieves this morning. Thea's doing very well, Elspeth. She should be able to come home soon. She's even put on a little weight."

"I've noticed," she said, with a smile. "I'll never be able to thank you enough, Dr. Cabot. You saved her life . . ."

"Stephen," he corrected her. "Please call me Stephen. No one has for a long time. One begins to lose his identity as a person when everyone calls him 'Doctor.' I'd like you, of all people, to call me by my Christian name."

"There isn't anyone else who calls you Stephen?" she asked, with surprise, and he shook his head, staring at her with a serious expression on his handsome face. She recalled Doña Isabella's last words about him and flushed. "I'll be happy to call you by your first name, Stephen, though perhaps some people won't understand my doing so."

"I hope they will. I don't know how to say this, Elspeth. I came over here particularly because I knew you'd be alone, and now I'm at a loss for words. I've developed a particular affection for you . . ."

He hesitated awkwardly, and Elspeth responded, "We're friends, Doc—Stephen. I'm fond of you, too." She considered the lonely, wonderful man who had saved her sister and befriended her—and it occurred to her how solitary his life probably was. His confession that no one called him by his first name saddened her. If anyone deserved friends it was he, but he had isolated himself from the rest of the community by serving the Indians. "You're the only real friend I have, too, now that Maria's gone," she told him. "My sister is my good friend, of course, but I haven't been able to tell her everything. You're a kind man, Stephen, and we share the same interests."

"That's what it's all about. Sharing. I've gone my own way for so long that I think I lost track of it. You're so young and fresh. Everything is new to you. I . . . you mean a great deal to me." He paused thoughtfully, and when he spoke again, he changed the subject entirely. "You're very good at that. What are you weaving?"

Elspeth sensed something in his attitude that she did not wish to consider, because if it were spoken it would ruin their friendship. She had read in a book that it was impossible for a man and woman to be merely friends, but she hoped that their friendship was the exception. "A little rug for Thea's room," she replied, as anxious to change the subject as he. "I wanted to make a covering for her bed, but I didn't bring much yarn. I can make that another time. Thea said they have Germantown yarn at the general store."

"You can get almost anything there," he agreed, relaxing visibly. "You've a fine view here. You can't be much more than a mile from the foothills."

"The captain says the mountains are crawling with hostile Indians."

He laughed incredulously. "Hostile? I'm up there often. I've never seen anyone but Pueblos, and if you know me, you'll recognize that I've been looking. They were a little suspicious of my medicine, at first, but they've never been threatening. I've been as far as Taos, about eighty miles north, without having any difficulty. It's quite nice there, a lovely old Spanish village. I should like you to see it sometime."

"No Apache?" Elspeth asked. "No Comanche?"

"Not in the three years I've been here."

"Where are the Ute? They kidnapped Maria."

"Much further north. Carson has them pretty well under control. I think I told you that he's the Ute agent, though he makes his home in Taos. I don't think he interferes much when it comes to an occasional sortie against the Navajo. He hasn't much patience with the Navajo. He was an army scout for so long that some people say he thinks like an Indian. You never did tell me what part you took in your friend's escape, my dear."

She knew his interest and kindness and that nothing she said would go any further, but she was reluctant to discuss Valerio with anyone. "I only provided a little help," she demurred. "The captain and Don Diego would kill me if they knew."

"I daresay," he said, with admiration. "All the same, it was a bold thing to do. Don Diego claims they escaped into those mountains, and I don't question that. It's the only place they could have gone, and the mountains are vast enough to conceal a couple of Navajo, though they'd have had a long ride from there, God knows.''

"How long?'' She could not refrain from asking. He thought for a moment.

"I'm trying to think like an Indian,'' he said at last. "The tribal lands have no boundaries, and I have no idea where the Navajo homeland begins. They'd have to descend from the Sangre de Cristos at some point and cross the high plateau to the range in the west to escape detection. Perhaps they'd be in their own territory by then. The Jicarilla Apache and Navajo both roam that area, and only they know their own boundaries, if they exist at all.''

"You told me at the ball that the Apache speak the same language. There wouldn't be any trouble if they'd encountered them?''

"I don't know. No one really knows. They must have been one tribe once, but they're different in every way, now. Something divided them. The Apache speak the same language, but faster, using a smattering of Spanish words. They're certainly more aggressive when it comes to fighting. They're feared and hated for their atrocities, which resemble those of the Comanche, with whom they've probably had contact. Aside from the Navajo raiding sheep, they keep pretty much to themselves. In my opinion, they're a peaceful people, but my opinion doesn't count. An Indian is an Indian in this part of the country.''

"And, 'The only good Indian is a dead Indian,' '' she quoted the captain. "It's so unfair! If someone took our country, we'd fight, too.''

"This is *our* country,'' he reminded her, "and the Indians are a menace to commerce and its settlement. And mining, of course. The government's convinced that the area's as rich in mineral deposits as California and Nevada.''

She did not mention the captain's interest in gold. There was no point in it, really. Their inheritance had brought them here because of the gold, and her indignation over his actions had dispersed. She could not imagine any place she would rather be, unless it was that mythical canyon in the north.

"May I offer you some coffee?'' she asked suddenly, recalling her manners. "Forgive my hospitality. When we're together,

I'm so absorbed in our conversation that I forget about everything else.''

"That's the nicest compliment I've ever received,'' he told her seriously, though there was a smile in his eyes. "No, thank you. I must be off. I enjoy being with you, too, Elspeth. We're kindred spirits, I think. At any rate, you're the only person who'll listen to me, and I tend to get carried away when we discuss the Indians.''

He rose and replaced his wide-brimmed hat, and she walked with him to his horse. She was so fond him, and she empathized with his loneliness, but she hoped he would never attempt to propose again. It would be difficult to hurt a friend. Before he mounted, he leaned down and kissed her briefly on the cheek.

"You are a pretty picture,'' he said. "I'll see you next week, Elspeth.'' He started to ride away and drew in his reins suddenly. "My God, I nearly forgot. The captain and Don Diego are leaving tomorrow. They'll be gone for a while, I guess, because Concepcion is coming to stay with you.''

She was not sure when she first became aware that she was being watched. The captain had been gone for over a week, and she had been spending more time at her loom. The sensation had been with her for some time before she recognized it for what it was. She glanced toward the hills and surveyed the mountain ridges above them, because the feeling seemed to originate from there. Her first thought was that Valerio might have returned, but she was certain he would reveal his presence if it were he. She trusted Stephen Cabot's information about the inhabitants of the mountain more than the captain's, but she began to take precautions when she rode to the hacienda to see Thea, leaving in the morning instead of late afternoon so she would not be riding at dusk.

She was grateful for Concepcion's presence. The lively Mexican woman distracted her from thinking about the feeling too much. When she dismissed the idea of hostile Indians observing her, she recalled the rough prospectors she had seen in town and found them even more unnerving. Solitary and unkempt, some of the prospectors had lost touch with reality to the extent that she equated them with madmen. One afternoon, the feeling was so strong that she considered sending the peons into the foothills, but she reconsidered such drastic action. If some curious Pueblos were watching her weave, it would only make trouble for them; if it was some crazy prospector, someone might get hurt. Elspeth had not had much contact with the peons, but in the captain's absence she felt responsible for them.

Finally, rather than abandon her weaving, she consulted Concepcion as they sat outside enjoying the cool evening air. Though the heat of early August was intense, thunder rumbled hopefully in the distance, and Elspeth had covered her loom with a tarp.

"Have you ever felt someone was watching you, even when you don't know he's there?" she asked casually. "Sometimes when I'm alone, I think I'm being watched, Concepcion."

"I know that feeling," the older woman said, warming to the subject. "Every woman experiences it, I think. We're sensitive to such things. We all have some of the second sight." She crossed herself and lowered her voice. "The Church discourages speaking of such things, but what do the priests know? They're men. When I walk into a house, I know at once if it's empty or someone's there—even if they're in another room."

"Have you felt we're being watched here?"

Concepcion shook her head thoughtfully. "If I did, I'd suspect the peons, and I'd give them a piece of my mind."

Elspeth did not want to alarm the woman so she did not pursue the subject directly. "My family believe in second sight, and think it runs in families. My mother had it."

"Old Juanita in our village had the strongest gift I've ever known. Some people thought she was a witch, because she foretold disasters."

"Did they occur?"

"Not always the way she predicted them, unless you thought about it later. She said a swarm of devils would descend upon us at harvest time. The men thought she meant grasshoppers. The women were praying in the chapel when the Apache raided. Red devils!" She shivered at the memory. "If I live to be a hundred, I'll never forget their war cry."

Elspeth remained silent. She did not wish to have Concepcion relive the terror of that raid again. "It would be terrible to foresee things one has no control to change," she said at last. "My sister thinks I've inherited our mother's gift, but I'm not convinced."

"When people live close to the earth, it is common, senorita. It's as if the Lord provides us with an extra sense to protect ourselves and our children. When there is nothing but the corn in the fields and the wide sky above, sometimes more than faith is necessary. It's a mistake not to follow your intuition, senorita."

Elspeth realized she was living closer to the earth than she ever had before; perhaps it had activated a latent sensitivity. There really was a watcher in the hills. She had not found it frightening at first. She had created her fear by imagining the prospectors from Santa Fe. Her initial impression had been that it was curious Indians. She was determined to follow Concepcion's advice and see what happened, to leave herself open to the impressions she was receiving.

The thunder had been growling at the edges of the sky and gave a mighty roar in the middle of the night. Flashes of splintered lightning illuminated her room. She jumped out of bed and ran to secure the tarpaulin over the loom. The rain was falling so heavily that it ricocheted from the ground, splashing the hem of her nightgown. After her task was completed, she stood with her face raised to the hard rain, exulting in its wildness. She had never encountered such a storm. The earth seemed to be flowing away beneath her bare feet. If Concepcion had not awakened, she would have remained outside longer. She was drenched to the skin when the older woman pushed her into the kitchen.

"*Santa Maria,*" Concepcion said as she fetched a dry nightgown and some towels. "Dry yourself, you silly girl. Standing out in a lightning storm! No one goes out on a night like this."

The storm passed as quickly as it came. By morning, only a few puddles marked its fury. The dry earth had greedily consumed the rain, and the sky was so blue that Elspeth almost doubted there had been a rainstorm. Small pools were trapped in the folds of the tarp and she removed it from the loom with care. The loom seemed dry, but she leaned over to test her rug for dampness. She gasped with surprise. A turquoise earring lay on its surface. Valerio *was* here. Her heart began to pound. With the earring in her hand, she looked toward the hills. Something was catching the sunlight among the rocks, blinking too irregularly to be a reflection off mica. Disregarding the captain's warning, she ran to saddle her horse, trying not to lose the location of the light as she cinched the girth.

She led her horse away from the farm and mounted only when she was certain Concepcion could no longer hear the hoofbeats. Ascending into the foothills, she did not consider where her meeting with Valerio might lead. She had never felt more completely alive than she did as she followed the beckoning light above her. She lost sight of it when she reached the pine-clad ridges and experienced a momentary anxiety that she had lost him. She reined in suddenly when he appeared before her on a pinto pony. He was everything she remembered, and the forest around him receded from her vision. His clear, handsome features had been engraved in her heart for so long that it responded by beating rapidly in his presence. He wore a rough hand-loomed cotton shirt over his buckskin trousers, and dark strands of hair escaped from his red headband and the Navajo chongo knot at the nape of his neck. He rode forward with a smile and took her reins without speaking, leading her upward through the trees until they reached a spring that fed a small pond.

"This place is safe," he assured her at last, though he made no move to assist her from the saddle. She dismounted easily and stared up at him. He was more beautiful than she remembered, his expression more relaxed, and his dark eyes met hers directly.

"I felt someone watching," she said breathlessly. "I didn't think it was you. I really didn't think you would ride such a long way to see me."

"I gave you my word," he said, studying her face. "I do not break my word. I wanted to be near you, so I am here."

"I'm happy you're here. I didn't know I could be this happy." She drew a deep breath to compose herself. "How is Maria?"

"She is well. She is with our family, and does not know I've returned here. Your brother-in-law is not at your house," he observed. "You've been alone with the Mexican woman for several days. I watched you riding to the hacienda."

"My sister is still there. I visit her every day. She's coming home soon."

"And the Spaniard?"

His contemptuous tone made her uneasy. Maria had undoubtedly revealed everything she suffered from Don Diego. "He's gone off somewhere with the captain," she said. "You aren't planning anything foolish?"

"Foolish?" he said more mildly. "Everything I'm doing is foolish. I haven't come for the Spaniard, if that's what you mean. I considered it, but being with you was far more important."

"You must be careful, Valerio. The New Mexicans consider themselves at war with your people."

"I am invisible here."

"Not as invisible as you think. I found you," she said with concern. "They say the Dineh raid their sheep on the Rio Grande and . . ."

He smoothed away her frown with his fingertips and smiled innocently. "We've always raided their sheep, just as they have raided ours. We aren't at war with anyone. You saw me because I wanted you to see me. I've been here for almost a week."

"I like what I see," she said impulsively. "I couldn't bear it if anything happened to you. I've thought about you so much."

"I've thought of you. My family knows what you did for my sister. They call you"—he paused to translate the Navajo term into Spanish—"Helping Woman."

She wondered if Indians kissed one another, and felt she would die if they did not. The last time she was with him, he had only brushed her cheek with his. The color rose to her face at the thought and she lowered her gaze. "We know so little about each other," she whispered. "You speak Spanish better than I."

"I was in a Mexican household for seven years, a slave like my sister. I was only a boy, but all I thought of was escaping. The Spaniards were bad, the Mexicans no better. What you did for my sister gives me hope about the Americans."

She wanted to assure him that her people would not allow slavery, but what she had seen at the Governor's Ball restrained her. "Whatever happens between our people, we mustn't let it affect us, Valerio. I know that isn't your real name, but it's the only one I know. My name is Elspeth."

"I know. My people call me Tall Man, but you can use Valerio if you like. My sister told me much about you. About your sister's long illness and your trouble with your brother-in-law. I want to help you. I want to know you better. Will you come when I signal to you?"

"If I can. I'll certainly try. I don't know when the captain will return. What did you use to signal me?"

He handed her a Mexican silver coin, polished until it looked newly minted. "I trade with one of the Pueblos. Most of them fear us, because of an old dispute, but this man is my friend. He gave me this, so I can signal like an Apache." He smiled, revealing even, white teeth. "I will be here."

"Please be careful," she repeated. "I wouldn't forgive myself if anything happened to you. But I'm happy that you're here."

"You must not stay too long. They will be suspicious," he said, gathering up her reins so she could mount Plata and resting his hand on the horse's neck after she was in the saddle. "I will be cautious, but I must be near you. You are beauty."

She was touched by the way he expressed his affection. "You are beauty, Valerio. I'll watch for your signal."

She rode to the hacienda when she left the mountains, her spirits so uplifted that she noticed nothing along the way. She wanted to tell Thea about Valerio; they had always shared their experiences and thoughts. But, as soon as she was in the inner garden at her sister's side, she knew this was one thing she could not share with her.

"You're all flushed," Thea said, smiling, "and you seem so happy. You haven't looked like this before. If I weren't certain my little sister would tell me, I'd suspect she was in love."

Elspeth flushed even more, conflicted by the guilt of not being frank with Thea, who was looking very well herself. "I've almost finished the rug for your room," she said awkwardly. "If I'm happy, it's because I rather like being at the house alone, doing what I like when I like. And Concepcion's such good company, really. Perhaps I'm lazy, but she shares the work."

"My news may disappoint you then," Thea said gently. "I guess you really didn't see Dr. Cabot this morning. I'm coming home as soon as Robert returns, Elspeth. I know things haven't been easy for you. There wasn't much I could do about it, but I shan't put up with it any longer. I've had a lot of time to think since I've been confined here. I feel like myself again."

"I'm delighted that you're coming home," Elspeth said sincerely, though she wondered when Dr. Cabot had left for her place, fearing the possibility that he might have seen her riding from the hills. She did not like to deceive Thea and her good friend, but at the moment she could only think of Valerio. "We'll have to find someplace to put the loom before the weather changes. I put a tarp over it last night. There isn't room for it in the house."

"Oh, dear," Thea sighed, with smiling eyes, "the loom again! If that doesn't set Robert off, nothing will. I'll just have to insist that he build a shed for it, so we can weave during the winter, the way we used to do. They say it snows here in the winter. I can hardly imagine it. It's practically a desert."

"Concepcion told me that the snow isn't very heavy," Elspeth remarked, wondering how everything could seem so normal between them, after what had happened this morning. She studied Thea closely, tempted to tell her, but she knew she dared not. She knew she could never tell her and it made her hurt inside. She wondered if it was her hopeful imagination, or if Thea really did appear to have finally defeated her illness. "You look so well, Thea. Better than I've seen you in years. What did Dr. Cabot say?"

"Just that. I'm cured, Elspeth. My lungs are completely clear, and I'm to take more exercise now. When Robert returns, I can go home with him. I'm still a little weak, but I'll take care of that in no time. I can't imagine how you missed Dr. Cabot. He was anxious to tell you the good news. I've never met a finer man, and he's very fond of you. Perhaps, within a short time, you'll . . . What is it, Elspeth? You just drifted off, as if you weren't with me at all."

"It's nothing," Elspeth said as she leaned over to kiss her sister's cheek. "I'm just happy, that's all. I must find Francisco for his lesson. He should be finished riding, now." She hugged her impulsively. "I love you, Thea."

Thea was surprised to hear the words spoken aloud, and she returned the embrace. "I love you, too, Elspeth. You're one of the two dearest people in the world to me."

Elspeth considered the short time she might have with Valerio as she walked toward the stables. When the captain returned, it would be difficult to ride to the mountains without his being aware of her activities. If Valerio had simply captured her this morning, she would have been less conflicted; because it would have removed making a choice. He was far too noble to steal her, as his sister had been stolen, though. She wondered if he would eventually ask her to come with him, and her heart rose at the prospect. She had dreamed of being with him, and living among his people. She wanted to be with him, but she did not want to hurt Thea.

Francisco darted from the house before she reached the stables, and she noted that he was not in his riding clothes. He was in a lively mood as he ran to meet her, and he took her hand as he looked up at her.

"Have you heard?" he asked, with excitement. "Aunt Isabella's had a message from Father. He'll be returning later in the week. He promised to take me riding outside the walls before he left. I'm so weary of riding in the area of the stables. I'm a better rider than you. A girl can never ride as well as a boy!"

"You must speak English when you're with me," she admonished distractedly. "My sister didn't know about such a message."

"She does by now. Aunt Isabella was going to her when I left. Will you really become my mother when Father returns?"

Elspeth thought she must have misunderstood his Castilian with everything that was on her mind. "I don't understand. I asked you to speak English."

"Before he went away, he asked me if I'd like to have you for my mother, and I said *yes*! He told me that's the way it would be, then. Really, Elspeth, you should learn Spanish more than I should learn English, if you're going to be the wife of an hidalgo!"

Elspeth felt slightly sick, as if she had been in the sun too long. "You're making this up, Francisco. Your father's never indicated anything of the sort . . ."

"I wasn't supposed to say anything," he admitted. "Even my aunts don't know. But it's the truth. I couldn't keep quiet any longer. If I have to have a mother, I'd rather it was you than anyone else."

"I know nothing about the matter," she managed to say, trying to control her fury over Don Diego's presumption, after the way he had treated Maria. "You're too excited for a lesson today, Francicso, and I don't feel very well. I'll return tomorrow."

She rode home as if she were being lashed by a whip, trying not to explore the consequences of what she had been told. She told herself it did not concern her, to put it out of her mind, but she was aware of the bad feeling her refusal of Don Diego would cause. He was a proud, arrogant man, and his sisters had been so kind to Thea. The captain would like nothing better than to tie his family to Don Diego's through marriage; he would make her life miserable for being uncooperative. The sight of a hawk rising into the sky, with a snake coiling in its talons, brought her close to tears.

Concepcion was waiting for her with her arms crossed when she rode into the yard, and Elspeth realized she had a more immediate concern from the expression on her duenna's face. "I decided to go to the hacienda early," she explained as she dismounted. "I'll take care of Plata, Concepcion, and we can have lunch."

She was not to get off so easily. Concepcion followed her into the small corral and did not leave her while she took off her saddle and covered her horse with a sweat rug. "You've been riding like a crazy woman," she admonished. "Who gave you permission to ride so fast? You must never leave without telling me, senorita. I was sick with worry. Why did you leave so early? There are some supplies we need from the hacienda and they'll have to wait until tomorrow."

"I'll see to them," Elspeth replied tersely. "You can tell me what you need tonight, Concepcion. I may be leaving early in the morning again. There's been news that the captain and Don Diego are returning soon."

Concepcion was sobered by the information. "If you're going to give the peons the extra rations you promised them, you must do it before then."

"Yes," Elspeth said, "yes. Tomorrow. I'll see about it then. They'll have their rations before the captain returns. God knows, they need them."

"The nice doctor came to see you. He was cross with me for not knowing where you were. But he thought the hacienda was the only place you'd go, so he wasn't alarmed. Not as worried as I was. I know you, senorita, and what crazy things you might do. It's all well and good to have spirit, but you must consider other people."

"He didn't see me?" Elspeth asked. "I understood that our paths nearly crossed."

"If he'd seen you would he have been so worried? He cares

about you, senorita. You should be kind to him. He would be a fine husband for you.''

"Why is everyone trying to marry me off?" Elspeth asked, with asperity, the tears she had been holding back running down her dusty cheeks. "I have feelings of my own. I can't be responsible for *everyone's* feelings, Concepcion.''

"You're overtired," Concepcion said more gently, "and hungry, too. *Madre de Dios*, I wouldn't be your age again for anything.''

Chapter 8

She felt strangely heavy as she went about her chores the following morning, glancing often toward the mountains in the hope of catching Valerio's signal, the only brightness in her life. She had not slept well, tossing and adjusting her pillow until almost dawn, picturing in her mind the events that might ensue upon the captain's arrival. No matter how she considered them, they were unpleasant, and even coolheaded reasoning did not dispel her visions of family strife. If anything, it made them worse. Thea was cured, and Elspeth was no longer needed in the captain's household; he had the double incentive of relieving himself of her presence as well as tying his family to Don Diego's. When she flatly refused to follow his wishes, she did not like to imagine what might ensue. She knew only that her position would be more untenable than before.

Her arms felt heavy when she drew the water and carried it to the kitchen, where Concepcion was waiting to dictate the list of supplies that would be needed for the peons before the captain's return. Elspeth wrote them down at the kitchen table over her untouched breakfast. She knew she could not see the flashing light from Valerio's silver coin until the sun rose higher, so it was safe to spend this short time indoors, and she added even more provisions to the list than Concepcion dictated. I might as well be hung for a sheep as a lamb, she reasoned. When the trouble comes, the captain won't be concerned about the provisions I've issued to the poor peons.

"Concepcion," she said suddenly, wondering why she had not thought to ask before, "how long does it take a peon to pay off his debt in labor? Pedro's hardly older than I, but some of the others are close to middle age. I don't really understand the peonage system."

Concepcion remained silent for a few minutes, and her gaze did not meet Elspeth's, who realized at once that the Mexican servant was conflicted between her loyalty to her employer and her friendship toward herself. "It depends," she said at last. "It depends on the size of the debt on the paper they signed."

"You mean upon how much they had to borrow?"

Concepcion frowned uncertainly and began to clear the table, and Elspeth leaned forward, put her hand upon her wrist lightly. The older women sighed heavily, and she lowered her eyes. "Senorita, it is better not to discuss such things. It's always been this way . . ."

"The peons can't read," Elspeth realized aloud. Even Concepcion had found it necessary to dictate her supply lists. "They don't know what's written on the papers they sign, do they?"

Concepcion shook her head. "A few pesos is a lot of money to them, senorita. Some of them don't even borrow that. They sign on to work for their room and board and the clothes on their backs. They never work off their time, because they have to borrow more and sign another paper with their mark."

"They're indentured," Elspeth said, without surprise. "Slaves."

"It's always been like that," Concepcion repeated, turning her back, "just as it is in Mexico."

A flood of indignation filled Elspeth, directed against Don Diego as much as the system he embraced. She changed the figures on her list, increasing the amount of beans, cornmeal, and coffee in the hope that the peons could sell the surplus for cash in town. She realized it was an ineffectual gesture, but it was the only one she could make. The sun was higher, and she moved toward the door.

"I'll be leaving shortly," she told Concepcion dutifully, though she withheld her destination. She had to see Valerio, but she didn't know whether to expect his signal today. "I'm going to weave awhile before I go."

"Wear your hat," Concepcion ordered, and Elspeth complied by taking it from the hook on the door and crushing its limp straw down onto her head as she left.

She was at her loom for only a short time, planning an alternate route into the mountains, when the longed-for beacon flickered from the same rocky prominence as the day before. Her heart leaped at the sight of it, and she went to the corral to mount Plata at once. An arroyo cut through the pale pink landscape less than a quarter of a mile from the house, and she descended into it so her progress to the hills would go unseen. When she finally approached the foothills, she ascended recklessly in her hurry to reach Valerio. She found the spring where they had met the day before, and her spirit plunged when she did not find him there. The strain of the night before, and her indignation about the peons, produced a momentary confusion. She did not know what to do next. She finally dismounted and knelt on the mossy bank, splashing water on her face to clear her thoughts. Her hands were trembling, and she held them out to observe them, realizing she could not endure much more.

She did not hear him, but she sensed his approach and rose to face him with relief. She had to restrain herself from rushing into his arms. Instead, she burst into tears, a reaction Valerio observed with curiosity.

"I'm sorry," she said, wiping her eyes. "I don't do this often. Everything's gone wrong since yesterday. The captain's returning, and Don Diego wants to marry me. I don't know what to do. I didn't sleep at all last night."

She recognized at once that she should not have mentioned Don Diego. Valerio's usually calm eyes became as hard as obsidian; his handsome, sharply angled face looked almost cruel.

"He'll never have you," he said, hardly moving his lips as if he were speaking his native language.

"I won't have him!" she said forcefully, alarmed by his reaction. "No one can make me marry him, Valerio. I can handle it myself. My brother-in-law will undoubtedly want it, but I shall never marry that man."

His expression softened. "There is another way." His gaze measured her reaction. "Come with me. I will look after you forever, and I will show you beautiful things."

Elspeth gazed at him helplessly. "I want to go with you,"

she said sincerely, "but I must consider my sister. She should be home before long."

He glanced away from her. "We have no word for love like white people. We don't understand what you mean by that word. I need you. I need you more than I've ever needed anyone."

"I need you, too," she said. "I love you, Valerio, but I don't know what to do about it."

He drew her into his arms and pressed her face against his chest, stroking her hair in silence, and she slipped her arms around him. His lips touched her forehead. "We will know what to do when the time is right. Perhaps when your sister comes home, she will be well again. There is nothing to fear. I'll be here watching over you."

"I feel safe here with you," she confessed, raising his hand to her lips. "I don't feel that way with anyone else."

"The Mexicans I was with kissed each other on the mouth," he suggested. She smiled and rose on tiptoe to brush his lips with her own. His arms tightened around her as he prolonged the kiss, revealing himself to be more experienced than she. All of her troubles disappeared now that she was in his arms. She had never known what it meant to need a man, to actually want him, until now.

"I love you, my darling," she whispered. "You're everything that's beautiful. But," she said with regret, "I must go, now. If anyone notices my absence or the direction I ride, I couldn't come anymore." She reached into her pocket and placed the two earrings in his hand. "I brought them this time. They are both together again as they should be."

"Keep them," he said, closing her fingers around them, "as a pledge between us."

She made several trips to be with him over the next few days without anyone becoming aware of it. He told her about his people and how happy she would be with them. He never called her by name; it was not proper among the Dineh. One mentioned a name only to others, but never to the person who bore it. She would remember in future not to call him Valerio. He taught her some Dineh phrases, and laughed boyishly at her mispronunciation, and smiled proudly when she spoke correctly. The language was difficult. She wondered if she could ever learn it, minimizing the use of vocal organs as it did, hardly moving the lips.

"I didn't think your people kissed," she confessed in his arms. "I was afraid you didn't."

"I was sixteen when the Mexican woman began to fancy me," he said, without embarrassment. "My people do not kiss, but I learned."

She realized it was not a confession; he felt no shame over the affair with the Mexican woman. He was as matter-of-fact about it as he was about everything else. "Did you love her?" she asked, and he smiled down at her.

"I escaped from the Mexicans without any regret. I've never loved anyone but you."

Sometimes they sat beside the pool with their fingers interlocked, not feeling any need to speak, communicating without words. But there was another, lighter side to him that she had not expected, as playful and full of humor as a child. He liked to tease her. He would disappear so suddenly and completely that he became a part of the forest, and she joined into the game of hide-and-seek with amusement. She was never able to find him. He would jump out unexpectedly and lift her in his arms. When she tried to hide from him, he found her within moments, usually approaching from behind and frightening her with a sudden embrace.

"You must learn to track," he told her. "At least, you must learn to conceal yourself better. It's important. I will teach you."

One morning, she sensed him behind her when she knelt at the pond to drink and splashed him with water. He retaliated by attempting to dunk her face, and they rolled on the mossy edge as she struggled against him. They both fell into the cold pond and emerged laughing with Elspeth's skirts floating around her like a lily pad. He embraced her and kissed her wet face before he assisted her from the water.

"I'm drenched," she cried as she pushed her hair back and gazed at her dress in dismay, and he laughed affectionately.

"Just as you were on the night of the Male Rain. You greeted the lightning without fear and let the rain fall on your face."

"You *were* there," she said, recalling the thinness of her drenched nightgown. "What am I to do about this?" she asked, slightly flustered, as she shook the folds of her skirt. "I can't go to the hacienda half-drowned."

"It will dry shortly," he said without concern. But she knew it would dry wrinkled, and it was soiled besides.

"I must go home to change. I don't know what I'll tell Concepcion."

Concepcion was not at the house. Elspeth was relieved at first as she changed her clothing and tidied her hair; then, she became vaguely disturbed by the woman's absence. She thought that Concepcion might be out in the back garden, where they were growing vegetables for the kitchen, but she found only young Pedro there with his hoe. He took off his wide-brimmed straw hat when he saw her.

"We want to thank you for all the extra rations, senorita," he said, with lowered eyes. "No one has ever done this for us before."

"Tell the men they are welcome, and please conceal everything, Pedro. The captain will be back soon. Have you seen Concepcion?"

"She took the supply wagon back to the hacienda, senorita."

"When?" Elspeth asked, realizing how disturbed Concepcion would be when she did not find her there.

Pedro shrugged his white-clad shoulders languidly, "I don't know, senorita. I saw her leave, but I don't know the time. She should be there by now."

Elspeth had been fortunate in her meetings with Valerio until now, but she experienced an anxiety so sudden and acute that she did not know what to do. She thought of going to the hacienda with some explanation of her absence, but she could not bring herself to do so. By now, Concepcion would have put everything together in her mind, realizing that she had not spent as much time at the hacienda as she had pretended. She went back to her loom to think as she worked on Thea's rug. It would be better to confront Concepcion here than in the presence of the de la Cruz sisters, she decided. And, perhaps, Concepcion would say nothing at the hacienda; she would have to answer for Elspeth's whereabouts if she did.

She finished the rug and sought for something else to calm her mind. Though it was not the day for cleaning house, she put a dampened cloth over the broom and removed the fine dust that filtered in constantly from all the floors, and followed that activity by thoroughly dusting the furniture, activities that Concepcion largely ignored. I should have gone to the hacienda at once, she considered later in the day as she prepared a stew for dinner, for herself and the missing woman. Perhaps I could have explained myself then; now, it is I who have been missing from the hacienda for a day. She ate very little as the sun was setting, wondering if she should still ride to the hacienda; by now she was really worried. She tidied the kitchen, glancing frequently from the narrow window into the darkness. Concepcion had never left her alone at night; perhaps she had been taken ill at the hacienda. But, if she had, surely someone would have been sent to stay with her. She tried to read for a while, but could not concentrate on the page of her book. She completed her evening chores and retired to her room.

Sleep would not come, no matter what she did to summon it. Whatever had happened today would surely put obstacles between herself and Valerio. What would he think if she did not answer his summons in the morning? There was no way to get a message to him. He was certain of her love; he would not think she had simply abandoned him. But what if she could not get to him within a few days, a week? He might put himself in danger to come to her.

She was finally beginning to doze around eleven o'clock, her body's weariness overcoming the activity of her mind, when she was startled by footsteps in the kitchen. Concepcion had returned at last. She rose quickly, her mind a jumble from all of her speculations. She had to know what had kept her so long, even if it meant a strong reprimand. She rushed to the kitchen in her nightgown, with her hair loose around her shoulders, and was stunned to see the captain sitting at the table.

"Elspeth!" he greeted her as she reached for her shawl. "You're a blonde. You must have spent all your time outside since I've been gone."

"I've had more time to weave," she stammered, "and I ride to the hacienda every day . . ."

She stared at him, waiting for him to disprove the latter statement, but he leaned back and gazed at her without speaking. "Would you like something to eat?" she asked, moving toward the fireplace. "I didn't expect you so soon."

"No, I dined with the de la Cruzes. Come, sit with me for a moment."

He did not look like a man who had been prospecting. He

had bathed and shaved and changed his clothing at the hacienda. She had approached only a few steps before she smelled the alcohol and grew wary.

"You weren't at the hacienda today," he said. "Concepcion couldn't understand why you weren't there. I instructed her to remain there, since I was coming home tonight. Where were you?"

"I went riding," she said cautiously. "She wasn't here when I returned. I couldn't imagine what had happened to her. Are you sure you wouldn't like a cup of tea? I'd like one."

He appeared satisfied by the explanation, but he did not take his gaze from her as she stirred up the fire. He finally opened a leather pouch and dumped some ore samples on the table. "Take a look at these," he said good-naturedly as he held one up in his hand.

"You found the mine," she said, with surprise, and approached to examine the gold-flecked sample of quartz with interest.

"No," he admitted, putting his free hand over hers, "but we may have found a vein. Why don't you ever call me Robert?" She tried to withdraw her hand, but he clung to it tightly and stared at her in a way he never had before. "It's always been 'Captain Morrison' this, and 'Captain' that. Hell, I'm not in the army anymore. It isn't very friendly, Elspeth."

"You're the head of the family. It's a term of respect," she told him, wishing he would release her hand. His attitude was beginning to alarm her. His face was flushed and his tan eyes were feverish.

"Did you miss me when I was gone?" he asked, pulling her toward him. She resisted and actively tried to disengage his grip.

"I was accustomed to your being here," she tried to placate him. She knew she must not give in to the panic that was getting closer to the surface by the minute. She must reason with him. "Concepcion and I didn't take as much pains with meals."

He rose to his feet and pulled her to him more tightly than he had when they were at the ball. She began to struggle, turning her face away from his searching lips. "Stop it," she commanded. "You don't know what you're doing. You're drunk, Captain. You're Thea's *husband* . . ."

"It isn't easy being Thea's husband," he said through clenched teeth as he attempted to subdue her. "You don't know anything about men. Why do you think I didn't stay with her tonight? My return and the long dinner exhausted her, and the Spanish women went to her room with her. I've wanted you since that night at the Governor's Ball."

Her struggle increased his determination. Locked in conflict, they overturned the table. He released her hand to control her better, and Elspeth instinctively clawed at his face, no longer reasonable in her effort to free herself.

"You little bitch!" he cried as he touched his cheek and stared at the blood on his hand.

She seized the moment to flee to her room and latched the door behind her with shaking hands. As his obscenities reached her from outside, she dragged her heavy trunk to block the door. Her knees suddenly went weak and she sat down on the trunk in tears.

"If that's what you want," his voice said threateningly, "that's the way it will be. I've been putting Don Diego off, but he wants you more than I do. He's willing to marry you for what he wants. And you'll do as I say. As you pointed out, I'm the head of this family. It's to our advantage to be connected to those people."

Elspeth remained silent, her heart pounding in her ears, and she felt as if it would break in her distress for poor Thea as much as for herself. The only thing that kept her from feeling totally helpless was Valerio's nearness.

"If you mention this to Thea," the captain warned harshly, "I won't answer for the consequences. Do you hear that?"

The captain was even worse than she had ever thought. She would never hurt her sister, who had such innocent trust in her husband, but she could not bring herself to speak to him. She sat weeping softly until she heard him stagger away and slam the door to the master bedroom behind him.

She huddled on her bed in the dark for some time before her mind cleared enough to make the decision that would change her life. She could not remain under the same roof with him after tonight, but she was conflicted regarding Thea. After some consideration, she lit a candle and took out her lap desk to write her sister a letter. She made several false starts in her attempt to explain that she was in love with a man of whom Thea and her husband would disapprove. She told her sister that she had done everything not to hurt her, but the time had come to make her own decisions, and she had decided to go away with the man she loved so they could marry:

> I am leaving tonight with the only man I shall ever love, Thea. He is kind and gentle, and will be good to me. Please, do not worry about me, for I shall be safely in the east. I shall contact you as soon as possible to assure you of my well-being. Please do not upset yourself over me. I love you, and I shall miss you, my dear sister.
>
> Elspeth

She felt that the letter was unsatisfactory, but she could think of no way to improve it with further untruths. She dressed quickly in a blouse and dark skirt which, though too heavy for the season, she thought would be less conspicuous than any of her other clothing. At the first sign of false dawn, she cautiously opened her door and heard the captain snoring, deeply asleep in his own room. With only her hairbrush and the stationery in her writing box, she put it in her shawl and slipped into the kitchen, where she gathered some bread and fruit and, as an afterthought, a kitchen knife, placing them into the shawl, as well, and tied it together tightly. Drawing a deep breath in her effort to maintain silence, she left the house and made her way to the shelter where the peons were sleeping.

She knelt quietly and shook young Pedro's shoulder, cautioning him to remain silent as she forced the letter into his hand.

"Do not deliver this to the hacienda until evening," she whispered, "no matter what happens. It is for my sister. Do you understand?"

"*Sí*, senorita," he mumbled as he stuffed the envelope into his shirt and turned over to continue his slumber.

One of the other peons muttered in his sleep, and Elspeth remained still, holding her breath until she was certain he had not awakened. When she went to the corral, she feared one of the horses would nicker and betray her presence, but both Plata and the captain's horse were too familiar with her to make any sound. After she saddled Plata, she did not look behind her as she led the mare by the reins, not mounting until she was well out of range of the house in the diminishing darkness.

She tried to put Thea, the only person that really mattered, out of her mind. What lay ahead of her would be completely foreign, she realized, almost as if she had been reborn. Daydreaming about living with Valerio among his people had been one thing, but the reality that faced her made her chest tighten with trepidation. The thought of Valerio not being where she expected to find him struck her with momentary terror. She wondered where he went during the times that he did not signal for her to come. She knew he had to hunt; and, in order to do it, he had to employ great stealth in mountains inhabited by other tribes and white men. If he isn't there, she thought, with sudden determination, I shall wait for him. She could be invisible, too.

She breathed deeply as she ascended into the foothills, where the trail seemed to disappear between the times that she used it. Valerio would be there, not far from the pond. He had to be. Her heart swelled when she thought of him. Everything had been in preparation for this moment.

Part 2

All is beautiful.

Now the Mother Earth
And the Father Sky
  Meeting, joining one another,
  Helpmates ever, they.

All is beautiful.

Life-that-never-passes,
Happiness in all things,
  Meeting, joining one another,
  Helpmates ever, they.

All is beautiful,
All is beautiful, indeed

—FROM NAVAJO SONG OF THE EARTH

Chapter 9

He stood bare-chested within a formation of rocks, greeting the rising sun by sprinkling fine yellow powder in each of the four directions. Elspeth knew he was aware of her presence and waited in silence until he completed his prayer. His blankets were spread beneath an overhanging rock, half covered by brush, and his pony grazed nearby, unfettered like a wild thing. Strips of venison were drying on a rack of stripped branches next to a deerskin he had been treating. His camp was a marvel of economy, his few belongings stacked near the brush shelter, with his bow and quiver close at hand. She watched him as she had on the first day she had seen him; there was no more beautiful sight in the world to her. When he finally secured his medicine bag to his waist and moved toward her soundlessly, he seemed almost unreal, a being that had sprung from the earth and sky and the rocks around them, until he stroked her cheek gently with the back of his fingers and drew her against his chest.

"The day has begun in harmony," he said softly. "That was my prayer."

She could not tell him about last night; she did not want to spoil the moment. There would be time for speaking of such things later. She enjoyed the moment of serenity in his arms for a moment before she whispered, "I want to go with you, Valerio. I'll be missed soon, but I don't think they'll look here."

"We will start for Dineyah at once," he said, tilting her chin

125

so he could look into her eyes. "You're sure this is what you want? There will be no turning back when we leave."

"I'm sure," she assured him. "I've never been so sure of anything. I've wanted to be with you since I first saw you."

He moved away from her with an easy, unhurried grace and began to gather his belongings. Before she could assist him, he had rolled the deerskin into his sleeping blankets, secured them with a strip of leather, and dismantled the meat rack, scattering its branches on the forest floor and covering them with pine needles. There was no unnecessary motion. Everything was carried out as if he had done it often before. He slipped his reins around his pony's muzzle and tied the bag of venison and extra blankets securely on its back. He surveyed his camp for a moment and swept the area with a branch. When he was through there was no trace of his having been there for over a week. Together, they led the pony back to the pond where Elspeth had left Plata.

Before she realized what he was doing, he unsaddled Plata and tossed her saddle into the pond, where it sank slowly until it was completely submerged. She opened her lips to object, but he told her quietly, "You cannot ride with your legs at one side of your horse like a white woman. You are Dineh, now."

To reinforce her new identity, he draped the blanket he had been carrying over her hair and shoulders and embraced her encouragingly. She was dismayed when he spread a saddle blanket on Plata's back and tied her bundle securely at the horse's neck. How can I ride without stirrups? she wondered, but she did not question his actions. She knew that she had many things to learn. Within less than half an hour of her arrival, when the birds that had been chirping in the semidarkness began to hop from branch to branch in the early sunlight, she found herself riding uncomfortably astride, with Valerio leading Plata by the reins from his pony. Everything had been swept away to obscure their having been there, and Valerio avoided earthen trails now, as he did any surface that would take the imprint of the horses' hooves. She marveled at his inborn caution. Perhaps he had really been invisible in the days he had spent here.

She recognized the necessity for silence as they rode higher into the mountains, probably taking the same route he had taken with Maria. She had to concentrate all her attention on riding astride with only the blanket between her thighs and the short silver hairs of Plata's coat, which chafed her unprotected legs. She had never realized that a horse's back was so wide or its spine so prominent and wondered how long she could endure the misery of this kind of riding.

They did not stop until the sun was directly above them. The forest was thicker here, and a small spring trickled into a hollow in the granite. They ate some of the bread and fruit Elspeth had brought and drank cold water from the stream, using their hands as drinking vessels. After Valerio filled a leather bottle and attached it to her horse, he knelt beside her and kissed her forehead.

"This place is safe for a while," he assured her, "but I must scout ahead. This is Pueblo territory, and there are white men in these mountains, too. Rest for a while. I'll return soon."

She sweltered in the heat beneath the woolen blanket for what seemed an eternity. Her legs burned from the perspiration that ran in rivulets down her body, and she leaned down to examine them. The chafed skin had begun to bleed where her knees had gripped the horse. She wanted to bathe them, but despite the nearness of the water, she remained behind a blind of foliage with the horses. They must put as much distance between themselves and the captain's farm as possible. She occupied herself by tearing strips from her petticoat to tie around her knees for protection while Plata nudged her with a soft muzzle.

Valerio crept up on her so silently that she was unaware of him until his shadow fell across her. She covered her legs with her skirt, but not quickly enough for his keen eyes. He crouched beside her to inspect the damage despite her protestations. "It's worse than I thought," he said as he lowered her skirt again. "I didn't see any sign of Pueblos or of those crazy white men who dig for gold. We have to keep moving," he said gently. "If you can ride until sundown, we can rest."

"If I had to ride to your homeland without stopping, I could do so," she replied gamely. "I'd do anything to be with you, Valerio."

"I would not ask that of you," he said. "You must let your legs hang loosely instead of gripping your knees as if you were controlling your horse. That will come later."

He took the saddle blanket from his pony and placed it over

the one on Plata for extra padding. When Elspeth protested, he shook his head. "My horse and I move as one. I don't need a blanket. You will learn to ride like that in time."

She was more comfortable on the next lap of their journey, though the blanket made her face sweat even in the high mountains. Moving easily with the stride of the horse, with Valerio leading her, she began to enjoy the calm of the wilderness and the fresh scent of the trees and shrubs. The sun was in the west and a light breeze had arisen when they came to a rocky gully surrounded by thick trees. Valerio dismounted lithely and smiled up at her. They had arrived at their destination for the day, their first camp along the way. Elspeth wondered if she could dismount alone on her weakened legs without stirrups to assist her. He had never helped her down from her horse, and she was certain he would not do so, now. Indian women were capable of looking after themselves, apparently. She was relieved when he approached to lift her to the ground. She was even more grateful when he removed the blanket under which she had sweltered all day so the cool breeze could reach her body.

"Only I know this place," he told her. "You don't have to wear the blanket here."

He led her to a peculiar ground-level indentation in the rocks, which extended inward for some distance. "You see," he said, fingering a few ashes on the floor of his hiding place, "no other ashes have joined those I left here. There is also water nearby."

He handed her the water bag and let her slake her thirst before he drank from it. She walked unsteadily to a fallen tree trunk and sat down on its rough, lichened surface, wanting nothing more than to remain here forever, or at least until her legs had healed. He followed her and poured the contents of the water bag over her head, making her gasp. The shock of the refreshing water passed quickly and she laughed aloud.

"You can laugh, so you will survive," he said, with a smile, before sitting down to rest at her feet. His face was illuminated by a sun ray that penetrated the canopy of branches above them. "I will make some moccasins that will protect your legs. They won't be Dineh moccasins, but more like those the Apache wear. I have to remove the iron shoes on your horse, too. Our horses are unshod. They make less noise and are more difficult to track. It will not cause Plata discomfort. She will be treading on the earth as she was meant to do."

She smiled and touched his face. "I'm beginning to learn your secret of invisibility, but I still have so much to learn. You must begin to teach me your language, so I will be able to speak to your family when we arrive."

"You will learn, a little at a time, like a child—the way I learned Spanish. Why don't you refresh yourself in the water while I set up our camp?"

While he prepared his usual brush blind at the opening of the cave, Elspeth washed herself in the icy water, using her petticoat as both washcloth and towel and wringing the water out of it down the front of her blouse. The shelter, which looked like brush growing at the foot of the rocks, was finished when she completed her bath, and she carried the blankets and spread them on the earth behind it, intent on doing her share of the work. Their sleeping arrangements had not entered her mind until she had put their blankets side by side in the security of their shelter. She wondered if she had invited Valerio to share her bed and paused with indecision. She could not change the position of the blankets now; that would look even more peculiar. If he noticed, he gave no indication of it. Apparently, the sleeping arrangement was quite natural to him.

She assisted in the difficult task of removing Plata's horseshoes, which took some time because of the inadequacy of their improvised tools. He had learned some blacksmithing when he was with the Mexican family, and it made the task easier. After he bathed, they lingered over their meal of fruit and jerky until it was nearly dark. "We must sleep," he said at last, taking his place on his blanket, and she crawled into the enclosure gingerly and sat down on the blanket next to his, biting her lip with apprehension, not certain what to expect when they lay down together. She loved him, but she did not know much about such things. She also ached in places she thought it was impossible to ache, and she was tired to her very bones.

"Sleep," he said softly as he wrapped her blanket around her. "Sleep as long as you want in the morning. When you're with my people, you'll be expected to rise at dawn or you'll be considered lazy. But we are still far away from my people."

He bent to kiss her, and she slipped her arms around his neck. "I love you," she whispered against his cheek. "Everything you do makes me love you more. I'll rise at the same time you do, Valerio."

"And I love you," he said, holding her for a moment before lying back on his blanket in the darkness. "You have shown great spirit today. After tonight, we must not call each other by name, though, so you won't forget and do so in front of my family. When we are alone, we may say anything we wish, but never before others. And you must remember never to call them by name to their faces. It is not polite."

"I'll remember," she said, with a smile, settling down in the soft folds of the blanket. Her long period of learning had begun.

The sun was already up when she dragged herself from sleep and shivered in the chill of early morning. He was no longer at her side and had not awakened her at dawn; though she had slept deeply, she recalled that they had huddled together for warmth during the night. His blanket was gone, so Elspeth gathered hers up before crawling outside. She shook the ants and twigs from it and was not surprised to see Valerio's blanket airing in the sun on a bush. She draped her own near his, considering the airing of the blankets a sensible solution against pests. His pony grazed near Plata, so she knew he had not gone far. The deerskin he had brought was spread on the ground, and she knelt to feel it, because she knew it was destined to become her moccasins. It was supple, but not as smooth as she expected it to be, and she did not welcome its surface against her sore legs. She had thought moccasins were as soft as the buckskin trousers Valerio wore.

She washed in the cold creek nearby, discreetly removing one article of clothing at a time and letting it dry on the rocks before she replaced it. Her dark skirt and blouse needed ironing badly, she thought, and smiled at how deeply ingrained her old habits were. Her clothing would never be ironed again and no one would notice. The horses appeared content, but she lifted one of Plata's hooves to inspect it and probed it gently with her fingers. She did not know much about horses, even how deeply a blacksmith's nails went into a hoof, but Plata's hooves were clean, with no sign of infection. The mare did not react even when Elspeth exerted considerable pressure. If anything, her horse seemed livelier today, as if relieved to be free of the metal encumbrances she had worn for so long.

"You're an Indian pony now, Plata," Elspeth said, gently stroking her muzzle. "It may come as a shock to an old lady like you. We both have a lot to learn, but it shouldn't be too difficult. I already know what to do with my blanket in the morning."

She sensed Valerio's presence and turned to find him staring at her with a bemused expression on his face. She wondered if it was permitted to speak to horses.

"I've never heard you speak your own language before," he said as he descended from the rocks with a bundle of leafy branches in his arms. "It is completely strange to me. I forgot that Spanish isn't your native language, either."

"I want to learn yours," she said. "You must start speaking to me in it. I learn better that way. Why did you gather those branches?"

"To cure the buckskin. It will take several days. It is woman's work, but I have watched my mother."

"And I'll watch you, so I'll know how to do it in the future. What do the leaves and branches do?"

"They preserve the leather, soften it. It is *čéč il*, and it tans. We don't have a pot to boil it in, but I've found a shallow rock that might not break from the heat of the fire."

She touched the oak-shaped leaves and repeated the word to the best of her ability, but he had to prompt her several times before he was satisfied. "I will speak to you in my language today. You must not move your lips so much."

During the tedious task of curing the hide without the proper equipment, he patiently repeated words for her, never laughing when she got them wrong. When his hands were free, he embraced her proudly when she said something to his satisfaction, the best way to learn a language Elspeth ever imagined. He welcomed the diversion, too, over the next few days, while he worked on the skin, pounding it with fist-sized stones until it became as soft and supple as suede. When he measured her feet against it, he taught her the word for foot, and that for knife when he carefully cut the leather, avoiding the hole left by his arrow.

"If these were ceremonial moccasins, the skin would be free of the mark that killed the animal," he explained. "Anything that touches you is ceremonial in my mind . . . pure and untouched by all evil."

He spoke of the ceremonials as he stitched the moccasins, translating the names for Enemy Way, Blessing Way, and the other Sings into Spanish for her. "A Sing cures the mind and body and restores *hozro*, harmony," he explained. "Some of them last for a week, and every word of the chants must be perfect. My uncle, Hosteen Yazzie, knows most of the chants. He is a noted Singer."

Though she was pleased with the high moccasins when she tried them on, even now they were not finished. He filled a hole with damp sand and put them in it overnight, so they would fit perfectly when she put them on damp the next morning. Because they were above her knees, he had slit them on the outside and patiently inserted laces to hold them fast. "These are not like any moccasins I've ever seen," he told her when they were finished and on her legs. "Not even Apache wear them this high, but they won't show under your clothes."

To Elspeth, it was like having nothing on her well-healed legs at all; they were like a second, protective skin, and she embraced him gratefully.

"We must leave this place," he told her. "We've lingered too long, made too much smoke. I must hunt soon, and I have to do it somewhere else."

She was able to ride Plata without being led in her new moccasins, exerting gentle pressure on Plata's sides with her knees and holding her seat well when she became accustomed to the feel of the horse. The blanket was still an encumbrance, but she was freer to observe her surroundings as they moved cautiously through the mountains. The Sangre de Cristos had been populated with villages since the early Spanish days, and by the pueblos of the Indians before them, and Valerio was always alert and watchful, ready to rein in and change their course to avoid an encounter. He knew where the Mexican and Pueblo settlements were and avoided them easily, but his sharp eyes and keen hearing were constantly strained for the unexpected. They camped briefly, for only a night at a time; he seemed anxious to put the mountains behind them. He particularly avoided the ancient cave dwellings that abounded in the area, though Elspeth thought they would be a good place to camp. One evening, after he had constructed a brush shelter and they had smoothed their blankets beneath it, Elspeth risked making a suggestion.

"Wouldn't it be safer to travel at night? We're so vulnerable during the day. Why can't we sleep then, and ride when no one's about?''

He sat in their shelter with his face dappled by the sunlight fading through its branches. "No one goes out at night if it can be avoided," he replied. "We can deal with the threats of daylight, but the night is peopled with things beyond understanding."

She recalled the remarks about the Navajo and Apache being afraid of the dark. "What sort of things? You've ventured out in the dark before."

"When it was necessary for Maria. But now I am responsible for your well-being, and I wouldn't risk that kind of danger. You're everything to me."

"What danger?" she pressed. "Wild animals are just as likely to prowl during the day, aren't they? We haven't seen anything but deer so far. Of course, we've heard wolves during the night . . ."

"It isn't the animals," he said, taking her hands and holding them between his. "We are in harmony with the animals. And I'm not really afraid for myself. There are creatures of the night you know nothing about. Witches and spirits which we do not speak about . . ."

"Ghosts?" she asked, with surprise. "Even if they existed, they couldn't hurt us. Besides, spirits haunt houses. They don't roam around outside."

He smiled slightly, but his dark eyes were serious. "You're wrong about the harm they can do," he told her. "They bring sickness and madness. I've never met one, but I know people who have, and the only cure is in my own country. We are in a strange place. Someone may have died on the very spot we're camping, or an improperly buried body could be nearby. I scout the area every evening for that, because the evil that was in a man can manifest itself at night, bringing disaster with it."

"What about the good in him?"

"That is freed with his last breath. Only the evil lingers; and then, only if he isn't buried properly."

Elspeth shivered in spite of herself and inspected the flimsy walls of their brush shelter. "What do you mean by a proper burial?"

"It's better not to speak of these things," he said, and drew her into his arms. "You have nothing to fear when you're with

me. You must sleep now. We will rise before the sun to cross
the valley below and gain the mountains in the west. We'll be
safe there.''

They had never slept in each other's arms. He had always
turned his back to her after he kissed her good night, though
Elspeth would have preferred to sleep in his arms. There was
temptation there, of course, and she knew that he experienced
it, too. A silent agreement had risen between them that they
would not make love until they were married in Dineyah, but
every night she wished that the agreement did not exist. Often,
she awoke to find them huddling together in the cold mountain
night, and she was able to stroke his hair and face so lightly that
it did not disturb his sleep.

He awakened her in the chill hour before dawn, and they
descended by a circuitous route from the mountains under a
moon that hung so low that it illuminated the way like a huge
lantern. When they reached the valley floor, he paused to listen,
and spoke to her so softly that she had to strain her ears to hear
him.

"There are some ranches in the valley. We cannot speak from
now on. We'll cross the Rio Grande before daylight. It's low
this time of year so you must not fear the water.''

She gazed across the dark valley and saw no lights to mark
the ranch houses. "I trust you completely,'' she whispered.
"I'll do whatever you do.''

He reached from his horse and clasped her hand with reassurance. "Move like a shadow. I've done it many times, and
they haven't missed a sheep.''

She opened her lips to express her opinion on that subject,
but he had already moved ahead of her and she had to loosen
Plata's reins to keep up with him. She wished he had not mentioned the sheep. If this was an area the Navajo raided, surely
the ranchers would be cautious. But Valerio took them through
open pastures where not even the barking of a dog was heard,
and they crossed the river just before dawn without any difficulty. She had hardly emerged on the far bank when he gave her
a single quiet order.

"Ride swiftly now!''

She followed at a gallop over the open range as the sun was
rising, passing through flocks of merino sheep which scatted like

gray and white clouds around them and stared back at a distance
with stupid, placid faces. He finally reined in his pony, and they
rode slowly for a while to rest their horses. Elspeth's mouth was
dry, but he did not offer her the water bottle until they were well
into the foothills of the Jemez Mountains.

"The worst is behind us," he told her as she passed the leather
bottle back to him. There was a relaxed, almost triumphant
expression on his face. "The ranchers have grown fat and lazy."

So complacent that it was time to raid them? she wondered.
When the time was right, she must discuss future raiding with
him.

"Your mare's done well for a horse that's been fed oats," he
remarked. "She will be able to graze all she wants here."

"There is nothing to avoid in these mountains?"

He replied only with a smile, and she had a moment of foreboding. She wished she had the map in Don Diego's library.
She had no idea where they were, except that they were moving
west, with the Sangre de Cristos behind them. Why were these
mountains unlike the others? She sensed their wildness as they
rode higher and suddenly felt very far from civilization, as if
everything she knew were receding gradually behind her. Instead of feeling free as she had expected, something troubled
her. She felt as if she were being observed on all sides by an
unfriendly presence and wondered if Valerio's evil spirits ever
came out in the daylight. He rode ahead more boldly than before, almost recklessly, as if to announce his arrival.

Before midday, they reached a small lake, and he dismounted
in a sheltered area near the water. Without scouting the area
beforehand, he spread her blanket under a tree and indicated
that she rest while he tended the horses. There were questions
she wanted to ask, but she complied in silence, so weary that
she soon fell into a deep sleep. When she awoke, his bow was
resting nearby—next to two skinned rabbits—and he was watching her. She stretched and smiled up at him, wondering how
long he had been there without her knowledge. The trepidation
she had experienced earlier had been dissipated by sleep. She
must have imagined they were being watched because she was
tired and tense from the forced ride across the dangerous valley.

"Are you hungry?" he asked. "We'll have a feast this evening. In the meantime, there is only jerky."

Her gaze wandered longingly toward the lake as she chewed

the tough venison, and as if he had read her mind, he handed her some pithy pieces of what appeared to be plant stalk.

"Soapweed," he told her. "Yucca root. It's much sweeter than the lye soap the Mexicans made me wash with. You want to bathe. When I've finished here, I will join you."

"Is it all right?" she asked. "I haven't had a real bath for days. My clothes feel like they're part of me."

"It's all right. Soapweed is good for the hair, too. It makes it shine in the sun."

"Mine needs something," she said with a smile, her hand closing around the pieces of root. "I'll wash my clothes, too," she decided, reaching for her blanket for the sake of modesty.

She ran toward the lake and quickly undressed in the plentiful bushes at its edge, slapping away an annoying cloud of gnats while she did so. Wearing only her torn petticoat and her camisole, she stepped into the water and gasped. It was chillingly cold until she submerged her body and became accustomed to it; then, she lathered herself all over with the foaming root. The abundance of water was a luxury she had not enjoyed since they began their journey. She returned for her clothes and scrubbed them as thoroughly as she had cleaned herself. Her hair was wet and heavy on her neck when she went back to hang them on the bushes, fighting off the gnats with one hand. The sight of Valerio startled her. Clad only in his breechcloth, he had come to join her, and she backed into deeper water because her thin cotton garments were clinging to her body. She watched him dive into the water with only her shoulders and head visible above it. She had never become completely accustomed to his disturbing beauty, and she was more conscious of it now. He laughed as he lathered his long, black hair and bronze body and submerged to rinse himself, repeating the ritual several times before swimming with a long stroke into deep water. Elspeth could not swim; she watched with admiration.

When he realized why she had not followed him, he returned and draped her arms around his neck before swimming out again. She was so aware of his closeness that she forgot her fear of the water. He shifted her and held her hands so that she floated in front of him, and she looked into his eyes, no longer conscious of her clinging garments. The faint stirrings of desire she had felt before did not compare with the sensation that swept over her now and reflected itself in his eyes. He drew her closer, until their lips and bodies were clinging in the water, and, with one arm tightly around her waist, he slowly swam toward the bank. The wilderness receded around them as she gave herself to him on the grassy bank and clung to him as if their souls, as well as their bodies, had joined.

"You are beauty," he whispered against her neck as they lay entwined. "We will be one always. You are all I want from life."

She stroked his damp hair and bronze shoulders, too overcome to speak for a moment. Finally, she managed in a small voice, "I didn't know it would be like this. We belong to each other completely. We'll always be together."

They remained beside the lake for almost a week. Elspeth would have been content to remain there forever. They could not pass each other without touching, and she began to learn his language, which was now her language, too. She learned it like a child, without understanding its syntax or concerning herself with its mechanics. Her life had fallen into a different, slower rhythm than she had known before, and she could learn more easily in this peaceful environment. She did not feel as though she were living in the wilderness with Valerio so near; their brush shelter was home when she desired to retire to it. The animals she saw were not afraid of humans; indeed, their company was desirable. She coaxed the bushy-tailed gray squirrels almost to her hand, though the tiny striped chipmunks were more cautious, staring from a distance with bright, slightly protuberant eyes and skittering off when she tried to approach them. The only predator they sighted was so lovely that she lacked any fear of it. The great tawny cat, with its buff-colored triangular face, appeared often to lie in the sun on a prominence above them, and she and Valerio observed it quietly.

"The mountain lion is shy of people," Valerio told her. "He is watching us just as we are watching him. We're in his territory, but he does not look upon us as game. I've never heard of him attacking anything but small animals and deer. The People live in harmony with the animals. Even snakes. If you are alert, it's easy to walk around Snake."

"You kill animals to live."

"We always say a prayer for the animal when we do so—to speed his departing spirit and ask him to forgive us for the necessary act. All of the animals brought the earth to life and are sacred.''

He told her that the animals were born of First Man and First Woman, and that made them brothers to all men. Coyote, the fifth child born, could not speak, so breathed into him were the four evil Wind Spirits and he began to howl and talk. His voice warned the People of coming disasters, and it was Coyote who, in a moment of mischief, hurled the stars into the sky.

''After the People took two pieces of black agate and made Talking God and Hogan God, they laid out the constellations on the floor of their hogan with the pieces left over. But before they could make more, Coyote returned from the East with the Fire God and hurled the stars into the sky. Fire God gave them their light.''

When they spoke of his family, Elspeth noticed that his mother's name appeared more often than the others. He explained that women were in charge of the family; the children they had were theirs. In important matters, they consulted the men, but they were in charge of their own property and could distribute it as they chose.

''My clan is Rocks-Beside-the-Water, and I am born for Salt, my father's clan. My mother is the head of my family. Everyone looks to Many Beads for instruction and guidance where we live. When a man marries, he goes to live with the family of his bride, though he may never look upon the face of his mother-in-law.''

''How can you bring me to your mother's house?'' she asked. ''You're supposed to go to the home of your wife.''

''I've thought about that. I am my mother's only son, and she is grateful to you for helping my sister. That will ease our way, I think. My mother is not married, now; perhaps, she will keep her only son at home. My uncle is a very wise Singer, too. If he is called upon, he will give the best advice. A Singer is to us what a priest is to the Mexicans.''

''He's a medicine man?''

''No,'' he said, with a smile, shaking his head. ''There are no medicine men, though the white people think so. There are medicine women, who treat illness with herbs and plants, but the Singer uses such things only in rituals. He has memorized the holy chants and knows the sand paintings. My uncle knows more chants than most Singers. He lives with us.''

''Why doesn't he live with his wife's family?''

"He is old. He has no wife or children. My mother asked him to live with us. My father went away when I was small. My mother married twice after that, but her husbands were lazy, so she put their belongings outside the hogan. She is alone now."

Elspeth frowned. "She just sent them away? Divorced them? A woman can do that?"

"Of course. It is permitted. Just as it is permitted for a man to leave and go to another wife. People shouldn't live together if they are unhappy."

"We will be happy," she said, touching his face. "I'll never send you away . . . if you'll never leave me."

"Some men and women were meant to stay together," he assured her, kissing her hand. "My sister, Many Tears Woman, is not happy with her husband, but she has not sent him away yet. My sister, Big Woman, is always happy—and so is her husband."

"How many sisters have you? Do they all live with your mother?"

"Three. Smiling Girl—the one you know as Maria—is not married yet, but she will be soon, I think. We were all born for Salt. There are no children by the other husbands. Girls always stay at their mother's place."

"I must remember their names before we get there. Of course," she sighed, "I'm not supposed to speak their names, am I? There is more than your language to learn." Another more disturbing thought occurred to her. "What will happen if your mother doesn't allow us to stay with her?"

"That won't happen," he said boldly. Then, as if considering the prospect for the first time, he added, "If it did, we would still stay together always. Things would be more difficult for us, but I will look after you, *querida.* I'd rather have you with my family when I'm away, though, and I think that is the way it will be. Do you have a clan? It is important to know your clan name when we meet my mother. And knowing your clan prevents the evil of intermarriage; our children should know yours."

"It isn't likely that they'd marry any of my people," she told him, with a smile. "My name is Williams. There are thousands of people with that name, none of whom know their lineage for more than a few generations."

"Your clan is Williams?" he asked, and she replied hesitantly, wishing that the Welsh were as clannish as the Scots.

"Not really. But a surname prevents intermarriage, too. Our customs are different from yours."

"I know," he said, with understanding, "but you must have a clan when you meet Many Beads. She wouldn't understand if you didn't."

Elspeth gazed out over the twilit lake and felt the first twinge of anxiety about meeting his mother. Their future rested in her hands. "The Welsh are Celts," she said. "I suppose that is my clan. I guess I'm Celt, born for Williams. Do you think that will do?"

"Yes," he considered, "I think so. Many Beads must know that white people are different. We must leave in the morning. We are not far from Dineyah now."

When Valerio said a destination was not far, it usually took them days to reach it, so she was not concerned about time. She did not want to leave this place, where they had been so happy, but she knew they must continue on their way. She tried to calm her fears about meeting his mother, who had never seen a white person before but who was a woman who wanted her son's happiness. Customs may differ, but some things are universal, she felt, and somehow she must convey to Many Beads how much she, too, loved Valerio.

Chapter 10

The western slope of the mountain was more rocky and barren, and she had a definite sensation that they were being watched, an intuition so strong that she wanted to call out to Valerio, riding ahead of her. They had not traversed terrain like this before, and she scanned the crags above them cautiously from under her blanket, starting at the motion of a coyote loping away in the heat. Even Valerio seemed to be riding straighter on his pony, as if to advertise that he was a warrior, alert for the unexpected. But, after a while, she relaxed her vigilance, no longer sensing danger. There had probably been nothing to worry about. If there had been any peril, Valerio would have warned her before they left the lake; she had probably misread his apparent caution. He had told her that these mountains were safe, and she could understand why no one came here. These bare ridges had a strange feeling to them, almost as if the tawny slopes had a menace of their own. They rounded a ledge, and her heart nearly stopped with terror. On a rock above them, outlined against the blue sky, two Indian braves sat loosely on their pinto ponies, and she knew at once that they were not Navajo. They were like no Indians she had seen, with long, loose hair, naked except for their breechcloths and high moccasins. As lean and sharp as predatory animals, they observed from a distance without moving, and she was so frightened that she gave Plata rein in the hope of reaching Valerio.

"Don't change your pace," he said in a voice loud enough for only her to hear. "Don't look at them. They're Apache. We're in their land, but they won't harm us."

The very word Apache increased her panic, but she obeyed his instructions, finding it difficult not to see what the braves were doing. She had felt much more comfortable with the mountain lion. The picture of them remained clear in her mind: the way they sat their horses with arrogant ease, conveying prowess with their stance. She remembered everything she had heard about Apache, expected an arrow to strike her breast at any moment, or to hear the scream Concepcion said she would never forget when they attacked. Valerio behaved as if they did not exist, riding easily and carelessly, as if he were unaware of them. She recalled Dr. Cabot telling her that the Navajo and Apache had once been one tribe; they spoke the same language, but something had happened to separate them. Perhaps that was the reason no arrow had torn into her yet.

They descended the grade slowly, with the Apache behind them. Her back was exposed to them. Cold perspiration trickled down her sides, and her mouth was so dry that she could hardly swallow. After about half an hour, Valerio surprised her by pausing to rest the horses. She joined him and he passed her the water bottle. She drank from it quickly, so she would be able to speak.

"I've never been so terrified," she confessed, still not glancing behind them. "Are they following us?"

"No. They want to avoid us as much as we do them."

"They didn't seem to be afraid," she said. "You speak the same language. Why do you avoid one another?"

"If our eyes meet, the world would end."

"The world would end? I don't understand."

"We were one People many years ago, it is said, but something happened. The Apache left, and it became known that the world would end if we met face-to-face. Some of them still call themselves Dineh, but they have forgotten our Way. They've traded with the Comanche, and they've become cruel. But they never bother us."

"I was so frightened. You said these mountains were safe."

"They are. I come this way often, and they know me by sight and avoid me. Nothing's harmed us in all the time we've been here, has it?"

She remembered the lake and their unrestrained affection there and drew in her breath. "We were being watched! You knew they were there, and you didn't warn me."

"We were completely alone," he told her patiently. "They knew we were there, and they gave us a wide berth. There is nothing to concern us but the weather, now." He indicated the mesquite-dotted plain below them. "We must cross that before the rains come."

He pressed her to ride quickly as they traversed the desert. She did not understand his haste or why he continually glanced at the dark clouds gathering many miles away to the north, but she followed at a gallop without questioning his wisdom. She would have appreciated a refreshing downpour to wash away the dust they raised in their headlong dash for the western hills. She wondered if rainstorms were another phobia of his people, like spirits walking in the night and their avoidance of the gaze of an Apache. When they gained higher ground, he paused to look back, and she did not have time to ask him about it, because the dry land they had traversed suddenly flowed away below them as a torrent of water rushed across the desert and rampaged over the land. Only the tight-rooted brush clung desperately to the diminishing earth; no horseman could have survived the flood. She had heard the expression "flash flood" at the hacienda, but she had not conceived the devastation of water carrying broken trees and boulders in its wake.

"We might have drowned," she marveled as she dismounted. "We could have drowned in the desert."

"The season of the Male Rains is upon us," he said as he walked to her side. "The water from the storm in the north is coming this way. It will soon be at the Sacred Mountain."

"*Male* Rain?" she asked, with a smile. "Is there Female Rain, too?"

"Of course," he said as he put his arms around her. "Everything is either Male or Female. The strong Male Rain makes the earth fruitful, but it can be destructive, too. The Female Rain is as gentle and soft as you, *querida*." He bent to kiss her as the first drops of the approaching storm spattered on the bare rocks around them. "It will be safer to remain here; we'll be caught in the storm anyway. I'll make a shelter with the blankets. The force of the rain will diminish by the time the storm strikes here.''

She felt safe in his arms when the rain pattered against their blanket roof and the lightning illuminated the darkness of their refuge. She thought of the power of the Male Rain when he made love to her, appreciated the wisdom of creation for making everything male or female. The horses whinnied outside as if from a great distance. If the earth had flowed away beneath them, Elspeth would not have noticed.

After a few hours' ride the next morning, the earth changed dramatically to an intense rose color which made the sky appear even wider and more blue, and trees began to appear around them. Even before he told her that they were in Dineyah, she knew they had finally reached his homeland, but it was some time before she noticed any dwellings. The hogans, roofed with the same red earth that surrounded them, were almost invisible to the eye, as much a part of the earth as the red sandstone outcroppings near them. She realized that she had probably passed others before her vision became adjusted to their presence and the languid activity taking place near some of them. Since they were not in the fabled canyon stronghold, *Tsegi*, she was surprised by the number of families living here on the high plateau.

"It's beautiful," she told Valerio. "We must be near the canyon since there are so many families living here.''

He smiled, sunlight and shadow accentuating his features. "The white men think that everyone lives in the canyon. They don't know how large our homeland really is, extending in all directions as far as a man can ride. It will be afternoon before we reach Tsegi.''

Though his spirits had been good during the whole journey, he was more relaxed and cheerful here. He did not ride close enough to the hogans to greet his tribesmen; Elspeth suspected that he did not wish to expose her to them before he spoke to his family. But, even at a distance, no one raised a hand to greet him, and this began to disturb her. Had they recognized at once that she was not one of them, even at a distance?

"They don't seem very friendly. Is it because I'm with you?''

"No. It is because I'm not their kinsman. It is I who should make the first overture. They would show us hospitality in any hogan, no matter how little they have to offer, but I would be regarded with some suspicion, because I have no blood ties with them.''

"You told me you have no chief. Your clans are independent and suspicious. What do you do when there is war?"

"We don't have war, unless we're threatened by the Ute or Comanche; then, we join together to defend ourselves. But you must not worry about that. Even the Ute, our greatest enemy, would not enter the canyon. We're more vulnerable in the winter when we move out of Tsegi, but these people''—he indicated the hogans scattered sparsely around them—''are in danger all year.''

"Why don't you remain in the canyon in the winter so you'd be safe?"

"There's no forage left by winter. If the sheep don't survive, neither do we."

A cornfield rustled near every hogan, a patch of green and gold on the red land, and Elspeth was convinced that the Dineh would not actually starve without their sheep, though they would be cold without their wool, which provided clothing and blankets. She was struck by the openness of this land, and the peace surrounding her; this, more than physical features, was the signature of this place with its absence of fences and walls. A young shepherd, driving his flock in silence, might have been herding white clouds that had become disoriented by so much space and moved onto the land instead of remaining in the sky.

The storm had not passed beyond the Chuska Mountains, and the red earth was dry, with stunted trees, since they had left them. A stand of cottonwood trees ahead alerted Elspeth to a change of scenery, but not to the full impact of the change until they suddenly stopped on the edge of the canyon. The streaked, red sandstone cliffs below extended, wind-sculptured, for as far as she could see, but she could not discern any habitation on the banks of the meandering water in the valley seventy feet below.

"We are home," Valerio said. "Do you think you can descend here?"

She leaned forward cautiously on Plata's back to look for a path, but only tumbled stones met her eyes. "Can you actually get down here? I see now why they say the canyon is impenetrable.''

"Those who know the canyon can descend in several places,"

he said when he observed her reaction to the depth. "I better take you by the entrance the Spaniards once found, though it will take longer."

He pointed downward to a dark, horizonal opening left in the ruddy canyon wall. "That is a famous cave," he said. "The People fortified themselves there long ago, when the Spaniards came. The Spaniards fired on them from up here for many days and finally killed them. That place is *chindi*; the spirits of the dead still linger there. The Spaniards call this branch of the canyon Del Muerto, because of the heavy losses here. The officer finally led his men through Chinle Wash, where we are going, the only entrance into the canyons. The first man who entered that cave met a Dineh woman with a knife. They struggled there, and both fell from the cliff. We call that place *'ah tah ho do nilly,'* Two Fell Off. The Spaniards took the ears of those who died there, but they did not come back again."

Elspeth recalled the perfume and music at the Governor's Ball and shuddered at the recollection. She could not tell Valerio that the ears still hung on a wall in the palace. She found it difficult to imagine such violence in such a peaceful place as this. "Does anyone live in the Canyon of the Dead?" she asked.

"Yes. It isn't all *chindi*. I will take you there sometime."

Chinle Wash, the only open access to the canyons, was flowing turgid pink water from the rains when they reached it. Elspeth asked if she could freshen herself when they paused to rest before retracing their steps on the floor of the canyon. She was weary from the long ride, and fine red dust covered both of them. After she bathed her face and arms in the silty water, she found a sheltered spot and attempted to brush the tangles from her hair. She would have liked to submerge herself completely in the fast-running water, but Valerio cautioned her about quicksand. She would have to meet his family as she was, with her skirt dusty over her torn petticoat. The blanket had protected the rest of her, and she replaced it carefully before they continued their ride, more nervous than she had expected at the prospect of meeting his mother, who would decide the future course of her life with Valerio.

In the late afternoon, weariness gradually began to replace her nervousness as they rode through the canyon the Dineh called Tsegi, and the Spaniards, attempting to reproduce the name, designated as "de Chelly" in writing, though they pronounced it "de Shay." They crossed the Wash several times in their progress to secure footing on the other side, until its course changed and they had to cross the rock-strewn water again. The Wash meandered through the canyon even when the water was running rapidly, and she tried to remain alert because Plata did not fancy the moving water. The earth on either side of the Wash widened, revealing cornfields and peach trees on the fertile banks, and settlements of scattered hogans, which had been invisible from the rim above. Children ran out to follow them for a distance, chattering together with excitement. Though they were clad only in small blankets sewn at the sides, they were the happiest children Elspeth had ever seen, completely at ease and free in their wild environment, their large, dark eyes shining up at her from their smiling faces. She wanted to return their smiles, but it was necessary to hold her blanket more closely around her face to conceal her white skin. They had never seen a white person, and she wondered if they would run from her in terror or be as fascinated with her as she was with them.

"Where are the men?" she asked Valerio when the most recent group of youngsters had fallen behind. "We've passed several hogans, but the only people I've seen have been old women and children."

"They may be away," he answered guardedly. "The younger women are doing their chores or weaving. It is safe to leave the women and children alone here."

She thought of the Mexican sheep ranches they had passed through in the east; this was something they must discuss. He did not seem to realize how high the feeling against the Navajo was in Santa Fe. She must warn him, try to impress it upon all of the People through him, if possible, before it was too late. She observed the flocks grazing in the canyon, Mexican merino sheep, attended by children and a few old women. She had attempted to speak to Valerio about the raiding several times, only to be informed that it was the Dineh way. They raided the Mexicans, and the Mexicans, given the opportunity, raided them. It had always been that way. When she called it stealing, he had laughed; apparently, no one looked upon it that way. They only took what they needed; no one was harmed by it.

Toward evening, they reached the settlement of several ho-gans situated far apart in a grove of lacy tamarisk trees. He did not have to tell her that this was his "mother's place," as he referred to it in his own language. Several children materialized from the stand of trees calling his name joyfully, and he swung one of them up onto his horse. These would be Big Woman's children, Elspeth surmised; she was the only sister who had children. When they dismounted, Elspeth caught the boy and his two younger sisters sneaking glances when they thought she was not looking. Since her face was almost covered by the dusty blanket, they soon abandoned their curiosity and ran ahead to alert their elders. Elspeth followed Valerio in silence, sensing that he was as anxious as she about meeting his mother. The hogans fascinated her as they passed each of them on their way. The lower walls were composed of stacked branches, plastered with the same red clay that composed their rounded roofs, and there was a brush shelter near each of them where the inhabitants could perform their daily tasks during the day out of the heat. Even in a family community, the dwellings were spaced widely apart, with trees between them to insure privacy. The recently harvested cornfield extended to the foot of the cliff, with peach trees growing unevenly enough to seem wild, not in neat rows like the orchards she had seen in the past. Yellow squash were still hiding beneath their broad leaves in the sandy soil closer to the Wash, and across the water, Elspeth observed a crumbling cliff dwelling, which she called to Valerio's attention.

"The Ancient Ones built it, the Anasazi," he told her. "They left this place before the Dineh came here many years ago. No one knows why. There are many dwellings like that in the cliffs of the canyons. Who knows what ancient evil is still within them? We avoid them."

Many Beads and her daughters emerged from a brush shelter where Indian corn was drying, its yellow, blue, and red kernels as colorful as rows of beads. Elspeth recognized Valerio's mother by the tangled strings of uncut turquoise which covered her chest and gave her her name. Her hair was bound into a chongo knot like her daughters', with loose strands escaping over her lined forehead, and the expression on her handsome face left no doubt about who controlled the family. The oriental fold of her eyes had been transmitted to her three daughters, but it was less evident in Valerio and the young boy. Mother and son did not embrace, but their feeling for one another was almost palpable.

"Ya tay," Valerio greeted her, and she responded with the same words and indicated that they sit.

Elspeth sank down slightly apart from the family and tried to place the other women by their names, while Valerio and his mother conversed. Smiling Girl, Maria, was finding it difficult not to detach herself from her sisters to greet her friend. She was not the same young woman Elspeth had known at the hacienda only a few months before; the tightness had left her face, and her dark eyes were happy and alive. While he was explaining her presence to his mother, Many Beads's face was so impassive that Elspeth was not sure whether she was pleased or displeased. Big Woman, the mother of the children, was not only taller than the other women but plump all over, and she had the cheerful nature usually attributed to stoutness. Elspeth sensed that nothing would bother her much, but she was not as sure of Many Tears Woman, the eldest daughter, whose face wore the mark of some unimaginable grief. She was slender almost to the point of thinness, and she bore herself with a curious dignity that belied her despair. She would be the most difficult to win as a friend; indeed, Elspeth already sensed her disapproval. The children were, of course, Oldest Boy, Oldest Girl, and Small Girl, the names they would bear until something more distinctive about them gave them another nickname later. While their elders conversed, they continued to cast forbidden glances in her direction, openly curious. From where she sat, Elspeth suddenly became aware of yet another woman—of whom Valerio had not spoken—standing in the distance under the tamarisk trees, too far away to be seen clearly. Elspeth tried to dismiss her as a visitor, but she knew that she belonged here, though in what capacity she did not understand.

"My mother greets you," Valerio said at last, half turning toward her. "She thanks you for helping my sister. She asks that you remove the blanket so that she can see you."

She tried to do so gracefully, with her head held high, but she was so nervous that she thought she might burst into tears at any moment. Big Woman gasped audibly, and Many Tears Woman compressed her lips tightly when they saw her. Only Many Beads retained her composure, though she had never seen a white woman, either. Perhaps because she was not one of them, they did not consider it bad manners to stare at the stranger with blond streaks in her hair and eyes the color of blue-green water.

Elspeth endured their scrutiny with as much composure as she could. A smile began to play on the lips of Big Woman; she did not find what she saw unpleasant. But Many Tears Woman's distaste was evident, and Valerio's mother's face revealed nothing. Maria—Smiling Girl—could not contain herself any longer and jumped to her feet to come and sit beside Elspeth, who nearly wept over the friendly gesture.

"I thought my brother had gone to get you," Maria whispered in Spanish. "He asked me about you all the time. I'm so happy to see you!" She lowered her voice even more, though the other women could not understand her. "I know my mother will accept you as her own. Please be patient. We do things more slowly than the white people."

Elspeth glanced down at her dusty skirt and realized she probably looked like a beggar, though she must not behave like one before these women. She must walk a careful line between too much pride and humility. She tried to smile at Maria, but she could not control her lips. Her friend's small hand insinuated itself into hers beneath the folds of her skirt, and she began to feel better as the warmth of the little hand spread through her body.

"Thank you," she said to Maria. "I'm so glad you're here. What has your mother said concerning our marriage?"

"Nothing. My brother hasn't mentioned it yet."

Many Beads had a pot of water brought to them, and they drank from it with a gourd. Elspeth's mouth was so dry that she could not quench her thirst, but she drank slowly, in small sips, in an attempt not to show weakness. Maria acted as her interpreter when the older woman repeated her gratitude for Elspeth's assistance at the hacienda.

"Smiling Girl is my friend," Elspeth replied. "It was my pleasure to get her away from that place and back among her own people."

"You have left your people to come here," Many Beads said.

Elspeth could not determine if there was reproach in the statement. Family was everything to the Dineh; Valerio had indicated as much. How would she explain forsaking her own people without mentioning her love for Valerio? "I will miss my sister," she told Many Beads. "I love her very much. She is married, though, and I was not happy in my brother-in-law's house.

Among my people, men are the head of the family, and women are dependent upon them for everything.''

The women consulted together briefly, unable to credit such a statement, pursing their lips and shaking their heads over the strange ways of the whites. Only Many Tears Woman made no comment, staring instead with narrow-eyed suspicion at the young woman who did not belong here.

"You only have one sister?" Many Beads asked. "What about your mother and father?"

"They're . . ." Elspeth almost said they were dead, which would have shocked even Maria. "My mother and father left us some time ago. My sister and I only had my brother-in-law. My sister needed me for a while, but she does not need me now.''

"Her brother-in-law wanted her to marry the Spaniard," Valerio interjected, and Elspeth felt the pressure of Maria's hand increase. "She could not do that.''

Though Don Diego's name was not mentioned, it was clear that there was only one Spaniard to them. Their hatred for him was revealed in their faces momentarily, but Many Beads commented only, "No. She could not do that," before changing the subject to free herself of angry thoughts. She volunteered the names and ages of those around her and inquired Elspeth's age so directly that she almost had to suppress a smile. She could not imagine the women in her society volunteering their ages so directly, especially after they reached forty, and Many Beads was fifty.

"I'm seventeen," she replied, and they seemed surprised.

"You are very old not to be married," Many Beads stated frankly, and Maria added, "I'm sixteen, and that is very old. I'll tell them that girls marry later where you come from.''

Elspeth could not tell if the explanation satisfied Many Beads or not, because she frowned and spoke to Valerio. She appeared worried about something, and Elspeth wished she did not have to wait for a translation of what she said.

"My mother is concerned that you might have been followed," Maria said. "My brother is assuring her that no one besides us knows where you are. He made a joke," she said, with a smile. "He said that we should know that if a bear was stalking him, he would end up stalking the bear.''

Everyone but Many Tears Woman smiled at the jest. Many Tears Woman appeared bored with the conversation, though she kept her irritation to herself. Elspeth did not understand her, but her intuition told her that her unhappiness was internal and not directed only at herself.

"We owe much to Helping Woman, because she helped my daughter return to us," Many Beads said at last. "She can stay with us as long as she wishes. Her presence will be remarked upon. Our neighbors will think we have captured a white woman, and that will worry them. We will explain to them what she has done for us and tell them that our debt must be paid."

Before Elspeth could thank her, Valerio said, "I want her for my wife."

Maria smiled, but her sisters glanced at their mother, each reflecting her own feelings. Big Woman was surprised, but she was too kind to show disfavor; Many Tears Woman was shocked and indignant. Neither of them spoke, and Many Beads kept her own counsel, an inscrutable expression on her wide face.

"If I do not marry a Dineh," Valerio continued, "I'll never have to leave to live with another family. I want to remain here, where my mother has no man of her own kin, except for Hosteen Yazzie, who is growing old. I will never want any other girl. We need each other."

His mother's long silence alarmed Elspeth. She knew that everything Valerio had said was contrary to tradition; Many Beads would have to give it much thought. She felt herself shivering and found it difficult to control her expression, and had to bite her lower lip to keep it from trembling. She clung to Maria's hand like a lifeline, while her friend waited impatiently for her mother to break the uncomfortable silence so she could interpret her words.

"You have ridden a long way," Many Beads said at last. "You are tired and hungry. We will eat and sleep, my son. Such matters are never decided in a moment, and what you ask requires consideration. We are happy to have you back home."

"You will sleep in my mother's hogan," Maria informed Elspeth as they ate mutton stew from the mutual pot with chunks of corn bread. "Tall Man will stay with Hosteen Yazzie, who has not been well. I had to carry his food to him a while ago. It is well that you stay with my mother. She will come to know you better."

Elspeth accepted some dark, dried peaches and nibbled at

them distractedly. It had not been realistic to imagine that she
and Valerio would marry at once, but she felt she could not bear
the separation after sleeping in his arms at night. Her gaze followed him when he left them, walking dejectedly through the
trees with his blanket under his arm. The woman who had been
standing in the stand of trees had vanished; she wondered if she
had really seen her at all. Everything was so strange, even the
pungent taste of the food, and she must face it alone on her first
night here. At least, she had Maria.

"I thought I saw a woman standing over there earlier," she
remarked, "Dressed in dark colors. I couldn't see her face."

Maria was silent for a moment, as though she were reluctant
to speak of the figure Elspeth had seen, perhaps a little embar-
rassed by it. "We will talk about such things later," she said at
last. "My family would not want me to speak about it now. We
are not bad people, but sometimes good people have the badness
of others thrust upon them."

Her sisters began to clear away the meal before Elspeth could
question her further. They scoured the cooking pot with sand
and washed it out with water, placing it against Many Beads's
hogan until it was used again, and Maria left her side to extin-
guish the fire. Big Woman brought Elspeth a clay pot of water
and indicated by gestures that she could wash herself with it.
She cleaned her face and hands and washed as far as her elbows;
perhaps tomorrow she could bathe completely. For the moment,
she adhered only to instructions, like a small child. When the
necessary cleaning up was completed, Big Woman and Many
Tears Woman took their leave to go to their own hogans, which
were hidden by the trees, and Many Beads ushered Elspeth into
her own dwelling. Her arms were heaped with sheepskins and
blankets, which had apparently been airing outside someplace.
Maria disappeared for a short time and entered with some folded
blankets, too.

In the dim light of evening, it was difficult to make out much
detail inside, but Elspeth noticed at once that a large loom was
suspended from the rafters, and the sight of it made her feel
more comfortable. The rest of the hogan seemed almost bare,
the earthen floor smooth and well swept, and clothing and other
essentials neatly concealed against the walls. A few words passed
between Maria and her mother when they were laying the bedding, and Maria whispered to Elspeth later, when they lay be-

side each other, "Mother knows about the fine weaving you did on your kind of loom and that I tried to explain ours to you. She just told me she would teach you. She's never shown anyone but her daughters before. She is the best weaver I know. I think she likes you."

"I hope so. She's very kind. Do you think she'll allow your brother to marry me?"

Maria placed her hand over Elspeth's in the soft sheepskin. "She has great affection for him. I think it would please her if he remained with us. He couldn't do that if he married a Dineh girl. But," she sighed deeply, "everything depends upon her uncle. Hosteen Yazzie will decide. He is very wise. Only he knows what will please the Holy People."

A few syllables from Many Beads silenced the girls, and, though her entire future might be decided the next day, Elspeth could not stay awake. The accumulated weariness of the journey seemed to have caught up with her and, on the comfortable bedding, with a real roof over her head, she soon fell asleep.

Chapter 11

She did not hear the household stirring until the sun was nearly up, and she rose quickly, realizing that she had slept later than was proper. Many Beads's and Maria's bedding was already gone. She could hear them outside preparing the morning meal. Not wishing to appear lazy, she began to roll her bedding hastily, but the sunlight penetrating from the door made her pause to look around her. The order inside the hogan, which she had sensed the night before, was confirmed by daylight, but she had not anticipated the warm colors around her. Skeins of yarn hung from the rafters near the loom in shades ranging from creamy yellow to deep brown, and she wondered how they had obtained such hues. The rug on the loom was a large one, beautifully crafted, the pattern different from the other rugs she had seen. She glanced around to find a pattern for the design, but the weaver seemed to have woven out of her head. Rose-colored pottery stood in rows on a shelf placed in one of the niches made by the joined poles of the timber walls; indeed, all of Many Beads's worldly goods appeared to be tidily tucked away in such niches. Only a water jar inside the door and some fleecy wool, recently carded, attested to the hogan's habitation. The circle of stones marking the fireplace directly beneath the smoke hole in the roof looked as if it had never known ashes, and, though the tamped earth floor could not have been swept this morning, it was as clean as any floor Elspeth had seen.

"*Su, Su!*" a voice said outside, and Elspeth hastened to exit the hogan with her bedding. Many Beads was chasing a dog away from the cooking while Maria crouched to fashion flat bread between her hands near the fire. She greeted Elspeth with a smile and noted her anxiety about rising late while Elspeth was still wondering if she should apologize for the breach of etiquette.

"My mother decided to let you sleep," she said comfortably. "It is your first day here, and you have traveled far. After we eat, I'll wash your hair and brush it."

The children arrived when the last bread was cooked, but they had apparently eaten at their own hogan. The two younger ones hovered around the fire, interested in Elspeth, but Oldest Boy left, after greeting his grandmother, to open the corral and take the sheep to graze for the day. Valerio had not been idle since sunrise. He came bearing a load of wood for his mother, which he stacked in the pile beside the door. He observed Elspeth while he ate, his eyes so full of affection that she had to restrain herself from touching him. She wondered what was proper between young people who wished to marry, but she sensed that any familiarity would be frowned upon. She returned his gaze, searching his face for some indication of what Hosteen Yazzie might have told him during the night, but he gave no indication that his uncle had spoken to him. When Maria left to carry bread to the old man, Elspeth attempted to help Many Beads clean up, but the older woman was so methodical in her motions that it made her feel clumsy, and she soon stood aside to observe her actions.

"My mother doesn't expect you to help. You are a guest," Valerio told her when Many Beads was out of hearing. "She will show you what to do later."

"What did your uncle say about us?" she whispered.

"I spoke to him. He knows everything, but he had little to say. He will take a sweat bath later, and then he will pray. He is very wise, *querida*. We must await his decision. If he decides against the marriage, we will still be together."

When Many Beads returned, she sat down with them with her callused hands folded in her lap, obviously ready to discuss their problem, or at least hear more for her consideration of it. In Maria's absence, Valerio had to translate for Elspeth.

"If you were married, what kind of children would you have?" she asked. "Pinto children, half-Dineh and half-white?"

"Beautiful children," he replied, "because they would be born in harmony. I have seen the child of a Pueblo woman and a white man. It was a good child, and it looked like the Pueblo."

She is like any mother, Elspeth thought; her concerns are the same. She suppressed a smile when she tried to imagine the pinto child that had worried Many Beads. Valerio and his mother discussed something for a while, and she expected something equally fanciful when he turned to her.

"My mother asked if we had lain together," he said to her discomfort. She flushed deeply and averted her eyes, certain that everything was lost, now; Valerio would not deceive his mother. "I told her we wanted to wait until we were married," he continued, without embarrassment, "but we were alone for many nights, and we needed each other. That you were meant only for me, and I, for you."

Elspeth glanced at his face, which was as composed as if he were discussing the weather. She tried to emulate his calm, though her heart was pounding heavily. She was not accustomed to hearing such private matters discussed so openly; indeed, she had never heard anyone speak about them before. She was certain that the knowledge of their lovemaking would prejudice his mother against her.

"She wanted to know if you were already with child," he continued. "I had not considered that possibility, but I told her that if you were, it would give me the greatest happiness. For we will stay together always; nothing can part us. Our happiness would be more complete if we could be married and remain here with her."

Elspeth managed to hide her discomfort. Too much was at stake to allow her modesty to interfere. She swallowed hard and gathered all her courage to address Many Beads in a language that was foreign to her. "Tall Man is my husband. I am his wife. We need each other, so I came here. It is beautiful."

Many Beads was momentarily astonished to hear such words from a white woman, but Valerio smiled at Elspeth and spoke to his mother. "My wife speaks both the American language and Spanish. She is learning our language. She is learning our Way."

A high, nasal chant reached them from some distance away, cadenced but sung in falsetto, and Elspeth realized that the Hosteen was praying in his sweat bath. The sound thrilled her, as

Valerio's had done when he chanted in the saddle, but she was not eager to meet the old man who would decide her future. He was so steeped in tradition that he was almost certain to deny their request. Valerio had explained to her that Hosteen Yazzie was a widower, who had lived for many years with his family. He was not actually Valerio's uncle, but his mother's; all family members were designated by their relationship, regardless of generation. The children of one sister became the children of all, and the children referred to all the sisters as "mother"; and this great-uncle was called only "uncle" by Many Beads's children. She had found the kinship terms confusing at the lake; they were becoming clearer after observing the closeness of this family, but she still was in no haste to confront the old Singer.

Maria appeared with some fresh-cut soapweed in her hand. True to her word, she was going to groom Elspeth for the dreaded occasion. Valerio left to take care of the horses, saying something about a new foal, and Many Beads went into the hogan to weave. When she was alone with Maria, Elspeth expressed her anxiety about meeting Hosteen Yazzie.

"He won't like me. I'm afraid of him. I'm so dusty and dirty all over that washing my hair won't be enough. Is there anywhere I can take a bath? Wash my clothes?"

Maria regarded her cheerfully. "Your clothes are no more dusty than ours, my friend. If your hands and face are clean, and your hair shines, who will notice the rest of you?"

"I will. Isn't there some secluded place where I can bathe in the river?"

"There is quicksand there. We never bathe in the Wash. The Mexican women made me bathe all over in a tub at the hacienda, but we don't have anything like that here. And it isn't modest to take all of your clothes off at once. Even in the sweathouse, we leave something on."

Elspeth, who had always bathed once a week and taken sponge baths in between, suddenly realized how unreasonable she was being in a place where water was at a premium. "I'm sorry," she told Maria. "I'll do as you do, of course."

"You'll have new clothes soon," Maria consoled her as she ladled water into a clay pot to wash her hair. "Big Woman is sewing two blankets together today, and we will make some moccasins, too. You won't need those funny ones here."

If the personal hygiene differed from her own, they made up

for it in the care of their hair. Elspeth, luxuriating in the shampoo and brushing under Maria's gentle hands, began to feel almost drowsy under their unhurried care. After her faux pas over the bath, she did not volunteer the hairbrush concealed in her writing box, submitting to a brush made from a small bundle of twigs instead. The process took longer, but time was one thing that was not in short supply, and the women experienced no guilt over how it was used. She sensed that hair grooming was the one luxury they allowed themselves, and cheerfully performed for one another, a time to socialize. Maria spoke to her constantly while she dressed her hair, and in that short period, Elspeth learned several useful things.

"You must always wear your hair this way," Maria instructed her, "bound with wool to hold it in place. If there is no one to dress your hair, you may leave it loose around your shoulders, but you must never braid it. Only witches braid their hair, tormenting it into twisted strands that are not in harmony. I was so frightened when I saw the Mexican women, because some of them braided their hair. It took me some time to recognize that it was just their fashion and had nothing to do with witchcraft. I mention this word because you are new here. We usually don't speak of such evil things. If you mention a witch, he might hear you and turn his wicked powers on you. I'm not afraid, because I'm using the Spanish word."

"He? I thought they were usually women," Elspeth said, encouraging her to speak further.

"They can be, but more often they are men who have lost *hozro* and have a sickness in their minds that makes them do evil things. Harmony could be restored by a ceremonial, but they have usually strayed too far from the Way to ask for one."

"You believe that if one does evil it is because his mind is sick? Your view is more charitable than ours. Will a ceremonial also help someone who is unhappy and ill-tempered?"

"Yes . . . well, usually," Maria replied. "You are speaking of Many Tears Woman, aren't you? That is different. She is the way she is because she cannot bear a child. She has done everything to bring this about, but still she is barren—and jealous of women who can have children, I think. She is bitter, but not evil. There. Your hair looks beautiful."

Elspeth touched her hair and wished she had a mirror. She regretted that the grooming was over, because it might be some time before Maria was this talkative again, and she had so much to ask. She had hardly framed her questions in her mind when they were interrupted by the appearance of Hosteen Yazzie, followed by Valerio and his two older sisters.

The ancient, bandy-legged old man wore buckskin trousers and a homespun shirt, which was tucked in carelessly at the waist. A necklace of heavy, rough turquoise hung from his neck, and he carried his medicine pouch and a staff decorated with blue feathers. Maria rose to greet him, and Elspeth followed her example as Many Beads emerged from the hogan to join them. He crouched easily in spite of his age and indicated that they sit with him; his bowed legs permitted him to sit tailor-fashion without discomfort. Though he did not look at her, Elspeth studied him carefully. His white hair was gathered into a chongo but escaped from beneath his headband unnoticed, as if he did not have time for personal grooming; but it was his face that arrested her full attention. Brown and deeply seamed from the sun, there was not an unwrinkled place on its surface, and, though his left eye was milky from a cataract, his right remained sharp and keen beneath the fold of skin above it. She had expected him to be slightly fanatical, but his expression was peaceful and mild, as if he had seen much, contemplated it, and incorporated it into the Way that was known as Beauty.

Many Beads put her problem to him at length, in one long, unaccented harangue, though she must have realized that Valerio had already spoken to him. Maria did not interpret for her, and Elspeth felt uneasy. Even Valerio did not glance in her direction while his mother spoke. The serious problem she presented seemed to be something to be dealt with between themselves alone. She could not tell whether the Hosteen was looking at her or not while he listened in silence to what Many Beads had to say. She felt nothing but peace emanating from the old man, but it did not communicate itself to her. She lowered her eyes and studied her hands in an effort to maintain her composure and did not look up again, even after Many Beads completed her dissertation. She was unaware that the old man had risen until she saw his moccasins in front of her. Silence had fallen over the small group of people gathered together to decide her fate, a silence broken only by the call of a bird further down the canyon. He touched the top of her head and raised her face gently with his blue-feathered staff, so he could study her carefully. He spoke in a normal tone, his voice unusually strong for his age, and Maria interpreted for him.

" 'I had a dream last night. Dawn Maiden and Corn Maiden came to me bearing gifts of turquoise and shell and cornsilk, all prosperous signs. Dawn Maiden also brought a pool of blue-green water in which I could see what others could not. I did not understand the meaning of these symbols until now. This girl has hair like cornsilk and a face as pale as shell. Her eyes are like blue-green water; she sees what others cannot. The Holy People were telling me that she brings us nothing but good.' "

He moved away to join the others, and Elspeth was startled to see the dark form under the tamarisk trees again. The unexplained woman hovered like a phantom, and, for a moment, Elspeth wondered if she was a ghost. If there was one thing the People did not like to hear about, it was spirits, so she could not mention what she had seen. Living here as they did, surrounded by the canyon walls between the earth and the sky, with no illumination in the house at night, their awe of the supernatural was understandable; she was beginning to feel it herself. She glanced at the others to see if any of them had seen the figure. Either they had not, or it was someone familiar to them. When she looked back in the direction of the mysterious woman, she saw only the eerie lace of the trees, and she shivered slightly, though it was full daylight and the sun was warm.

" 'The girl has helped us in the past,' " Maria continued her translation of Hosteen Yazzie's words, " 'and she will do so again. Tradition cannot be broken to suit our own wishes; under other circumstances, I could not have honored the wishes of my nephew. But I cannot dismiss my dream or what I have seen in the girl's eyes, which have no back to them and see everything. If others ask why she was allowed to stay and marry Tall Man, tell them about my dream. While Tall Man builds the hogan for the ceremony, I will tell her about the Holy People and how the Dineh came here.' "

"As soon as your hogan's built, you can be married," Maria said happily grasping Elspeth's hand. "We will truly be sisters then!"

"I'll help him," Elspeth said. "We can build it faster that way."

"You can't help him. He has to do this by himself. If my

brothers-in-law were here, they could help. It would only take a few days, but they are not here. I will stay by your side while you learn from my uncle."

The betrothed couple were allowed to walk together as far as the Wash, within sight of Many Beads and her daughters. They had been separated for almost twenty-four hours, and Elspeth was happy to be with him, even under the women's chaperonage.

"I need you in my arms, and I can't even take your hand," Valerio said. "No hogan will ever rise as quickly as ours, *querida*."

"I'm so happy that I've been accepted. I hope I can fulfill your uncle's expectations. He is old and deeply religious. He doesn't imagine things, does he?"

"No. Sometimes, he sees beyond the reality of others, though. To me, your hair and eyes are those of the woman I love, but Hosteen Yazzie sees farther. No one had to tell me you'd be good for me."

"Perhaps he had the dream because you spoke to him about me last night. You did speak to him, didn't you?"

"I told him how much I need you, but I didn't describe you. I wouldn't question the Hosteen's dreams. Your eyes may see what others do not, but I want them to see only me."

She did not tell him that others had remarked the same thing about her. She was too grateful just to be with him. She did not even think to ask him about the dark woman who had observed them from the stand of trees. "I love you," she said. "From this day on, my eyes will see only you."

"And I will only see you," he told her. "Nothing can separate us. Except the stares of my mother and my sisters, right now," he added, with a smile. "It's difficult not to touch you, but it will only be a few days. Did you know that my mother spoke up in favor of our marriage?"

"No," Elspeth said, with surprise. "I thought she was speaking against it, but I'm glad she approves. She really doesn't want to lose you, does she?"

"I think she likes you, though of course it was her wish that I remain with my own family. Of course," he added, with a smile deep in his eyes, "that's why I'm marrying you, instead of a Dineh girl, too. This way, I can remain at home."

The remark startled her for a moment, until she realized that he was teasing her. "You must build our house quickly," she responded, with a smile. "I'm only marrying you so I can have a roof over my head."

Life centered around the hogan, though the women spent most of their time outside at this time of year. Maria's first duty in the morning was to sweep the earthen floor after putting the bedding out to air, while Many Beads prepared the fire for the morning meal. Elspeth was not encouraged to assist them, though Many Beads told her to watch, because she would soon have a home of her own. Indeed, all instruction was given by showing how things were done.

"We have no word for *teaching* as the Spanish do," Maria told her. "Our word means *show*."

Elspeth divided her days between the women and Hosteen Yazzie, who explained the Creation story which Maria translated for her in the shelter outside of his hogan. First Woman was born from the mist before First Man, and they lived together for some time before the Rainbow People and Crystal People completed them by entering into their bodies and filling them with desire. They came together as man and wife, and from them issued the other Holy People, as well as the animals and insects. They traveled far, in all four directions, before they found the *Ah-rah-Suzzi*, the Enemy Ancestors, the forefathers of the cliff dwellers, where two rivers crossed, a black one from east to west and a blue river from south to north. Four mountains rose on the four sides, and Coyote brought gifts from each of them to the place where First Man and First Woman made their home. Then, First Man had a dream, and going to White Mountain, he found a disc of turquoise which became the Sun. First Woman brought a large white shell from the west, which later became the Moon.

The stories of First Man and First Woman became very involved, a legend which had been embroidered on for hundreds of years, and Elspeth wondered why the Hosteen took such pains to relate it to her, instead of instructing her in the ways of a good wife. Everything he recounted involved the four directions and precise numbers. Spider spun five webs around the Sun and Moon to make them bright. Coyote, the trickster, through whom unexpected things happened, was indirectly responsible for creating the stars. When the People made Talking God and Hogan God out of agate, they planned seventeen constellations out with remaining chips, and Coyote hurled them into the sky. Finally, destruction rocked the earth in all four directions on succeeding days, and the earth and sky struck together, producing a dark rain cloud which was followed by rainbows. On the fourth morning, Salt Woman walked to where the rainbow hung and found at its end, in a patch of grama grass, a beautiful white baby, whose body gave off light. This was Woman-Who-Changes, or Changing Woman, who created the first Dineh.

"Now you know how our people were created," the Hosteen concluded, "and why your white skin did not frighten me. We are all descended from Changing Woman, who had skin like yours, and your coming only bodes good for us."

Elspeth remained silent for a moment, trying to find a reply that would discourage him from expecting too much of her. "I am not a Holy Person," she said at last. "I am only a woman who wants to live in peace with my husband."

"That is all a woman should wish," he replied, "just as a man should wish to live in peace with his wife."

His story had taken many hours, and though her legs were cramped from sitting in one position so long, Elspeth felt strangely calm. She was more anxious than ever to learn the language so she could speak directly to him in the future. She wanted to know everything about her new people, and she was interested in their religion, which white people knew nothing about.

"Why was he smudged with red earth?" she asked Maria as they walked back through the trees.

"He has dried himself with earth after purifying himself in the sweat hogan—in preparation for your wedding ceremony tomorrow. Your hogan will be finished by then."

Water was heated in a clay pot that evening so she could bathe herself in the privacy of Many Beads's hogan, and she was provided with a soft, finely woven blanket dress afterward. There was a short discussion about the unusual moccasins Valerio had made for her, and Elspeth explained the reason for them.

"You will soon be able to ride without them," Many Beads assured her. "Until then, you may wear them. We will make you new ones."

A fire illuminated the hogan that evening, and the women sat together for a while. Fresh branches had been brought in and lay against the walls at floor level, their fragrance freshening the air. "They keep insects away," Maria explained when she noticed Elspeth looking at them. "Something in the leaves drives away the insects. I'll show you where to gather them so you won't be overrun with pests. The women usually give the bride some instruction on the night before her wedding, but your situation is so different that they have decided not to speak of such things. My mother says you have already made Tall Man happy in bed, so it is not necessary."

Elspeth flushed and glanced at Many Beads. Apparently, her relationship with Valerio was common knowledge, though no one seemed particularly disturbed about it, least of all his own mother. "Isn't a girl supposed to be a virgin when she marries?" she asked Maria. "Dineh girls, I mean."

"Yes. But occasionally couples cannot wait . . . like you and Tall Man. When that happens, they are encouraged to marry each other, unless the marriage would not be suitable. Our marriages are arranged by our parents and those of the groom, but, if either the girl or boy objects to the marriage, they don't have to marry. People should at least like each other before they marry. In most cases, they have seen each other at ceremonials and fallen in love."

Many Beads was weaving a basket she had begun earlier in the day, and Elspeth watched her, wondering if she would be able to accomplish the craft with equal ease with practice. She was surprised when Valerio's mother addressed her.

"This basket is for your wedding cake. It will be decorated with corn pollen, happiness pollen dusted from the feathers of bluebirds or yellow warblers. My uncle catches the birds in their nests and sprinkles pollen over their wings while he holds them by the legs. As they flutter, the happiness pollen is shaken from their feathers. Then, he lets the birds go and gathers it up from the cloth he has used. It is very holy. It will bless your union. Tomorrow, we will cook lots of meat and bread for the wedding guests."

Elspeth smiled her appreciation, but she whispered to Maria, "Guests? I thought this would be kept within the family."

"They will all be kinsmen," Maria assured her. "It's a pity you have none of your own. Your wedding will be like every other wedding; nothing will be kept secret, my friend. A gathering of the clan is a good time for the Hosteen to let them know how he feels about you.''

"What if the men don't like me when they return?''

Maria laughed easily. "It won't matter. They do what my mother says. They married into her family knowing how it would be.''

"They won't cause trouble then?''

"My mother doesn't like troublesome men, any more than she does lazy men or gamblers. My sisters' husbands must behave themselves.''

Many Beads smiled when she completed the basket, and Big Woman's appreciation of her work confirmed what Maria said. These people smiled and laughed a good deal, and they were remarkably gentle with the children. Only Many Tears Woman had nothing to smile about, but her personal woe was tolerated with sympathy and understanding. Elspeth, who had felt uncomfortable in her presence at first, was no longer afraid of this sister who wore her misery like a cloak. She was grateful to have been accepted into this family, determined to earn their approval.

Hosteen Yazzie dedicated her hogan on the morning of her wedding, and Maria explained the ceremony to her. As he rubbed the supporting timbers with white cornmeal, beginning at the south and circling the wall to left, he chanted:

> May my house be blessed,
> From my head to my feet,
> Where I lie and all above me,
> All around me, may it be blessed.

Many Beads placed a blanket over the door, and the old man made her a poker of green wood to build the first fire inside, feeding it with a morsel of food to make it happy. As the first smoke rose through the hole in the roof, Elspeth was so touched that she had to blink the tears from her eyes. She glanced at Valerio and found him looking at her; they both smiled in the knowledge that they would live here together always. They would be married in the evening and never be separated again. The preparations for the wedding feast were already underway.

Many Beads had killed a sheep, and her daughters began to

bake bread as soon as they returned from the dedication. They prepared corn cakes sweetened with honey and wrapped them in corn leaves, which they placed into a pit in the ground lined with heated rocks to bake. Elspeth, who was not allowed to help, observed the cooking process carefully, conscious that she would be keeping her own house tomorrow. The amount of food seemed excessive, and she wondered how many kinsmen were coming.

Oldest Boy arrived with a message for Maria, who washed her hands from the bread-making and approached Elspeth. "The Hosteen wants to see you, and I am to come, too. I'm so glad we're having sweet corn cakes! They are very special. It's only possible to make them while there is still fresh corn, and Oldest Boy found the honey yesterday."

As they walked toward the old man's hogan through the gently blowing trees, Elspeth wondered if this was part of the wedding ceremony, too, like a minister's instruction of a young couple in her own society. But, when she asked Maria about it, her friend laughed.

"If you were a Dineh girl, he would not need to speak to you. You would know about the wedding ceremony and what is expected of you. I think he wants to explain all that."

Elspeth knew the locations of all the hogans, and who dwelled in them, but she glanced at them as they passed through the trees. The chaos around Big Woman's dwelling indicated that she was as easygoing about her housekeeping as everything else. Many Tears Woman was fastidiously neat; her bedding hung carefully in a neat row, indicating that she gave the utmost attention to even the most ordinary task. There was something almost unlived-in about her hogan, and Elspeth looked away, thoughtfully, wondering how she herself would react if she were incapable of bearing children. The Hosteen's hogan was situated between two paws of red rock extending from the canyon wall, giving him even more privacy than the others. She hoped that he would invite her inside, because she was curious about it, but he sat in the same brush shelter where he had instructed her before.

He did not rise to greet them, but remained with his bare, crooked legs crossed beneath him, his half-naked body covered with red dust, as if he had taken another sweat bath. Elspeth immediately sensed the spiritual power that came from him, as she had in his presence before. He indicated that they sit on the ground before him, and they did so with their legs to one side, the position Many Beads used when she was weaving.

"You came by choice," he told her, "and I know you will follow the way of the People. This afternoon, I will explain this to our kinsmen and tell them that I have a special purpose in allowing you to marry into our family, a purpose I feel but which is not yet clear to me. Do you have a clan? It is important that your children know their mother's clan."

Valerio had warned her about this, and Elspeth replied, "My people do not have clans as you do. We have family names instead. My name is Williams."

Maria translated her words in the strange language that made Elspeth stare at the lips of the person speaking it, and the old man repeated her name with some difficulty. "Your children will be called Williams, then, born for Rocks-Beside-the-Water. They will know who they are. Now I will tell you about the ceremony tonight, so that you will know what to do and not make it bad by doing something wrong. Everything must be perfect in every ceremony. We don't want another mistake with a strange woman in our family."

The instructions were relatively simple, but he went over them twice so that she would understand. Elspeth was curious about his remark about the other strange woman, but she felt she should not ask about her. She and Maria walked through the tamarisk trees without speaking, which was unusual for them, and it was Maria who finally broke the silence.

"We call her Mexican Woman," she said. "It is a long story, and one you will not like. My father brought her here as a slave many years ago. She was very young then, they say. He wanted her for a second wife, but Many Beads would not allow that. She was jealous. When she finally divorced him, he did not take the woman with him. Mexican Woman married one of our kinsmen. After he was no more, she was not accepted by anyone, and she would have perished if Many Beads had not taken her in. She is a little mad, and you mustn't befriend her."

"She was taken as a slave," Elspeth said. "I didn't think the People took slaves."

"It doesn't happen often. When Tall Man and I were captured, my mother thought it was because we had kept Mexican

Woman here for so many years. She asked her if she wanted to go back to her people, but she would not go."

"I've seen her," Elspeth said. "I didn't think she was real. She wears black like a Mexican widow. She must have loved her husband."

"You mustn't speak of her. She wears a cross around her neck, and she braids her hair sometimes."

"Surely, you don't think she's a witch?"

"If we were sure of that, we wouldn't let her stay here. She isn't right in the head, though, and she won't have a ceremonial."

"Where does she live? I know all of the hogans here."

"She lives alone, farther up the canyon. She helps with the digging at planting time, but my mother doesn't let her touch the seed or help with the lambing. She helps with other things, too . . ." Maria's voice trailed off as if she were reluctant to speak about that. "We shouldn't be speaking about her on the day of your wedding."

Moved by compassion for the solitary woman who had not come here by choice, Elspeth ignored the warning. "Does she still speak Spanish after so many years?"

"I don't know. I never speak to her. And you mustn't, either. Your children might be deformed."

Elspeth was not prepared for the number of kinsmen who arrived for the wedding. Maria told her that Hosteen Yazzie was speaking to them in a brush shelter that had been constructed near the new hogan, where her mother and sisters were preparing the food while she dressed Elspeth's hair in Many Beads's house. When the old man finally came to escort her to her hogan, taking the place of her father, she was conscious of the curious stares of those still assembled near the shelter. The closest relatives had entered the hogan before her, and the interior was already warm with the heat of their bodies. Valerio's immediate family was seated at the north side. The Hosteen led Elspeth around the hogan to the south, to her place of honor beside her bridegroom, where she was seated on a clean white sheepskin. Valerio smiled at her as she joined him, and suddenly all her nervousness seeped away. This was the moment they had been awaiting, and it did not matter that she had no family to represent her. She thought of Thea with a feeling of poignancy, but she quickly suppressed the emotion. She would have liked her sister to attend her wedding, but she could not picture Thea in this setting.

Acting for her father, the Hosteen set a clay pot of water and a gourd before her, and Elspeth poured water over Valerio's hands. He, in turn, cleansed her hands with the water, his eyes gazing into hers. A white line had been drawn to the east in front of them, and the new ceremonial basket filled with corn-meal mush was placed upon it. The Hosteen knelt to draw a cross of happiness pollen in the four directions on the cornmeal, sifting it skillfully through his fingers; then, he made a circle of pollen around the edge, stopping short to leave a "spirit opening" in the circle while he sang the Corn Song. Valerio took a pinch of mush from the east side of the basket, and Elspeth followed his example until they had each eaten from all four sides. The remaining cornmeal was presented to Valerio's family to eat, while Many Beads prayed for the happiness of the young couple. The bride and groom then drank from the same small bowl of water, and they were married. Many Beads entreated them to care for each other, and, there being no one in Elspeth's family to do the same, the guests began to stir and leave the married couple alone in their hogan. The family would feast by the fire outside until nightfall, but no one would enter the hogan again.

Valerio took her into his arms. "We are together at last, *querida*," he whispered. "Nothing will ever separate us again."

Chapter 12

The cottonwoods were a glow of yellow and the air was growing brisk when Valerio interrupted Elspeth's daily work to take her on a ride through the canyon. During her first month of marriage, she had tried to become more Navajo than the Navajo, though she now thought of them only as the Dineh. Accustomed to some structure in her life, she had made up a schedule to accomplish everything that had to be done in a day, but she still did not seem to have enough time for all the chores expected of her. She had observed the other women, who seemed to do things randomly, as the spirit moved them, leaving for tomorrow what could not be completed today, but it was not in her nature and training to follow their example. Valerio had constructed a loom outside of their hogan and weaving was her only recreation. Maria had instructed her in carding and spinning before Many Beads came to help her with her weaving, and Elspeth found that carding the unwashed wool was harder than she had imagined, and spinning it between her fingers even more difficult. She persevered with blistered hands as diligently as she tried to learn the language, though, and with greater success. The words continued to sound flat and unpronounced to her unaccustomed ear. Until she recognized that it was built on verbs instead of nouns, she almost despaired learning it. She finally began to converse with the children who came to watch her. When she made a mistake, they laughed at her and she joined in the laughter, but she was certain never to make the

171

same mistake again. Valerio was patient with her, though sometimes in the privacy of their hogan, he too, laughed at what she was trying to say. When she seemed hurt by his amusement, he explained that the People were given to punning as a form of humor and entreated her to forgive him for laughing at her particular use of a word. Then, in the blaze of autumn, he made her leave everything to familiarize her with the vastness of their homeland, and took her farther into the canyon than she had been before.

"It is time you learned to ride without your high moccasins," he suggested, after presenting her with the new ones that Big Woman had fashioned for her, but it was quickly apparent that his real purpose was to relieve her of the drudgery she had imposed upon herself.

If the high wind-carved red walls of the canyon had been spectacular in late summer, they surpassed themselves with the coloring foliage at their base at this time of year. Elspeth had already observed some of the changing moods of the canyon, for one day was rarely exactly like another, altering almost as dramatically as the brilliantly colored sunrises and extravagant sunsets. Sometimes, a curtain of dark rain hung in the distance, far away inside of the canyon, only to change abruptly as the sun came through or a rainbow danced from wall to wall against the gray sky. No day was like another. And, as they rode together, crossing the Wash frequently to gain a foothold for their mounts, she began to observe other wonders, the most significant of which were the mineral tapestries on the canyon walls. Created by moisture over many years, the dark streaks reminded her of the colors in the blankets, though they shone with a patina she did not comprehend. As the light changed, so did the hues of this amazingly beautiful phenomenon, and she paused to let Plata drink in the Wash so she could continue to observe one of them.

"If I could weave that, I would be content with my weaving," she remarked. "There is beauty everywhere. I don't think there is a more beautiful place in the world. The Holy People must have woven the colors on the sandstone walls."

"You work too hard," he said. "All the women say so. You should live your life in a more relaxed way, as they do."

"I have so much to learn," she said, with a smile, "that I have to work hard. In the time I've been here, I still haven't touched my loom, but Maria says I shall learn to weave soon. We've carded the wool and spun the warp, and we began to dye some wool yesterday. I'm busy, but I'm very happy. I've never known such happiness.''

"You've made me happy, *querida*, but even I wish you didn't try to do so much. You have forgotten what I told about harmony, and *hozro* does not come to one who is pressed for time. You have all the time in the world to learn what you wish to learn, and you will not become one of the Dinch until you attain harmony with everything around you.''

The miracle occurred shortly after she began to weave. Even Many Beads was pleased at how quickly Elspeth was able to control the upright loom. Her first small blanket, which was like those young girls attempted, had edges as even as those of an accomplished weaver, and, with a little more instruction, she was able to pick out a design, attaching different colors by tying on separate small spools of yarn without difficulty. She was so content at her loom that Many Beads left her to experiment by herself, and Maria came less often to sit at her side.

"My mother said you are a natural weaver," Maria reported to her, "and such weavers are rare. Your work already surpasses mine," she added, with a smile of pride in her friend's accomplishment. "You can make up your own designs. If you need us, we are here.''

"I'm afraid to attempt your designs. I don't understand their significance yet," Elspeth said, "and I don't want to offend anyone in my attempts.''

"They are simple. Each weaver creates her own. I will explain their significance some time.''

Maria often wore the full cotton skirt in which she had escaped from the hacienda, and it was much admired by the other women in their thin blanket dresses. The skirt did not seem to awaken memories in her, and Elspeth wondered how her friend had so quickly overcome the ordeal that she had been submitted to in captivity. Neither of them mentioned Don Diego, as if they both chose to forget the episode, though sometimes they spoke of Thea, who was never far from Elspeth's mind. She was completely happy in her new life until the unfortunate question of the sheep arose. Until then, she had not realized that she had come to Valerio indigent.

Sheep were as important to survival as corn in this wild land, and they were held in common between husband and wife, though the whole family flock was tended together. They provided not only meat, but the skins for sleeping, and the wool that the women wove. Valerio possessed some sheep in the flock, but as a bachelor, he had not needed many; he had mentioned that he must replenish his stock soon to provide for his own family. He also had several horses, which he tended along with those of his brothers-in-law while they were away. The return of Slim Man and Shouting Man, driving a sizable flock of sheep and some goats before them, precipitated the unpleasantness. Many Beads sent a message from her hogan suggesting that each of her daughters should contribute a few sheep to be marked for their new sister, who had none of her own.

The suggestion was ill-timed. The men had herded the sheep for a long distance, and they had not yet adjusted to the changes that had occurred in the family in their absence. They did not know what to think of the white woman Valerio had married; or indeed, of the fact that Many Beads's favored son would be remaining here to live with them. Big Woman's husband, Shouting Man, went uncharacteristically silent, and Slim Man, who had to live with Many Tears Woman, walked away rather than deal with the matter. If Many Beads could have greeted them face-to-face and discussed her idea with her usual persuasion, the outcome might have been quite different. Until now, Elspeth had not observed the difficulties which could be brought about by the mother-in-law taboo, though she knew that Many Beads and her daughters' husbands were not allowed to meet face-to-face. To avoid such a meeting, the result of which was not made clear, someone in the family would say to either party, "There's an owl over there," so they could take appropriate action. Because Many Beads had been warned of the return of the men, she had remained in her hogan and sent the fateful suggestion through Maria; the women were left to deal with it between themselves.

Elspeth wanted to return to her own hogan, remove herself from the growing tension, but Valerio restrained her with a glance. "It isn't fair," she said. "They've come a long way with the sheep. They shouldn't be asked to share them."

"My mother is referring to the entire flock, not just these animals," he explained. "I have contributed to that flock more than they have. My mother chose this moment, when they have extra sheep, out of fairness. She is appealing to their generosity, and the People are generous. She doesn't want me to go raiding so late in the year. It is already the time of 'Half-Cold.' The 'Big Winds' would be here by the time I returned.''

If they were generous, it was not evident in their expressions, which were grudging at best. Even Big Woman considered the matter with a heavy face; she had a family to support, and her husband was already displeased. Many Tears Woman was vocal in her objections; though Valerio did not interpret what she said, her total opposition was evident. Her husband had turned his back on the suggestion, and she had to please him, too. Elspeth looked around for Maria to interpret the squabble, but her good-natured friend had disappeared quietly. Perhaps she could not endure this discord any more than Elspeth. She caught the word ''children'' in Many Tears Woman's angry speech and did not quite know what to make of it. Was she arguing that she would not support Elspeth's children? There seemed no other interpretation, for surely she would not bring up her own childlessness in connection with this subject. Elspeth appealed to Valerio with a glance, but he remained firm, without speaking, almost as if he were allowing his sisters to judge themselves, or observing how far they would go.

Maria ended the dispute abruptly. She appeared from the direction of the corral, driving about a dozen sheep before her with a smile on her face, as if she were unaware of the situation. ''My mother wants these sheep earmarked for my new sister,'' she told Elspeth. ''They are her contribution. All except one. That is mine. Since I am unmarried, I don't have many sheep of my own. She asked me to bring one ram, so the flock will increase at the time of lambing.''

When she repeated what she had said to her sisters in their own language, the effect of her generosity—more than that of Many Beads's—brought shame to Big Woman's face. She glanced at her husband and immediately offered half the number that her mother had contributed. Only Many Tears Woman remained adamant. She stared at Elspeth with the same distaste she had exhibited on the day of her arrival, and Maria interpreted uncomfortably, '' 'Tall Man has spent too much time getting a woman this year. He has not added to my flock, so why should I give up what is mine?' ''

"He has brought sheep to our mother in the past, who has given them to you," Maria said mildly. "It is the same thing."

Many Tears Woman was firm, though it meant that Valerio would have to go raiding at an unpropitious time of the year. Elspeth recognized that her sister-in-law's action was directed at her and tried to comprehend it. Valerio had assured her that envy was not part of the Navajo Way. Still, people were people, she decided, and Many Tears Woman is a disappointed, bitter woman. Though she found it difficult, she tried not to dislike her. If I am ever really able to attain *hozro*, she thought, I must not let such things bother me.

"You must think of it this way," Valerio said when the others were gone and he was clipping the ears of the sheep. "The family will be on the canyon rim when I return, and I won't have to drive our sheep so far."

Though Elspeth was opposed to the raiding and had expressed her warnings to Valerio about the temper of the Americans regarding the raids, she already recognized the necessity to replenish the flocks. The People could not live through the winter without enough to eat, and they had to reserve some stock for breeding. She and Valerio were in a particularly vulnerable position; if they consumed only one animal a month, there would only be a few lambs in the spring. She was surprised at the shift in her own thinking as she helped Valerio prepare to leave. She would be uneasy until he returned safely, but she knew she must hide her anxiety over his welfare if she was to be a good Dineh wife. At the last moment, Shouting Man decided to accompany him, and she felt easier in her mind. At least, he would not be alone. When Valerio had said that they would be together always, she had thought that was the way it would be, without considering that he would be leaving her for weeks, perhaps even months at a time.

"If you need anything, my mother will help you," he assured her on the morning he left. "That is why the family is so important, *querida*. You will never be alone. You'll be so busy you'll hardly miss me."

"I'll miss you every moment," she said, embracing him outside of their hogan. "Please be careful, my darling. When you return, you'll be surprised by how much I've learned while you were away. Return soon."

She thought she might have another surprise for him, but she did not mention it, because she did not want to divide his attention from what he was doing, and she was not absolutely sure yet. Without a calendar, it was difficult to tell, but she had not had a period since her wedding. The thought of bearing a child so far away from everything she was accustomed to was a little frightening, but, she reasoned, the other women did it without much difficulty. Conscious of her condition, she tried to emulate the easy, relaxed pace of Many Beads and her daughters when working at the communal task of preparing the corn for winter. Most of it would come with them when they left the canyon, but the seed corn for the following year was stored in a cellar dug out of the earth behind Many Beads's hogan.

She took turns with Maria in tending the sheep and came to recognize her own animals by sight instead of their earmarking. Maria helped her grind the corn allocated to her. Besides spinning wool, Elspeth found the preparation of the meal on a metate her most gruelling task, though her hands were growing callused enough to do either without much discomfort. If women had a high place in the family, they earned it by doing most of the work. The men did the heavy labor of constructing and repairing corrals and bringing in wood and water, but most of their time was spent at leisure. Slim Man, the only man left with the family, spent a lot of time caring for the horses and riding from one Sing to another seeking impromptu races, a pastime of which Many Beads openly disapproved, since she suspected betting was involved.

"If he is a gambler, you should get another husband," she told Many Tears Woman when they were bundling the corn for their approaching exodus from the canyon. "He should be here packing the horses instead of racing them. A wastrel is no good to anyone. The sheep you withheld from Tall Man's family, and your horses, will be lost on a bet."

"He is the husband I want," Many Tears Woman replied, without taking her mother's criticism very seriously. "I'm not sure he's betting yet. He rode a long way to get the sheep and needs some relaxation."

"He could relax you out of all of your property," Big Woman said good-naturedly, without reproaching her sister for the action that had deprived them of the help of her husband and brother in moving their belongings to winter quarters.

Elspeth was able to understand some of the conversation, and Maria put its full context into Spanish for her later. "Many Tears Woman needs that man," Maria commented. "Unless he ruins her, she won't consider sending him away."

Elspeth, who knew what it was to love a man, was amazed that the women advised one another so openly and with so little acrimony between them. "I expected Many Tears Woman to react more strongly to such criticism," she said.

"We are a family and depend on one another," Maria replied. "If one person doesn't carry his full weight, the family may be better off without him. My mother doesn't have anything against Slim Man except his possible gambling, which had to be brought out in the open for the good of all of us."

At Many Beads's suggestion, Maria stayed with Elspeth at night during Valerio's absence. Elspeth appreciated her mother-in-law's consideration. She missed Valerio terribly, and she would have been miserable alone in the hogan where they had spent so many happy nights together. She might have been a little frightened, too. When the darkness fell it was almost total, and she had heard stories of witches hurling corpse dust through smoke holes to put a spell on the sleepers within. In the light of day, she dismissed such tales completely, but they had a way of returning to bring primitive terror at night. In spite of Hosteen Yazzie's injunctions regarding her, few of the kinsmen had visited Many Beads since the wedding, and those who did were uneasy in Elspeth's presence. Late at night, it occurred to her that if one of those kinsmen was unsettled enough to believe himself a witch, it was highly plausible that his malevolence would be directed at her. Maria's almost childish enthusiasm for ghost stories did little to reassure her as the sun began to fall, either. Often, after she had frightened both herself and Elspeth with her stories, the two young women clung together and fell asleep in each other's arms.

Though Elspeth could dismiss the idea of witches, the hostility inherent in the phenomenon troubled her, and no more so than when she learned of the Skinwalkers, witches who draped themselves in the skins of animals and roamed the night to do their mischief.

"They meet in caves hung with the skins of wolves and bears, which they can put on and turn into animals," Maria told her. "They scour the land at night, digging up bodies and searching for their victims. If you see a wolf during the day with its tail hanging straight down, it must be killed, for there is a man beneath that skin. Real wolves hold their tails straight out behind them. To become such a witch, a man must sacrifice the person dearest to him; after that, he fears nothing, for he is not like other men. They shoot evil beads into a sand painting made with ashes instead of the holy colors; they can kill their victims that way from a great distance. Sometimes, a Singer can find the bead during a ceremonial and save that person's life, but usually he dies."

"If you know where the caves are," Elspeth could not restrain herself from asking, "why doesn't someone destroy them?"

"Only the Skinwalkers know where they are. And, if anyone wished to destroy them, he would surely die."

Maria had never mentioned death before, and probably did so now only because she was speaking Spanish. When a person died, he euphemistically "went away." She recalled Valerio mentioning that he built shelters at night on their journey "because someone might have been improperly buried" where they were camping. Though Maria's stories always upset her later, Elspeth decided to pursue the subject while she was so talkative.

"Why do the Skinwalkers dig up bodies?" she asked. "Is it for corpse dust?"

"Yes, but they rob them, too. They take any jewelry in the graves. If a man was a warrior, they take his sinews for magic."

"I haven't seen a cemetery," Elspeth said, but the word was not in Maria's Spanish vocabulary. "Where are the dead buried?"

"They are hidden in the rocks and covered with stones, but the Skinwalkers can find them," Maria said, with a shiver. "They must be properly buried, or the bad part of them will come back to haunt the living. Or, sometimes, things left undone may bring them back. Many Beads saw my grandmother standing beside her loom where she had been weaving before she died. Instead of being frightened, Many Beads assured her that she would finish the rug and the ghost went away. My mother sent it back to rest. Wouldn't it be awful to be a ghost, alone out there in the night? Only small children are good enough not to come back, they say."

Elspeth smiled and took Maria's cold hands between her own. "You don't have anything to worry about," she assured her friend affectionately. "There's as much good in you as in a child. Who, besides yourself, has so much good in her heart that she feels sorry for the ghosts she fears so much?"

The exodus from the canyons began as if a signal had been given, though no messages had passed between its inhabitants. One day the family was still packing its belongings, and, on the next, everyone began to walk or ride toward the great open mouth of Chinle Wash at approximately the same time. Under a gray sky, with shadows slanting into the red walls on either side, the colorful spectacle progressed, revealing more people than Elspeth thought inhabited de Chelly and its branches. The very young rode in the travois bearing all their household goods, and the old like Hosteen Yazzie rode on the extra horses, often lending their assistance in leading the unmounted ones. The women and older children herded the sheep and kept them from becoming intermingled with the flocks of others as they crossed and recrossed the meandering Wash as it progressed to the only broad exit from their stronghold, the place where Elspeth and Valerio had entered the canyon several months before. She and her sisters walked in the caravan, each bearing a bundle of goods and looking after the children, who were in a high state of excitement. Many Beads rode at the head of the party and chose the easiest route for her family to follow. Elspeth had chosen not to ride because of her pregnancy. She didn't reveal the reason for her decision, because she wanted Valerio to be the first to know. She knew that the pace would be relaxed, with frequent stops to rest along the way. Slim Man and Many Tears Woman did not accompany them. They had gone on ahead to prepare the winter quarters on the rim for habitation, and the method by which they left the canyon made Elspeth dizzy as she watched. They appeared to move up a vertical red sandstone wall like flies with bundles of supplies on their backs. Many Beads and her daughters laughed at Elspeth's open-mouthed incredulity over the feat, and her stupefication did not diminish when they explained how it was accomplished. Almost invisible in the face of the canyon wall and not noticed by Elspeth until now, there were small notches cut into the sandstone, just large enough to gain finger and toeholds on the hundred-foot-high surface.

"It isn't hard after you do it once," Maria said, still smiling as Elspeth held her hand to her throat. "It's a long way to the mouth of the canyon. If you're in a hurry, it's the only way to get out."

"*You've* done it?"

"Of course. We all have. The notches have always been there. The People have used them for hundreds of years."

"I'll never use them," Elspeth, who had been trying to be more Navajo than the Navajo, said firmly, and the women laughed again.

"If Tall Man appeared at the top right now," Big Woman teased her, "you'd climb up faster than any of us."

Her devotion to Valerio had not gone unnoticed, and Big Woman and Many Beads often teased her about it, gently admiring her single-minded attachment to him, though they would never have revealed their own emotions so obviously. They had decided that she was a good wife; their only concern was that her singular attachment did not interfere with her other family relationships.

Mexican Woman had joined them silently with her bundles of bedding, which she placed alongside theirs on one of the travois. She remained apart on the progress through the canyon, though she was quick to notice anything that had to be done and bore as much responsibility for the sheep and other belongings as the rest of them. Elspeth glanced often at the solitary figure who appeared to be one of them though she was not.

The snow began to fall shortly after their arrival at the winter hogans. Everyone said it had come early this year, and though no one spoke about it, Elspeth felt they shared her concern for Valerio and Shouting Man, who planned to return before the time of the "Strong Winds" in December, but the "Big Crust," which usually came in January, had come too soon.

"They will be all right," Big Woman commented, without conviction, as they watched the heavy flakes of snow descend. "They will be all right if the snow is not heavy and if the winds don't come."

She did not mention the men again as she settled into her hogan and went about her daily chores. Elspeth worked at her own chores, but it was not enough to keep her from thinking of Valerio. Only her weaving calmed her, and she sat at her loom

with the sun shining on the new-fallen snow for long hours at a
time. Her first, larger rug, had been taken off her loom to wear
against the chill in the air, and she decided to attempt a more
difficult pattern, using many small balls of yarn of various colors, which had to be woven in at precise intervals. The only
pattern in her mind was the mineral tapestries below on the
canyon walls, which reminded her of the women's rugs, and
with the colors she had on hand, she began to weave a stylized
conception of a tapestry that would be large enough for Valerio.
Next year, she would learn to dye her own yarn, and she would
dye enough so she would not have to depend on others and
would not have to work with such limited colors. She tried to
keep her mind on the future instead of the present as she wove.
Next year, I'll have my baby in a cradleboard beside me when
I weave, and Valerio will be with us as if he'd never been away.
She wove even after her feet got cold and she had to blow on
her fingers for warmth.

Every snowfall brought more foreboding, but the winds remained calm, and she knew that Valerio and her brother-in-law
were not fighting their way back through a blizzard. The snow
clung to the cottonwood branches and outlined the dull green of
the twisted junipers, but the sheep foraged successfully on the
weeds and bushes and nudged through its surface for grasses.
Maria accompanied Oldest Boy on his daily herding, and Slim
Man took over the shepherding after they heard a wolf howling
in the night. Fodder had been hauled from the canyon for the
horses. Elspeth, who had not been around so many animals
before, marveled at how heartily they endured the weather.

She wove all afternoon, until she was cautioned that she was
not using her time well. The warning came by an unexpected
messenger as she was tying a new color into her blanket under
a gray sky that threatened further snow. When Mexican Woman
approached, Elspeth was surprised; she had not seen her so
closely before, and she could not imagine why the solitary
woman was moving directly toward her. She was a handsome
middle-aged woman with large, dolorous eyes, her face half-
hidden by the old blanket in which she had wrapped herself.

"Many Beads sent me because we speak the same language,"
she explained. "She says that you work too long at your loom."
Elspeth was touched by her mother-in-law's concern for her,
until her strange visitor added, "She says that everything should

be done in moderation. No women spends more than a couple of hours at a time weaving. And she warns that your last blanket was not good because it was finished."

Elspeth thought she must have misunderstood, and her puzzled face brought a thin smile to Mexican Woman's lips. "They never finish anything completely," she explained. "Only the Holy People—Gods—are perfect and complete. You didn't leave a spirit opening in the blanket you're wearing. There should have been a line through one corner, from your pattern through the border."

"Maria told me," Elspeth admitted. "I forgot. Please tell Many Beads I won't forget again. She probably doesn't understand that my weaving is all that keeps my mind off my husband. That's why I spend so much time at my loom."

"It wouldn't matter," Mexican Woman said, her dark eyes studying the white woman who had chosen to come here. "You still shouldn't work longer than she thinks appropriate. I have lived here for over twenty years. I know the way they think."

Elspeth, who had expected the woman to exhibit some disturbance of mind, was impressed by her reasonableness. "We should have spoken sooner," she told the stranger. "We both speak Spanish, and you know so much more than I do."

"You were warned against speaking to me. I understood," the woman said, with a faint smile. "Because I perform certain services for them, they think I am unclean . . . a witch, perhaps. I do what I have to do to be of some value to them. I am here when they need me, but they don't like the constant reminder of my presence. That is why I live apart."

"I don't understand. They are the kindest people I've ever known. Is it because you've kept your own religion?"

Mexican Woman touched the crucifix around her neck. "That, too, but only because I won't submit to their ceremonials after burying the dead. Yes," she said when she observed Elspeth's surprise, "it is a task they dread so much they would rather leave it to someone else. You must beware of this in the future, since you are white, too. If you serve them in that way, they'll distrust you afterwards—unless you agree to a healing ceremony."

"They can't really think you're a witch," Elspeth said. "If they did, they wouldn't allow you to stay. Their fear of witches is very real."

"As long as the crops don't fail or a double-headed lamb isn't born, I am secure," the woman said, with irony. "How are you progressing with the language?"

"Not very well," Elspeth admitted. "It's difficult to speak without moving your lips."

"You have to learn it as a child to speak it well. You have an accent even when you speak Spanish. I probably have one, too, because I haven't spoken my own language for so long. I've stayed longer than I should to deliver Many Beads's message. I must leave now."

Elspeth attempted to delay her, because she liked the woman and wished to prolong their discussion. "Perhaps we could—"

"No," Mexican Woman said as she gathered her blanket around her to depart. "If you want to be one of them, you must avoid me. I could hurt you more than I could help you."

Elspeth stared after her as she made her way across the winter-blighted land. She would have liked to know her better, but the woman had spoken the truth. As kind as her family was, she knew their feelings about death, and Mexican Woman's adherence to her faith set her apart. She moved across the snow with a dignity that did not invite pathos, but Elspeth's heart went out to her. If it was within her power to make Mexican Woman's life more bearable, she would do so, even if it meant justifying her action to the family.

Chapter 13

The flock the men drove before them was almost indistinguishable in the flurries of snow that blew from the north. Oldest Boy saw the horses first and alerted the family of their return. They were already within calling distance when everyone except Many Beads ran out to meet them. She had to remain inside her hogan because she could not face her son-in-law. Their relief over the arrival turned quickly to concern when Valerio had to assist Shouting Man from his horse and half carried him into Big Woman's hogan. He put the injured man down on a sheepskin and began to unwind a filthy bandage from around his thigh as exclamations of concern sounded from those around them. The wound was ugly, blue and swollen; its odor filled the warm interior. Elspeth's stomach turned, though she had not experienced any sickness during her pregnancy before. She shooed the children off to their grandmother's and began to boil water over the fire. Her hands shook visibly in spite of her effort to control them; the smell in the room was the odor of death. Big Woman sat at her husband's side, but he was too feverish to answer her questions. Valerio dispatched Maria for healing herbs and Hosteen Yazzie before crouching down beside Elspeth.

"I did not want you to worry," he said, "but he could hardly ride. We had to stop often. The snow was too deep to find herbs after I used those in my medicine pouch."

"What happened?" she asked, wondering if the Hosteen could treat gangrene. "How did he get injured, Valerio?"

"We tried to take too many sheep. A dog barked, and the rancher shot at us."

His words jolted through her like the rifle report, and she cried, "It could have been you!"

He put a comforting hand on her shoulder. "It's never happened before. It won't happen again. I'm here with you, *querida*."

Hosteen Yazzie entered with his medicine bag, his face betraying nothing when he smelled the terrible odor. Elspeth carried the pot of hot water to him, but he ignored it, intent upon cutting away the dead tissue from Shouting Man's leg. The sight, combined with the cloying smell, was too much for her, and she rushed out to gulp deep breaths of the clean, cold air. The nausea came over her in waves, and she struggled against the impulse to retch. Slim Man entered the hogan without noticing her, and Valerio joined her a few minutes later.

"It will be all right," he assured her as he took her in his arms. "They will burn the bad flesh away. You're shaking. I didn't want my return to be like this."

"I've missed you," she murmured in the warmth of his embrace. "You mustn't go raiding again. We'll find a way to barter for sheep, so you don't have to put your life in danger."

Even as she spoke, she realized he would never barter for something for which everyone else risked danger. His silence reinforced her intuition. Tinkling bells milling around them in the snow penetrated her consciousness, and she was suddenly a practical Navajo wife again. "The wind's blowing harder. We must drive those animals into the corral or we won't be able to find them."

They spent the better part of an hour calling and clapping their hands until the sheep were safely secured within the log fences of the corral with the rest of the flock. She leaned against the haphazard, snow-covered fencing, perspiring and out of breath, but with a feeling of accomplishment. She had not only driven the sheep to safety; she had conquered her nausea and fear as well. Valerio kissed her cold lips and held her close.

"You are no longer without property," he said proudly. "You have a flock as big as my sisters'."

But at what a price? she thought. Is it really worth it? "Thank you," she said aloud, for gratitude was more important than criticism. "You said you could provide for me." A worrisome thought crossed her mind. "Did we get the lambs? I didn't see any lambs. They'll never survive the night in this storm."

He laughed aloud and held her closer. "There won't be any lambs until spring. But many of the ewes are carrying. It will be a good year."

"I'm carrying, too," she heard herself saying. "We'll have a baby then, too."

He gave a cry of delight and lifted her into the air by her waist. "Surely this will be a beautiful year. We'll be surrounded by beauty, *querida*, and so will our child. Is it possible to be too happy?"

"Not here," she said, with her arms around his neck. "Some people are afraid to tempt God by being happy, but you pray for happiness every day. The Holy People don't begrudge it when it comes."

The weather improved. After the first storms, the snow retreated, leaving only brush strokes of white on the land. Shouting Man lived, but he was lame and his sleep was troubled by dreams, which required a cure. There was discussion of having an Enemy Way ceremonial for him if the weather remained clear. Elspeth was more serene with Valerio beside her in their hogan. Her happiness could be contained in her arms, and she embraced it closely, wishing never to be parted from it again. With no crops to tend, there was less work to do at this time of the year. Firewood had to be cut and the sheep herded, but winter was a season of ease, when people recounted stories and, in general, did only the things they enjoyed. She began a blanket for her baby, and Valerio became preoccupied with some Mexican silver coins he had acquired from the Pueblos and, until now, had kept hidden in a buckskin pouch.

He attempted to shape the soft coins by hammering them on a smooth rock. He spent hours attempting to work the malleable metal into the jewelry he had seen on the Mexicans when he was a slave, but the results were disappointing and the silver acquired gritty imperfections in the process.

"I worked with metal when I was with the Mexicans," he said one afternoon, "but it was hard metal that I had to hammer after firing it."

With an expression of determination, he put one of the coins into a clay pot and set it on the fire in an attempt to soften the metal, but the pot cracked and the silver ran in rivulets from its side. Elspeth was distraught over the loss of his precious coin until she saw the excitement in his face.

"It melts," he exclaimed. "Now, I know how the ornaments were made."

He began to carve a pattern into a piece of sandstone with so much absorption that he was unaware of his surroundings, and Elspeth watched him, familiar with the emotion he was feeling. She experienced it when she was weaving, and she had known it long ago when she painted with watercolors. The sandstone was not difficult to carve, though he paused every few minutes to blow gritty sand away with his breath before continuing. When the inverted pattern was completed, she was impressed by its symmetry and beauty; he had carved skillfully, and the result was a delicate squash blossom in the stone.

"It's lovely," she said, with her hand upon his shoulder, "but what are you going to do with it?"

"Fire the remaining coins and pour the silver into it," he replied. "There will still be grit on the surface, but that can be polished away."

He procured the heaviest clay pot he could find, and they sat beside the fire with suspended breath that evening as they waited for the coins to melt. He extracted the pot from the fire at just the proper moment, ready to pour it into his cast, but the pot cracked before he could pour and the molten metal splattered his hand as it poured onto the floor.

Elspeth dressed the burn with animal fat, feeling the pain as if it were her own, though he did not reveal his discomfort; indeed, he still appeared to be thinking about what had gone wrong.

"It's all right," he reassured her, touching her cheek with his uninjured hand. "What I need is an iron pot like the white men have. I can get it through my Pueblo friend near Santa Fe. I will go there after the planting is done."

"Valerio," she objected, but he closed her lips with his fingers.

"I won't be raiding this time. There is nothing for you to fear."

"I fear the white men more than you do. They're at *war* with the People. Why won't you listen to me?"

"Where are their warriors? I haven't seen any, *querida*. How can they make war on us without warriors? The Americans aren't like the Spanish and the Mexicans. We can trust them, just as I trust you. I won't leave you for many months. You know I wouldn't leave you now. They have no more reason to fear me than I have them. We aren't at war, *querida*. Our only real enemy is the Ute."

The Enemy Way ceremonial a few weeks later included the Mexican who shot Shouting Man in the category of enemies, and Elspeth thought it prudent to keep a low profile, because she, too, was white. The slight chill in the air required blankets for warmth, so she was able to observe without being conspicuous, and her advanced pregnancy excused her from cooking side by side with the guests who were assisting in that task. A large medicine hogan and several other shelters had been constructed for the occasion, one of which was devoted entirely to the preparation of food. She carried her contributions for the feasting there when she knew that only the women in her family were present. Many Beads reproved her for carrying the heavy pots full of stew, but Elspeth wanted to participate in the work as much as possible without attracting attention to herself.

The most careful attention was given to every detail of the ritual. Valerio was chosen by Hosteen Yazzie to cut the cedar for the Rattle-Stick, which would later bear three deer hooves and two eagle feathers and some ritualistic cuts that had to be carved exactly. The stick had to be cut from a perfect piece of cedar, without mark or blemish, and it had to be the length of a man's forearm. It took Valerio an entire day to find the proper stick and return it for the Singer's approval.

Before all the guests and relatives arrived, the Hosteen and his assistants made the ceremonial drum after dark one night. While he sang the Drum Song, a goatskin was wet gradually with water and pulled tightly over the top of a large clay pot and secured there with bow strings. Three small holes were pricked into the top of the drum with a moccasin needle to give it life. The men sang through the night in the "Old Language," which few could understand, least of all Elspeth, who had not completely mastered the living language.

"A scalp is necessary for this ceremonial," Valerio told her, "but that's hard to find. We haven't taken scalps within the memory of anyone here. A knot of hair is used instead, but it must be the hair of the kind of enemy who harmed Shouting Man. It's been buried beyond the eastern side of the medicine hogan, and it will be 'killed' on the last day of the ceremony.''

Elspeth was curious. "Where did they get a knot of Mexican hair?'' she asked. ''I should think he would object to that almost as violently as to being scalped.''

"Mexican Woman gave my mother some of hers. It was a dangerous thing to do, but she's fond of Shouting Man's family.''

"It was a kind gesture, but why dangerous?''

"The person whose hair is used for a scalp will die within two years,'' he said simply. "Mexican Woman was very brave.''

Elspeth smiled. Mexican Woman did not adhere to Navajo custom and knew very well that there was no risk, but she said in her favor, "It was both brave and kind.''

The ceremonial was to last for three days, and the patient, Shouting Man, was lodged in the medicine hogan for most of that time, since it was he who was to be cured of his lameness and the bad dreams that had resulted from his injury. Though Elspeth did not know what was taking place in the medicine hogan, it seemed that Shouting Man was relatively forgotten in the dancing and socializing that followed. All the eligible young bachelors from miles around were in attendance, and on the second day, the carefully chaperoned girls, wearing beautiful blankets of their own weaving, were presented. She had watched the dancing for some time before she realized that it was not the young men, but the girls, who were choosing their partners. Maria danced with the same partner several times and, though she made an attempt at being demure, she was enjoying herself thoroughly. Her face was flushed in the firelight, and her dark eyes smiled when she danced with a slim young man with a face that might have earned him the nickname Handsome Man.

"They had the same ceremonial for her when she came back from the hacienda,'' Valerio said. "It is time she had a husband. She is already very old to be unmarried.''

The ceremony must have healed the terrible scars in Maria's mind, Elspeth thought. That's why she was so cheerful by the time I arrived here. She had been restored to *hozro* and made pure again, and she could now dance with the other maidens seeking husbands. She hoped that she had found one at last in the attentive young man with whom she was dancing.

At dawn the following morning, a noisy commotion about a quarter of a mile from the encampment brought Elspeth from her hogan. She was further alarmed when the young men in the camp leaped on their horses and rode toward the sound at top speed, whooping and yelling.

"It isn't a real battle," Valerio said, putting his arms around her from behind and kissing her neck. "The young men have gone to face the Enemy, but the Enemy is only other young men who went out before them. It's part of the ceremonial. They'll all return soon, and they'll be very hungry."

"I better take the bread I made to the cooking shelter," she said. "And they'll need the pot of stew on the fire."

"I'll carry the pot for you," he said, and moved through the door to get it with Elspeth following at his heels.

"You can't do that," she objected. "What would people think? A man doesn't carry food for his woman."

"This man does," he responded as he wrapped a skin around the bubbling pot to lift it. "The men can make fun of me at their peril. None of them have a woman like mine."

The women in the family had been cooking as early as Elspeth and only Many Tears Woman looked unfavorably upon Valerio's assistance. She had been more unfriendly since Elspeth's pregnancy became apparent, and Elspeth sympathized with her and understood her reaction. Maria was patting flat bread between her palms, slightly apart from the others, and Elspeth joined her since the guests had not yet arrived to help.

"Only the men really enjoy themselves at these ceremonials," Many Beads grumbled as she stirred the pots on the rectangular fire. "The women do all the work. You are a good husband," she told her son. "I've told her not to carry heavy things."

"He spoils her," Many Tears Woman commented glumly.

"You spoil her, too, Mother. How many sheep have you had to kill for her?"

"The same number that you gave," Many Beads said curtly. "She will learn to slaughter sheep in time. She's never killed anything in her life. That must be very hard on a girl."

Valerio smiled and drifted off, perhaps to challenge any man who had a comment on his behavior, and Elspeth whispered to Maria, "You had a handsome dancing partner last night. The same partner several times."

Maria flushed and averted her eyes, but there was a smile on her lips. "Lone Raider's Son," she murmured. "A good young man from the right sort of family. I think he likes me."

"I'm sure he likes you. How could anyone help it?" Elspeth teased her in the Navajo fashion. "I suppose there will be much more cooking soon, and a wedding cake to be baked."

Maria was silent for a moment, and her face grew serious. "If his father comes to my family with a gift. But his father may not come. Everyone knows about my captivity and what happened do me during that time . . ."

"Everything?" Elspeth asked as she put a round of bread in the grease, which sizzled and spattered in the cold air.

"Only that I'm not a virgin. Only my family knows about the other things. They were very angry. They could not understand it. They could hardly believe it."

"You danced with the maidens last night," Elspeth encouraged her. "Ritually, you are a maiden."

Maria sighed deeply. "I hope Lone Raider and his wife see it that way. If they don't . . ."

"Yes?"

"Lone Raider's Son and I could go off together. He'd have to marry me then. He may want me that much."

When everyone had eaten, the Hosteen led them into the ceremonial hogan, and Maria and Elspeth followed, both covering their faces with their blankets. They insinuated themselves between the guests and sat in the shadows behind the family. Elspeth was surprised to see that Shouting Man and his wife had been thoroughly blackened by some compound and that Big Woman was naked to the waist, her large breasts exposed without shame before the crowd. Hosteen Yazzie sang the Giving Medicine Song, pausing only to administer a decoction to the blackened couple. Water was then added to the potion and the couple was washed with the liquid, starting at their feet and ending at their mouths. Their smudged faces were tranquil, but they were not to remain clean for long. Black ashes with the pungent odor of cedar were taken from a small fire and applied again to their feet first, and then their bodies. The old man started another song and painted a red band across their chins from ear to ear, giving the startling illusion that their throats had been cut. Elspeth gasped and Maria noted her reaction.

"The earth ashes will keep the ghosts from reentering their bodies," she whispered. "Two pinches of earth will be put into Shouting Man's moccasins to cure him."

"Why are they both being treated?" Elspeth kept her voice at a whisper, too, though it was unlikely that she would be heard because of the singing.

"A man and his wife are one person," Maria explained. "They are the same, just as you and my brother are the same person."

Elspeth was relieved to emerge into the bright, cool day and paused for a moment on the threshold of the medicine hogan, amid the milling crowd, to regain her equilibrium. She had a dull pain in her lower back from sitting so long.

She would have liked to go to her own dwelling to rest, but only the Killing of the Scalp remained to be witnessed, and she wanted to follow the ceremonial through to its end.

A toothless old man with unruly hair emerged from the crowd bearing a poker in one hand and a bow and arrow in the other. He feinted with his poker in the direction of the post marking where the "scalp" had been buried, and retreated a few feet to string his bow. He was the lone player in the scene. Elspeth had expected some of the young warriors who had fought the mock battle to participate in this final part of the ritual.

"The old man has been paid to kill the scalp," Maria explained. "Only a very old man with nothing to live for would do it, for he is only supposed to live a year or two afterwards, they say. I know of an old man who has lived for many years, though, and makes his living killing scalps."

Shouting Man limped out of the medicine hogan with a companion who was painted as black as he was, and as the two men approached the scalp, the old man gave a loud yell and released his arrow into the ground next to the post. He then proceeded to beat the ground over the scalp with his poker and threw some ashes over his kill. Shouting Man turned toward the east and stood still for a moment before beckoning the rays of the sun toward his body with both hands.

"He's inhaling the sun," Maria said. "The cure is almost complete. He will be better, now."

Elspeth put her hand over her lower back, wondering why the pain seemed to be increasing. There had been so much to take in that she was almost relieved that it was over. The only clear impression that emerged in her mind was that the 'scalp' that had just been killed and sprinkled with ashes was a knot of Mexican Woman's hair. The dull pain was spreading to her lower abdomen now, and she wanted more than ever to lie down.

"I know I shouldn't lie down during the day," she told Maria, "but I'd better go to my hogan. I feel strange. I ache."

Maria observed that Elspeth was holding both sides of her abdomen. "I'll take you there," she said, with a smile. "I think your time has come. Your child wants to inhale the sun, too. It is good. My mother must be told. She and the other women will help."

Her baby was born during the final feasting and singing that night, and that, too, was a good sign. Hosteen Yazzie left the guests when he heard that Elspeth was in labor and spent the following hours sitting at one side of her hogan, chanting and waving a bunch of eagle feathers. Many Beads and two older women, who were guests, attended her in such a matter-of-fact manner that she did not think of being afraid. One of the women loosened Elspeth's hair, because that would make the birth easier, and Many Beads built a soft mound of earth on the floor of the hogan, which she covered with a clean sheepskin from her own house. The only misunderstanding between the patient and her attendants was Elspeth's inclination to lie down. That was not permitted; it was unnatural. A woven belt was tied into a loop from the ceiling beam above the sheepskin, and Elspeth was instructed to hang on to it when the contractions seized her. Aided by gravity in this position, the birth was relatively quick and much easier than she had anticipated. As the cord was cut and Many Beads bathed the lustily crying baby in cold water, the Hosteen chanted:

> The Early Dawn found a baby,
> To the East, he found a baby;
> The baby was eager to be born.
> The baby has a happy voice,
> The Everlasting, Peaceful baby.

"You have a son," Many Beads told her after she was at last allowed to lie down. "A beautiful baby. Now I am sure this marriage is blessed. He even has the blue spot."

The tiny, squirming infant was placed into her arms wrapped in a soft sheepskin after his shocking bath, and, as Elspeth touched his face and hands for the first time, a rush of love flooded through her. His cries subsided as soon as he reached her arms, and he made little sucking sounds with his lips.

"Blue spot?" she asked suddenly, inspecting him for a birthmark. "Where is it?"

Many Beads flipped him gently onto his stomach with confident hands and indicated a spot at the base of his spine. "You have become Dineh," she said. "Completely Dineh. Even your hair has grown dark living among us. Only Dineh babies have the blue spot, which will fade shortly."

"The Apache have it, too," one of the other women volunteered. "So I have heard, anyway."

Elspeth was too absorbed with her baby to explain that her hair had become dark because there was no sun in the winter. The Hosteen began to discuss a naming ceremony for her child, and Many Beads removed a string of turquoise from her neck and placed it around Elspeth's.

"You are a good wife. You have worked hard," she said. "You've given us a good baby."

"You are kind, Mother," Elspeth said, touched by the gesture, which made her feel completely accepted. "I know the Hosteen will choose the war name for my son, but I would like to name him, too. Is that permitted?"

"If that is what you want," the fond grandmother agreed, "but won't he have too many names? He will earn the name by which he'll be called later, probably Tall Man's Son. What name do you have in mind?"

"Sky," Elspeth said simply. She had given it much thought. "There is so much sky here, and it is always beautiful. I want my son to grow straight and tall toward the sky and to be as generous and beautiful."

The women were surprised over her choice of a name; it was not a customary one among the People. Many Beads consulted Hosteen Yazzie briefly, and he did not object to *Yotááh* as an additional name.

Many Beads smiled and offered Elspeth some warm gruel.

"You must drink this. It will restore your strength. Tall Man is waiting to see his son. Soon, everyone in the family will want to see him, but not until you've had some rest."

The women remained during Valerio's visit. Elspeth would rather have had this time alone with him, but she knew the others stayed out of concern for her and the baby. Someone would remain with her for several days to assist her in caring for Sky. Valerio nearly made the mistake of kissing her when he knelt beside her, but he only brushed her lips in a manner that would not be noticed and rested his cheek against hers.

"I love you," he whispered in Spanish. "When we are alone, I'll take you into my arms and kiss you as I should." Then, aloud in his own language, he said, "You are a good wife. I have come to see my son."

She opened the flap of sheepskin over the baby's face to show him to his father and was surprised when Valerio took the baby into his arms as fondly as she had. The women smiled their approval as he examined the child, allowing the tiny fingers to grasp his own with an expression of love on his face. Apparently it was not considered unmanly for a warrior to cradle an infant in his arms like a woman. Nor did he take the baby outside into the cold air to proclaim that he had fathered a son as Elspeth half expected. Their gazes met and held, and his eyes expressed the depth of his feeling in a way that words could not have done.

"He is a fine son," he said at last, returning the baby to her reluctantly. "I will make a cradleboard that will make him grow straight and strong, a beautiful cradleboard with a headpiece like a rainbow. You must rest, now." He leaned toward her again before he rose to go and placed his hand around the side of her face. "I love you," he said softly. "I've never been so happy, *querida*. You are my life, and our son is part of both of us."

Chapter 14

Sky was laced into his cradleboard by the time the sheep were driven back into the canyon again in the spring. Valerio took great care in building it, while his son rested in a basket of laced twigs with his head always facing the hogan fire. He selected a perfect young pine, which had not been struck by lightning and was not near a place that a bear might have come, for bears and snakes were evil, and cut a piece out of the best part of the tree. Elspeth watched him carefully take the bark off and cut a small piece for the footboard and a triangle for the head, time-consuming work, because he whittled so carefully. He bent a good piece of oak over the fire for the hood and cut four holes to tie it to the cradleboard, then made holes on the sides for the buckskin lacings. Each piece was sprinkled with corn pollen as it was made and once again before he painted the fully constructed board with sheep tallow and red paint inside and out. The soft inner bark was shredded for the lining and a small blanket laid over it with a small buckskin curtain to protect the baby's face. The lacing strings started at the bottom and crossed, going upward, so the baby would lie as the tree grew, upward.

Sky remained in the cradleboard only a few hours at a time before being cleaned and allowed to kick his legs, and Elspeth found the board safer and more convenient than an ordinary cradle. She held it on Plata in front of her when the family returned to the canyon, taking the long way through the Wash again, accompanied by Hosteen Yazzie and Shouting Man, who was now called Limping Man. The rest of the family drove the sheep down the steep slope into Tsegi, shouting and raising a cloud of red dust. They arrived before Elspeth and her companions, but she would not have missed the spring ride through the green floor of the canyon beneath its shimmering cottonwoods.

Her hogan had been opened and aired by the time she arrived, and the sheep were all in the corral. Maria was sweeping the floor of the hogan with the subdued demeanor that had characterized her for the past two months. Lone Raider had not called upon her family; she had seen nothing of his son since the ceremonial. She was in love with the young man, and it was a difficult time for her. She had not mentioned her distress to Elspeth, but Elspeth knew what was troubling her and went out of her way to try to raise her spirits. Maria's single distraction was the baby, of whom she was inordinately fond, and she rushed to take the cradleboard from the horse so Elspeth could dismount.

"You took such a long time," she said. "I thought you'd never get here. I'll help you with your belongings."

"The Hosteen is old," Elspeth explained. "He has many stories to tell. He's been showing me where to find medicine plants and how to use them. He stopped to gather some along the way. It probably delayed us."

"He'll try to make a medicine woman of you," Maria said, with a faint smile. "He tried with my mother a long time ago, and he wanted me to learn, but it didn't interest me. You don't have to do it unless you like it."

"I think I might, if it doesn't interfere with my weaving. Where's Tall Man?"

"The men have gone back for the firewood we threw into the canyon," Maria said, without taking her gaze from the baby. She put the cradleboard down and began to unlace it, and Elspeth realized that Maria was becoming a second mother to her little son; when she really needed a child of her own.

They bathed the baby and allowed him to kick in the sun, as she had done so often during the trek into the canyon. "This is the place I like best," Elspeth said. "I feel right here, different than anywhere else."

"In harmony," Maria reflected, brushing a fly away from the baby. "Yes, I used to feel that way, too. If that feeling doesn't come back soon, I'll need a ceremonial. I was wrong about Lone Raider's Son liking me as much as I like him. If he did, he would have come to me whether his father approved or not.''

"Do they live in the canyon?" Elspeth asked, relieved that the matter had come out into the open. "Will they be returning here, too?"

"Yes, but quite a distance away, and this is the busiest time of the year. If he had wanted to court me, he should have done it sooner.'' She brushed a tear from her cheek with the back of her hand. "I didn't know it would be so painful to need someone so much. I think I must resign myself to being a spinster. No good man will have me after what happened at the hacienda."

"You're wrong," Elspeth told her confidently. "Only a good man deserves you. If it is not Lone Raider's Son, it will be someone better than he. I know that isn't much consolation right now, because I know what it is to need one certain man, my sister.'' Something occurred to her suddenly; she wondered why she had not thought of it before. "Perhaps some circumstance has arisen which has kept Lone Raider's Son from you. Couldn't one of the men ride to their place and find out?''

Maria's face brightened visibly. "No one can be spared now, but after the busy time is over, would you suggest it to Mother? I can't do it, you know."

"If you want me to," Elspeth said, smiling and taking her hand. "I just want to see you happy again."

The lambing was the most intense period of work Elspeth had encountered; some days, she took time out only to nurse her baby. The whole family was involved and, within a week, the flock had almost doubled. Separate pens had to be made for the ewes who did not accept their lambs. The rejected newborn lambs were tied to their mothers in the hope that their proximity would induce the ewes to nurse them. In the few cases where that failed, the children adopted the small orphans and fed them by saturating a cloth with the ewe's milk and allowing the lambs to suck on it. The men were as busy as the women, rebuilding the corral to accommodate the burgeoning flock and attending a mare that had also foaled. In spite of the long hours of work, lambing was a joyous time, and everyone who participated smiled and laughed a great deal, not over their good fortune, but at the miracle of life and the antics of the lambs, themselves.

Big Woman's younger children each adopted a lamb they had fed and spent their playtime later caring for their pets.

As soon as things settled down, it was time to break the earth and plant the corn and squash, activities carried out in a more leisurely fashion. The housekeeping, which had never been attended to with much organization but somehow got finished every day, did not hinder the women from other pursuits. Many Beads visited her grandson every afternoon, usually accompanied by either Big Woman or Maria, and Valerio found time to erect Elspeth's loom in its customary place beneath the tamarisk trees. The respite was short, though. The crops had hardly been sowed before it was time to shear the sheep, and great mounds of wool soon lay outside of the corral on blankets. When the sheep were driven out to graze after the shearing, they looked naked, and Elspeth and Maria laughed together at their appearance.

"They'll be cooler this way," Elspeth remarked, sending Maria into another paroxysm of laughing.

"They are so funny without their wool," she said. "They always make me laugh. They look surprised and their legs are spindly." Then, she grew suddenly serious. "We'll start carding the wool tomorrow. You won't forget what we spoke about?"

Elspeth assured her that she would put the matter to Many Beads, but she had another matter to attend to first, something she had put off too long with all of the activity around her. When she and Valerio were alone in their hogan, she took out the small pouch which contained her baby's dried umbilical cord. She had not wanted to bury it at the corral of the camp on the rim where he was born, though it should have been buried there to insure his well-being. Tsegi was his home, the place where he belonged, and Many Beads had assured her that she had buried the cords of all of her children in the canyon, too. That evening, Valerio dug a small hole in the earth near the corral, and they buried the pouch together.

"Now he truly belongs here," Valerio said as he rose and dusted his hands. "If he ever goes away, he will always come back to the place where he belongs."

"I wonder how many generations are represented here?" Elspeth said. "Your family has been here for such a long time."

"My grandmother's family, and her grandmother's family before her," he agreed. "Too many to count. This is our homeland and Sky's, too. You were not born here, but I know that you'll never leave; it's your home, now, too." He paused for a moment in the gathering darkness, and she knew he had something on his mind even before he spoke. "I must leave for a while, *querida*. We spoke of it during the winter, remember?"

"Your Pueblo friend near Santa Fe," Elspeth murmured in a dazed voice; in her happiness, she had forgotten. "Must you go so far for a vessel in which to melt your silver?"

"It's a long ride, but it's safer to deal with someone you know, and I am sure of the Pueblo. He sheltered me for a long time when I escaped from the Mexicans. He is a good man, almost like a father to me."

"Then I suppose you must go. Take the blanket I wove during the winter for trading goods. Perhaps he can get you more silver, too." She wanted to tell him she would hate it when he was away from her, but she restrained herself. Neither of them would be completely happy when they were apart, and he must pursue his interest in silver as she did hers in weaving.

"I've been thinking," he said as they walked back toward their hogan. "If you want to send a message to your sister, I can carry it for you. You never speak of her, but I can see you thinking of her sometimes. She must think of you, too, and would be glad to hear that you are well."

Elspeth had not opened her writing box since she came here, except to extract a piece of paper to draw a pattern for a rug. She had thought of Thea a good deal during the winter, especially when Sky was born. The possibility of getting a letter to her was tempting. "It would be too dangerous," she objected. "You mustn't go near the farm or the hacienda."

"My friend could see that it reached her. He goes down to trade pottery in town."

The prospect was so appealing that she tried to think of a way to get the letter to Thea from town. As kind as Valerio's friend seemed to be, it would not do to have an Indian delivering it by hand. The only thing that came to mind lessened the possibility of Thea receiving the letter at all, but it seemed safe. "Do you think your friend would drop the message on the walk in front of the post office? Does he know where the post office—the place where they send letters—is?"

"If he doesn't, he would find it. I promise you, your message will get to your sister."

The fact that the letter did not have a stamp would not matter, she decided. If someone picked it up and took it inside, the post office would take care of the rest. Thea would have to pay the postage, but no one would know where the lost letter originated.

She took out her letter box and composed a reassuring letter beside the fire that night, cautiously avoiding any reference to her surroundings. As she wrote, she felt so much closer to Thea that she wanted to tell her everything, but she knew her sister would worry if she knew where she was. Thea knew nothing of the Navajo except what she had heard in Santa Fe. She told her about her son and said that she was happier than she had ever believed possible. She found it difficult not to inquire about Thea's well-being, but the question would not be answered anyway. There could be no reply to this letter.

After she sealed it and addressed the envelope, she joined Valerio on their sheepskin bed. He took her into his arms, and she realized with a rush of love that there would not be any nights like this for a while. Their secret and private ritual of undressing entirely when they made love would stop for many weeks when he went on his peaceful journey. She held him close, not wishing to part from him for a moment.

Alone at night with her baby sleeping in his cradleboard beside her, she began to think of things that did not trouble her when she had been safe in Valerio's arms. Though night came late in the summer, the darkness was almost complete, and she recalled all the stories Maria had told her. That of a witch sprinkling corpse dust through the smoke hole to bring misfortune became foremost in her mind. The possible misfortune did not trouble her, but the vehicle used was odious enough to make her shiver. She understood the fear of the dark that made white men laugh at the Indians. When darkness fell like a black shroud in this wild country, and voices seem to speak on the wind, anyone might become fearful, even if they did not believe in the supernatural.

Maria was unable to stay with her as she had done in the winter when the men were out on the raid. Limping Man's visit to Lone Raider's family confirmed that only a misadventure could have kept his son from pursuing his courtship. Within a week of the Enemy Way ceremonial, his father had encountered a bear bringing her young out of hibernation and had been badly mauled. The rest of the family, deprived of the injured man's assistance, had been working harder than usual during the lambing and planting. A five-day Mountain Chant had been sung to cure Lone Raider from his contamination by the bear, and a nine-day chant was planned next winter, when such ceremonials usually took place. The patient was up and around and soon he would be able to ride again. His brother would call upon Maria's family soon, for he had no objection to the marriage. In the meantime, the happy Maria had been urged by her mother to remain with her, so no aspersions could be cast upon her reputation, which could not be defended if she was out of Many Beads's sight. Elspeth suspected that Many Beads's real concern was that the young couple, in their impatience over the long delay, might find a way to meet in secret.

Relieved and happy over Maria's approaching wedding, Elspeth spent long hours during the day weaving the finest blanket dress she could imagine for her friend. But the harmony she achieved during the day did not carry her through the lonely nights and the trepidation that came with them, and she did not wish to reveal her weakness by confessing it to the family. She tried to get to sleep before night fell, and sometimes she was able to avoid the period of darkness in slumber. But, more often, she lay awake in fear of her own fear, unable to sleep. On one such night, her heart nearly stopped when she heard a footstep near her door. She lay paralyzed on her sheepskin, grasping the cradleboard close to her and picturing a demented man dressed in an animal skin hovering outside of the hogan. She could almost hear his abnormal breathing; in fact, she was certain she heard it, labored and wheezing. If I scream, will anyone come out into the night? she wondered frantically, moving closer to the wall with her baby. If I don't scream, will he come inside? The rug hanging over the door moved and a dark figure became visible against the even darker night.

"Are you sleeping?" a woman's voice said in Spanish. "I must speak to you, Helping Woman."

Elspeth's relief left her limp for a moment. She finally managed to stand, but her legs were weak. "Mexican Woman? You don't know what a fright you gave me. Please come in, if you can see in this darkness."

"I brought a candle," Mexican Woman said, and a small flame caught and flickered in the slumbering embers of the fireplace. "I make them from tallow. They don't know about it. I don't think they would like it."

She breathed heavily and Elspeth detected the wheezing sound again. At least, her ears had not deceived her. "Are you all right?" she asked, moving to the woman's side to assist her. "You don't sound well."

"I have come to ask a favor of you," Mexican Woman said. She sank to the floor and drew Elspeth down with her. "I wouldn't have bothered you, but you're the only person who can help me."

"I can get some herbs from Many Beads. Your chest doesn't sound right."

"I've had their herbs," Many Beads said breathlessly, "and usually they are effective. But this is something different. My heart beats irregularly, and my legs . . ." She moved the candle so Elspeth could see her swollen ankles. "Whatever it is, I think it won't go away until I do. And that's what I wanted to speak to you about. When I'm gone, they will probably turn to you to perform the death duties. I told you that before. Helping Woman, would you see that I get a Christian burial?"

Elspeth remained silent for a moment. Having someone request burial was too far from her experience for a prompt reply.

"You will live a long time," she said lamely. "We don't have to talk about this now."

"You think you can't prepare a body for burial," Mexican Woman said wearily. "I thought so, too, once, but it isn't difficult after you've done it once. They'll ask you to bury me in their manner, and that's all right, too. But my mind will be much easier if I know I'll have a Christian burial, too. Just a few words said over my grave that my God will understand."

"The only funerals I've attended were those of my parents," Elspeth told her. "The Twenty-third Psalm is all I remember . . ."

"The Psalm is good," Mexican Woman encouraged her, "but the part when the priest sprinkles holy water is better. Do you remember that?"

"I'm not a Catholic, Mexican Woman."

"I will teach you. I remember it, even after such a long time. 'Ashes to ashes and dust to dust . . .' "

". . . 'in sure and certain hope of the Resurrection unto eternal life,' " Elspeth murmured, as much to her surprise as that of Mexican Woman. "But it's from *The Book of Common Prayer.* It isn't Catholic at all."

"I don't know about that book," Mexican Woman told her, "but it is the same. And you know it. That's all I ask of you."

Elspeth sighed and took her hand. "All right, if it will make you feel better. But I'm still going to ask Hosteen Yazzie for some herbs for your chest and legs."

The women were helping Maria grind the corn for her wedding cake when Valerio rode in unexpectedly, leaped from his horse, and hastened toward them. Elspeth rose on her knees before the metate with fine cornmeal on her hands, grateful for his early return but startled by his manner. He greeted his mother courteously, but his troubled gaze sought that of his wife.

"I have much to tell you," he told Many Beads, "but I must speak to my wife first."

The other women were taken aback by the breach of manners, and Elspeth found it alarming, because it was not like him. Something's happened to Thea, she thought. Something terrible has happened. She brushed the flour from her hands and rose to follow him into the grove of tamarisks. When they were completely alone, he turned and opened his arms to her. She rushed into them and buried her head against his chest.

"It's Thea, isn't it?" she murmured. "What's happened?"

"Your sister's in good health, *querida,*" he assured her, "but something very strange is taking place. The white men are preparing to fight one another. Your brother-in-law is dressed like a bluecoat and men are volunteering at the fort in Santa Fe. My friend said they are expecting an attack from the Texans. We don't know what to make of it. I don't know how to explain it to my family."

Elspeth had forgotten the rumors of war and she found the news disturbing. Surely, if a civil war had started it would not be fought here in the West. "There was talk about it before I left," she said, "about the North fighting the South if it was necessary. The South must have seceded . . ."

"What do you mean by the North and the South? Are they all Americans? Are the Americans fighting the Americans?"

"Yes, they must be. The disagreement was over the South keeping slaves, Valerio. The president didn't like it, but the South was determined to keep the slaves. That's all I can tell you. The Texans must have sided with the South. If they're coming, will my sister be safe in Santa Fe?"

"There are many soldiers there, and Texas is far away," he said, "with the Apache in between. They'd have to march up the Rio Grande. I don't think they'd have a chance. You mustn't worry about your sister. She does not seem worried, and there is a baby in her house. She sits beside it in the sun in the morning."

"You didn't send the letter with the Pueblo," she accused him. "You went yourself."

"When I heard about the war, I had to see if she was all right," he defended his action mildly. "You love your sister and I love you. I left the message by her door before dawn and watched from my usual place. She read it many times while she sat beside her child. I observed her for several days. She is well and happy with her child. My friend said that the other side wears gray. He overheard it selling pottery in the Plaza. They are two different people, now—like the Dineh and the Apache— aren't they? They are divided."

She nodded unhappily; then, she remembered that there had been a full complement of soldiers at Fort Marcy. Why were they asking for volunteers? She recalled the discussion at the ball at the Governor's Palace that had almost resulted in a duel. "Did your friend say anything about soldier's leaving the fort, Valerio?"

"Many of them left, riding toward the south," he said. "That was what first alerted him that something was happening." He considered that information for a moment and said almost in a whisper, "They weren't riding in columns. They left at different times, a few men riding together. Yes. They were riding to join the Texans, weren't they?"

"It's possible," she said. "No, it's likely. There were Southern soldiers at the fort."

"I must tell Many Beads," he said, with growing excitement. "Everyone in the canyon must know. This war will make our raids easier. While they are fighting one another, they won't be at war with us."

She stared at him with a sinking heart. "You mustn't

tell anyone, Valerio. You mustn't take advantage of the situation . . ."

"Why not?" he asked. "For the first time in many years, the land belongs to us."

She recognized that she might argue with him, but not with all of the tribes in the Territory. At this very moment, the Apache were probably considering their options in much the same way, and that possibility made her feel cold, though the afternoon was warm.

"I brought back the iron pot," he told her casually as they walked back to his mother's hogan. "And more silver coins . . . much silver, *querida*. The Pueblo liked your rug." When she did not reply, he tried another tactic. "I will go back to watch your sister's farm again. If she is in any danger, I will protect her. You must not worry about your sister."

"If the Apache look upon this war as you do," she said angrily, "there may be good reason to worry about my sister and her child."

And every other white family in the Territory, she thought, though she did not express that concern aloud.

"You don't understand," he said. "We are not Apache. We do not harm people unless they try to harm us. The Mescalero Apache won't come that far north, anyway. And the soldiers at the fort can protect themselves against the Jicarillas if they venture so far out of their hills. You are Dineh, now, *querida*. You must see things as we do."

She did not want to cast a shadow over Maria's wedding, so she tried to put the unpleasantness from her mind. She and Valerio had never disagreed before.

Elspeth hid her feelings behind an expressionless face when Valerio told his mother and sisters about the American conflict. The women, who had been engrossed in the preparations for the wedding, listened in silence for the most part, though Many Beads put the same questions to her son that he asked Elspeth earlier. She did not seem to be speculating upon the advantage of the war to her people; she just seemed mildly surprised and interested in the ways of the white man. But Many Beads never revealed everything she was thinking. Big Woman and Many Tears Woman continued their work placidly, but Maria, who should have been grinding all the corn for her wedding cake, watched Elspeth with concern and abandoned her task to speak to her softly in Spanish.

"You're concerned about your sister," she said. "I would be concerned about my family, too. Do you think she is in danger?"

Elspeth had no intention of spoiling this happy time for her friend. She could not tell her that the only danger she feared was an Indian uprising. "No," she said, with a difficult smile. "I can't imagine the Texans getting all the way to Santa Fe, can you? There are forts along the Rio Grande. They would be stopped before they got that far."

"You're unhappy that the white men are fighting one another then. I can see in your eyes that something is upsetting you."

"A little," Elspeth replied, disappointed that no matter how carefully she composed her features, her eyes expressed her feelings. "I'd heard these things discussed in Santa Fe, but I didn't think they'd happen. You mustn't be concerned for me, my sister. It will pass."

The sound of horses leaving the compound made them turn to look. Valerio and his brothers-in-law were riding rapidly to inform the other men in the canyon of the news. Elspeth's heart constricted as though a hand were squeezing it, but she tried to breathe normally and did not look at Maria. "If you don't grind the corn for your wedding cake, there might not be a wedding," she said as lightly as possible. "Lone Rider's Son will go back to his mother's place after all the trouble we've had getting him this far."

Maria laughed happily. "He didn't go with my brother to spread the news," she said. "He's still working on our hogan. I think he'll remain. But," she sighed, "there's a lot of work to do before evening. I better start grinding."

"And I'd better start regrinding your corn," Elspeth told her. "Nothing is more important than your wedding."

The men did not return for dinner. Many Beads said they probably would not be back until dawn, because they had a long way to ride. She was certain they would be back in time for the wedding; it would be unthinkable for them to miss it. Elspeth picked up her cradleboard and walked slowly back to her hogan, disappointed and unhappy that Valerio would not be spending his first night at home with her, but more troubled about the reason that had made them quarrel and taken him away.

She nursed Sky and cleaned him for the night. He was naked, kicking and making happy sounds, when a woman cleared her throat outside the door to announce her presence. No one entered another person's hogan without being invited, and Elspeth opened the blanket over the door to find Many Beads standing at a short distance in the twilight. She had never called this late in the day before, and Elspeth wondered if her mother-in-law had noted her disquietude, too.

Many Beads played with her grandson and made small talk about the wedding before revealing the real purpose of her visit, as politeness dictated. Elspeth tried to appear completely at ease in her presence and had no intention of confiding the details of her dispute with her husband. Until now, she had been able to keep their lives private and beyond the open discussions and advice of the other women, and she had no intention of changing that. She loved and respected Many Beads, but had never solicited her for advice regarding her marriage. She was surprised at how well the older woman summed up the situation when she finally mentioned it.

"If a man does not provide for his family, his children do not belong to him," Many Beads said. "He only borrows them. When my son goes raiding, he is looking after you and his baby. With the white men fighting one another, there will be more raids, I think. You didn't like it during the winter, but you'll have to change your attitude."

"It's dangerous," Elspeth defended herself. "Perhaps more dangerous than you know. Did my husband tell you that the white men consider themselves at war with the People because of the raiding? It's wrong, because the Americans won't allow it. I've heard their views. They intend to have peace in the Territory at any cost."

A sardonic glimmer came to Many Beads's eyes. "The people who desire this peace are fighting one another. While they're doing that, they can't fight us as well. While they make war, we will increase our flocks."

"We have enough sheep already," Elspeth protested. "So many that we had to build a larger corral to hold them. There is no reason for the men to raid this year."

"It's a good year," Many Beads agreed. "You have never

seen a bad one. We can never have too many sheep, and the men must provide them for us.''

"Limping Man nearly got killed last winter. Is it necessary to die for unnecessary sheep?'' Elspeth asked. "I couldn't live without Tall Man, Mother. He is my life.''

"You say you could not live without him,'' Many Beads said, "but you could. I have survived two children being taken into captivity, never expecting to see them again. I have survived marriage with three husbands whose belongings I finally had to put outside of my hogan. We are speaking of survival, daughter, and that depends upon the flocks. Big Woman is expecting another baby. Smiling Girl will marry tomorrow, and she will have babies, too. If the men do not provide for the children, they are not men. You must encourage your husband, not make him weak. You must stand by his side. Your loyalty must be with us. You have behaved very well until today. I was proud until I saw your face when the warriors departed to bear the news that the land is ours again.''

Elspeth averted her eyes before the criticism, and Many Beads rose to leave. "I must sleep well tonight,'' she said. "There is much to do tomorrow. The wedding of my daughter must be a fine one. The guests have already begun to arrive, and the men are speaking of nothing but the war between the whites.''

"Has Tall Man returned?'' Elspeth asked as she bound Sky back into his cradleboard. "It will be a fine wedding, Mother. I won't do anything to spoil it.''

"My son has ridden far into the canyon. Others will bear the news even farther. The news of this war will not ruin the wedding; if anything, it will make it more festive. I want you to be happy, too. Smiling Girl is very fond of you and will want to share her happiness.''

Chapter 15

Lone Raider's family sat at the north side of the new hogan and the family of Many Beads at the south during the wedding ceremony, and the presence of the groom's family was the only difference between Maria's wedding and Elspeth's. Hosteen Yazzie acted as father for Maria, just as he had for her, and Elspeth found herself reliving the ceremony. As Maria poured the gourd of water over her groom's hands, Valerio took Elspeth's hand and their eyes met and held, all the tenderness between them stirring once again, their dispute of the previous day forgotten. Elspeth did not have to remind herself that she belonged to him and his people; that was all she had ever wanted. She would never question their ways again. When the wedding was over and the young couple was left alone in their hogan during the general feasting, she and Valerio slipped away to walk along the Wash in the dusk.

"I feel as if I'd married all over again," she whispered, "as if tonight were the first in our life together. I need you, Valerio. I love you."

He took her hand in both of his and paused in the solitude between the high canyon walls, with the sound of the singing far away. "I need you, *querida*. Nothing will separate us for long. I want you like a bridegroom on his wedding night."

They embraced and held each other closely. They had been apart for only a few weeks, but even that was too long. They walked back to their hogan, pausing to kiss among the tamarisk trees, their desire growing as the singing swelled in happiness for the bride and groom. When he finally took her on their sheepskins, Elspeth was so open and vulnerable to his loving, her surrender so complete, that she knew she had conceived again. She was so certain about it that she mentioned it to him as she lay in his arms.

"How can you know that?" he asked gently, holding her close and smiling at her fancy.

"I felt like Changing Woman being impregnated by the Sun," she murmured. "I felt as if a lightning of generation passed through me, more than at any time before. I've conceived your child, and in nine months you'll see that what I say is true."

Her condition became apparent much sooner than that, of course, at the same time that Maria's did, and the two young women shared each other's happiness. The men were gone for long periods during the summer, sometimes raiding but more often scouting to determine the progress of the white man's war. Elspeth and Maria were inseparable. They shared their daily tasks with Sky beside them in his cradleboard, concentrating on their weaving and household duties to divert their minds from their concern over their husbands' safety. They assumed the duties of the men in their absence, chopping wood and carrying their water from the Wash, and threw themselves wholeheartedly into the corn harvest by shucking the ears with the other women and putting them out to dry for winter. The men seemed to be gone for an interminable length of time, but Elspeth and Maria kept their personal thoughts and fears regarding this to themselves. Elspeth was not even certain that her friend shared her anxiety regarding the men. If she did, she covered it with her constant cheerfulness. Aside from the absence of their husbands, it was a generally happy time.

She had washed Maria's hair and was carefully dressing it in the sunlight one morning when Big Woman approached, heavy with the child she would soon deliver. "My mother is concerned," she said as she sat down beside them. "No one has seen Mexican Woman today, and she did not leave her hogan yesterday. The last time we saw her was the day before when she came for the medicine my mother made for her."

Elspeth's hands went idle in Maria's hair at the announcement. During the past few months she, too, had gathered herbs for Mexican Woman under Hosteen Yazzie's supervision, and they seemed to have helped her dropsical condition. The swelling had left her legs, and she had participated in the harvest and the baking of the sweet corn cakes. "Hasn't anyone looked in on her?" she asked.

"No," Big Woman said, averting her eyes. "We are afraid to, now. My mother would like you to do so."

Elspeth had to suppress momentary indignation at the oversight, though she understood the women's feelings. She handed the stick hairbrush to Big Woman so she could finish Maria's hair and walked rapidly in the direction of Mexican Woman's hogan, some distance down the canyon. They should have mentioned it yesterday, she thought. The poor woman's probably been lying there in her illness alone. She may have even died as they suspected. She called out Mexican Woman's name in front of her hogan as politeness required, but she did not wait for an answer before entering. Even before she pulled the blanket aside at the door, she knew that the women's fears had been realized. The scent of death was unmistakable, but she mustered the courage to enter, conscious of her promise to the woman many months before. Mexican Woman had not been dead long, but the heat of summer was intense. Elspeth made a cursory examination of the body, but discovered only that the poor creature had held her crucifix to her lips when she died. Sympathy brought tears to her eyes, but she was quickly forced outside by the odor.

The women were standing a short distance away awaiting her verdict. She observed the fear in their faces and realized her position at once. She had been contaminated by the dead, as Mexican Woman was before her, and she had to make her position clear at once.

"This hogan is *chindi*," she warned them, feigning fear instead of grief over what lay within. "I have entered without knowing it. I must be cleansed."

"You will be cleansed," Many Beads said, "but not until you have buried the body. Mexican Woman is no longer with us to perform such tasks."

"I have been tricked into this," Elspeth responded. "If Tall Man were here, he would not allow this. You have tricked me like Coyote."

"You are not like the other one," Many Beads assured her,

carefully not mentioning the name of the deceased. "You are one of us. You will be doing us a service. Many Tears Woman will instruct you and assist with the burial."

"If that is what my mother asks," Elspeth said. "But I was tricked into this and find the task repugnant. I am frightened, too."

She followed Many Tears Woman's instructions in preparing the body, though her sister-in-law did not enter the hogan. She reversed the moccasins on Mexican Woman's feet so that her ghost could not return from the grave and sewed a blanket around the body, tying the ends of the yarn with complicated granny knots to further impede the ghost. When she was finished, the women knocked a hole in the north wall of the hogan and everyone disappeared except for the thin, unpleasant Many Tears Woman. Elspeth wondered how she could perform the Christian burial she had promised Mexican Woman with this sister-in-law present. They passed the body through the hole in the wall and she wrapped it in still another blanket on the ground before they put it over the back of a horse.

"I will take you to the burial place," Many Tears Woman informed her. "We must go there quickly and return by another route before dark."

Elspeth thought she was familiar with the canyon, but she and Many Tears Woman rode to a craggy, barren spot where a red talus slope ran into the Wash like blood amid the fallen rocks. The walls had been eroded almost into shelves here, and Many Tears Woman selected one they could easily reach as the place for the burial. The strength of both of them was needed to carry the cocoon of blankets to the shelf, and Many Tears Woman showed her silently how to heap the loose rocks over it until a mound marked the spot. Elspeth closed her eyes and recited the Twenty-third Psalm in her mind. The valley was not green here, but the Lord was surely Mexican Woman's shepherd. She was tempted to put a cross over the grave, but there was no wood available. As her sister-in-law walked back to the horses, Elspeth paused to inscribe one of the stones with the symbol, using a harder one to incise the sandstone. She knew it would not last long, but she felt she had kept her word to Mexican Woman.

" 'Earth to Earth, ashes to ashes, dust to dust,' " she murmured, " 'in sure and certain hope of the Resurrection unto eternal life, through our Lord Jesus Christ.' "

The words sounded unlikely in this spot, where resurrection was feared rather than encouraged, but she did not have time to think about it because Many Tears Woman had already mounted her horse, impatient to leave. They crossed and recrossed the water many times on their return route, making confusion into the damp sands on either side of the Wash. Poor Mexican Woman's ghost would never find its way back, Elspeth thought, but she knew it would not want to leave the place where Mexican Woman had finally found peace and rest. Many Tears Woman spoke to her only once during the long ride. Elspeth was so surprised by the sound of her voice that, at first, she did not realize what she was saying.

"It's the animals," she said, and when Elspeth did not comprehend, she added, "All of the rocks. They keep the animals away."

Hosteen Yazzie performed their ritual cleansing before nightfall, but it did not prevent the show of blood she had that night. Lifting the heavy burden and riding so long, combined with the prescribed sweat bath, had brought it on, she thought, and she kept the matter to herself for several days because she felt the other women would interpret it otherwise, as ghost-sickness to her unborn child. After a few days, she became alarmed and consulted the Hosteen instead of the women.

He invited her inside his hogan for the first time while he prepared an infusion of herbs for her. "You were right to come to me," he said in a matter-of-fact manner. "The bleeding is caused by the things you said and is not ghost-sickness, but the women are superstitious. They live by their emotions instead of their minds. This should stop the bleeding. If it doesn't, return to me."

Elspeth was fascinated by the interior of his dwelling, which was not as she had expected it to be. Instead of a clutter of ritualistic objects, it was orderly. The various colors of sand for his paintings were kept in a neat row of pots, varying in size by the amount of the color needed; the rafters were hung with drying herbs, which exuded fragrant and pungent odors. The ritual feathers and sticks were stacked against the wall beside the skins of small animals used in his ceremonials, and leather medicine pouches, beautifully painted, were suspended from the rafters apart from the herbs.

The Hosteen's clouded vision missed very little. As he urged her to drink the bitter concoction he had prepared, he studied her face.

"You wonder what all these herbs are," he said. "They come from many places secret to me. You helped me gather herbs when we came back to the canyon. I only had to show you a plant once and, after that, you never made a mistake. I am old. Someone else will be needed to collect and give these medicines. I think you are interested in them."

"Yes," she replied. Maria had forewarned her of this moment, but she had begun to think it would never come. "To be able to help people with the medicines would make me happy. There are so many herbs," she added, indicating those drying above them. "I don't think I could ever learn to use them all, or to find them in the secret places."

"I will leave soon to gather more," he said. Elspeth found his toothless speech difficult to understand and had to watch his lips constantly. "You will come with me. I will show you the secret places and tell you the properties of the plants. Your baby will accompany us in his cradleboard. Babies are no trouble. When Tall Man returns, he will join us. He helped me collect herbs when he was a boy. He knows where I go this time of year."

She was anxious to learn the medicinal properties of plants and welcomed this chance. "I will go," she said, "if the medicine you just gave me stops the bleeding."

"Prepare to leave in two days' time then. The medicine you drank is good. The women will prepare food for us. They know how much we will need."

Many Beads and her daughters approved of Elspeth's decision to learn medicine from the Hosteen; the knowledge would be for their mutual good in the future when the old man "went away" and could no longer help them. During the months they remained in the canyon and, later, when the family migrated to its winter home on the rim, she spent many hours with Hosteen Yazzie. He instructed her in the preparations from the plants they had gathered and the ailments that were cured by them. Unfamiliar with the names of the wildflowers and shrubs of the region, she soon recognized many of them and referred to them by their Navajo names, some of which described their properties in a colorful way: *aliz be-yi-e'-ol* meant urine spurter and was a diuretic; *y-o-dini aze* was toothache medicine; *ko-aze*, fire medicine, was used for burns. Most of the botanical names referred to the appearance of the plants without describing their properties, though, and the Hosteen patiently imparted his knowledge of them to her during the dim winter days, showing her how to combine them in infusions and salves. She soon realized that her period of training might extend over several years and she mentioned this to Valerio as she lay in his arms one night.

"The more I learn, the more I need to know," she said. "There are hundreds of plants. I'll be as old as the Hosteen before I'm as wise."

He laughed softly. "Probably. That is the advantage of old age, *querida*. But everything you learn will be helpful. I'm proud of you for doing what you're doing. The prospect of so much learning discouraged the other women. You healed the burn on Oldest Boy's leg already, all by yourself."

"And the sores on Many Tears Woman's goat. Don't forget that," she reminded him as she snuggled closer. "I didn't expect to be paid for it, though the turquoise she gave me is nice. A simple thank you would have been enough."

"Many Tears Woman resents you more than ever, now," he said equitably. "I suppose she thought that paying you was the only thing she could do. Now that you and Smiling Girl are great with child, you are more of a reproach to her than ever."

"Perhaps she'll feel more comfortable when the babies come. After Big Woman's baby was born, Many Tears Woman helped her care for him. It's the pregnancy that seems to bother her. I wish there were some way to lift her spirits, poor woman."

"My sister has an envious nature," he said, wrapping the blankets around them securely. "She was like that even before she married. It's getting colder, *querida*. The Big Winds have come early. It will be a hard winter."

Severe winters had been referred to in the past, but Elspeth had never experienced one. All activity was devoted to trying to save the flock and keeping the hogans warm. Everything else was abandoned. Partly woven rugs were left on their looms, and Valerio's silver remained untouched in its pouch within the metal pot he had obtained. If the flock had not been so large, the family might have perished, and all their efforts were expended upon retaining enough animals to breed in the spring. Food was not in short supply, because the women cooked the sheep that died from the cold and lack of forage. Both the men and the women continually carried extra firewood, the men gathering it from the snow-covered plateau and splitting it, and the women carrying it into the fires in their hogans. In the evenings, they huddled beside their fires, too exhausted to tell stories as they had the year before, the younger animals, brought inside for protection, milling around them in the darkness.

"It would be worse if there weren't any food," Elspeth remarked to Maria one morning when they were cooking the stew for the midday meal. "Will there be enough animals left to breed? If there aren't, it will mean the men will have to raid again."

"I know you don't like that," Maria said, "but the men will have to go. Even if the flock that remains is large enough, the animals may be too thin and hungry to breed this year. Winters like this don't happen often, but they can be very serious. Other families will suffer more. My mother is already sharing our food with them. I'm glad we have enough to share."

"She's good and generous," Elspeth said, with affection for her mother-in-law. "There aren't many women like her."

Maria expressed mild surprise. "She is only doing what anyone would do," she said. "It is our way. The poorest family will share its food with a neighbor, regardless how little it has. There won't be any large ceremonials this winter, though. Aside from the difficulty for guests getting here, there isn't enough firewood to cook for all of them. I'll miss that, but it will better next year."

"The Hosteen said there would be a Blessing Way before our time comes," Elspeth said. "He said it was important. He performed the ceremonial for Big Woman, but he didn't perform it for me when Sky was born."

"He planned to, but Sky came earlier than any of us expected. We'll have our Blessing Way together," Maria said, with a smile. She lowered her voice, though no one was within hearing. "I bet I have mine before you do. We won't make wagers, because Mother hates gambling, but I bet my baby will be born first."

Elspeth laughed quietly. "Only if it was conceived on your

wedding night, my sister, because that was when my child was conceived.''

"How do you know?'' Maria asked, with interest, but Elspeth only smiled. "Tell me,'' her friend persisted good-naturedly. "How do you know?''

"I just know,'' Elspeth replied. "But if you want to bet, I'll bet that my baby will be born before yours. Maybe they'll be born at the same time and neither of us will win.''

"They'd be like twins,'' Maria said, with delight. "That would be better than winning. How nice it would be if our babies were born on the same day. We'll be mothers to each other's children anyway, but how good it would be to make twins of them.''

Both of the babies were born before the Blessing Way could be sung, but they were not destined to be twins in spirit, because Elspeth's child was stillborn. As she hung from the strap from the ceiling rafter listening for its first cry, the silence in her hogan was magnified by the stillness of the women attending her. She turned her face to the wall afterward and wept, unable to share her sorrow even with Valerio, who quietly buried the infant. The fear surrounding deaths did not apply to babies, who had no evil in them. She did not know until later that Big Woman had suggested that the misfortune was caused by Elspeth's burial of Mexican Woman, who was certainly a witch, now. Valerio banned the women from his hogan and attempted to console his wife alone.

"These things happen,'' he said, stroking her hair, "for no reason we can understand. The fact that the child was born before the Blessing Way ceremonial had nothing to do with it. You had nothing to do with it.''

"I know,'' Elspeth said, weeping against his chest, "but the baby was yours, my darling, and I lost her.''

"There will be other children, *querida*. You must not give yourself over to unhappiness. I can't bear to see you unhappy. You must get up and make yourself useful again. It is the only way to overcome misery. You've worked hard all winter. Now, you must do something enjoyable, perhaps return to your weaving. You always find peace in that.''

Many Beads and her daughters did not call the following day, and Elspeth thought it was out of consideration for her feelings, though it might have something to do with Maria's approaching delivery. She knew Maria would have come if she had been allowed and suspected that some taboo prevented her friend from visiting under the circumstances. She did not mention it to Valerio, who remained with her all day as she attempted to focus her attention on stringing the warp for a rug. She had not woven since early autumn, when she had begun to study under Hosteen Yazzie. Her fingers had become tender and unpracticed at the loom, and she found it difficult to think of a pattern. Valerio put his iron pot on the fire and placed several silver coins in it, as if he, too, needed distraction, and she became more interested in his work than her own when he began to pour the liquid silver into his mold.

"How long will it take it to cool?" she asked, leaning forward to observe the sand-casting.

"I don't know, *querida*," he replied. "I'll let it harden at its own speed, though. I don't want to cool it outside."

He ruined the first casting by trying to unmold it too soon and had to remelt the silver, skimming off the granules of sand that came to the surface while Elspeth cleaned the mold, carefully restoring the delicate edges of the pattern. When he cast the silver again, he did so cautiously and poured a single large drop on another piece of sandstone. "This time, we'll see how long it takes for the drop to cool and grow hard," he said. "That way, we can tell how long it will take for the larger piece." He covered it with charcoal from the fire, a method he had not used on the first piece. "My Pueblo friend told me I should do this," he explained. "I forgot before. He said it prevents the holes in the metal caused by air bubbles. He called it 'silver spitting.' "

They were so engrossed in their work—and the avoidance of thinking of anything else—that they worked late into the night, melting the metal in the crucible and recasting it without success until Valerio finally had to break his mold to free the silver.

"I will carve a new one tomorrow," he said at last. "I'm doing something wrong. Maybe the silver will come out of the cast easier if I grease it with mutton fat."

They were so exhausted when they lay down on the warm sheepskins that they went to sleep immediately, falling gratefully into the blissful, healing darkness. Elspeth woke only once during the night. A strong wind moaned against the wall of the hogan, and for a moment, she thought she heard chanting, but she went back to sleep to escape the hollow aching in her chest.

The sense of loss returned in full strength the following morning when she was preparing their meal. Not even Sky's antics as he toddled over the floor distracted her from it; Valerio, intent upon his own method of dealing with unhappiness, began to carve another sandstone mold. Sky required minimal supervision. One did not hear constant admonitions for children to be careful among the Dineh. If they were not in actual imminent danger, they were allowed to discover for themselves that the fire was hot, and that they would bump their heads if they fell against the doorpost. After his first burst of early morning energy, he settled down beside Elspeth at her loom. She hugged him until he began to squirm with panic in her desperate, unnatural embrace. Then, as if he sensed something was wrong, he cuddled against her, watching her shuttle pass before his eyes as she wove the first few rows of her blanket. The wind had died down, and the silence was almost total. Elspeth began to lose herself in her weaving. When her hands and mind were busy, an invisible wall went up to protect her from the intrusion of her pain. Her breasts began to ache as they filled with milk, but she found she could overcome the discomfort if she did not associate it directly with her loss.

Valerio was showing her the handsome design he had carved when footsteps were heard outside, an indication that someone had come to call and was waiting to be recognized, for usually one did not hear the fall of moccasins on earth or snow. Valerio rose to admit his mother, and Elspeth took her batten out of her loom before she left it, an action that had become automatic; it was bad luck to leave a batten in an unattended loom. She was surprised at the expression on Many Beads's usually stoic face. The skin was drawn tightly over her strong cheeks, but the rest of her face seemed to have caved inward, making her look like an old woman, and her oriental eyes were puffy and red, as if she had been crying. Tears sprang to Elspeth's eyes at the sight of this courageous woman's grief, and she moved forward to embrace her, a liberty she had never taken before.

"Sit, Mother," she said softly as she led her to the fire. Valerio crouched across from them and stared at his mother with a troubled face. He had never seen her this way, either.

"It is a bad winter," Many Beads said at last, wiping her tears away with the back of her hand. "The most terrible time I have ever known."

Neither Elspeth nor Valerio commented; they watched Many Beads expectantly, instead. Surely, Elspeth thought, the death of my baby, as painful as it is to me, has not brought my mother to this. Many Beads let out a dismal wail, no longer able to control herself, and Elspeth held her in her arms, looking toward Valerio with alarm.

"You have come to tell us something, Mother," he said in a loud, firm voice, "something we will not like to hear."

"First, you lose your child," Many Beads sobbed. "Now, a child has lost its mother. My youngest daughter left us early this morning. My happy little girl is gone."

The words struck like stones in a pond, and Elspeth was so stunned that her mind recorded them only by their ripples. She told herself she had misunderstood the Navajo words with all their euphemisms, but when she looked at Valerio, she knew she had understood. His face had gone gray and tears started to his eyes.

"Gone?" Elspeth repeated numbly, realizing that if this catastrophe were true, she must not mention Smiling Girl's name again. Her mind still refused to believe what she had heard.

"And her baby?" Valerio asked, confirming the identity of the deceased. "Is the child well?"

"Yes," Many Beads said, pushing her fists into her eyes until it must have hurt. "Yes. A fine, strong boy . . . but he has no mother. Many Tears Woman is feeding him gruel from the edge of a cloth like an orphaned lamb. All of the goats are dry. It has been a cruel winter."

"I have milk," Elspeth told her through her tears. "Her baby will be all right. Our babies were going to be our little twins, but now the twins are only one."

Many Beads did not dismiss the offer, but she had come for another purpose. "Later," she said, drying her tears purposefully. "There is much to be done, my daughter. We need your help again."

Before Elspeth understood what help was needed, Valerio's closely controlled temper flared. With the tears running down his face, he responded, "You have no right to ask this. Big Woman said we lost our baby because my wife gave you such help the last time. My wife helps you generously and you spit in her face."

"Big Woman should not have said that," Many Beads said. "Besides, it is different this time. My poor little daughter—your favorite sister—was not a Mexican witch."

"Neither was the Mexican woman," Valerio said firmly. "Big Woman expressed what all of you were thinking. My wife is still weak and grieving the loss of our child. She could not help you anyway, Mother. I will do it—"

"No," Elspeth interrupted, "I want to do it. I loved Mar—your sister. No blame can fall on me for this. There was no evil in her, but only good. She was my friend."

"They will expect it of you in the future, and you'll get no thanks for your help," he cautioned, but Elspeth rose unsteadily to her feet and Many Beads followed her example.

"I will help you," Valerio said. "Mother, wrap my son up warmly and take him to your hogan. And tell the Hosteen that we will need a cleansing ceremony tonight."

"If there had been a Blessing Way," his mother said, "perhaps none of this would have happened."

Elspeth recalled her mother's stories about the Sin Eaters in old Wales, itinerants paid to eat bread and ale over the departed, taking on their sins as they did so. The customs of the People were no more primitive, and she did not resent them using her for a task they abhorred. After she lovingly prepared Maria's young body, Valerio went to lay it in the canyon below, where Elspeth could not accompany him.

"I did everything I could," the openly grieving Hosteen Yazzie told Elspeth. "I used the medicine to stop the bleeding and the placenta medicine, but the hemorrhage would not stop. There may be remedies for such things, but I do not know them. They are not in the medicine of the Dineh."

"They are not in the white man's medicine, either," she tried to console him, though she felt as if her own heart was breaking. "For some things, there is no cure, Uncle. When that happens, the white men say, 'It was meant to be,' though why it should have happened to my sister and friend I do not know."

The hungry cries of Maria's baby reached them from Many Beads's hogan and Elspeth glanced miserably in that direction, but the old man put his hand on her arm. "Not yet," he said.

"They will not admit you until after the ritual, and I cannot perform that until evening."

"Many Tears Woman is trying to look after him. I hate to take him from her. She's wanted a child so much. But we'll lose him, too, if he doesn't have nourishment. My friend would want me to help her son."

"The decision is not yours alone," he said. "There is a way that will please everyone, I think."

They went to Many Beads's hogan immediately after the Ghost-Sickness ceremony had been sung over Elspeth and Valerio. Once they had been purified, they could mingle with the others and touch the children again. The women were trying to calm the baby beside the fire, and Many Tears Woman stared at them with suspicion and held the baby closer. Big Woman was nursing her own child, her large breasts exposed under her blanket, but her face had none of its usual placidity.

"The child won't nurse," she told the Hosteen. "My own baby cries a lot, too. I don't think I have enough milk for both of them."

Many Beads, who sat with Sky on her knees, exhausted by the events of the day, said nothing. Worn by grief, she detached herself from the events around her, and left everything to the Hosteen. Elspeth's wits were as dulled as her mother-in-law's, but she felt she had to say something.

"The babies were going to be our twins, that was our wish. Now, there is only one baby, and I have milk. Our sister would have wanted me to care for him. The babies were to belong to both of us."

Many Tears Woman narrowed her eyes and clasped the screaming baby tighter to her chest, as if she could give it sustenance. She had never been completely stable, and not having a child was at the root of her disorder. She was not going to give the baby up; she had laid claim to him. A bowl of corn gruel and a cloth twisted to make a teat lay on the floor at her knees, but still the infant screamed. The Hosteen stepped forward unsteadily.

"The child will be the next to leave us unless he has nourishment," he said. "Feeding him gruel with a cloth is like trying to save a baby bird that has fallen from its nest. How often does anyone save a baby bird? This child is happier than others: he has two mothers to care for him. One to feed him and one to look after his other needs. The child will belong to both of you. He will grow strong and happy with so much affection.''

Many Tears Woman hesitated, her gaze searching Elspeth's face for confirmation of the old man's words, and Elspeth told her quietly, "He will belong to both of us, my sister. You shall give him a name."

"That is more than fair," Many Beads said, breaking her silence. "Give the baby to my son's wife, daughter. What has been offered is not only fair, but necessary."

Many Tears Woman relinquished the squirming bundle and knelt beside Elspeth when she took the baby to her breast. Elspeth could feel the love and concern that emanated from the troubled woman, and she smiled at her. "What do you want to call him?" she asked.

"Not an odd name like you gave your own son," Many Tears Woman said without malice. "And I cannot call him the son of my husband, because Lone Raider's Son is his father. I will call him Two Mothers Baby, I think."

No one raised an objection, though the name was as unconventional as Sky's. The name was not to endure long anyway. Maria was so much in their hearts that everyone soon referred to the infant as Surviving Child. And if Elspeth had any trepidation about sharing the baby with her sister-in-law, it faded quickly in the company of Many Tears Woman in the days that followed. Maria's child filled her own arms, easing the pain of her loss, and Many Tears Woman responded with such maternal warmth that Elspeth considered giving her another name, for she was certain that she would never weep again.

The winter had been a bad one, but the weather cleared early, and the sky was so warm and blue that the men moved the women into the canyon early. At first, Elspeth thought it was because they shared the same longing to be in a happier place, but the real reason was soon apparent. The flock had to be replenished; there would be no lambs this spring. No sooner were the women settled than Valerio and his brothers-in-law rode off on a raid. Lone Raider's Son, miserable over his wife's death, packed his things and returned to his own family, leaving his infant son behind with Maria's family; a child belonged to its mother's clan. Many Beads said that he would be greatly missed during these hard times, but he must visit his son often. Slim Man watched him leave with a grim expression on his face, spat, and remarked that every man in the family was needed to drive sheep home, and Lone Raider's Son had let them down by leaving so abruptly.

Chapter 16

The women turned the earth and did the planting, and the time that followed was peaceful and happy. Without realizing it, Elspeth had begun to think and feel like a Navajo. She paused in her work to enjoy the beauty of the earth and sky and to admire the spectacular sunsets, glowing with red and gold and purple, each one completely unlike another. Many Beads showed her how to dye wool. She watched purple bee plant turn dull yellow as it boiled in the pot, and red onion skin turn brown. Lichen gathered from rocks turned a surprising orange, and black greasewood, soft beige. And she continued her work with the Hosteen, carrying a cradleboard again and leaving Sky with his other "mothers." She enjoyed the antics of the children with the other women. Her chores became as disorganized as theirs, but somehow were accomplished in the course of the quiet days. She was in *hozro* with her surroundings at last.

She was no longer afraid of the nights, though she spent them alone with her children. Somehow, by participating in Maria's burial rites, her fears of the supernatural were banished. The night no longer held any fears for her; though she always missed Valerio when he was away, she no longer needed anyone to keep ungrounded fears at bay. She was completely attuned to the rhythm of her life and in a serene frame of mind, when the most extraordinary thing that had ever happened to her occurred one afternoon.

She was weaving in front of her hogan, with the baby in his cradleboard beside her, intent upon making another rug to replace the one Valerio had traded for his silver, a rug that would be for him alone. Sky was visiting his grandmother, who often came by to visit and play with the children, and, on several occasions, had taken Sky to her hogan for the entire afternoon. A light breeze fluttered the leaves of the tamarisk trees with their delicate pink spring plumes. She had just selected a small spool of yarn to incorporate into her pattern, as she had several times before, and when she looked up she became aware of a woman standing under a nearby tree in the line of her vision. A sensation of detachment from the normal course of time came over her, as if the moment and everything it contained had been painted on a canvas. The woman, as corporeal as everything around her, was Maria; her presence brought no discomfort, though Elspeth was rationally aware that her friend was dead. The vision was peaceful, and Maria smiled at Elspeth in a particularly gentle manner, as if she approved of what she saw. Elspeth returned the smile and whispered her name. She might have beckoned her closer, but she did not want to break the spell. Maria smiled at her with understanding, as though she could read what was in her heart; then, before Elspeth's eyes, the figure faded away and disappeared.

Elspeth remained by her loom with the spool of yarn still in her hand. She felt the exact moment in time, when everything became normal again, like a person emerging from an episode of déjà vu. She did not even consider the experiences akin, though; she knew the vision had not originated in her mind. She had seen Maria, and, somehow, the baby was the link that made it possible. Her natural impulse under the circumstances was to tell someone about it, but she recognized the obstacle to doing that at once. The family would not have experienced the same peace she did over the incident.

The men drove a considerable flock into the canyon before the corn began to sprout, raising a cloud of red dust around them. That the raid was successful was clear, but in the dust and confusion, she could not find Valerio. Her heart nearly stopped when she realized he had not returned with his brothers-in-law. She went to Slim Man and Limping Man to ask frantically about her husband, but they were not prepared to discuss his absence until the whole story of the raid was recounted to their wives so they could impart the information to Many Beads, who had sequestered herself in her hogan so she would not encounter her daughters' husbands. Elspeth joined her mother-in-law with both of the children so that she would hear the news at the same time she did. They sat in the semidarkness of the warm hogan without speaking, each preparing herself for the worst while trying to remain calm and optimistic.

Big Woman lumbered into their presence bearing her cradleboard after a short while, and the smile on her broad face was reassuring.

"Tall Man was not needed to drive the sheep home," she told them. "The flock isn't that large, because they had to cut out the ewes with nursing lambs. He left them at the Rio Grande and rode east, they say. He did not say where he was going, but they think it was to see the Pueblo who harbored him after his escape and gave him the silver."

"Does he need more silver?" Many Beads asked Elspeth, who was at a loss for words, still trembling over his not returning from the raid.

"He didn't take any trade goods," she said, with a dry mouth, already suspecting where he had gone. She had forgotten about the war in New Mexico, lost herself in the peace of the canyon after the terrible events of the winter, but Valerio had not forgotten, and his curiosity had driven him to Santa Fe. For the first time in many months, she experienced guilt about her lack of concern for Thea. She had not thought of her once since the heavy winter had forced all of them to work to survive and the subsequent birth of the babies. She could not tell Many Beads that Valerio had gone east, perhaps at his peril, to gather news of the white man's war and her family.

"He needs tools," she said, averting her eyes. The statement was true, but it was a sin of omission. How could she describe a hand bellows? "There is a thing that increases the heat of the fire to cast silver," she said lamely, "and an anvil, too . . . a thing to hammer the metal on."

"We will just have to wait," Many Beads concluded. "Perhaps he will bring news about the war the white men were fighting." She paused thoughtfully, and added almost hopefully, "Perhaps they have all killed one another, and we won't be bothered by them anymore."

* * *

He appeared one evening a few weeks later and entered their hogan nonchalantly, as if he had done nothing out of the ordinary. The tongue-lashing she had prepared was lost in his strong embrace and his delight in seeing the children. With Sky on his lap, he watched her while she prepared a meal for him.

"I heard from a Ramah man that the gray coats were marching up the Rio Grande," he said. "He said they had overcome the forts in the south and were laying waste to all the land behind them. Only fools would destroy food supplies they might need in case of retreat. They were arrogant." His voice was calm and reassuring. "By the time I got close enough to see what was happening, there was a strange flag flying over the Governor's Palace, with a blue cross instead of stripes."

Elspeth nearly dropped the pottery bowl she had been filling with stew. "The American flag was gone?" she exclaimed with alarm.

"Only for a little while," he said, placing Sky on the floor so that he could eat. "There was a battle in the mountains near Apache Junction. I could hear the shells and I saw the smoke. 'The bluecoats are no match for them,' I thought, but late that afternoon I could see the gray coats retreating to the south without a supply train, with nothing to sustain them. I told you that they destroyed the fields. When I went into town the next day, your flag was over the Governor's Palace again."

"You went into town?"

"There was a great deal of commotion. No one noticed two Pueblos wearing blankets."

"You were with your friend the whole time?"

"We watched the smoke of the battle together. We learned later that the bluecoats came from behind at the junction and destroyed their enemy's supply train. They have gone back to Texas. With nothing to eat along the way," he added, with a smile, as he bit off some bread.

"Did they destroy my sister's fields?"

"Yes, but she is all right," he assured her, reaching to take her hand firmly. "She and her child were at the hacienda. Her house is standing, but her fields were burned. That is a strange thing, too. Don Diego's fields weren't touched. I didn't see her husband. He was probably with the soldiers."

"If Don Diego's sisters have taken Thea in, she is safe,"

Elspeth considered. "Please don't go there again, Valerio. The news you bring isn't worth your life to me."

He took her into his arms and kissed her gently. "I will not worry you by going back. The white men and their war interest me only to the extent that it concerns us. My spirit is uneasy when I'm without you, *querida*. Everything I do is for you."

Elspeth's relief was clouded only by the knowledge that he would continue raiding, but she knew she could not change that. The raiding was for her and his family. The following winter might be as devastating as the last, and the flock was still below the necessary size because there had been no lambs in the spring.

"What does this mean?" Many Beads inquired when Valerio repeated his story to her the next day. "Are the bluecoats stronger than we thought they were?"

"Not in numbers," he said. "They are few, but they are clever. The fact that they destroyed their enemy's supplies instead of striking at their larger force shows that."

"What sort of people fight among themselves?" Many Beads asked, as she had done when she first heard about the war. "The Dineh do not fight the Dineh. It would be madness to do so. The Holy People would be angry."

"They're fighting over a principle," Elspeth said. "Two of your children were taken into slavery, so you must understand that."

"It won't prevent the Ute from taking our children as slaves. That is something to fight over. We would fight to protect our homeland and her families, but not over an idea."

"There is also the love of fighting," Valerio interjected. "The Apache are raiding in the south, and this is not good for us. The Apache like to fight."

"What the Apache do does not concern us," his mother said. "They do not tend fields or raise flocks. They are lazy and forced to raid all the time. What the Apache do doesn't matter."

"It does matter," Elspeth told her respectfully. "The white men consider all the raids as the same. They group you and the Apache and other tribes together under the name *Indian*."

"I don't understand that word," Many Beads replied. "How can anyone think the Dineh and the Apache are the same? Or the Ute and Comanche are like us?"

"The Pueblos are divided into several villages, speaking different languages," Valerio said, "but we think of them all as Pueblos. That is the way the white men think of the other tribes and ourselves."

"It's unfortunate," Elspeth told her, "but it's true. Whatever the Ute do in the north, the Comanche in the east, and the Apache in the south might affect us very much. The outrages are all committed by Indians in the white man's mind."

"I do not understand the white man," Many Beads said, and shook her head.

"And he does not understand you," Elspeth cautioned. "You must remember that."

"Then it doesn't matter whether we raid or not, in the white man's mind," Many Beads said. "We will be blamed for it in either case. If the bluecoats come, we can defend ourselves, just as we are defending ourselves from the Ute. There are warriors enough in the north to drive them away. There are many Dineh in Dineyah. We don't all live in the canyon."

Valerio and his brothers-in-law paused long enough between raids to help with the shearing. In his spare time, he worked with his silver, and with the help of the small bellows and other tools he had secured from his friend, he made a stylized squash-blossom design in his mold and polished it almost to perfection with fine sand. He smiled as he put it on the turquoise necklace Many Beads had given Elspeth.

"It's beautiful," she said. "I'm so proud of you. But shouldn't your mother have it? She's a more important person than I."

"Not to me," he told her. "But your suggestion is wise. I have enough silver to make one for her, too."

He was working on his mother's pendant when three men rode in on lathered horses and dismounted near their hogan. Lone Raider's Son, whom they had not seen since early spring, approached Valerio.

"The bluecoats have built a fort not two days' ride from here," he said, without the usual amenities. "The men who are with me are from the east. Their fields and hogans have been destroyed and their flocks driven away by the Ute and some bluecoats."

Valerio rose quickly to speak to the men, and Elspeth felt a chill of apprehension. She sensed that retaliation for the raids had begun. She stood near the hogan with Sky clutching her skirt, his wide, dark eyes staring at the riders with curiosity. Elspeth was unable to understand what the men were saying without being close enough to watch their lips, and she almost missed the implication of the name spoken in broken English: *Kit Carson*. Her heart constricted, and she stepped forward to join them.

"What about Kit Carson?" she asked the strangers, who observed the blue-eyed Dineh woman narrowly.

"You know of this man?" Valerio asked her. "They call him The Rope Thrower."

"Yes, I've heard of him," she said. "He was an army scout before he became the Ute agent. He's supposed to keep the Ute under control. What is he doing in Dineyah?"

"Destroying the homes and fields of the People," Lone Raider's Son said. "The bluecoats have summoned our chiefs to the new fort. 'Chiefs,' they said, but we have no chiefs. Some of our headmen will have to go. Their message is that they only want to talk to them."

"Did The Rope Thrower send the summons?" Valerio asked. "I don't think he can be trusted if he's with the Ute."

"A bluecoat chief from Santa Fe sent for the headmen," Lone Raider's Son told them, but, when Elspeth pressed him for the officer's name, he was unable to give it. He volunteered the man's rank in such broken English that it took Elspeth a moment to understand it. She finally decided he must be attempting to say "Territorial Commander," but she did not know who the present commander was.

"He is an important man," she said at last. "A very important man, who should be trustworthy. This has to concern the raids," she told Valerio. "What they've done in the east was a warning. Now, they want to talk."

"My father is going," Lone Raider's Son said to Valerio. "He wants you to go, too, because you speak Spanish."

"Tell your father that I will accompany them," Valerio said. "When must we be there?"

"Within five days," Lone Raider's Son said as he mounted his horse. "We must leave here at dawn, three days from now. I have to tell others."

Elspeth and Valerio stood together in silence as the men rode away. The baby began to cry in his cradleboard, and Elspeth went to attend him, troubled by the way the news had been delivered. For the first time since she had been here, a matter that concerned only males had arisen, and that it was a serious matter she had no doubt. Valerio left to inform his brothers-in-law and her gaze followed him until he was out of sight. She recalled what Dr. Cabot had said to her about the army's lack of understanding of the Navajo, which included the conviction that they had chiefs. No matter what the headmen who went to the fort agreed to, it would surely be violated by others, who were not there. And, how, she wondered, had Kit Carson become involved in this? Certainly not as a free agent leading his Ute. When the answer finally occurred to her, it was so simple that she wondered why she had not thought of it at once. There was a war going on, and manpower was spread thin, so they had sent Carson and his Ute to do the job. The conclusion chilled her. Did they know about the long animosity between the Navajo and the Ute? Had they any idea that they might be starting an intertribal war?

"I want to go with you," she told Valerio that evening. "I speak their language."

"No," he said firmly. "They might recognize that you're white. I couldn't risk that. No women will be going, *querida*."

"Some of the headmen are old," she argued. "They should have someone to cook for them. If a few other women went, no one would notice another 'squaw' with a cradleboard. Look . . . my hands and arms are dark from working in the sun. I can cover my hair with a blanket."

"You are everything to me. If they discovered you and took you away, I'd pursue you for as long as I live. It's too hot to wear a blanket."

"*They* don't know that," she said, with a smile. "They think squaws wear blankets all the time. I know the way they think, Valerio. I can understand what they say among themselves."

The logic of her argument was not lost on him, but his concern for her welfare made him stand firm. "There's some sense in what you say, but I couldn't risk it. There may be other dangers, too."

"I think Many Beads should have some say in the matter," she suggested. "It's an enterprise of the men, but she is wise. You surely don't question your mother's wisdom?"

"My mother doesn't love you as much as I do," he said. "She may be more careless regarding your welfare."

Elspeth was so adamant that they consulted Many Beads the next morning. She was deeply concerned by the sudden meeting with the Americans and the story she had heard about the Ute raids in the east. She considered Elspeth's suggestion for several minutes, with her grandchildren playing around her. The decision was not an easy one for her.

"Until now," she said at last, "the Americans have left us alone. They have never come so near. We have heard rumors of some of the headmen in the east talking to them, but we did not know what was said. Doesn't it strike you, my son, that your wife's presence in our family is a blessing? Once again, she is able to help us. If anything is wrong when you enter the fort, she will notice it, perhaps. If the bluecoats say anything treacherous in their own language, she will understand their words."

"Wrong?" Elspeth asked.

"It has happened before. Not to the Dineh, but to Apache. Men, women, and children massacred when they went to hear the bluecoats in peace."

"The Apache are feared and hated," Elspeth said, with a steady voice, though the revelation gave her some misgivings. "The Dineh do not commit atrocities." But, she thought in English for the first time in several years, to the white man an Indian is an Indian. "I will be alert for anything wrong at the fort. I think I would notice it."

"I must discuss it with my uncle," Many Beads said. "The plan frightens me a little. One woman from a family would be enough. No family should take a greater risk. If my uncle thinks it is a good plan, the headmen will have to bring their own women. Not too many. Just enough to obscure the presence of my daughter."

"You are braver than I thought," Many Tears Woman remarked as she dressed Elspeth's hair before the trip. "I did not like you once. I did not give myself a chance to know you and that was my loss."

"I'm not brave," Elspeth said. "I just don't think there will be any trouble. But I'm glad you like me, now. I didn't know what to make of you at first, either."

"I know you must take our baby with you, because he has to

be nursed. I wish it were otherwise, but I know you will look after him. You love him as much as I do, and I would lay down my life for him.''

"You must not worry about him," Elspeth said, turning to face her. "I swear to you that if danger presents itself, Surviving Child will not be harmed. I would do more than lay down my life for him, my sister. I would reveal my identity to save our child and Valerio. That would be worse than leaving this earth. You will care for Sky while I'm away, no matter how long it is.''

Their eyes met with perfect understanding. "I will care for Sky as if he were my own," Many Tears Woman agreed.

"Valerio and I must ride to join the others, now," Elspeth said, drawing in her breath. The trepidation that had seized her when she was discussing her plan with Many Beads had not left her. Her reassurance to Many Tears Woman was in the nature of a lie. She did not know what to expect at the fort, and the possibilities had troubled her so much the night before that she had finally decided that the worst possible outcome, an ambush, might be deflected by the desperate action she confided to Many Tears Woman. She did not want to believe that the army was leading them into an ambush. She found it difficult to credit the rumor about the Apache massacre. She thought she knew the Americans. But, she reasoned, if any treachery was contemplated, they would not carry it out under the eyes of one of their own women.

The army installation was small, dwarfed by the breadth of the pink plain and the red rock formations near it. The American flag flew boldly from behind the wooden walls of the fort, and Elspeth felt a grudging admiration for the soldiers who served under that flag, in the heart of Dineyah, far away from reinforcements. The sign painted over the gate read FORT DEFIANCE; it could not have been more aptly named by men who thought they faced a warlike tribe.

The band of Dineh paused a safe distance from the forbidding gateway to assess their situation. Their eyes scanned the ramparts for armed soldiers, but there were none visible. As they conferred among themselves, the wide gateway opened from within and a soldier rode out carrying a flag of truce. They observed him with self-contained suspicion as he approached.

"General Carleton, the territorial commander, greets you,''

the lieutenant said in Spanish. "He invites you inside in peace so the talks can commence."

Valerio interpreted the greeting to the headmen, few of whom knew any Spanish, and the mounted group followed the rider cautiously, every eye alert. As they passed through the gate, Elspeth was as alert as any of them, her gaze scanning the compound for anything that might be amiss. Most of the soldiers were clearly visible and wore only the side arms in their leather holsters. If there were men within the building with rifles trained upon them, they were well hidden, and she did not sense their presence. Tables had been brought out and set in a line before the administration building, though no one occupied them at the moment. The Americans obviously intended to speak to the headmen from there. She glanced at Valerio to indicate that everything seemed what it appeared, and he communicated the message to the others, who dismounted and held the reins of their horses. They had ridden a long distance and it was late afternoon. She knew they did not want to stay in the fort overnight; it was imperative that the talks begin at once. Perhaps the Americans felt the same way about the Dineh remaining within the walls, because officers began to file out of the building to fill the chairs behind the long table, bearing papers and briefcases. She was not near enough to hear what they said between themselves, so she carried her cradleboard to a shade tree not far from the table and sat down beneath it. No one even glanced toward the Navajo "squaw" with her baby seeking the shade.

The headmen settled on the ground to face the bluecoats, with their dignity unruffled, and Elspeth was proud of their demeanor, though her attention was still directed toward the windows of the buildings and on the faces of the soldiers. The possibility of Captain Morrison being among them had crossed her mind, but none of the men were familiar to her. General Carleton was easily recognized by his insignia, a small, dark-haired man with a determined face and eyes so pale they seemed almost colorless. He was not a man to be crossed, she recognized: his was the face of a fanatic. The chair beside him was empty; indeed, all of the officers seemed to be awaiting someone before they began the meeting. A tall man dressed in buckskin and with shoulder-length hair suddenly appeared, accompanied by two Indian scouts. Elspeth recognized Kit Carson from the pictures she had seen in the Eastern tabloids, and she felt a chill of alarm. Where were his other Ute, those who had been raiding the eastern part of Dineyah? And what was he doing here, sitting beside a general of the U.S. Army? An audible murmur went through the Navajo delegation sitting cross-legged on the ground, and Valerio raised their objection in Spanish.

"You insult us by having Ute present at this meeting," he said. "The Ute are our enemy. There will be no talks while they are here."

"Colonel Carson is the Ute agent," the interpreter announced. "He has a commission in our army. The Ute are in his party. You must hear us out."

He did not apologize for the insult, Elspeth noted. The Ute had been brought here to convey a point: the enemy of the People is on the side of the U. S. Army. The depredation in the east had sanction. The Navajo headmen conferred among themselves and remained seated to hear what the general had to say. But, first, a roll call was taken, and Valerio translated the names of the headmen into Spanish for the record.

"Who's the buck whose interpreting for them?" a captain asked the officer next to him; and, for a moment, English was strange to Elspeth's ears. "It isn't the old men who'd do the fighting, it's men like him."

"I was thinking the same thing. Good-looking devil; I wouldn't like to fight him." The officer passed a message down the table, and Valerio was asked his name.

"Tall Man," he replied, without hesitation. "I was called Valerio after the Ute sold me into slavery. The Ute have taken many slaves."

"You had him pegged right," the captain told his companion. "He has a grievance. If the general had any sense, he'd take him out right now."

Elspeth fought back her alarm as she waited for that message to be sent down the table to the general, but the captain did not bother to communicate his observation. "They'll accede to the general's order," the captain said, "or Carson will be all over them with his savages."

The general spoke to the small delegation in English, which was translated into bad Navajo and Spanish by his interpreter.

"The United States Government will no longer put up with your depredations in the New Mexico Territory. You have not kept your treaties. You have lied to us. Carry this message back to your people. You must return all the sheep you have stolen. All Navajo must come in, either here or at Fort Wingate, to be transported to a new reservation at Bosque Redondo. You have three months to do so. After that, we will be in a state of war against you.''

The Navajo were struck dumb by the proclamation; then, Valerio conferred with the headmen for several minutes. Elspeth was torn between watching him and listening to the conversation at the table.

''That took the wind out of their sails,'' the captain remarked, ''without even mentioning that Carson and his Ute will be busy in the meantime.''

''They may hide in their canyon. It's said there's a canyon somewhere big enough to hide them all.''

''The Spaniards exaggerated. There's no such place. If they defy us, there will be no place to hide. The interpreter's getting ready to speak . . .''

Valerio rose to his feet to deliver the reply. ''You cannot take us from our sacred land,'' he said. ''*Our* land, Dineyah. By what right do you demand that we surrender to you and the Ute?''

''We have every right,'' General Carleton responded icily. ''The president in Washington has agreed to this in order to make the Territory safe for settlers. We will locate you on the reservation in the southeast where you can grow crops and learn to behave yourselves. Irrigation canals are already being dug for your crops. The government will feed you until the first harvest. Several hundred Apache have already been taken there to farm.''

''You use our enemies, the Ute,'' Valerio said, with narrowed eyes, ''to make us live among Apache. This is not just. We have never made war on you.''

''You have no choice in the matter. You will turn yourselves in at the specified forts within three months and bring all the sheep you've stolen with you. If every Navajo has not come in by that time, we'll hunt you down like animals and capture you.''

Elspeth was as astounded as the headmen, who were not chiefs and could not possibly alert all the People. She wanted to explain this to the Americans, but she recognized that it would have little effect, except that it would reveal her identity. The

People could never comply with such an order, and her uneasiness began to grow. Several of the headmen began to address the general directly in Navajo, but when Valerio attempted to interpret their objections, General Carleton ignored the furor and rose from the table, mopping his face with his handkerchief in the heat. The other officers followed his example, dispersing into small groups. The general moved toward the shade tree under which Elspeth sat and lighted a cigar, and Colonel Carson followed him.

"We should get them out of here," the general said. "They're getting too agitated."

"They'll come in," Carson said. "They'll hear about Canyon Bonito soon and realize that we back up our words."

"Yes. The destruction of grain and driving off livestock in a forty-mile radius should get the message across. Are you leaving for Fort Wingate tomorrow?"

"At first light," Carson replied. "I'll send one of my scouts to bring more Ute. With a hundred Ute warriors and the troops, we can subdue the Navajo nation by making sorties. They know they can't survive through the winter without food. They'll come in, General. It's the most merciful way. As little bloodshed as possible."

"I'm not squeamish about that," the general said, puffing his cigar. "I'll bet your Ute aren't, either. What are they getting out of this?"

"Captives they can sell in the Territory. The women and children will be better cared for in New Mexican homes. I don't share your enthusiasm for the reservation site."

"You do your job, and I'll do mine, Colonel. You always were an Indian lover. If they don't come in on time, every male will be shot on sight. That's my way of settling the Indian problem in the Territory. Once it's taken care of, its mineral wealth can be explored."

Elspeth's face was almost covered by her blanket, but she observed the expression in the general's eyes. She had seen it in her brother-in-law's in the past, the gleam that only gold inspired. She recognized that the general was not interested in prospecting as Captain Morrison had been, but opening up the Territory for the exploitation of minerals would certainly further his career. He was an ambitious man.

"We're planning facilities for eight hundred to a thousand

Navajo,'' he said. ''If the Ute can take some of the women and children off our supply list, we'd be grateful. What the devil's this squaw doing here?'' he demanded, suddenly aware of her. ''Doesn't she know they're all supposed to stay together?''

''She's just taking the shade with her papoose,'' Colonel Carson said, glancing down at Elspeth. She averted her eyes and tried to remain calm, ignoring the suggestion that she go elsewhere, which had been spoken in English. Her heart pounded in her ears under their scrutiny, but she forced herself to maintain her relaxed position. She would not have recognized Kit Carson's face from the etchings she had seen in the Boston newspaper, which portrayed him with noble features and wide eyes, romantic and adventurous. Even in youth he could not have been like that, and he was now middle-aged. His hair still reached his collar, but it receded over his stern, high-cheekboned face, and his eyes were so narrow that she could not make out their color. She saw no compassion in that Missouri-frontiersman face, only a distrustful nature. Perhaps his life as trapper, army scout, and Indian fighter had drained away what humanity he possessed. He had once been married to an Indian girl, but Elspeth did not trust his reputation as friend to the Indians. The only tribe he supported now was the Ute, and he had chosen to use them against her people. She was relieved when he told her shortly, in Navajo, to rejoin the headmen, who had risen indignantly and were preparing to leave.

Chapter 17

Autumn, with its splendor of golden-crowned cottonwoods and temperate days, was overcast by the meeting at Fort Defiance. The People decided to remain in the canyon and invited those on the rim to join them in their stronghold. Instead of the usual exodus from the canyon for winter forage, men, women, and children poured into Tsegi with their animals and belongings, straining the hospitality that had been extended and arousing concern about the meager grazing land. Such congestion might have caused short tempers in another setting with different people, but, somehow, harmony was maintained and even laughter occasionally heard. They were drawn together in a common cause and made preparations to withstand an intrusion that they did not seriously contemplate. They harvested the corn and stored it in the root cellar as usual. The women even paused to weave in the afternoon. Only Elspeth seemed to take an invasion of Tsegi seriously. She had looked into the faces of the men who planned to solve the problem of the Navajo, and they were ruthless, their determination unmistakable.

The headmen had decided to a man not to give their people up on the appointed date even before Elspeth revealed what she had overheard.

"They are dangerous men," she told them when they camped at night after they left Fort Defiance. "They will carry out their threats. No fort has ever been so close to Tsegi before. They can scout from there and explore the area. They could find the entrance at Chinle Wash.''

"If they do, we will defend it,'' Lone Raider said. "We drove off the Spaniards, and we can drive these men away, from within Tsegi. I don't like the Ute being involved in this business. Several times over the years, the Ute have located the entrance to the canyon. We fought them off, but these warriors may be their sons; the information could have been passed from their fathers.''

Silence fell over the men around the campfire. The flickering flames highlighted the strong features of the old men as they thought of previous wars. They were wise and experienced and good. Elspeth sensed that they did not like the prospect of a war. The Navajo were peaceful. Their blood did not boil at the sound of war drums like that of the Apache.

"The bluecoats won't be able to enter the canyon unless a Ute shows the way,'' another headman said, with decision. "The chances of that are minimal. The Ute have not come to Tsegi in my lifetime, so there is no son, or son-of-a-son with the knowledge.''

"The Rope Thrower is a fine scout,'' Elspeth intervened. "He led the white explorer, Fremont, through the wild country, all the way to Calif—the great water in the west.''

"Tall Man's wife is thinking like a white woman, now,'' Lone Raider jested. "She has found a white hero.''

"Not a hero,'' she defended herself. "But he's proven that he's good at what he does. I'm not suggesting that you give yourselves to him. I'm one of you, and I would not surrender. You must consider a way to defend the canyon if The Rope Thrower discovers its entrance.''

Elspeth had not observed any preparations to fight during the two months since that conversation. Valerio reported that a clan near the entrance was fortifying itself on top of a large, anvil-shaped rock, which stood in the middle of the junction between Tsegi and Black Rock Canyon, not far from the entrance. "They're carrying supplies up by ladders which they can pull up behind them,'' he said. "They look like ants on the face of that huge rock formation. If the soldiers come, they plan to sit out the seige. They call the place *Tse'laa*, the fortress.''

"Do you think it will work? If the soldiers do come?''

"I don't know,'' he sighed. "It would depend on the season.

If they were trapped up there during the winter, they might freeze. People are laughing at them.''

"At least, they have a plan," she considered. "Everyone else is too complacent.''

"You are really concerned about The Rope Thrower, aren't you?'' he asked, touching her hair. "Lookouts have been placed in the rocks commanding the entrance, *querida*. We wouldn't be taken unaware. If they come, we can shoot down at them from there.''

"They have guns. Your arrows would be no match for them, Valerio.''

"Their guns can't shoot what they don't see. Don't worry, *querida*. The women and children might appear complacent, but the men are not.''

"Will you slaughter some sheep for me?'' she asked Many Tears Woman when her sister stopped by to play with the baby one morning. "I want to dry the meat.''

"Your drying rack is covered with the antelope your husband shot,'' Many Tears Woman replied. "I don't know what's gotten into you. Mutton doesn't dry like venison, you know. Have you ever seen dried mutton? The fat makes it go rancid. It tastes bad.''

"Will it make people sick?''

"Only the taste. We have plenty of sheep, too many with the flocks the people from the rim have brought. There's no need to store their meat. If you kill your sheep now, you won't have their wool in the spring.''

"I want to try it,'' Elspeth said. "Just with a couple of sheep. You know I don't like to ask you, but I still can't bring myself to kill them. It'll be two less animals to feed. The grazing land will soon be depleted.''

Many Tears Woman laughed. "I'll never understand you. You were brave enough to go to the fort with the men, but you can't slaughter a sheep. Of course, I'll do it for you, but you won't like the taste. It seems wasteful.''

She had been grinding corn in an attempt to store as much imperishable food as possible in the event of an attack; so far, no one had questioned her activities or where she was storing the supplies. Valerio was taking his turn as a lookout, so he did not observe her frantic preparations. The deadline was drawing nearer, but the complacency of the canyon dwellers was un-shaken. Except for the short incursion into Canyon del Muerto by the Spaniards, the natural fortress had been inviolable. No news had reached them regarding Carson's projected raid in Canyon Bonito to the east. They were cut off from the outside world; there was no tribal unity. If there had been one strong chief to lead them, they could have opposed the Americans, at least for a while. Without such leadership, a unified defense of their homeland was impossible.

She reasoned with herself that it was probably foolish to hide supplies; if it was, there was no harm done, though, and she could retrieve them for use later. Whatever happened, it would be a difficult winter in the canyon because of all of the extra mouths to feed. Too much meat on her racks would cause com-ment, so she had Many Tears Woman slaughter one sheep a week and contributed some of the fresh meat to the table to feed their guests, arguing each time that there was not enough forage. She did not want to watch her flock starve with the others when it was exhausted. The special tie that existed between the two mothers of Maria's baby was so strong that her sister-in-law did not question her wisdom again. Storing the food in a place apart from the communal root cellar was the most difficult part of her plan, but she accomplished even that over a period of time, using her interest in medicinal herbs as a cover.

Her concern about the deadline General Carleton had set was so strong when she returned to the canyon that she was unable to calm it by weaving. She had quickly abandoned her loom for her other activities, one of which was further training with Hos-teen Yazzie, the only person who shared her concern about the proximity of the American troops. He had failed visibly over the autumn, and he was anxious to impart as much of his knowl-edge to Elspeth as possible, so it would not be lost if he left them.

"You will teach someone else when your time comes," he told her when they were searching for herbs. "Someone in our family has always known these cures, so you must impart them, too. I have lived a long time. Sometimes, now, I think too long. I don't want to be here to see the People taken from the canyon. I pray more than usual nowadays. You share my fear. I've seen it in your face, the constant frown between your eyes. You sense what others do not."

"I haven't sensed anything regarding this," she told him as she assisted him up a rocky slope. "It's my reason that's troubling me. While you pray, I'm driven to horde supplies. The winter worries me."

"The white men coming into Tsegi worry you more," he said. "Let's sit for a while. The plants will wait to be gathered."

They rested next to a juniper. She was concerned about the Hosteen's progressive weakness. A fine tremor had developed in his gnarled hands over the past weeks, and he had to wipe away the saliva that gathered at the edges of his thin lips before he spoke. "There are healers among the People who diagnose illness by hand trembling," he joked. "My hands tell me only that I am too old for what's happening to us."

"Is there an herb to cure such tremors?" she asked, and he laughed slightly.

"Not for my affliction, little niece. I can show you how to make a potion for palsy, though."

"Has anyone . . ." she began, and hesitated, wondering if she should approach the subject, ". . . has anyone ever blessed a place that is *chindi*? Among the white men, there are Singers who can remove the spell from an evil place."

He studied her seriously with his rheumy eyes. "I don't know that anyone has ever tried this," he said at last. "For one thing, no one will approach a *chindi* place. Do you have a particular one in mind? A tree blasted by lightning? A hogan in which someone has departed from us?"

"The dwelling of the Ancient Ones across the Wash," she suggested. "I've never understood why the cliff-houses are forbidden. No one is likely to fall from them. They are high in the rock walls of the canyon, but not as high as the People climb by using the slits cut into its face."

"I should never have questioned such things," the old man replied, "but I have thought about them. The ancient ruins have always been *chindi* because corpses have been found in them. The Ancient Ones buried bodies in their floors, it is said. A very dangerous custom."

"Yes, if it was a general custom," Elspeth said. "But what if there were no bodies in the ruins across the Wash? Would it still be *chindi*? Wouldn't prayers cure it so it wouldn't harm anyone?"

"We will never know that. There is no way we can know,

because no one will go there," the Hosteen said. "A long time ago, someone discovered bodies in one of the ruins. He must have fallen ill from corpse-sickness."

She put her arms around her knees and attempted to sound calm. "There are no corpses there," she told him. "There are a few sound walls, and the rest is rubble. There's a pit behind one of the walls, but there's nothing in it. I've been there. I've explored the whole place. Most of the walls have fallen outward into a talus slope. There are no bodies there. It would be an excellent place to store food supplies in the event of an attack."

He was silent for so long that she thought he feared contamination. The lines in his face deepened, and he gazed contemplatively at the floor of the canyon, the narrow strip of land on which they lived between the soaring red walls. The cornfields had been harvested. The Wash, which roared with the spring runoff, had gone underground now; only the golden cottonwoods and the tamarisk trees marked its course, their roots sustained by its moisture. She did not know what Hosteen Yazzie was thinking, but she felt she should not have mentioned visiting the cliff-house. His belief that the ruins were haunted, forbidden, had been with him for a lifetime; it was ingrained into his very bones. She wanted to ask his forgiveness for her transgression, but found it difficult to verbalize her apology, as if mentioning the *chindi* place might upset him more.

"You've never been in the canyon in winter," he said, touching the corners of his lips with the back of his feeble hand. "It is cold like no other place is cold. The warm air rises, and the cold is trapped beneath it. Animals freeze to death. Men would freeze if they didn't have fires." Elspeth wondered if he had begun to wander, because he made no reference to the cliff dwelling. "The canyon looks so narrow from here. If riders found the entrance, they might sweep through it in a few days. Do you think the Ancient Ones remained here during the winter?"

The question surprised her. "I don't know," she replied, "but it seems probable. There are no dwellings on the rim. They probably didn't migrate; perhaps, they didn't have sheep. Their dwellings were sturdy—or they wouldn't have lasted this long. The pit where I stored my supplies was lined with slabs of stone, and there was a flat stone nearby which I used for a cover to keep out any moisture. The cover fit perfectly, though it was difficult to move it into place. Yes, I think they must have remained here in the winter. They'd have had to gather firewood from the rim beforehand, though, just as our men are gathering it, now.''

"Take me to the *chindi* place," he said, rising unsteadily to his feet. "If there are no corpses there, it may be safe. I want to look at the walls that are standing. I may have a plan."

She was so relieved that she jumped up to support him. "You are the first person who has mentioned a plan," she said. "I was careful about anyone seeing me go there, but won't two of us be observed?''

"No one looks in the direction of the ancient dwellings," he assured her. "They avoid them completely. Two of us can be as careful as one if we use the shelter of the trees and then the shadows.''

Elspeth thought he would be completely exhausted by the time they reached the level of the ruin, but the old man was curiously elated by the adventure. He wanted to see the pit into which she had put her horde of supplies, and he stood before the tallest wall, with his back to the cliff, and examined it for a long time.

"It is wider at the base to support the weight above it," he commented. "It isn't as thick as you thought. This must have been a room, from its distance from the cliff. It seems to be solid, but it's built of mud from the Wash below." He knelt down to examine the rubble beneath it and crumbled a piece between his hands. "The mud was mixed with weeds and small branches," he observed. "We could build the wall to the top of the cave again, I think."

"*Adobe,*" she murmured, the Spanish word slipping into her speech unaware, and she explained, "The Mexicans use something like this, but they build with . . ." There was no Navajo word for "brick," so she attempted to explain with her hands. "They mix the mud with straw and they don't build a wall in one piece like this. It's easier that way. We could probably extend the wall, but I don't understand—"

"I want to see the rest," the Hosteen said, making his way carefully through the rubble in the shadows.

"It's on several levels," she said, taking his arm so he would not fall. "A wall here and there seems to indicate separate dwellings, but that's the highest one."

She ventured forward ahead of him, onto an area she had inspected only visually before. She noticed what appeared to be signs of fire on the blackened rubble and it occurred to her that she had not explored the ruin as completely as she had indicated to the Hosteen. If they found what seemed to be a human bone anywhere, whatever plan the old man had in mind would be abandoned at once. She kicked through the sand and debris cautiously, but all she uncovered were a few shards of pottery. As she turned to encourage him forward, the earth sucked at her feet like quicksand and she leaped clear of the spot in alarm. She and the Hosteen watched with superstitious horror as the fine debris funneled inward, moving as rapidly as sand in an hourglass. The Hosteen exclaimed softly, and Elspeth's heart beat in her ears. If an ancient spirit or a phantasm from a lost religion had appeared, neither of them could have moved. The debris disappeared, leaving a perfectly round, dark hole where it had been.

"I don't like this," the old man managed after a while. "What do we know about the Ancient Ones? They may have left traps for intruders, or this place is *chindi*."

"I think it's just a hole," Elspeth said, with relief. "It was clogged with debris, and I disturbed it by standing there."

"I don't think I like this hole," he persisted. "Who knows what it may contain?"

He was right, of course. There still might be a burial in the floor. "I'll look," Elspeth volunteered. "It may be just another storage pit. We shouldn't have been frightened."

She moved cautiously to the rim of the hole, which was several feet in circumference, and knelt down to peer into it. She expected it to be shallow and was surprised to find it so deep, its floor illuminated by a shaft of light coming through the wall at its base. The light in itself was curious. It did not appear to be a random ray from a break in the outer wall; and it was not large enough for a window.

"It looks like a small cave, a natural one," she said over her shoulder. "I can't tell without going down there. Light's coming through at the bottom, and the floor's covered by debris."

"Don't go down," the Hosteen told her. "There could be snakes . . . at least."

She stood up and brushed the dust from her woven dress. "I'd need a ladder," she said as she rejoined him. "I'm curious to see what's down there. If it's a cave, it isn't visible from the approach."

"We will return," the old man agreed, "but not alone, I think. We'll wait until Tall Man can come with us. He can explore this place with a torch. I'll explain to him why I think this place is not *chindi*, though I don't think it would matter that much to him. Even as a child, he went where he should not go. I won't tell him what I thought when the hole was making itself," he added, with a wheezing laugh. "You won't tell him what you thought, either."

Hosteen Yazzie procured enough yucca rope to make a ladder while they awaited Valerio's return. Elspeth marveled at the change their project had brought about in the old man. His step was livelier; the hand tremor was not so pronounced. Motivated by a plan he had not yet revealed, he began to take sweat baths to purify himself every day. His songs could be heard throughout the encampment, and Many Beads remarked upon it when she visited her grandchildren.

"He's preparing himself for a ceremonial," she told Elspeth, "but no one has requested one. The strain of having so many people around has affected him, I think. Old people are more comfortable when they are surrounded by their own."

"His mind is clearer than usual when I speak to him," Elspeth defended him mildly. It would not do to have the family imagining signs of senility in the only person who might help them. "He was depressed by the American order. He felt helpless, hopeless, I think. He must have come to grips with it, now. This is difficult for you, too. Are the extra relatives a strain?"

Sky struggled happily in his grandmother's embrace, but Many Beads did not smile as easily as she had in the past. "They are no problem. The grazing land is, though," she said. "Oldest Boy has to herd the flock deeper into the canyon. It's a long day for a boy. And, of course," she paused as though uncertain about speaking the words aloud, "the Americans prey on my mind, too. We've heard nothing about what's happening outside. That's unusual. News travels fast in Dineyah. I wish I knew what is happening. Whether any clans have adhered to the order."

"Our men aren't riding from here," Elspeth reasoned. "The

other men probably aren't riding abroad, either, and that's how news is carried."

Many Beads released Sky and dispatched him to play by patting his bottom. "Why do I feel I can talk to you?" she asked. "I keep my silence when I'm with my own children. What you said about feeling helpless applies to me, as well. I think a great deal when I'm at my loom. I don't feel like weaving, but it's the only time I have to myself. I worry about my family, about what would happen if the soldiers come. I try to hide it from the others; I'm sure they worry, too."

"Everyone's concern has been well hidden," Elspeth said. "I thought I was the only one who worried."

"You know the way their minds work. Do you think they would kill us if they came here? Will they really shoot at the men for not surrendering? We have only a short time left."

Elspeth stared down at her hands, which were folded in her lap. "I don't think they would kill women and children. You know about the permission given to the Ute, though. It's terrible to consider. They'll try to shoot the men who hold out, there's no doubt about that. I've said from the first that we should have some sort of plan, but the men wouldn't listen."

"They don't always make the best decisions," Many Beads said. "They have to prove their bravery. They'd throw their lives away to protect their families. That is foolhardy, but there's little hope of changing them. We are more practical, and not given to wasteful heroics."

While everyone else was occupied around the morning cooking fire, the Hosteen and his small party departed for the ruin unnoticed. He had spoken to Valerio the previous afternoon, shortly after his return; though he had not been completely frank with his nephew, Valerio was eager to explore the cave.

"My eyes are weary from acting as a lookout," he told Elspeth later. "Every muscle in my body is tense. The Hosteen's proposal surprised me, but it's just what I need. For some reason, he seems to want me to prove that the cliff dwelling is not *chindi*, I think. He wants to prove there are no bodies in the cave."

"I think so," Elspeth replied carefully. Since speaking of a plan with Many Beads, she had been considering the Hosteen's actions, and she sensed what he had in mind. She did not like to deceive Valerio, but she did not know how he would accept the idea; besides, it would be better for Hosteen Yazzie, a man whom he respected, to reveal the reason for the interest in the ruin, instead of her. "It's a good place to store extra food for the winter," she ventured. "There are so many people here, now. I'd already started to do it and asked the Hosteen if there was any way the place could be purified."

"No place on earth is *chindi* to you, is it?" he asked, with a smile, and she shook her head.

"Not yet," she admitted.

"I've never seen a cave there. Forbidding something gives it a special attraction. I explored most of the cliff dwellings in Tsegi when I was a boy. With my heart in my throat, because I knew there was danger there. The Ancient Ones were the ancestors of the Pueblos, I think. Some things in their dwellings are the same."

They reached the ruin in less than an hour and spent a few minutes examining the walls before Valerio lit his torch from a coal he had brought in his metal pot. He leaned forward to look through the hole and glanced at Elspeth with widened eyes to express that he had never seen it before. Elspeth smiled uncomfortably. She realized for the first time how it felt to be caught up in others' secrets. Valerio could just as easily have voiced his reaction, because the Hosteen knew that he had explored the ruin in the past. Remembering how much each person knew was confusing. When the men dropped the rope ladder, her heart constricted with fear.

"Be careful," she cautioned Valerio, unnecessarily, for he had already placed his knife between his teeth in preparation for the descent. He disappeared so quickly that the hole appeared to have swallowed him. She knelt down at the rim to follow his progress, but the light from the torch only illuminated Valerio when he reached the bottom.

He moved in cautious silence beneath her, and she looked toward the Hosteen, who stood a safe distance away. "The space is larger than we thought," she said, her voice falling almost to a whisper. "I can't see anything but his torch."

Her concern was apparent, and the old man patted his medicine bag. "I have everything here," he assured her, "for ghost-sickness or snakebite."

Valerio's voice sounded hollow when he called up to her,

"Come down. It's all right. There's nothing down here but the rubble that fell through the hole."

The rope ladder was secured at the top on some outcroppings of rock, but Elspeth had not experienced anything more terrifying than climbing down its shaky rungs. Halfway down, she gripped it with both hands and clung to it, unable to will herself to go further. Valerio grasped the bottom of the rope to steady it. She took several deep breaths and continued the descent cautiously, until she felt his arm around her waist and solid ground beneath her feet. Even with such reassurance, she found it difficult to breathe and had to wipe the perspiration from her face. The cave was man-made out of the sandstone, a perfectly circular room with smoothly hewn walls, but it was incredibly hot and stuffy; the air might have been trapped there for a thousand years.

"It's a kiva," Valerio told her, "a ceremonial chamber. I've found a few in the other ruins. They wouldn't bury anyone here." He held up the torch so she could see the walls, which were blackened by smoke. "They've built fires down here, many fires."

"They did stay here during the winter, then. No one in his right mind would build a fire down here before the cold weather came, unless it was used for a sweat bath."

"It wouldn't be used for that," he said, lowering the torch toward the opening admitting the shaft of light. "I talked to my Pueblo friend about the ruins, but I wasn't allowed into the great kiva there. This opening is a ventilation shaft. When the entrance was closed, it was the only air they had."

"They *closed* the entrance?" Elspeth said, with a shudder. "I don't think I could stand that . . . ."

"In the Pueblo kivas, the holy men remain several days during a ceremonial. This is too small for that purpose. It wouldn't hold many men; perhaps it was just a place to pray." He handed her the torch and crouched down to peer through the air shaft. "You can see the canyon below from here," he considered, "as far as our hogans."

The Hosteen's voice reached them from what seemed a long distance, and Elspeth turned to Valerio. "He's concerned about us. He doesn't know what's happening down here. We'd better go up."

"Not before I kiss you by torchlight," he said, drawing her

close. "I've missed you, *querida*. You're in my mind all the time when I'm away. When my eyes grow weary from straining them against the approach of soldiers in the sun, they remain alert because I'm thinking of you. This is a trying time."

"Yes," she agreed, with her arms around him, "and it may get worse, my darling. I'd rather be at your side at the canyon entrance than waiting for word of you here."

"I wish it could be that way, but you're safer here if anything happens. The important thing to me is that you and the children are safe. The Hosteen's calling out again. We better join him."

Ascending the ladder, with Valerio's hand steadying her from below, was easier than it had been going down. The sunlight hurt her eyes as she emerged from the kiva; she had to block its rays with her arm. Valerio emerged after her and smothered the torch in the broken masonry on the ground.

"It's safe down there," he told the old man. "If the rubble on the floor was cleared away, you could use it for any purpose you choose. I'd like to look at those walls again, unless you're going to perform your ceremony now."

"The walls first," Hosteen Yazzie said. "I want to discuss something with you, nephew. You may not approve of what I have to say, but you must listen to me."

They stood next to the cliff, looking up at the partially crumbled masonry of the wall, and Valerio leaned his weight against it to test its strength. Fine dust trickled down its surface, but it withstood the pressure.

"It's like adobe," Elspeth volunteered. "It's held up for a long time."

"Wattle," he said. "The Ancient Ones were good builders."

The old man placed his open hand on the wall. "Some of the People are preparing to occupy the flat top of a rock," he said. "I don't know if that's a good idea or not. I think we should have a plan, too, though. If we repaired some of these walls, we could move up here if trouble comes. We may not have to, but we should plan ahead. Now that we know the cave is safe, we could use it, too."

"That thought came to me in the kiva," Valerio said, with some irony. "I think it was meant to, wasn't it? Until I came here, I couldn't understand why you were exploring a *chindi* place, Uncle. The cave wouldn't accommodate more than ten people. It would be warm in the winter, perhaps too warm. The air is bad. I could take care of that by driving more shafts through the stone.'' He scanned the area critically. ''No one could remain in the kiva for a long period of time; it isn't large enough for all the people living with us. The walls could provide a blind for exercise. People could survive without too much discomfort behind them.''

''While some were in the warm hole, the others could be outside,'' the Hosteen considered. ''No one would see them here if we repaired the walls a little. Do you agree that it is a good plan?''

Valerio nodded. ''I'd feel better if I knew the women and children were safe. This place has an added advantage. It is high enough to see the valley below clearly, but not too high to shoot down on intruders. We'll repair the walls.''

''But we won't tell the others about it yet,'' the old man cautioned. ''Not until the time comes . . . if it does. The thought of coming here would fill them with panic if they aren't under duress. It would destroy *hozro* and make them unhappy.''

''We can do it in secret. It shouldn't take long.''

''We'll need a better ladder,'' Elspeth suggested, ''with wooden rungs. It must be strong if Big Woman's going to use it.''

Valerio laughed and put his arm around her shoulders. ''You didn't like that ladder, did you?'' he asked. ''I promise you we'll make the strongest one you've ever seen. We wouldn't want Big Woman to be afraid if she had to use it.''

Chapter 18

Frost rimed the fallen leaves on the floor of the canyon, and a chill wind began to blow. Limping Man accompanied his son in herding the flock, because they had to remain away several days at a time, going ever deeper into Tsegi's fastness in search of grazing. A few people straggled into their traditional fortress after the deadline had passed, bringing stories from outside. The farms to the east had been destroyed by The Rope Thrower and his Ute, who harrassed the People from Fort Wingate. Thirteen Dineh had been killed and twenty women and children captured. Those who had been holding out had surrendered themselves at the fort.

"There are no more People from the Chuska Mountains to Canyon Bonito," an emaciated young man shivering in his blanket reported. "The land is as bare as the badlands of Bisti, no animals and no farms. My brother and I are young. We are warriors. We've come to make a stand in Tsegi."

"Are they killing the men on sight?" Many Beads asked quietly as she served him more stew beneath the eyes of her relatives. "If the men go to the fort now, will they shoot them?"

"Those who were killed were opposing them," the young man replied. "No one was shot who surrendered with his family. They say they will give the People food and firewood. They say they don't want to shoot us, but we all must go to the forts. If we don't, they will come to get us."

A murmur went over the group in Many Beads's hogan. Elspeth sensed that their guests were having second thoughts and studied their faces. There were more women and children than men among them, and the few men were past middle age. They had lived harmoniously with the family, but they were rim dwellers who did not have as much faith in the canyon as its inhabitants. The young men had come without horses and climbed down the notches in the canyon wall, its only inlet besides Chinle Wash twenty miles to the west. Many Beads's farm was the first one they reached.

"You must rest here for a while," Many Beads told them. "You need food and rest. You're welcome to stay as long as you wish."

"We will spend the night," the young man replied. "We've come to defend the entrance to Tsegi. They might come at any time. We've seen it happen. We've brought our weapons, and we want to fight."

Their weapons were slim bows and quivers of arrows. Instead of bolstering the courage of the family, their youthful bravado had a demoralizing effect. Attack seemed inevitable, though no one had found the canyon yet. Within hours, Many Beads's relatives decided to give themselves up at Fort Defiance.

"We are used to the high plateau," her cousin told her. "We feel trapped in here with no place to go. Our sheep are depleting your grazing. Soon, it will be winter, and we'd be more of a hardship on you. We'll leave tomorrow morning, while we have horses to ride. We'll surrender ourselves, and our sheep, to the white men. They will look after us. I feel I must do this for our women and children. I don't want them to be captured by Ute."

Many Beads objected, but her daughters and Elspeth remained silent. They had their children to consider, and the man's decision made good sense to them. Elspeth had been concerned about the refuge in the cliff dwelling for some time. She had stocked it as much as she could without being observed, carried as much food and as many warm sheepskins as she could against the possibility of an attack, but she knew they could not stay there for longer than a month if all of the kinsmen remained. If they left, the family would be secure there for several months, until the danger had passed. She felt guilty for not thinking in terms of the customary hospitality of the People, until Hosteen Yazzie arrived at the hogan after hearing of the decision.

"Each family must do what is best for them," he told Many

Beads, who sat despondently beside her loom. "You have done everything you could for them. You have shared with them during the winter even when we were on the rim. Now they want to go, and you must respect their wishes. Everything they say is true. The fewer people who remain here, the better chance they have." He glanced at Elspeth, and there was perfect understanding between them. "Your kinsmen are being considerate, but they are also looking after themselves. You did not ask them to leave."

"They haven't discovered the canyon yet," Valerio said, holding Sky on his lap. "We should be safe when the snow begins to fall. I don't think they'd risk a winter campaign in unfamiliar territory even with Ute scouts."

"Will you be able to remain here after the snow?" Elspeth asked as she added wood to the fire. The days were shorter, already, and the early darkness brought a chill with it. Outside of the periphery of the fire, one could feel the cold. "We miss you when you're away. I can't tell you how much, Valerio."

"I miss you. And this fellow here," he said, looking down at his son. "He's grown since I was here last. And the baby will be walking soon. I'll be here more often after it snows. We've decided to remain alert, but each man will spend less time as a lookout, because it will be more difficult in the cold. You'll need more firewood. I'll get you some tomorrow."

Sky looked up and announced, "I can carry wood. I'm strong. Can I go with you tomorrow? You can show me how to track again."

Valerio brushed his son's hair back from his forehead and smiled. "I need the help of a strong man. We'll go deep into the canyon on horseback and gather a lot of wood. Later, I'll show you how to track a rabbit in the snow. It sounds easy, but you must learn what the signs mean. You must sleep, now, because we'll leave at sunrise."

"Will we see Oldest Boy and Limping Man with the sheep?" the little boy asked, with enthusiasm. "I want to see where they take the sheep. Oldest Boy saw a wolf. It ran away when he threw a stone at it. I want to see the wolf, too."

"We may go that far," Valerio assured him, lifting the child in his arms to put him to bed. "Sleep, my son, and dream of rabbits in the snow."

Elspeth attended to the baby before she bent to kiss her son good night. "Good night, Sky, my dear baby," she said. "You have a big day ahead of you tomorrow."

"I'm not a baby," he protested sleepily. "I'm a boy . . ."

"Of course you are," she murmured, with her cheek against his. "You'll be a big boy soon."

Valerio smiled as he watched them, and she noticed the weariness in his face. He had ridden a great distance to be with them, and the strain of standing watch at the mouth of the canyon was beginning to show. She took his hand when they returned to the fire and brought it to her lips.

"It can't be easy watching for them to come," she said. "You must be prepared for action at any time."

"Yes," he admitted. "And I have to watch the others, too. The young men from the east are so tense that they might give us away if they saw anything. They're anxious to fight, *querida*. So anxious that they probably wouldn't follow the plan."

"What is the plan?"

"To prevent as much loss of life as possible. The lookouts would signal to those below so that riders could be sent through the canyons to warn the people there. We'd assess the enemy's strength and shoot our arrows from concealment. And, of course," he said, with a smile, "that clan would scramble to the top of their rock."

Elspeth smiled bleakly and rested her head upon his shoulder so he would not see the tears in her eyes. The plan was pathetic, and he might be there when it went into effect. Without rifles, defense was impossible; the men knew it and were concentrating on saving lives. The Navajo were clever, the most artistic tribe in the Territory, but they did not have warlike inclinations. They had defended themselves against the Ute in the past, but the Ute did not have rifles then.

"If we hold out in the canyon for the winter, will they leave us in peace?" she asked.

"I think so. It wouldn't be easy for us, though. I don't want you to worry," he said, kissing her hair. "I know you are aware of the circumstances we'd have to face, but I don't want you to dwell on them. We must live one day at a time. If it were in my power, I'd never let you out of my arms. Time would stop right here."

She raised her face to meet his lips. "We'll hold on to every moment," she whispered. "When we're together, I don't want to think of anything else."

They roamed the canyon together in the succeeding week and gathered as much firewood as they could find for the entire family. Their breath steamed the cold air, and the work was not easy, but they were content in each other's company; it was a happy time. Sky contributed his share to the bundles of wood; though the branches he carried were small, his parents encouraged him with praise. They heated their mutton stew over a fire at noon and rested beneath the graying sky. Elspeth, who had never been this deep into Tsegi before, sat with her arms around her knees and looked up at the red sandstone walls with wonder. They were a hundred feet high here, with frost in their ridges, and were as spectacular under the washed-out sky as when the blue canopy of summer emphasized their ruddy shades. She appreciated them in silence, and Valerio was silent for a long time, too. A moving form caught her eye, loping along a slope, and she watched it for some time without being able to identify the animal from such a distance.

"There's your wolf," Valerio told Sky. "He's a big fellow, but he's alone."

Sky ran to get a rock to hurl at the wolf, but Valerio took it from his hand with a smile. "He's far away. He isn't bothering you. You have no sheep to protect."

"That's the second one that's been seen," Elspeth commented. "Do they usually come into the canyon at this time of year? I've never seen them in the summer."

"Our sheep are usually on the rim by now. There must not be any sheep at all up there. Wolves have never been much of a problem. When the snow is heavy, they cut out the weak animals."

"Do they ever attack people?"

"I've never known them to, or heard of it. They've come down only because of the sheep. If they get too close to the flock, Sky can throw his rock, but I don't think it will be necessary. If you listen closely at night," he told his son, "you might hear them sing."

He put his head back and imitated the wailing of a wolf, and Sky laughed. He imitated his father, but he sounded like a cub, and his parents smiled. The next moment, he was on his feet searching for bits of wood again, his intention of stoning the wolf forgotten.

"We should follow his example," Elspeth said. "We haven't found as much wood as I expected."

"There's never much wood here," Valerio said, gazing toward the rim where it was usually collected. "I'll climb up and throw some down."

"No!" Elspeth said, restraining him with her hand. "If there are no sheep there, it is a bad sign. They've probably been driven away."

"Only by the families who own them. Your mind is too quick. I thought you'd overlook what I said. If the soldiers had been there, they'd be in the canyon by now. The people up there probably went to turn themselves in. We must go back now. The darkness falls early."

A few flakes of snow began to fall as they rode back and Elspeth looked up into the lowering gray sky. She glanced at Valerio and her son riding together on his pinto pony and apprehension stirred in her. The season of their deliverance from the threat of the army had arrived, but they still had to make it through the winter without enough wood.

Two feet of snow blanketed the canyon floor and icicles streaked the mineral patterns of its walls before the Big Wind. The sheep managed to sustain themselves on lichens, frozen foliage, and their own fat, but at least one was lost every few days. The women cooked some of the meat and allowed the rest to freeze before secreting it in the root cellar. The hogans were draped with carefully scraped sheepskins, which could hardly be distinguished from the snow.

"This must suit your nature," Many Tears Woman said when she and Elspeth were dressing a carcass. "The weather's doing your slaughtering for you."

There was no reproach in her words; indeed; they were spoken almost lightly. Many Tears Woman had revealed remarkable strength as their circumstances grew worse, a quality Elspeth would not have attributed to her before Surviving Child was born. Her tall, slender figure could be seen outside at all hours of the day, regardless of the weather, as she went about the tasks that discouraged the others in such cruel weather. Big Woman crouched in her hogan surrounded by her children in an attempt to keep warm, and Many Beads was occupied with preparing the sheepskins so they would not attract wolves when they were put outside to air. The only periods when Many Tears Woman seemed to come in for warmth were after the baby's feedings, when she rejoiced in cleaning him and holding him beside the fire.

"I may not be able to nurse him," she told Elspeth, "but I can tell that he knows I'm his mother, too. See how he smiles at me."

Her observation was not wishful thinking. Maria's baby was bonded as surely to Many Tears Woman as he was to Elspeth; even Valerio noticed it. "He has made a full woman out of my sister, and he truly has two mothers. More than the other children, who call their aunts Mother, and whose aunts treat them as their own."

Valerio was preparing to leave and, for the first time, Elspeth felt her own strength would not sustain her. In spite of the hardships, their month together had been as close and loving as when they had married almost four years before. And, because they had been living for their moments together, her mind had been distracted from the worsening conditions in the camp, exemplified most by the steady loss of sheep.

"We must speak to Hosteen Yazzie before I leave," he told her as they lay in each other's arms. "The family should be told about the cliff-house while I'm here to support the Hosteen's decision."

"You don't think the soldiers might still come?" she asked. "You said they wouldn't continue their campaign in the winter, Valerio."

"I'm not concerned about that," he reassured her. "It's the weather that bothers me. The cold is intense; there isn't enough wood. If things get any worse, the family could relocate to the place we've prepared. The kiva would be easier to warm. It's wasteful to feed so many fires."

"It doesn't matter what ceremonial has been sung there," Big Woman said stubbornly when they were gathered in Many Beads's hogan. "I'll never go to a place that is *chindi*. I'd rather perish here in the cold."

"Your husband feels otherwise," Valerio said patiently from

where he sat beside Hosteen Yazzie, who had drawn close to the central fire to warm himself. A meeting of the whole family would have been awkward, because of the mother-in-law taboo, so he and the old man had discussed their plan with Limping Man and Slim Man in the Hosteen's hogan before speaking to the women. The men had remained silent at first, but, in the end, they had agreed that conditions warranted the drastic measure. Slim Man was leaving with Valerio; Big Woman's crippled husband would remain here to look after the women and children.

"I don't care what my husband has agreed to," the large woman surrounded by her children argued. "It has always been an evil place, and that can't be changed. I'm shocked to hear that you and my uncle have been there. I don't understand your thinking." She put her arm around her seven-year-old daughter and placed a hand on her baby's cradleboard. Her half-grown son, Oldest Boy, was already sitting with the men; his face was impossible to read. "I don't want my children to get ghost-sickness. I've never liked living so close to that place."

Many Beads remained silent until her daughters expressed their views, her strong-boned face, wrinkled by deepening lines of concern for her family, did not reveal her thoughts as she listened. Many Tears Woman sat quietly beside her mother, one hand restraining the baby from crawling too near the fire, her attention focused only on him. Elspeth decided it was time for her to speak, for her words might carry greater weight with Big Woman than those of the men.

"There is no ghost-sickness there," she said evenly. "I've been going there for months to prepare a safe shelter for us in case we were attacked. I have not become ill. If the soldiers had come, we'd have had to retreat there, and no one would have been allowed to stay behind. There are enough supplies there for a month, and the cave is lined with sheepskins. We could carry extra food with us." Big Woman turned deaf ears on her argument, but Many Tears Woman smiled faintly, recalling the fleeces of the sheep she had helped dress after they had frozen. She regarded Elspeth with admiration tempered by slight resentment over not being taken into the secret preparations. Elspeth sensed that Many Tears Woman would not oppose the plan; her existence was tied to their baby by a cord of devotion stronger than if he had once been attached to her body. "I was uneasy at first, too," she said, concentrating on Big Woman, raising her voice firmly to demand her attention. "The place was strange to me, and I knew its reputation. But, after our uncle said his prayers over it, my uneasiness vanished. We explored the cliff dwelling completely and found nothing threatening there. I've been back alone many times."

She did not mention her terror on the flimsy ladder, or the supersitious fear that had gripped her when, as the Hosteen expressed it, the hole "made itself." Hosteen Yazzie seized that moment to press the argument further.

"The place is clean. It's warmer than here and would be safe if the time came. Now, there is no threat of soldiers, but it can still save your lives. The winter will get colder. The time of the Big Crust is not far away. The wood will not last that long. If you are miserable now, it is nothing compared to what you face, and only your husband will be here to help you move to that place."

"I won't go," Big Woman said, with finality. "No one can make me take my children there. I won't live with ancient ghosts. I won't expose my children to madness."

Elspeth drew in her breath with frustration, but Valerio's hand on her arm checked the harsh words that came to her lips. He leveled his gaze at his mother, who had kept her own counsel until now, and Many Beads understood the unspoken message: in the end, the decision would rest with her. Hosteen Yazzie was a holy man and had the wisdom of age. He was highly respected. But, in practical matters, the family looked to the matriarch, who understood their fears and who was all-loving.

"There is an alternative," she said. "Not a pleasant one, but it would keep us from inhabiting the cliff dwelling. While my son and his family were gathering wood, we had some visitors, a family of women and children and old people, who could not endure the privation any longer. They were ragged and half-frozen, short of food. My daughters," she said, with a glance at Big Woman, "brought them food here in my hogan. They had made the decision to turn themselves in at the fort, and nothing we could say would change their minds. We would have taken them in, but they wouldn't accept our hospitality, because they knew it would lessen our chances for survival. Have you met any other people like them?" she asked Valerio.

"No," he said, with surprise. "No one's even spoken of surrendering. Conditions are bad, but everyone is determined to stay in Tsegi."

"We gave them extra food, and they went on their way. They would surely have perished here, but the bluecoats have promised food and shelter and warm fires. A new reservation on which to live. There are no ghosts at the fort, or on the reservation. No Ancient Ones, nothing *chindi*. Since what we are speaking of is survival, this is an alternative to going to the cliff dwelling. There are the Ute, of course, we must not forget them. The Rope Thrower is permitting them to take women and children as captives to be sold as your younger sister was, but there's a good chance we would not encounter them. I think it is something to consider."

She spoke solemnly, as if she had dwelled on the matter; for a moment, even Valerio thought she was serious. He drew in his breath and waited for the others to express their opposition, which they did, loudly and in chorus, with Big Woman's strong voice dominating the others.

"We can't leave our land," she said. "It is part of us. We know its moods and its seasons. We've never known anything else. Who knows what might await us on that reservation, so far away?" Her arm tightened around her daughter. "Oldest Girl will be a woman soon. I don't want her to suffer as a captive. The Ute would take her first, and I couldn't bear it. If my children became slaves, I couldn't bear it. We must never turn ourselves in. I'd even go to that *chindi* cliff dwelling to prevent it."

Elspeth recognized Many Beads's subtlety in changing her daughter's mind. She studied her mother-in-law's face, but it revealed no subterfuge. She nodded her head quietly, without a flicker of expression in her eyes.

"It is decided then," she said at last. "We will stay here and do whatever we must to survive the winter. When the wood is gone, we will move to the warmer place in the canyon wall. My son's wife says there is enough food there. It won't be necessary to supply it further. We will have to return to the farm every day to care for the animals anyway. We can leave our food supply in the root cellar, where we know it is safe, and draw on it as we need it. I will go to the cliff dwelling tomorrow to see what it's like. My uncle's assurance is enough for me. I have never questioned his wisdom."

* * *

They were loathe to leave their familiar homes, though, and they were still occupying two of the hogans when the Big Crust came. In order to conserve firewood, Elspeth and her children moved in with Many Beads and Many Tears Woman when the men left. The hogan was crowded, but they lived together peacefully. It was not uncommon for many people to occupy a hogan, and, in a sense, Many Beads's children had simply come home. There was no more family with her than before the marriages of her daughters. Big Woman and Limping Man remained in their own hogan with their three children, not out of selfishness, but because of the mother-in-law taboo. Hosteen Yazzie had been invited to join both households, and he chose to join that of Big Woman, because he felt that his niece needed his support more than the other women, who felt more comfortable with the inevitability of the cliff dwelling.

"I want her to maintain *hozro*," he told Elspeth when she helped him move his ceremonial essentials to his new home. "I pray often, and it may give her enough confidence not to panic when the time comes. I've concealed the new rope ladder in that bundle of blankets. Be careful when you lift it, the wooden steps your husband helped me make are heavy. I don't want my niece to see it. She might object to the idea of using it to descend into the hole. And, what is worse, the wooden steps would make good firewood if she wanted to remain here longer. It is essential that we have the ladder. I would leave it with Many Beads, but I'll need Limping Man to carry it when we leave."

He left most of his herbs and ceremonial implements behind in his hogan, and surveyed them sadly before turning his back to go through the door. His medicine bag was well supplied, but he would probably concoct no more remedies for the winter. Everything would be waiting for him when they descended from the cliff dwelling in the spring. Elspeth empathized with his reluctance to leave his own abode; she had experienced an overwhelming poignance when she left the hogan in which she had lived since her marriage. She knew it must be harder for the old man, whose habits were more firmly set than hers.

"It's only for a little while," she tried to assure him as they trudged through a foot of crusted snow to Big Woman's hogan. "We'll be back in a few months, and our own homes will be waiting as if we'd never left them."

She did not understand the feeling that made her voice sound hollow. Hosteen Yazzie made no reply, to conserve the breath that steamed in labored puffs from his exertion. A sensation of foreboding seized her, and she paused briefly, with more than the weight of his belongings on her shoulders. She had never sensed disaster more strongly, and she attempted to put the dread in perspective. Their plan was a good one; she could see no possibility of its failure. I am just overwrought, she thought. Leaving my home and assisting the old man when he left his must have brought on this terrible sensation. Hoisting her burden more securely, she increased her pace to overtake him.

The sensation diminished in the weeks that followed as she became accustomed to the routine in Many Beads's hogan, but it did not leave completely. The women cooked on the small fire and huddled close to it at night with the children sleeping around them, their feet toward the fire for warmth as was the custom. With their feet warm, the rest of their bodies retained heat, and they slept better with their heads cool. Many Beads began to recount stories of the past to sustain their spirits, but she soon ran out of heroic tales and turned to memories of her eventful life instead; their personal nature was more engrossing to Many Tears Woman and Elspeth than tales of war. The strong, ageing woman bore no malice toward her feckless and unfaithful husbands.

"I married them because I was attracted by their beauty, without realizing other women might easily fall under its spell, as well. Men are stronger than women only in their bodies. If they are handsome, it is difficult for them to remain constant, because the glances of younger, prettier women flatter them. Men do not have as much responsibility as we do, and their minds are open to distractions to fill their time. Only one of my husbands gambled, but they all looked to other women, some no more than girls. You may think the fault was with me, as I did, but subsequent events relieved me of that burden. They all wanted to return to me in the end. One of them as recently as two summers ago, after marrying and fathering a family. Of course," she concluded, with a shrug of her shoulders, "I wouldn't take him back. A man can't live without a woman, but a woman can have a good life without a man. I was content with my life. I told him to look after his family better than he'd cared for mine. As it turns out, it was a wise decision. His family has need of him, now, and I hope he took my advice.''

Elspeth wondered if Many Beads had loved her husbands, but she found it difficult to explore her mother-in-law's emotions toward them, because there was no word for love. "You needed them once," she said cautiously, "but after they failed you, you needed them no more."

"They are still in my heart," Many Beads admitted. "More securely there than if they had returned. Some women aren't wise in their choices of men, and my judgment has been bad. I always fell under the spell of a beautiful face. My husbands are no longer with me; indeed, the father of my children has left us forever. But their faces are marked upon my heart as deeply as the figures the Ancient Ones chiseled into the canyon walls. I am never lonely for them. Those I truly need are here about me, my children and my grandchildren."

The woman's graciousness transcended passion. Elspeth admired her and felt that her character was worthy of emulation, though she doubted that a lesser woman like herself could attain such strength. She was grateful for Many Beads's confidences, which kept the creeping foreboding away for a few hours in the evening.

When it happened again, she was no more surprised than on the previous occasion, because everything seemed natural. She was beside the corral, where she went every morning to assess the condition of the diminishing flock. The familiar sensation that someone was watching her made her turn to look. The figure stood a short distance away, under the contorted branches of a bare peach tree. There was no question in her mind that the woman was Maria. Her features were as clear as though she stood there in life, in spite of the distance. The calm, understanding smile was no longer there, as it had been the first time. Concern and fear had replaced it, and her arm pointed desperately toward the cliff across the Wash. Elspeth did not want to look away from the phantom, but Maria's insistence finally made her gaze in the indicated direction. Only then did she experience fear. Maria was indicating the cliff dwelling. Elspeth recognized it as a warning. She stared at the figure to confirm it, not knowing whether she spoke aloud or just in her mind. Maria nodded forcefully and indicated the ruin again. When she was certain that Elspeth understood, her form faded, leaving only the winter-stricken tree where she had stood. Her appearance had lasted only a few seconds.

Shaken, Elspeth rushed toward Big Woman's hogan to tell Hosteen Yazzie, the only person who would listen to her, that they must leave at once. She would not tell him about Maria; she had not done so in the past. He must take her word that they were in danger, though even she did not know what it was.

She beckoned him from the doorway. Big Woman, occupied with her children, did not notice him leave. Elspeth knew that Limping Man was caring for the horses. Her knees were weak and her heart pounded. She leaned against the doorpost for support. When the old man saw her, a curious sound escaped from his throat.

"You must listen, Uncle," she said breathlessly. "You must *believe* me. We're in terrible danger. We must go to the cliffhouse at once. I don't know how I know this, but I do."

"We should have gone sooner," he said, studying her. "I believe you. I'll send the boy for Limping Man and deal with the woman here. Do you think you're able to get to Many Beads's place?"

She nodded, trying to resume normal breathing. "Have Limping Man bring the ladder. Without it, we're lost."

Despite Big Woman's protestations, the entire family made its way across the crusted Wash and ascended the slope to the ruined walls in the cliff, their moccasins leaving no tracks on the hard snow. The women had snatched up blankets and a few necessities, and only Big Woman complained as they lumbered across the hard snow and slipped on ice in their progress.

Many Beads prodded her daughter forward like an animal, her impatience with the bulky, frightened woman thinly masked. Sky scampered ahead of them like a young goat, impatient to see the place that had been forbidden until now. Maria's son, taken from his accustomed warmth, objected to the cold, and Many Tears Woman comforted him in her arms. Elspeth stayed behind with the Hosteen. Even with a walking staff, he had a difficult time getting a foothold on the icy slope. Limping Man walked beside them with the heavy bundle containing the ladder. His arms were strong, and his awkward gait did not hamper him as he picked his way up to the cliff.

"Who said we're in danger?" Big Woman panted. "Is this a

trick to get me to this place? There was no rider. Did anyone hear a rider? What was that?''

Several loud reports echoed and reverberated through the canyon and everyone stared in the direction of the sound, which came from the direction of the canyon entrance. Thunder was uncommon at this time of year, and when it came, it was a heavy, continuous rumble, which did not punctuate itself into separate bursts.

''A rock slide?'' Many Beads suggested, with a frown. ''An avalanche?''

Only Limping Man knew the significance of the sound, and he urged the family forward with sudden authority. ''We must gain cover. Move quickly, we're almost there,'' he said.

They reached the walls of the cliff dwelling before there was another burst of rifle fire.

Chapter 19

They did not light a fire in the kiva. The women wrapped the children in sheepskins and held them close for warmth in the darkness. The scant light from the ventilation shafts was blocked by the watchful faces of the two men and Elspeth. The Hosteen instructed everyone to remain silent, and, whether out of fear of the strange place or the certainty that their lives were in danger, they complied. Big Woman resorted to nursing her baby to keep him quiet.

Limping Man estimated that the shots had not been far away, but no force had revealed itself after several hours. Unable to remain in such a cramped position, Hosteen Yazzie abandoned his station, and a ray of light penetrated the interior. Elspeth moved from the crude shaft which Valerio had chiseled through the rock and took the old man's place, closer to Limping Man. She had a better view of the canyon floor from the wider opening.

"What's keeping them?" she whispered.

"I don't know," he said. "I've never heard gunfire in the canyon before. It seemed near, but it may have come from miles away."

"As far as the entrance to the canyon?" she asked, with trepidation. "They'd have to get beyond our lookouts there."

Valerio was there. The intrusion into their rock fortress took on an entirely different meaning in her mind. If the force had

271

gotten this far, it must have overcome the warriors defending the entrance.

She turned from the opening to look for Sky, and her eyes had to adjust to the darkness. They had pulled the stone across the opening after they descended, and it was as black as night inside. Many Tears Woman held the baby and Sky huddled close to her, as if he understood the danger. Big Woman, who had given them difficulty when she was forced to descend the ladder, exclaiming that she would not go beneath the earth while she was still alive, had settled down with her children around her. Many Beads sat upright, her attention focused on those watching through the shafts. The tension in her body made it clear that she recognized their position. Elspeth indicated the opening that she had abandoned, but Many Beads shook her head slightly, indicating that she preferred not to witness what was coming.

Limping Man drew in his breath, and Elspeth pressed her face against the shaft again. The unit of cavalry that had come in to view rode slowly, their horses' hooves penetrating the crusted snow. The riders surveyed the walls around them with their rifles at the ready. They looked directly at the cliff dwelling, and Elspeth withdrew her face from the opening, though even a few inches from it, she could observe them clearly. Satisfied that there was no sign of life in the ruin, the soldiers diverted their attention to the recently vacated hogans. They halted to confer briefly, an officer indicating several points in Many Beads's farm: the dwellings, the orchard, and the corral in which the half-starved sheep were milling. The officer was not Carson, and Elspeth noted that no Ute were in evidence.

Before she could communicate her observation to Limping Man, the soldiers filed out in three directions and struck the farm with a ferocity that left her speechless. While one group leveled the hogans, another set fire to the peach trees, which burned quickly, their smoke ascending with a shower of sparks into the cold air. Limping Man tensed, and Elspeth put a restraining hand on his arm, increasing its pressure to warn him that if he revealed himself it would jeopardize them all. A baby whimpered, startling her, until she realized that the soldiers were too intent on their destruction to hear, any more than she could hear the bleat of the sheep as they were slaughtered. She closed her eyes tightly to fight the grief and anger that rose in her over the depredation. If she had had a rifle at that moment, it would have been difficult to heed her warning to Limping Man.

"The horses," he said, "they've bolted!"

Panicked by the fire, the horses had broken free and were galloping away from the burning settlement, deeper into the canyon. The soldiers, occupied with leveling the farm, did not pursue them.

The family remained concealed in the kiva for several days, eating what little food they had brought with them sparingly. They did not dare move the stone that sealed them in until they were certain the soldiers had left the canyon. The mounted troops had moved further into Tsegi after destroying their farm, probably intent upon accomplishing the same devastation there.

Elspeth stirred herself out of her depression to care for her son and the Hosteen. She was concerned about the old man, who seemed to have given up after he viewed the work of the army. He sat huddled against the wall, staring blankly when he might have brought some consolation to the family. She wrapped him in sheepskins and remained by his side with Sky held closely against her. Until the troops passed this way again to leave by the Chinle exit, the family would be forced to remain as quietly as possible in this dark hole. Enforcing silence was not a problem, now. Everyone knew what had happened below and had seen it with their own eyes from the shafts. Despair was almost palpable in the darkness.

Elspeth slept fitfully, awoke at the slightest noise. When she could not sleep, she forced herself to consider what had happened. She could no longer ignore Big Woman's complaint that no rider had come to warn them. What happened when the soldiers entered the canyon? Why had no rider been sent? There may have been other shots they had not heard, a battle at the mouth of the canyon; in which case, their warriors had been overcome. She felt cold inside, but it was not the chill of conviction that they had all died. If Valerio were dead, she would know it. They were so close there would have been a tearing sensation if the connection between them had been severed.

He is alive, she told herself, he will come if we can wait long enough. There was only a month's supply of food, and they would have to make it last longer. After the soldiers left, they could return to the farm to see if they could salvage anything.

Perhaps the root cellar had escaped the flames; the slaughtered animals might still be safe to eat in this cold weather. They could light a fire and be more comfortable. When Valerio and Slim Man came, they would be able to hunt, perhaps. It would not be easy, but somehow they must survive here. The kiva was the only shelter they had, now. Even without a fire, it was not too uncomfortable. The warmth of their bodies fought off the chill. The most serious thing they had to fight was their growing depression. They must not give up hope. She would try, somehow, to counteract the effect of their losses. Many Beads was strong; she would help her. And she must make Hosteen Yazzie come around. He could keep their spirits high better than anyone.

She bent to listen to his breathing, which sounded so distant that it might not sustain itself, though she did not detect any congestion in his lungs. He was suffering from more than the exertion of coming up here. He had seen the Navajo Way, his Beauty Way, demolished and burned to ashes. He had no desire to live without it.

When the soldiers passed again, they were not alone. A small group of Navajo, mostly women and children, followed them, slowing their progress. Cold and hungry, they had surrendered to keep alive. If the soldiers had anticipated further resistance, they would not have encumbered themselves with so many captives. Limping Man's roan pony, with an old woman on its back, was led by one of the soldiers. Her brother-in-law wept openly at the sight. The other horses, which included Plata, were not in evidence. Apparently, they had eluded their captors and still might find their way home. They had not been shot, because no further gunfire had been heard. Smoke still smoldered from their farm across the Wash.

"What else could those people do?" Many Beads said beside their small fire that night. "They didn't have a good shelter as we have when their hogans were burned. Do you think it will be safe to go to our place in the morning?" she asked Limping Man.

He did not respond at once, and Many Beads had to repeat the question, addressing him for the first time directly as "My daughter's husband." Only then did Elspeth recognize that the mother-in-law taboo had been dispensed with in their time of peril. Limping Man needed a moment to adjust to the new relationship.

"Not in the morning," he said, without looking at Many Beads. "They may have camped for the night not far from here. They'd have to with so many captives. We should let another day pass before we show ourselves."

"We need the wood from the hogans before it burns away," Many Beads said. "We must salvage meat from the sheep, if we can."

"The wood won't burn entirely. It's caked with clay."

"Something's still burning down there. If it isn't wood, what is it?"

"Wool," Limping Man said heavily. "The carcasses of our sheep. Can't you smell it? It's been in my nose all day."

Big Woman, who had not once looked through the openings, bellowed softly, and Many Beads glanced at her with disdain. The sound stopped, but Big Woman could not refrain from weeping against her baby's cradleboard. Many Beads made it clear that she did not have the patience to console her family.

"We've lost everything," she said harshly. "We can sit here and bellow like animals, or we can do something useful. I don't want to hear any more groans of defeat. We have our lives and we have our children. We have what is most important. We need wood and water and food. This place must be cleaned. It stinks already. If we sit here and give up, we'll starve or freeze. Our bodies will get as dry as the mummies of the Anasazi found in other places like this. Our ghosts will inhabit this place forever."

The shocking speech had its effect. Big Woman dried her tears and everyone sat more erect, as if awaiting instructions.

"Will the sheep be safe to eat when we get to them?" Elspeth asked her mother-in-law.

"If there's anything left," she replied. "Cold weather preserves them. That is the kind of suggestion we need. If we don't use our heads they're no better than pumpkins sitting in the field."

Later, after everyone slept, Many Tears Woman reached out her hand to Elspeth, who lay beside her with Sky in her arms, and clung tightly when it was accepted. "Do you think our husbands are alive?" she asked softly. "I've been thinking about it since yesterday. Only your untroubled face has sustained me. I must hear what you really think, sister.''

"They are alive, and they'll join us soon," Elspeth told her. "If anything had happened to Tall Man, I'd feel it. You must sleep, now, so we can go back to search our farm tomorrow.''

Many Tears Woman was silent for so long that Elspeth thought she had fallen asleep and had begun to explore the men's chances again in her own mind.

"How did you know?" Many Tears Woman asked suddenly. "How did you know that we should flee to this place before the soldiers came?''

Elspeth was surprised by the question. She had not realized that anyone besides the Hosteen knew that she had initiated the flight. Perhaps she and Many Tears Woman had grown closer than she realized, bound together by their affection for Maria's baby. She did not try to lie to her. "I will tell you sometime, perhaps," she said in a sleepy voice to avoid further questions, "but not now. Someone cares for us very much. We aren't completely alone.''

The weather became more inclement. Snow fell as they scavenged the desolation of their farm, picking up only bits of wood that had not burned. A torch had been thrown into the root cellar, and nothing was salvageable there: the corn, the meal, and the dried peaches were gone. They would face starvation within a month unless the weather cleared enough for Limping Man to hunt small game. The wind grew stronger and whirled into a blizzard which left deep drifts against the walls of the cliff dwelling. They awoke shivering in the morning, but they had to conserve the wood Elspeth had managed to store behind the walls. A fire was more than a luxury, indulged in only when they could bear the cold no longer. They welcomed a thaw the following week, until the melting snow trickled into the kiva and dampened their bedding, necessitating a fire to dry it. A sudden freeze made the footing outside so treacherous that Big Woman and the smaller children were forced to remain in the kiva. Elspeth wrenched her knee when she went to get food from the storage pit and lay on the damp sheepskins for several days, unable to walk, and worrying about the food, which Many Beads had begun to ration. She was cold and hungry, more miserable than she had ever been, and still Valerio and Slim Man did not come.

"One of them must be injured," Many Beads told her. "Or maybe they are hunting without any more success than Limping Man. They wouldn't want to come here without food for the family. Tall Man knows where we are, and nothing would keep him away for long. He will be here any day, now. How is my uncle today?"

The task of looking after the Hosteen had fallen to Elspeth, because she was trained in medicines. She did not begrudge it, but his ailment was beyond her efforts. The old man had declined steadily since the day the soldiers destroyed their hogans. She managed to get a few sips of corn gruel through his lips several times a day, but he remained completely detached and seemed speechless. If his malady was of the spirit as Elspeth suspected, only another Singer could cure him; he was beyond saying prayers himself.

"He's about the same," she replied cautiously. She did not doubt Many Beads's affection for the old man, but she knew what was really on her mind. If he died here in the kiva, they would lose their only shelter. The place would be unequivocally *chindi*. "He may be a little better. I mixed some healing herbs into his gruel."

She had never lied to Many Beads before. She knew of no herb that would help him, but they had to maintain some peace of mind. The method used to preserve a dwelling in case of a death was to move the dying person to a comfortable place outside, but that was not feasible here. There was no comfortable place. She felt as if she were not fully in control of her thinking processes, because her mind closed immediately on the subject. Valerio was her only hope. He was strong, and he was diplomatic. They would listen to him. As the days went by, she depended upon him to save them from what was developing into a nightmare.

The relentless cold continued, penetrating through whatever they used against it. They finally had to build a fire. When her fingers were supple again, Elspeth suggested that they dress one another's hair. The occupation had always been friendly and soothing. It might make them feel more cheerful, though none of them was concerned with the way she looked. She combed

Big Woman's hair, which was oily and unwashed and smelled of smoke like her own, and she noticed for the first time how much weight the woman had lost on their inadequate diet. The skin hung in a fold beneath her chin, and even her shoulders were narrower. Though they did not chatter happily as they had once done, Big Woman sighed with appreciation beneath her hands. She was a simple, sensual person, and no one had been pleasanter or more open when all her needs had been met. Living in the kiva, under the present hardships, had been harder on her than the others. Elspeth glanced at the other women in the firelight and was shocked to observe the change in them. Their eyes were hollow, the skin stretched tautly over their strong-boned cheeks. She put her hand to her own face, but without a mirror, she could not assess how she looked. Her blanket dress, torn and stiff with perspiration, had felt loose around her body for some time.

Limping Man had gone in search of small game, but he returned empty-handed. He had found the three horses, though, and the sight of them was encouraging, though they were half-starved, their ribs showing in ridges and their pelvic bones prominent. Elspeth made the increasingly difficult climb down from the cliff dwelling to greet Plata.

"Poor old girl," she soothed, with her cheek against the mare's face and her arm over her neck. "You don't understand this sort of life, do you? Couldn't you find any fodder at all?"

"They will die," Limping Man said brusquely, visibly upset by the condition of the horses. "My roan was fortunate to be taken. Something must be looking over us for me to find them when I did. We must make a decision very soon. I can't speak to the other women about it, but you must understand. If we are to travel such a great distance, we'll need the horses, and they won't last very long here."

No one had expressed the thought aloud before, though everyone must have considered surrendering at Fort Defiance. Still clinging to her hope for Valerio, she did not reply. She knew he would come if they could wait a little longer.

The wood ran out, and it began to snow again. The children cried softly in their sleep, and Elspeth awakened, clutching at her sheepskin for warmth. She heard a voice in the darkness, though she was certain everyone else was asleep, huddled together to keep warm. A thin chant penetrated her consciousness and she moved quickly to Hosteen Yazzie's side. He had detached himself from the others and huddled against the wall, singing softly enough not to wake the sleepers. She bundled her own sheepskin around him, and as she leaned over she felt his breath against her hair. He was staring at the ceiling, though it was invisible in the total blackness of the kiva at night. A hand like a dry branch touched her face.

"Corn Girl? You have come," the old man whispered, disoriented enough to confuse her with his chant. "Carry me outside so I can see the stars."

"It's too cold," Elspeth said against his ear. "I can't take you up the ladder, Uncle. Go back to sleep. I'll stay with you to keep you warm."

"You won't have to stay long. You'll take care of them, won't you? They must do what I was too proud to do, my niece. I could never leave Dineyah. It is the only place I've ever known or wanted to be. But they are young. They must survive. The children must survive or the People will be lost. Take them to that place where there is food and warmth. You understand. From the first time I saw you, I knew you saw what others do not."

He seemed to know who she was, though he often referred to her as Corn Girl, as he had at their first meeting. She knew he was dying, had roused himself to speak these words, but she remained silent. She could not leave until Valerio came.

"He lives. You will see him again," the old man rasped. "What I say is true, Corn Girl. You must think of the others now. Corn Girl, I feel the *hozro*. Everything is in harmony again. It has come back to me . . ."

When his whispered words stopped, the silence was so intense that she could hear the blood beat behind her ears. She touched his face gently and held her fingers over his eyelids for several minutes to close them. She felt a curious peace as she folded his hands over his chest. There was no question about what they must do, now; his last breath decided that. She sat beside him until dawn cast its pale light through the shafts. Then, she woke Limping Man to tell him that the family must be ready to leave at first light.

"The Hosteen is leaving us," she explained. "I'll remain with him awhile. Be sure they take their warm things with them and pack whatever food is left in storage. I will join you by the time you get the horses.''

Hosteen Yazzie could not be buried without the dignity he deserved. She needed time to prepare his body in a respectful manner and sew it warmly into the tattered blanket that covered him to the chin. And it was important that the family did not know they had spent the night in company with a corpse, for who would say prayers for them now?

A steady wind moaned across the plain, though patches of red earth revealed themselves in the slushy snow; the temperature was several degrees higher here than in the icy canyon. Many Beads and Big Woman rode on two of the horses; they would have been incapable of the long trek otherwise. The older children rode with them from time to time, but they still had the resilience to walk. Elspeth had insisted that Many Tears Woman ride with the baby and Sky while she trudged along beside Limping Man. He should have been able to ride as well, because of his uneven gait, but the horses belonged to the women, and he was too proud to ride a mount that was not his own. Elspeth wrapped herself in her blanket to break the cold, but there was nothing she could do about her wet moccasins, which made sucking sounds in the half-melted snow and clung so tightly to her feet that she could not feel them after a while. She exchanged places with Many Tears Woman for a few hours, riding with the baby in front of her and Sky grasping her from behind, but once wetness had set into her shoes, she felt cold all over.

The fort was almost thirty miles from the canyon; it would take several days to reach it, and the land had been picked bare by those who had preceded them. Limping Man bent down occasionally to pick up any twig that had been missed, and Oldest Boy and Small Girl made short forays away from the slow-plodding horses to assist him. They tried to camp at night in places where there was some shelter from the wind and a little forage for the horses. They nursed their scant fire with quick-burning brush and slept fitfully, with their feet close to it, until it died. Under the present conditions, that was a mistake, because their moccasins shrank as they dried and felt a size too small the first morning, and the following night, they froze. Big Woman cut hers off and wrapped strips of her blanket around her feet, but the others could not spare any part of their blankets.

On the third day, they were joined by another family, ragged and starving, and they shared the last of their food with the old woman and her daughters, who had been scavenging the plain for over a week while they attempted to find the fort.

"My daughters' husbands were killed when the soldiers came," the toothless old woman whined in a thin voice. "They were shot on sight just as The Rope Thrower threatened, and we were afraid to come out of hiding for fear we would be shot, too. Now, it doesn't matter . . ."

Elspeth glanced at Limping Man, who listened in silence. She had forgotten about the threat until now. This was the first actual report of deaths that had been reported to them, and her chest constricted when she thought of Valerio despite the Hosteen's assurances. The old man may have had second sight, or he may have been trying to persuade her to make the family surrender. She began to lose heart that night, and by morning she felt too ill to think about anything clearly. Limping Man noticed her complete silence after they set out on the last day of their journey, cold and hungry, slowed down by the old woman's frail daughters. Many Beads had taken the baby and Sky up with her, so the old woman could ride Many Tears Woman's mount, Plata.

"Don't be afraid for me," he said. "I had already decided to leave you before we reach the fort. I would be no good to anyone shot. I have not told my wife yet. You will have to look after her."

Elspeth felt a twinge of guilt. She was so feverish that she had not considered what might happen to Limping Man after her thoughts went to Valerio. "What will you do?" she rasped, hardly recognizing her own voice.

"I can catch small game to live." He had not been very successful at that in the canyon. "I'll make my way toward the Holy Mountain in the west. I can't believe the soldiers went that far, not in winter. I'll wait until you come back, and meet you in the canyon then."

Elspeth's mind was not very clear, but it sounded like an implausible plan. Still, it was better than being shot by the soldiers, she supposed, uncertain whether she would make it all the way to the fort, herself.

The fire was warm, but she was shivering. She hardly knew where she was, though she vaguely recalled reaching Fort Defiance and the soldiers taking the horses away. A cough racked her chest painfully, and she turned toward the fire, unable to keep her eyes from closing. How long had she been here?

"What do we do with it?" Many Beads asked, trying to rouse Elspeth by shaking her arm. "They gave us this white powder. Should we drink it in water?"

Elspeth dragged herself up on one elbow to look at the bag of flour. "No. Cook it like cornmeal . . . make flat bread with it," she said groggily. "Where's Sky?"

"Right there beside you," Many Beads said, with a frown, placing her hand on Elspeth's forehead. "You're very sick. Why didn't you tell us you were so sick, my daughter?"

"Where's Plata?"

"They took the horses," her mother-in-law complained. "We won't see them again, I'll bet. They took them into a wooden shelter and they gave them some hay."

"Trust the cavalry," Elspeth said in English. "Nothing's too good for a horse . . ."

"What? You're raving! Your sickness of heart has spread to your body. One follows the other. Where is your medicine bag?"

She could not remember. The conversation of some passing soldiers caught her attention. They were speaking English, and she had been thinking in her own language a short time ago.

"General Carleton said not more than a thousand. We've already processed two thousand and they're still coming in. We're hard-pressed to feed them."

"We'll have to send more on to Fort Wingate. Let them take care of the problem. The general's reservation isn't going to hold them. I've never seen so many damned Indians. Some of them will have to start walking to Wingate tomorrow."

Fear stirred in Elspeth's heart, followed by intense hatred, and she was seized by a fit of coughing. Many Beads pressed a tin cup into her hands with concern.

"I mixed the coughing herb in some water," she said gently. "It might help you. You're very hot, but your medicine for that is gone."

Concerned by what she had just heard, Elspeth ignored the medicine. Her family was in no condition to walk all the way to Fort Wingate, and she was sure there were others worse off than they were. Many Beads lifted the cup to her lips and made her take a few sips.

"Come closer to the fire, my daughter. You can warm yourself and think restoring thoughts. I had no idea you were so ill."

Her voice was full of concern. She put her arm around her to draw her closer to the open fire, and Elspeth's blanket fell to her shoulders. Before Many Beads could replace it, they heard a loud exclamation.

"My God! A white woman!"

"It sure as hell is, and she's pretty sick. We better get her inside."

She seemed to be surrounded by blue-trousered legs. Many Tears Woman cried out, but her voice was lost in the scuffle that followed. Elspeth fought the soldiers with what little strength she had, hampered by Sky clinging to her blanket and Many Tears Woman holding on to her. Big Woman bellowed nearby as Elspeth was wrenched from her mother and dragged away from her family.

"Don't let them take me away!" she cried in Navajo. "I belong with you . . ."

"You're very sick, my daughter," Many Beads called after her. "They will look after you."

"The baby. My baby!" The distance between them was widening, and she held Sky's hand in a death grip, but Maria's child, the baby she had raised as her own, remained behind.

"Many Tears Woman will care for him," her mother-in-law's fading voice said. "Do not despair. You must live for Tall Man's Son . . ."

Part 3

Chapter 20

"She must have been with them for some time. Her boy's about four, I'd say. I've never heard of the Navajo stealing an American woman, but you never know what they might do. I wonder who she is?"

The words were familiar, but they made little sense to Elspeth, where she lay on a cot in the infirmary. Her struggle had sapped what strength she had; the loss of her family had left her mind even more confused. Disconnected thoughts in Navajo and Spanish drifted through her mind, but she could not fasten on anything. She had a physical sensation of still clinging to Sky's hand, but she was not certain he was there beside her.

"She's burning up with fever. If she makes it, she'll have quite a story to tell. She's young. Probably in her early twenties. Her moccasins were frozen to her feet. The corpsman had to cut them off."

"Well, the doctor's on his way. We'll see. I've never seen a case like this personally, but I suspect life won't be easy for her in our society if she lives. Ah, there you are, Doctor. We don't know of any white woman who's been stolen in the Territory, but there's one here in a bad way."

A warm, strong hand was placed over hers, and Elspeth smiled slightly, believing it to be Valerio, until the man's voice dispelled the illusion. She could not focus her eyes; the room seemed to moving around her.

"She has pneumonia, probably in both lungs. I'll have to get

287

her out of the filthy rags she's wearing. If you gentlemen don't mind?''

"Of course not. We're leaving. There's a child, too—an Indian boy, Doctor. You'd better have a look at him, too. He's a little bobcat, won't let anyone near him."

"Later. I have a dying woman on my hands. Incidentally, sir, she wasn't kidnapped by the Navajo. She went with them of her own accord, so you can't hold that against them, too. I'm leaving for Fort Wingate in a couple of days. I'll need an ambulance wagon for the woman and the boy. The facilities are better there."

"You *know* her?"

"Yes, I know her. She's been missing for five years. I'd appreciate it if you'd take care of the ambulance wagon. I know they aren't easy to come by."

She drifted in and out of consciousness in the jolting wagon, but she sensed Sky's nearness and the presence of the soft-spoken man. She called for Valerio several times, alternating between his Spanish name and *Dine nééz,* but she knew the man with her was not Valerio. Valerio was dead. The old man tricked her on his deathbed; she would never see him again.

"I don't know if you can hear me, Elspeth. I've done the only thing I could. I hope you don't hate me for it later." The gentle hands clasped hers tightly. "It won't be easy for you, but you couldn't have survived what those poor devils are going through. You have a fine, handsome son. He didn't take to me at first. I think it was the uniform. I finally got him to eat, though, and he can live in my quarters at Fort Wingate. You must try to take some broth. Lift your head a bit. The heat will ease the congestion in your lungs. Can't lift your head? I'll do it for you. You must live, my dear. You must live for all of us. You must think of your son."

Her head cleared briefly after she was transferred from the wagon to a more comfortable bed. She was conscious of the foreign odor of antiseptic and realized she was in a hospital of some sort. She fell asleep on the warm pillow, secure in the knowledge that the Kind Man was nearby. She was awakened later by the sound of men's voices in the distance.

"I didn't expect you to get here so soon," Kind Man was

saying. "You must have been right there at Fort Marcy. She's very ill. She's sleeping, so please don't wake her."

She tried to focus her eyes on the door as it opened. A man in uniform approached her bed, but it wasn't Kind Man she realized with a jolt. "No!" she screamed. *"Nooo . . ."*

Perspiration poured down her face. Her whole body felt wet as she scrambled weakly toward the pillow to protect herself from Captain Morrison. She hoped it was part of her delirium. She did not want to believe he was actually standing there. Kind Man intervened immediately. He wiped her face and attempted to calm her.

"The fever's broken, thank God," he said. "I don't know why she screamed at the sight of you, Captain. It might have been the uniform. I had the same problem with her son. If you'll step outside, I'll make her comfortable. She's on her way back to us now."

"She hasn't forgotten English, at least," the captain said, "unless that *No* was some damned Indian word."

She took stock of her surroundings that evening, the small, clean ward painted white and containing several other beds, which were unoccupied. The snow was still falling soundlessly outside the windows. Everything seemed unreal in the silence: the white cotton screen beside her bed; the white table and oil lamp beside it; and, most of all, the white nightgown she was wearing, probably donated by one of the military wives. She had finally recognized Dr. Cabot when the fever broke; he explained that they were at Fort Wingate. After seeing the captain, she had been afraid that it was Fort Marcy in Santa Fe. She had been ill for over a week, and she did not know where her family was, except that her mother-in-law and her sisters were out there in the cold with the children.

She had been unable to speak to Dr. Cabot at first; the words were there, and she understood him, but her English was halting. She had not spoken it for years. But, when he entered in the evening, it had suddenly come back to her, as though some connection between her brain and tongue, which had almost atrophied, had been restored.

"I don't want to see Captain Morrison," she said. "I never want to see him again."

"Then you shan't," he assured her. "Not for the time being at least. You must get your strength back."

He was the only person she trusted, the only person besides Sky that she wanted to see. He had already told her that she could see Sky the following day. He had looked after her son during her illness, and it was difficult not to call him Kind Man in Navajo instead of addressing him by his real name. She still had questions to ask, and she was not sure she would like the answers.

"The Dineh?" she asked. He fell silent for a moment, with a troubled expression on his face.

"They're on their way to a reservation," he said at last. "There's nothing we can do about it. Nothing anyone can do. It's two hundred miles away. It's called Bosque Redondo."

"I want to be with my family," she said. "My Dineh family. My baby is with them. If Valerio's alive, he will look for me there."

"You have another child?" he asked, observing her closely. "Your baby is with the Navajo?"

"Yes. He isn't actually mine, but I've cared for him since he was born. I feel that he's my own."

"I'll be stationed at Bosque Redondo," he said seriously. "I've requested duty there. I'll look for your family and write to you about them."

"Please take me with you," she begged, with tears in her eyes, but he shook his head.

"You and Sky will be better off with your sister, my dear. General Carleton's scheme about the reservation has already gone wrong. He thought there were no more than a thousand Navajo. Over six thousand are already there, with more coming in every day. I don't know how they're feeding them. The conditions must be terrible. It's no place for you, Elspeth."

"I want to be with them. I belong with them. Don't you understand?"

"Yes," he nodded, impressed by her determination, "but I simply can't allow it. Nor could I implement it. The army knows about you, now. Don't you want to see Thea and her children?"

"Yes," she said faintly, "but I don't want to stay with them. As soon as I'm better, I'll go to find Many Beads and the others if I have to walk all the way."

"Just as they're doing," he muttered. "There wasn't enough

transport for so many. Most of them are walking. Only the very old and the very young are in wagons. At least your baby is warm. Even without the war, there wouldn't have been transport for so many people. The whole thing's insane.''

She closed her eyes against the image of her family still walking in the snow. The children were probably riding in the wagons, but what about Many Beads and her sisters? And, if the war was still on, it might be even more dangerous to walk such a distance. Dr. Cabot assured her that there was no longer any fighting in New Mexico; the war was confined to the Southern states, where the battles were intense.

''It's been going on since 1862,'' he said, ''and it's now 1864. Captain Morrison reenlisted. I enlisted, too. Physicians were needed.''

The dates surprised her. She had not thought in terms of years for so long; the years had been broken into seasons, and she had not kept track of them.

''Tell me about yourself,'' he said suddenly. ''We nearly went out of our minds looking for you. We had no idea what sort of man you might have taken up with. Who he might be. Now, I assume that it was the Navajo slave girl's brother all along.''

''I loved him. From the first time I saw him I couldn't think of anything else. I didn't want anyone to worry about me. I tried to explain that to Thea in my letter.''

''If they'd known where you were, they'd have worried much more,'' he said, with a faint smile. ''Even I'd have been more concerned if I'd known you were living the life of an Indian. It can't have been easy for a white girl.''

''Easier than you might imagine,'' she said. ''I've never known such peace and closeness.''

''That brings up another point. What made you scream when the captain entered the infirmary? It wasn't the uniform, was it?''

She did not reply. She had learned to keep her own counsel and to preserve a stoic exterior. All that had happened so long ago, and there was no chance of its occurring again. Thea must never know about what happened between the captain and herself on the night she left.

''Very well,'' he said. ''I won't ask again. It troubled me when you were living there alone with him. You probably didn't know it, but I was mustering up the courage to ask you to marry me."

"No," she said, with a sigh, "I didn't know. You were my good friend then, just as you are now. I'm sorry. You needn't concern yourself about my being in his house anymore. I'm a different person, Doctor. I won't be there very long." She regarded him seriously. "Thinking is more complicated when I speak English. There are more levels to explore. When I was so sick that I didn't know who you were, I thought of you as Kind Man in my mind." She repeated the name in Navajo. "You've been so kind to Sky and me. The captain is Sly Coyote, and I may call him that to his face."

His gray eyes widened with humor. "I think you might. I'd like to be there to see his reaction."

"I won't speak to him unless I have to. That would be more diplomatic until I leave for the reservation."

The captain had brought his wagon to transport Elspeth back to his farm, and Thea had thoughtfully sent some of her clothing along. The warm gray dress no longer fit her. It was too tight across the bosom and otherwise seemed to hang on her, as if it belonged to someone else. She could not stand for more than a few moments, and she found it difficult to brush her hair. She stared at the image in the mirror, which might have been someone else's. Her aquamarine eyes were startling in her dark face, which looked strange to her because it did not have Dineh features. She had almost forgotten how she looked. When Dr. Cabot came to get her for the trip, her hair was still spread over her shoulders, the brush in her hand. Realizing how weak she was, he offered to help her.

"The chongo knot is most attractive. I've often wondered how it was done."

"It really takes two people," she replied, recalling the happy, leisurely moments with her sisters and blinking back the tears that rose in her eyes. "I can do it alone, though, if you'll find something to tie it with. It may take awhile, though."

He watched as she folded the smooth hair over her hand into the vertical chignon and held it as tightly as she could with her shaking hands. He handed her the strip of cotton bandage she had agreed upon, and she wound it carefully around the middle section of the hair bow to secure it in place. She wiped the dew of perspiration from her face after completing the simple task. She had never felt so weak.

"It isn't tight enough," she murmured. "It won't stay this way long."

"I think it's quite beautiful," he said. "You mustn't be discouraged by your weakness, my dear. You must rest for a long time, but you will be completely well. Come along now. I'll carry you to the wagon. The captain's waiting."

Sky was already in the back of the alien wagon, trying bravely not to cry. Elspeth held him tightly and stroked his black hair. "We aren't being taken by the enemy," she assured him. "We're going to see my sister. You have another mother you've never met. And a brother and sister, too."

She settled him comfortably before she felt she had to lie down on the cot that had been prepared for her with extra army blankets contributed by Dr. Cabot. She had never imagined that she would be lying in this wagon as helplessly as Thea during their trip five years ago, and she fought the depression that the loss of health brought.

"She's very weak," Dr. Cabot told the captain just outside. "She'll need rest and good nourishment. The sooner she's with your wife, the better."

"She hasn't even spoken to me," the captain retorted. "She might be looking at a stranger. She's always been ungrateful. Doesn't she realize the position she's putting us in by accepting her and her Indian brat into our home?"

"I think we'd better have a word alone," Dr. Cabot said, and she heard their footsteps crunching away in the snow.

She realized suddenly that she would be an embarrassment to the captain, though she knew that Thea would take another view. Thea would be happy to see her and her son. At any rate, it would only be for a short time. She would recover quickly, so she and Sky could make their way to her other family. Dr. Cabot put his head through the canvas flap to say good-bye.

"I'll send you word as soon as possible," he said. "I'm to look for Many Beads of the Rocks-Beside-the-Water Clan. I've written it down phonetically in Navajo. I'll have to learn the language quickly in order to communicate with my patients there."

Elspeth smiled faintly from her cot. "It isn't something you learn quickly. I'll be waiting for your letter. Thank you, Kind Man.''

When she was not sleeping, she amused Sky by teaching him a few words in English. Because of Dr. Cabot's kindness, he had adapted fairly well at the fort, but she knew Captain Morrison's household would not be as congenial. She wanted Sky to be able to speak to his cousins a little while he was there. His quick mind picked up the conventional greetings easily, and they progressed to some of the items in the wagon during the long trip. Most of the time, he sat looking out at the unfamiliar land they were passing through. There was little snow on the ground here, and Elspeth wondered if the People had progressed far enough south to be out of it altogether on their long walk to Bosque Redondo.

Her thoughts kept turning back to the shots they had heard in the canyon, wondering if there had been earlier rifle fire farther away that they had not heard. There must have been, she decided. The men guarding the entrance to the canyon surely stood their ground. Valerio and Slim Man had undoubtedly been wounded, at least. But, if he had been only wounded, he would have dragged himself back to her in the ensuing weeks. Still, in her heart, she could not believe that he was dead. She had to believe that he was alive and that he would see his family on the reservation. Kind Man, Dr. Stephen Cabot, would soon be there. He would tell her if Valerio arrived. She had to make certain she received his letters. As ill as she had been, she was determined to stand up to Captain Morrison. She had lived freely, with her head held high for so long that there was no possibility of being submissive again.

Thea embraced her tearfully outside of her adobe house and led her inside to sit by the kitchen fire. The room was familiar, but like a distant memory. The curtains were no longer the ones Elspeth had made, and there were toys on the floor. They interested Sky, but he made no move to touch them. He seemed uneasy in his new surroundings and Elspeth pulled him into her lap.

"I'm so relieved to see you," Thea said as she placed teacups on the table. "Your little boy is lovely. What is his name?"

Elspeth nearly gave his Navajo name, but she corrected herself before she spoke. "Sky. He'll answer to his English name." She asked him in Navajo to greet her sister as they had practiced in the wagon, and he stared at Thea for a moment with his wide dark eyes.

"Please to meet Aunt Thea," he finally murmured.

Thea laughed with surprise. "You've taught him English!"

"Only a few words. Where are your children? Dr. Cabot said you have two, a boy and a girl."

"They're sleeping. Little Robert's about Sky's age, and Elizabeth's—"

The captain had entered quietly. "We seem to have remembered our mother tongue," he said shortly. "She didn't speak a word during our trip."

Her sister scurried to the stove to put food into serving dishes. "Robert was expanding the house when the war came," she said, glancing at him. "The room I made up for you is small, but I've tried to make it comfortable."

They were silent at the table except for Elspeth's occasional quiet instructions to Sky. He had learned to handle a spoon at the fort, but she had to cut his meat for him. Thea drank tea while the others ate, nervously clicking her cup against her saucer. Elspeth realized that her sister was afraid to speak in the captain's presence. She recalled what it was like in this house when she also had to defer to him. The idea of Many Beads and her daughters submitting to such domestic tyranny, instead of treating men as equals, was ludicrous.

When the uncomfortable meal was over, Thea left to put hot bricks in the beds to warm the sheets. Apparently she did not have even one servant. Elspeth carried the dishes to the sink unsteadily and braced herself against it for a moment, her legs as weak as water. Sky followed her example, jumping from his chair to carry the gravy bowl as carefully as he handled everything. The captain lighted his pipe and observed them thoughtfully.

"Your presence here is awkward," he said at last. "I don't want anyone to know about you. It'd cause a scandal. There won't be any callers, and you're not to leave the house. Thea has her orders."

Elspeth knew his viewpoint from what she had overheard before they left the fort and did not think the remark required an answer. She began to wash the dishes.

Her silence must have felt threatening, and he added emphatically, "You won't tell my wife about what happened the night you left. I suspect you've recalled it now that you've regained your power of speech."

She turned to face him and held his gaze without expression. "I'd never hurt Thea," she said evenly. "I'm surprised you'd even mention it."

He flushed deeply and set his jaw. "You aren't the girl who left here, I can see that. You even look like an Indian with that hairdo. What do the bucks do in those camps, pass the squaws around? I've heard enough about them to know you aren't in a position to make moral judgments."

"If one of my brothers-in-law had touched me, he'd have been sent away in disgrace," she said, without betraying any emotion. "Incest is the ultimate taboo, and in-laws are the same as brothers and sisters. Whatever you've heard from your Indian-hating friends, the morality of my husband's people is stronger than your own."

"We won't have to see much of each other," he said, "but Thea has her instructions. I'm reporting back to Fort Marcy in the morning. There's still a war on, but I suppose you don't know anything about that."

Sky adapted quickly and brought his own culture to his new environment, taking on the tasks of carrying wood and water for the women, chores that Thea had considered beyond her son, Robert, until now. She appreciated the little boy's help; the Mexican handyman had been dismissed before the captain went to get Elspeth. Elspeth did what she could to help with the housework, but the effects of her illness were stubborn and it was not as much as she would have liked. Thea discouraged her from exerting herself too much.

"You looked after me when I needed you," she said. "Now, I have a chance to return the favor. Isn't it wonderful the way the children have taken to one another? When they're playing, you'd never know they didn't have a common language."

"They're more adaptable than adults," Elspeth observed as she watched them. "Little Robert knows that Sky's an Indian boy and he seems to admire it. And Sky's learned some English from him. It's a pity we can't all be as open as children."

Thea was interested to learn the details of Elspeth's life among the Navajo. Out of her husband's presence, she was as as intellectually curious as she had always been. When she learned that the women made many decisions and owned most of the family's wealth, she was delighted. "They sound more civilized than we are," she commented. "Sometimes, it's terrible to be at the mercy of a man. As you've probably noticed, things have not gone very well here. The farm wasn't doing well even before the Confederates came and burned our fields. He's spoken of moving farther west. I won't have any say in the matter if he makes that decision, though we'd be even more remote from civilization then."

"You don't see the de la Cruz family anymore," Elspeth said. It was a statement, because in the two weeks she had been here no one from the hacienda had called, even to bring supplies as in the past, and she did not think the captain's order about visitors would have restrained Don Diego's sisters from assisting Thea. "Their fields weren't burned when the Texans came."

"How did you know that? No, the hacienda wasn't touched, because Don Diego welcomed the Southerners. He was a slave owner, too, for what are the peons if not slaves? His sisters were good enough to take me in during the fighting, when Robert wasn't here. Now, the de la Cruzes are in disgrace for fraternizing with the Texans. I can't see them anymore. We have few friends. Most of them from army families at Fort Marcy. Elspeth?" she said, with a sudden frown. "How did you know that the de la Cruz fields weren't burned? Did Dr. Cabot tell you?"

Elspeth smiled. "No, Valerio told me. He heard about the fighting and came to see what was happening. He knew I'd be concerned about you."

"What a remarkable man. He took quite a chance. Are you ready to speak about him now?"

Elspeth recounted how she had left with Valerio, and told her sister something about her life with him, but when she came to those final days in the canyon, she could not maintain her composure. "I feel in my heart that he is alive. If he weren't, I'd know it. I feel that I'll see him again, Thea."

"Your instinct has never been wrong," Thea consoled her. "He'll know where to find you, Elspeth."

Elspeth shook her head. "He'll think I'm at the reservation

with his family. Dr. Cabot's going to look for them there. He told me in his letter that he's been unable to do so, but I'm certain he will, eventually. Over eight thousand Navajo are interned there now, and they only expected a thousand. It must be terrible. I'm so worried about my family. Perhaps the women and children Carson allowed his Ute to take as slaves are more fortunate than those at Bosque Redondo.''

"It's just as well that you became ill when you did," Thea said. "You've been through too much already."

"Why doesn't the captain bring a newspaper when he comes home on the weekends?" Elspeth asked. "I'm sure there must be something about what's happening at the reservation in the papers. I don't even know where it is, except that it's in the south. May I look at the maps?"

They searched the house, but they could not find the maps, a circumstance Thea could not understand. "They've always been here. I've had to dust around them. He must have them at the fort, though I can't imagine why. The army has better maps right there."

Spring came early in April, and with it Elspeth felt a resurgence of life, for she was accustomed to marking the year by the seasons, and the end of winter was always like a rebirth. The mountains turned green and the gama grass in the fallow field grew like the first shoots of sprouting corn. She was well enough to go into the field with Sky to pull the weeds for planting later, but her mind was not on the work. Her thoughts were occupied by her resolve. Though Dr. Cabot had not found her family, she began to plan her escape into captivity on the reservation. She did not tell Thea, because her sister would have stopped her, perhaps even told the captain out of concern for her. With the young sun dappling her face and the blue sky clear above her, she pulled weeds strenuously, her strength returning more each day. She began to put aside a small cache of food for the journey, extra biscuits from the table, a small supply of flour and sugar, which would not short her sister's pantry. She commandeered a battered skillet from its place behind the pots and pans in the cupboard. With a modest supply of oil, she and Sky could live on fried bread, dry biscuits, and water as they made their way south. She stored her supplies under her bed, wrapped in a shawl. They would have to leave soon, before the gentle sun gained its full strength and burned the flowering earth back into a desert. She wanted to discuss her feelings with Thea, in the hope she would understand. She did not want to leave as she had done before. She loved Thea. The six weeks she had spent with her had restored her ties with her. She did not want to cause anxiety and pain by her departure, but she could not risk being stopped, either. In her mind, the reservation and Valerio had become one, for she knew he would look for her there.

She wrote a letter to Thea the night before she planned to leave, repeating her previous pattern. She had decided to depart the following morning at dawn, not without guilt, but consumed by her need to be where Valerio could find her. She did not reveal her plans to Sky when they went to bed, confident that he would follow her in complete silence, no matter what she did. She rationalized that at least the captain would come home more often, instead of visiting his family on occasional weekends, once she was gone. He had put in his last appearance two weeks before, when he took his children into Santa Fe for the Easter festivities. He had not stopped for dinner when he returned with the weary little boy and girl; after ignoring herself and Sky while he had a cup of coffee, he departed once again for the fort. Elspeth's presence had upset the family's routine too much.

She was too excited to sleep well and kept going over her plan in her mind. When she finally dozed, she heard a child whining during the night, but, reassured by the light from Thea's lamp under the door as she passed, she fell into a heavy slumber. She began to dream, and her dream seemed to be reality, everything else that had transpired the real dream. She was at home in the canyon, happy and at peace with Valerio in the company of her family. She was weaving in front of her hogan with the children around her, and Valerio was shaping silver, his handsome face intent but conscious of his surroundings. He glanced up at her from time to time, and they smiled when their gazes met. In the distance, she could see the ancient cliff dwelling across the Wash, but it held no portent of the future. She caught a motion in her peripheral vision and glanced toward the lacy tamarisk trees. A dark figure was standing there, and she thought of Mexican Woman, whom she had seen in the stand of trees when she had first arrived with Valerio. A breeze stirred the delicate leaves ominously; the children and Valerio were no longer with her, but the figure remained. Elspeth realized that it was not Mexican

Woman but Maria in the same form, wraithlike but with some solidity, as she had appeared twice before. She did not speak, but Elspeth somehow heard her message: "You must not leave in the morning. If you do, the child will perish."

She opened her eyes with a start. A figure was standing over her with a lamp.

"Little Robert's burning up with fever," Thea said. "He's awfully ill, Elspeth."

Still trying to separate her dream from reality, Elspeth rose without remembering that she had been sleeping fully clothed in anticipation of the dawn. Thea was so upset she did not notice. Elspeth followed her to the children's room and placed her palm on little Robert's forehead. His temperature was very high and he was tossing his head on his pillow. She thought at once of the herbs she no longer had.

"Mama used to wash us with alcohol to bring our temperatures down," Thea murmured. "All I have is witch hazel."

"Fetch it, Thea. I'm sure she used it, too." She tried not to think of the dream, though it had indicated that the boy would die only if she did not remain to help. "You mustn't worry. Children run higher temperatures."

"He must have caught something when he went to town," Thea said as she returned with the bottle. "He was exhausted when Robert brought him home. Men haven't the faintest idea how a child should be cared for . . ."

The glands in the child's neck were swollen, and he developed a hacking cough before morning. "We must get a doctor," Elspeth said, still troubled by Maria's warning. "I've never treated anything like this."

"There isn't one. Not one we can trust. Not since Dr. Cabot left. Old Dr. Ibanez is worked off his feet, and you must remember how badly he treated me. There's the surgeon at the fort, but—"

"We must get a message to him."

"How? There's no one to send, and I can't ride that far, Elspeth."

"I can," Elspeth said, with decision. "This is an emergency."

"No!" Thea protested. "I'm sorry, but Robert's orders were firm and, I'm not even supposed to go to the hacienda. Her face brightened suddenly. "I shall, though. Doña Isabella will send a servant to tell Robert. He'll dispatch the surgeon if he can."

Elspeth gave Sky and little Elizabeth their breakfast and settled them on the kitchen floor with toys before she returned to sit beside the boy in Thea's absence. His eyes were sensitive to light and she drew the drapes. It was the first time she had to reflect on her dream. Maria had never appeared in a dream before. She wondered if the dream had been prompted only by the sounds of Thea treating her child. She had heard him whine earlier. She wanted to believe this reasonable explanation, but experience cautioned her to heed Maria's warnings. The message had been that if *she* left, the child would perish. Was there something she could do that the doctor could not?

Thea returned, windblown from her ride, and Elspeth prepared a meal, which they ate in shifts so that one of them was at the bedside all the time. After a few hours, she became restless, though it had hardly been enough time for the surgeon to get here.

"I'm going out to look for some herbs," she told Thea from the doorway of the sickroom. "I won't be gone long. I'll take Sky and Elizabeth with me."

"Do you think you should? The doctor will be here soon," Thea said. "I never let the children out of my sight when we're outdoors. There are snakes . . ."

"Sky and I know what to avoid," Elspeth said cheerfully, though she felt burdened with responsibility for her nephew. "I'll look after Elizabeth. If the doctor arrives before I return, so much the better, but this is something I have to do."

She and the children searched the area around the farm, but none of the plants she found would alleviate little Robert's temperature. She could not find *c'il disŏhí*, "furry plant," which was used for fever. She returned to the house within two hours. The doctor's buggy or horse should have been there by then, but there was no sign of him. Thea was washing her son with witch hazel again.

"Why doesn't he come?" she asked, with tears in her eyes. "He should have been here an hour ago. Isn't a child as important to the army as their soldiers?"

"I'm sure he is," Elspeth reassured her. "I've found something for his cough, Thea. I'll have to prepare it in the kitchen. I won't be long.''

An elusive thought tugged at her mind as she stood at the stove stirring the infusion with the children playing at her feet. The doctor had had more than enough time to get there. She was not fond of the army, but barring an emergency illness at the fort, she was certain they would have dispatched him for the child of one of their officers. She stopped stirring for a moment when she realized what was in the back of her mind. No one is supposed to see me or Sky. But, surely the captain would not withhold medical attention for his own son for that reason? No, she dismissed the thought, not even he would do that. She cooled the cough medicine and carried it into the sick boy's room.

"It smells dreadful," Thea commented as Elspeth forced a spoonful into the child's mouth. "Are you sure it's all right? It's made of boiled weeds, after all.''

"It's safe and it's effective. Don't worry about the medicine, my dear. The old man who taught me how to use herbs knew what he was doing. Thea, I'm going to have to take the horse for a while. Can you manage with all the children? I need another 'weed,' which would bring his fever down, and I may have to ride into the hills to find it.''

Chapter 21

By the time the captain rode in late in the evening, the child's symptoms had subsided, except for a runny nose. The *c'il disŏhí* Elspeth had found brought down his fever so completely that his father could not understand Thea's frantic request for the surgeon.

"It's only a simple childhood complaint," he said. "Can't you even cope with that? The army surgeon, indeed. I gave definite orders about your going to the hacienda, Thea. You disobeyed me."

"He *was* very ill," Thea attempted to defend herself. "If Elspeth hadn't found the herb she did, anything might have happened."

He picked up on that quickly enough. "I take it she didn't find her damned Indian herb in the house, where she belonged. Where did she go?"

"I rode into the foothills," Elspeth spoke up. "No one saw me. We needed something to bring little Robert's temperature down. The doctor didn't seem to be forthcoming."

"Don't leave the house again," he said, without looking at her. "I've taken a few days leave, so I'll be here if anything's needed. You've both behaved like chickens with their heads cut off about this. Panic doesn't solve anything."

The child came out in red spots the following day, confirming the suspicion of a childhood illness. He had the measles. Chil-

303

dren often died of pneumonia or brain fever as complications of the disease, and Elspeth and Thea continued their careful nursing. Elspeth noticed that the captain did not give any attention to his fields during his stay, and it troubled her. The rhythms of planting and harvesting were so ingrained in her that she could not understand his apathy.

"If you're going to plant," she remarked to Thea, "it should be done soon. What crops have you been raising?"

"None," Thea said, brushing her hair from her face with exhaustion. "The fields haven't been planted since the Texans burned them. I have only my kitchen garden. The war has changed everything, Elspeth."

Elspeth did not understand how it could affect the crops; if anything, there should be more demand for them. "It's a shame to waste perfectly good land. What have you been living on, Thea? A paying crop was supposed to sustain us when the captain was prospecting."

Thea shrugged vaguely. "His army pay, I suppose. We haven't discussed it. The peons just didn't return after the Texans left."

"What about your maid?" Elspeth asked, assuming she had been sent away just before her arrival.

"There was only one. You remember Concepcion? She was with us when the children were babies, but she hasn't been here for years. Robert dismissed her, and she went back to the hacienda."

"You've been doing all the work yourself?"

Thea smiled. "I'm well, now. There's no reason why I shouldn't. Robert lays in the wood. Carrying water was the only heavy work until Sky came. The fact is," she added, with less confidence, "I'm not very organized. You must have noticed. Robert's right when he says I don't cope well."

"If someone tells you something often enough, you begin to believe it." In her mind, Elspeth thought of it as murder by slow attrition. "I suppose you'd have had servants if he'd struck gold. Has he given up on that or has it just been interrupted by the war?"

"He never mentions it," Thea said. "I hope he's given it up. It isn't my place to say anything, but the war won't last forever, and he'll have to make a living when it's over. We'll really be dependent on the crops then, and I couldn't manage everything.

It's all I can do to take care of the house and children. Without another woman around, I don't even know how to care for a sick child.''

"Nonsense. Your confidence has eroded, that's all. You've done very well with little Robert.''

Elspeth did not want to leave Thea in such a situation; indeed, she could not do so until the child was completely well. The captain had been strangely silent during his stay, as if he were contemplating something. On the evening before he left, he put some papers on the table before her.

"Just sign these where I've marked X," he said. "They should have had your signature earlier.''

She picked them up to read them first to assure herself that they contained nothing regarding her Navajo marriage or Sky's legal position.

"Don't be silly,'' he told her. "Sign them. You've signed papers before without reading every word.''

"I want to read them,'' she repeated mildly, leaning forward to do so. The captain cursed and snatched the papers away, folded them, and put them back into his pocket.

"They aren't a peace treaty, for God's sake,'' he dismissed them. "You've grown very cautious living among those people. I'm surprised you can still read after five years of seeing nothing in print.'' He was angry and covering it with sarcasm. Elspeth did not know what to make of it. "This war's gone on too long,'' he grumbled, turning his back. "I'm thoroughly sick of it.''

Little Robert recovered quickly, but by the time he left his room, the other two children were coughing. Sky, who had never been ill before, sat on Elspeth's lap with his head against her shoulder, wracked by the cough. Both of the children had been dosed with Elspeth's herbs at the first sign of contracting the illness; Elizabeth's symptoms subsided, but Sky did not respond as well to the treatment.

"At least we know what it is, now,'' Thea said, "and how to treat them. Measles are so contagious. I remember that I had them first and you caught them from me. It was the same with chicken pox. Sky looks miserable, and he's so quiet. I think we should put him to bed right away to be on the safe side. The poor little fellow.''

Sky's illness was so severe that it was difficult to assure themselves that it was the same one from which Robert had just recovered. Only when his temperature became dangerously high did the Navajo medicine seem to have any effect. It was as if herbs and potions were not enough, what he really needed was a healing chant, a Sing to restore *hozro*. When the spots finally appeared, they covered his entire body, even the soles of his feet, and Elspeth's growing alarm would have turned into panic if she had less control of herself. She prepared a larger dose of *c'il disŏhí* than Hosteen Yazzie had recommended, and watched her son carefully to be sure that the herb did not have an ill effect on him.

"I can't understand it," Thea told her as she bathed her nephew in the last of the witch hazel. "Why is *he* so sick? He's much worse than the other children. I really think we should have a doctor this time."

Their eyes met over the tossing child. They both recognized the impossibility of seeking medical help for the Indian child. The captain had not sent the surgeon for his own child because of the boy's presence here. There was not a chance in the world he would reverse his caution, now. The dim room was hot; both women were perspiring.

"Bring a bucket of cold water," Elspeth instructed suddenly. "I'm going to wrap him in a wet sheet."

"He'll get pneumonia," Thea cautioned. "Children often have pneumonia after measles . . ."

"We'll deal with that if it happens. He won't live to have pneumonia if we don't get his temperature down."

Perhaps he would have contracted pneumonia anyway, in the light of what they learned later, but when Elspeth heard the rales in his chest the following day, she blamed herself. And, though she found it almost impossible to leave his bedside, she knew she must search for one of the four plants used as remedies for lung congestion. She had not seen them on her previous ride; she might have to go farther. She was not even sure that they grew at this elevation. Thea's eyes expressed that she did not want to be left alone caring for Sky; the responsibility was too heavy.

"I know how sick he is," Elspeth told her. "He has no hope at all if I don't try to help him. If I don't find one of the plants, he'll surely leave us. . . ."

The avoidance of the word *die* sounded strange in English; it was the Navajo way of speaking. She recalled her dream of Maria and what her friend had told her. Maria had said the same thing. And she had not been speaking of little Robert, who fell ill the same night; she had warned her about Sky. If Elspeth had left as she planned the following morning, her son would have fallen ill on their way to the reservation. He would surely have perished. By remaining here, he had a chance to survive; that had been implicit in the warning.

"He's going to be all right, Thea," she said more calmly. "You've nothing to worry about. I will find what we need."

She rode for several hours, dismounting often when she thought she saw one of the plants, not going into the hills but remaining at a lower elevation where they were more likely to grow. After examining the growth to the south of Thea's farm, she turned and rode north, just below the foothills of the Sangre de Cristos. Recognizing the risk of the proximity of the hacienda, she dismounted and walked cautiously toward the overgrown road and gully behind it, stopping to gather several medicinal herbs on the way. She would never be without her medicine bag again, she determined, as her gaze swept the wildflowers and weeds around her for those she desperately needed. The wall of the hacienda was less than a quarter of a mile away, and she could discern the usual activity there, when she caught sight of the *at-a-coh*, its "big leaves" almost covered by the other foliage. She gathered the leaves recklessly—and lost further caution when she saw some *ja-abani ilt-a-i* nearby. Two of the lung remedies were more than she had expected.

She was stuffing the "resembling a bat" leaves into her bag, collecting as much as she could, when she heard the warning shot and the shouted command in Spanish. She froze like a rabbit for a second, crouching in the overgrowth; then, scrambling on her hands and knees, she began to make her way toward the spot where she had left her horse. The embarrassment to the captain if she was detained did not concern her; the questions the de la Cruz family would ask, did. And the delay might be fatal to her son. She crawled through brambles and sharp grass without heeding the damage to her face and arms and made a dash into the open for her horse. The guards emerged from the overgrowth just as she mounted and, still too far away to see her clearly, they fired another shot. If it, too, was meant as a warning, their aim was not good. Elspeth felt the burning impact in her shoulder as she galloped away to avoid them.

She was resting on Sky's bed in their room when the captain returned unexpectedly the next morning. Sky had responded to the strong infusion of hot herbs. He was still coughing, but his chest was clearer already, and he had spoken to her several times. The pain in her shoulder had subsided, though she felt weak from the shock of the wound. Thea had dressed it while they were boiling the herbs; and, against her nature, she was prompted into pouring a jigger of whiskey into the raw shoulder muscle, the only treatment they knew. Fortunately, no bones had been broken; the bullet had entered and exited through soft tissue. Elspeth recalled Hosteen Yazzie's treatment of Shouting Man, but she knew her sister could not be coerced into cauterizing her shoulder with a hot poker. They both decided that she must remain in her room when the captain came home on the weekend if the scratches on her face had not gone away by then. Now, he had returned early, and she remained out of sight, for the marks were clearly visible.

She heard his raised voice, but could not make out his words because of the location of the new room. He was obviously disturbed about something. She wondered if the guards had recognized her. Thea opposed what the captain was saying enough to raise her voice, which eventually grew silent under the power of his. Then, and Elspeth could make nothing of this, she heard the wagon rattle past, moving in the direction of Santa Fe. She rose carefully and stood still for a moment to gain her equilibrium. The door opened before she reached it.

"He's lost his mind," Thea said in a loud whisper so she would not disturb Sky. "We've been ordered to pack our things . . . *everything*!"

They closed the door of the sickroom and moved to the kitchen, where Elspeth sank into one of the straight-backed chairs, resenting her physical helplessness. "I don't understand," she said. "Where does he want to go?"

"He wouldn't say, Elspeth." There was a touch of asperity in Thea's voice. "Don Diego reported a Navajo in the area, without mentioning that it was only a woman. Perhaps his guards lied to him. In any case, Robert's determined that we should leave. He's gone into town for supplies."

Did he think the Navajo was Valerio? Elspeth wondered. Was he afraid? But that did not make sense. If Valerio came for her, he would be rid of her forever; he would not have to worry about what people thought. She said as much to Thea, who interpreted it differently.

"You don't understand, Elspeth. You're a white woman, and in his eyes a white woman shouldn't be with Indians, no matter who she is. He may be thinking of that, but he didn't say so. He said he was fed up with everything here and we were leaving on Sunday. I told him that Sky had been very ill and Elizabeth wasn't really able to travel, but he wouldn't listen to me."

"I'll tell him it was I whom the guards saw," Elspeth said, closing her eyes against the little sparkling lights in her vision, "no other Navajo. There probably isn't one between here and the reservation."

"That wouldn't serve," Thea said quietly, pouring her a cup of tea. "It might make things worse. He wasn't here to see how sick Sky was and wouldn't understand your going so near the hacienda. You weren't supposed to leave at all. Oh! Speaking of the reservation. He left a letter on the table for you."

Elspeth opened Dr. Cabot's long-awaited letter without her usual enthusiasm, again deploring the loss of strength that caused floaters before her eyes. "You better read it to me," she said at last, and handed the single page to Thea.

"He's given his address as Fort Sumner," Thea observed. "You don't supposed he's been transferred? No . . . here it is." She read:

"You'll observe that the reservation's called Fort Sumner, now, though it isn't a fort or anything else that I can see. A barracks has been constructed for the military personnel on guard duty here; however, there's really no one to guard at the present time. Nearly all of the Navajo are ill, or are recovering from an illness. Many have died, Elspeth. I regret telling you this, but I feel I must be straightforward with you.

"These people have never been exposed to the white man's illnesses, something none of us considered at the onset. We've had smallpox and measles and people have died in large numbers. I've been worked off my feet. I tried to find your family before the outbreak, but there are over eight thousand people here now; it was like looking for a needle in a haystack. I will begin searching again as soon as possible. I speak a little of the language now, and that should help. I must implore you not to bring your son here, no matter how much you want to come. He would have the same lack of immunity as the others; you might lose him. Remain where you are. I shall keep you informed as often as possible.

"Please remain well, my dear, and be patient. I will write again as soon as possible. I must rest for a few hours, now.

Yours,
Stephen"

"How awful," Thea said as she handed the letter back to Elspeth. "That's why Sky's so sick! You weren't actually considering taking him to that place?"

Elspeth did not reply. She was deeply affected by the letter, concerned about her Navajo family. The warning in her dream took on another meaning. Had Maria meant that Elspeth was not to go to the reservation at all? Maria had said nothing of her own son. Was it possible that she did not know what was happening on Bosque Redondo? Or, that it was so far away, she had lost the connection with her family there?

For the time being, Elspeth had no control of her own destiny. She knew that somehow she would rejoin the People; but, for the present, she must not consider moving Sky when he was not well enough to travel. She was in no position to oppose the move.

The loom was finally left behind. The heavily laden wagon left the farm before dawn on Sunday morning, and after Sky was settled on the cot in the back, Elspeth stared in the direction of the mountains, awaiting the rising sun. Just as she was attuned to the seasons, the four directions had become deeply embedded in her consciousness. The door of her hogan had been in the east, where it caught the first dawn, and its interior had been divided into north and south for ceremonial purposes. Though the captain refused to tell them where he was taking them, and she might not know where she was, she would at least be able to tell the direction in which they were moving. As compasses were fixed on the north to aid travelers, her instinct was leveled on the east, and the wagon did not deviate in its course over several days. They were heading west, toward the section of the Territory known as Arizona, which extended all the way to California. Surely, he was not taking them to California, where gold still drew prospectors in droves? It would be much more difficult to get back from there.

She had not had the opportunity to post a letter to Stephen before they left, but she wrote one as the wagon lurched along over country so dry that it was dotted only with saltbush. The captain would have to stop at Fort Wingate; she would mail it from there. But the days passed in which they should have reached the fort, and it was nowhere in sight. The captain had neatly avoided it, probably by taking a wagon route slightly to the south, and this caused Elspeth some consternation. Fort Wingate was her only point of reference. The days were growing warmer, the sun stronger every morning, and they were still surrounded by the bleak desert land. Thea's children began to complain, cooped up without any activity during the day, and not allowed to run far from the fire in the evening when they stopped to camp. Only Sky raised no objections. He was recovering, but still too weak to take much interest in his surroundings.

Thea sat in front of the wagon next to her husband for most of the day, but when the afternoon heat became too intense, she crawled into the back with the others. Elspeth's arm was healing, and she exercised it regularly. She was soon able to lift Elizabeth into her lap when she told the children stories. They had been on the road for eight days, which she had carefully marked off on a paper in Thea's writing box, along with any possible landmarks she observed.

"It's so hot," Thea said as she drank from the warm canteen beside Sky's cot. "He seems better, don't you think? He isn't sleeping so much."

"He spoke to me this morning. He wanted to know if we were going back to Dineyah. Since I don't know where we're going, I told him we were going somewhere near there. Has the captain given any indication of his plans? Our supplies won't last forever."

"He's very closemouthed," Thea confessed. Then, she lowered her voice so the children could not hear. "He hasn't worn his uniform since we left. Have you noticed?"

"Yes, but it would only be covered with dust if he did,"

Elspeth said, sensing that Thea's statement indicated something more. "Something's troubling you."

Thea was reluctant to speak at first. When she did so, she said in a rush, "We're still at war, Elspeth! I don't know much about such things, but I know he's supposed to wear his uniform in wartime. And I don't think an officer can just resign, either."

Suddenly Elspeth understood the reason for his avoidance of Fort Wingate, but she did not want to add to her sister's concern. "He isn't the sort of man who'd desert, Thea. You mustn't worry about that. How do people get to California? On the maps I remember, it was a great distance away and across a desert."

"That isn't the way to go. There's a place called Ehrenburg on the Colorado River where you can take a small boat down the river to meet a sailing ship. I spoke to some of the ladies at Fort Marcy who were returning to San Francisco when the Texans entered the war."

"You *sail* to California?" Elspeth asked, with surprise, discouraged about the possibility of returning if they went there.

"Yes. There are several new forts across the area called Arizona for protection and rest. I can't remember their names; they've been built since the war began." Thea's voice fell. "I hope we aren't going that far."

Elspeth stared out of the arched back of the wagon, her hopes dashed by the prospect. Then something caught her eye in the landscape, but it did not register for a moment. The captain had been veering to the southwest since early that morning. An unexpected cry from her son focused her attention upon what she had been watching without seeing.

"Dineyah. Dineyah!" he said hoarsely, rising on one arm on his cot.

The red sandstone forms took shape before her eyes along with the stretch of red soil, and she put her head out of the wagon to observe the landscape. She could not believe what she saw. Though there were no clear landmarks, she felt they were near their Navajo homeland. Surely, there could not be another area so similar. The captain coaxed the horses as the wagon lurched with difficulty along a narrow track of road, rocking precariously as it hugged the side of the cliff wall. There was a sheer drop on the other side of them. They were descending into a small canyon, which had none of the soaring splendor of Tsegi, but Elspeth felt more cheerful than she had in months. Unwittingly, he seemed to have brought them to a place somewhere south of their homeland.

"What's Sky saying?" Thea asked as she struggled to reach the rear of the wagon. "He's very excited. My goodness," she said, with wonder, when she observed the landscape from Elspeth's side. "Everything's changed. I've never seen anything like it. Even the earth is red." Then, she grasped Elspeth's arm and clung to it. "Elspeth! There's nothing but space on one side of us!"

She did not unclasp her fingers until they reached the valley below. Green and full of wildflowers, it was surrounded on three sides by pine-covered hills, which no longer reminded Elspeth of Tsegi. They had left the red sandstone formations in the heights above; they could not be seen from here. The captain drew up the team and climbed down, covered with red dust and perspiration from the dangerous descent. The horses were foaming from their exertion and would have to rest for a while. The land was fertile, with none of the barrenness of Tsegi, and it bore no resemblance to the place where she had left her heart. In deference to Sky's excitement, she carried him down from the wagon and sat on a fallen tree trunk with him in her lap as the other children spilled from the wagon after Thea. She heard the welcome sound of water from beyond a stand of cottonwood trees and wondered if the captain would finally allow them to bathe. Sky nestled his head against her and she sensed his disappointment.

"We will return to Dineyah some day," she comforted him in Navajo. "When the People come back, we will go to meet them, never fear. You'll see it again."

"What do you think of it?" the captain asked them. "The soil looks good and the river will provide water. We've reached our new home."

"Here?" Thea asked. "Right here? It's beautiful country," she added, "but there isn't even a house."

"We'll build one," he said heartily. "We'll clear this land and farm it like the first settlers did on the plains. You'll be a real pioneer before you know it."

His children were wildly excited over the prospect, but Thea seemed dazed by the wilderness around her. Elspeth observed the scene with growing impatience. The captain had been a bad farmer even when he had peons; it was not likely he would change here.

"Is there a town nearby?" Thea asked. "There must be some place where we can get supplies and—"

"I'll take care of that," the captain replied shortly. "We can pitch our army tent on that flat space over there. We'll have to live in it until I get the cabin built."

"Where are we?" Elspeth asked, unable to remain silent any longer. "You might have made preparations for your family before your brought them here."

"Never mind where we are," he said. "Other people have pioneered and so shall we. I should think you'd feel at home in the wilderness. You're more Indian than white, now."

"Are there Indians here?" Thea asked quickly. "It's so remote, there must be Indians, maybe hostile ones."

He did not reply. He went to the wagon to unload the army tent, and Elspeth considered which tribes might inhabit the area. She did not think they had come far enough to encounter southern Apaches, but she felt vaguely uneasy. Until she knew where they were, she did not know what to expect.

The captain shot several diamondback rattlers during the first few days of clearing. He apparently mistook Sky's cries in Navajo for admiration, because he smiled at him for the first time. Thea and her children stayed inside the tent because of the snakes, and Elspeth joined her for a cup of coffee. Sky's health was improving in the open air; he had been helping with the brush as much as he could.

"Aren't you afraid to leave him out there?" Thea asked. "What has he been yelling when Robert shoots a snake?"

"Sky will be fine," Elspeth assured her, and laughed for the first time in months. "He's calling your husband names. The People don't kill snakes. Though Snake is evil, they avoid him or walk around him. Actually, I'm grateful for the gun here. We seem to have settled in a nest of them."

"I can't sleep in this tent another night," Thea declared, with tears in her eyes, "even with a rope around me to keep them away. Does that really work?"

"I don't know," Elspeth said, with a shrug; then, an idea occurred to her. "We can make a safer dwelling. If the captain chooses to remain in the tent, he can."

When the captain went to fell some trees for the cabin, she

and Sky cleared a space near where he intended to build the cabin. They gathered the thickest fallen branches to construct the base of the hogan while Thea and her children hovered close by to watch.

"Since you've come out of the tent," Elspeth said, wiping the perspiration from her face with a dirty hand, "you might as well help. First, we'll collect every bucket and basin we can find in the wagon."

She knew they would encounter fewer snakes if they walked in a group, talking and laughing, for snakes were basically timid creatures. They followed her to the river with the metal containers thinking they were going for water. Elspeth knelt to test the red mud on the bank and found it as satisfactory as that used for the hogans in Tsegi.

"I suppose you know what you're doing," Thea ventured doubtfully as she joined her in the mud with her skirt held above her knees. "You want us to carry *mud* in the containers instead of water?"

"Yes," Elspeth said, with a smile. "Will you help me scoop it up?"

The Morrison children had never had such a good time, and they had never been so dirty. By late afternoon, the walls of the hogan had been filled securely with the clay; the roof would have to wait until the following morning. The door faced east, toward the rising sun, in the ritual manner, but it also faced away from the cabin the captain was going to build.

"Ho-gan," little Robert repeated after Sky, and ran to his mother to share the new word. "Sky says it's a *ho-gan*. It must be like the house he lived in."

He had to share his knowledge with his father a short time later when he returned, sweating and dirty and exclaimed, "What the hell is *that*?"

Elspeth helped him build the cabin; Thea and the children, already skilled at caulking with clay, assisted in the final stages. It was not much of a house, or as symmetrical as it should have been, though Elspeth thought it would probably stand. Only after the field was cleared and ready for planting did she recognize how little he had planned in advance.

"We'll have to plant soon," she commented, not speaking

directly to her brother-in-law. His silence confirmed her suspicions. He had not brought any seed.

"I'll be away for a few days," he said at last. "I'll leave a rifle and some shells. I imagine your sister knows how to shoot," he told Thea. "With bow and arrow, at least," he added dryly.

"Leave extra ammunition," Elspeth said. "We'll both learn to shoot."

She calculated the time he would be away and the direction in which he rode and determined that there must be a settlement of some sort within a day's ride. She stored the information for future use.

"Has he given any indication where we are?" she asked Thea as they continued pulling weeds, with the rifle close at hand.

"No," her sister replied quietly. "Please forgive his behavior, Elspeth. He thinks you might run away. That's why we couldn't find the maps."

"You mustn't apologize for him, Thea. This isn't your doing. I was going to run away when we were in Santa Fe. He was right about that. But I wouldn't do it now and leave you here alone. He said he came here because of me; I feel responsible for the whole thing."

"He'd have come anyway," Thea said, recoiling from the sting of a plant and lifting her finger to her lips. "He brought his prospecting equipment with him. He forgot to bring seed, though. If this is going to be a farm, I suspect we'll be doing the farming."

"I'm accustomed to it, but I don't know how he can do this to you." She pulled a stubborn weed furiously and nearly fell backward when it came out with a clod of earth around its roots. "One of the reasons we held out in the canyon was because we feared the women and children would be taken as slaves."

Thea was silent for a moment, and when she spoke, her voice was thoughtful. "You aren't a slave, Elspeth. When you want to leave, I'll help you. I married him for 'better or for worse.' I didn't know it would be this bad, but I'm bound to him."

"Many Beads would have put his things outside of the hogan a long time ago," Elspeth muttered, but when Thea asked her to repeat what she had said, she demurred. She should not interfere. Thea had to make her own decisions. The People might not remain together for "better of for worse," but their customs did not apply here.

"I've been thinking," Thea said tentatively. "Robert was restless and impatient even before you came back. After the break with Don Diego, the 'lost mine' exploration ended, and he was too busy to prospect when he was in the army. It's a compulsion, you know, like drinking or gambling. I've seen some of the solitary old men who drifted into Santa Fe with their gold pans and picks tied to their mules . . ."

"Yes?"

"He's been careless in his planning. You remember how carefully he planned our trip from the East. I think," she paused, almost unable to articulate the words, "I think he deserted so he can prospect again. He used you as an excuse to leave Santa Fe. It's a terrible thing to say, I know, but why else would he be hiding here?"

"It's neither here nor there," Elspeth replied, "as far as we're concerned. We have the children to consider. We must make things as pleasant as possible for them. Everything will work out, Thea."

Even as she said it, she wondered how it would work out. As long as they did not know where they were, they were completely dependent upon the captain for supplies. She was more resourceful now than she had been when she depended upon him before, though. She knew how to live in the wilderness.

Chapter 22

The captain went into the hills several times during the summer, taking the horses laden with his supplies. Elspeth watched his departures uneasily. Without a horse or a clear destination, they were stranded here. There was no way to get help if it was needed. She confronted him with that possibility before his first excursion, but he had dismissed it as improbable.

"The children can't catch anything from other children here," he told her from his horse. "You have your Indian bag of tricks for minor indispositions. The snakes have been cleared away, and there's no way in hell they can break a leg if they're looked after properly. I'll only be gone a month."

The crops were growing well: corn, beans, and vegetables. The women and Sky had learned to fire the rifle, though its recoil nearly knocked Sky off his feet, and their aim was still uncertain.

Elspeth and her son hiked southward one morning in an attempt to find evidence of the captain's trail when he went for supplies. They were unable to explore very far; she did not want to leave Thea alone too long. Sky, whose line of vision was closer to the earth, and who had been taught to track by Valerio, picked up a stone that had been scarred by an iron horseshoe about a mile and a half from the cabin, near an outcropping of rock.

"He came this far," he told his mother, "but I don't know where he went from here. Maybe he rode up into the rocks."

Before Elspeth could stop him, the little boy scrambled up into the tumbled rocks, ignoring the possibility of snakes. He ignored her when she called out after him, so she began to climb, too. She had not gone far when Sky reappeared and slid down the granite face with ease.

"He didn't ride up here," he reported. He narrowed his eyes in thought, resembling his father so much that Elspeth felt a pang in her heart. "He could not vanish," he concluded reasonably, and his expression brightened slightly. "Maybe he set a false trail. When he goes for supplies, he may ride in a different direction and double back to hide his trail. Maybe he was going west, or north, or east, instead of south."

They made several expeditions to determine the direction of the captain's supply station that summer, but their efforts failed. They discovered a cliff dwelling not far to the north when they followed the river from the cabin. Long deserted, it resembled the ruins in Tsegi. They were excited over the discovery, because again it indicated that they were near the Navajo homeland. Sky was so elated that he ran toward the crumbling sandstone shelf to explore the ruins.

"*Chindi!*" Elspeth warned, without thinking. "You must never go there. The ghosts of the Ancient Ones are in that place, and Hosteen Yazzie is not here to banish them."

He returned reluctantly, and she reinforced the warning with the superstitions of his people as they made their way home. She often told him the myths and stories she knew so they would be clear in his mind when he rejoined the People, but, today, it struck her as good sense to forbid the exploration that children found so attractive. Sky could have a dangerous fall. Sky listened attentively, casting frequent glances over his shoulder in the direction of the cliff-house, which may or may not have been Anasazi. Surely, she thought, the cliff dwellings must be confined to one location; the range of their builders could not have been that great. They might be nearer to Dineyah than she had imagined. She considered stealing one of the captain's horses when he returned and riding as far north as possible. But she rejected the idea at once. Even if she and Sky found their homeland, none of the People would be in that desolation of flattened hogans and slaughtered sheep. The sensible thing to do was find the community that supplied the captain and post a letter to Dr. Cabot.

The captain did not return from his trip for the harvest, and the women and children worked long hours in the fields and late into the night to preserve the food in the jars he had the foresight to provide for them. They perspired over hot kettles of jarred tomatoes, green beans, and squash, but the satisfaction of watching the shelves fill for the winter offset their discomfort. The corn crop was good, and Elspeth hung the ears to dry in the Navajo manner, though she soon realized that they needed an earthen cellar to preserve the corn and the meager crop of potatoes in the cold weather. She selected a raised spot near the hogan and asked the boys to help her dig. When the storage room was as deep as the one at Many Beads's place, they lined it with branches and spread them with clay.

"We'll let it dry in the sun for a few days," she told the children, "then, we'll make a roof for it."

Little Robert and Elizabeth were as delighted as if they had built a playhouse and ran in and out of the space left for the door, until Sky was annoyed by their activity.

"It must dry hard," he told them. "It is not for play. It is to keep food for winter. If there is no food, you will be hungry."

Elspeth gathered the children around her. "If you want to play house, you can play in my hogan. Sky's right. You mustn't disturb the root cellar."

"We'll build our own hogan," little Robert said enthusiastically. "Will you help us, Sky? You know how to do it."

Elspeth and Thea rested on the porch of the cabin, where they could watch the children. With the canning completed and the root cellar nearly ready, they had time for a well-deserved rest. Thea had withstood the gruelling activity very well. The flush on her cheeks was from boiling kettles, Elspeth noted sharply; there had been no sign of the return of her old illness. The only indication of nervousness in their new environment was the rifle she always kept close at hand. They had heard a mountain lion crying during the night.

"What an alarming sound," she said. "Like a woman's crying. I didn't sleep much."

"I've never heard of one attacking anyone. Goodness knows,

they had the opportunity when we were in Tsegi. Children and sheep were milling around everywhere. The People respected the big cats, didn't even kill them for ceremonial purposes, and the cougars seemed to respond in turn.'' She ran her finger along the barrel of the rifle at her sister's side. ''Do we have enough ammunition?''

''Boxes and boxes. Why? Do you think we're going to need it?''

''No,'' Elspeth said quietly. Thea had more confidence in the captain than she had; for all they knew, he might never return. She had considered this possibility before. If anything happened to him when he was prospecting, they would be completely on their own, with neither horses nor the maps. ''It's getting cooler in the evening already. I think we should try to kill a deer. We need the meat. I could make moccasins for the children with the hide.''

''How *could* you, Elspeth? Those lovely, trusting creatures that come down to the river to drink! I thought you said the Navajo didn't kill animals.''

''I said they didn't kill anything they didn't eat. The meat will keep well in the root cellar. You don't have to watch, Thea.''

She kept her misgivings about the captain to herself. He refused to consider the perils of going into the hills alone, not the least of which was the possibility of hostile Indians. Elspeth had not seen any sign of Indians during the summer, but her senses had been sharply honed by living close to the land, and she knew they were not alone in the wilderness. If they were to survive, they must be self-sufficient. The idea of killing a deer was as repellent to her as slaughtering sheep had been, but the children could not continue to walk barefoot in country abounding with snakes and venomous insects. More than the venison, she needed the buckskin for moccasins.

She was determined to shoot carefully so the animal would not suffer. Valerio could accomplish this with bow and arrow, but she was not confident she could do it with a single shot. She had to muster all of her strength when she and Sky waited in the brush by the river the next morning.

They gutted the deer amidst a sweep of hornets attracted by the blood. To prevent being bitten, Elspeth and Sky covered their arms and faces with mud and disposed of the tantalizing viscera by digging a hole, which also accommodated the ant-lered head. No Navajo collected the antlers of the animal he had slain out of necessity and which he propitiated by ritual apology. Elspeth did not know the words, but she asked the deer's for-giveness solemnly in the language of the People, so that Sky would know that this was the way it was done. If she had been with Many Beads and her family, she would have kept the organs as special delicacies, which also bestowed the animal's best qualities on those who ate them, but she did not think Thea would appreciate the heart and liver of an animal she considered cruelly slain. After washing the carcass in the river, she and Sky half carried and half dragged it back to the cabin, where she suspended it from a tree by a rope in order to skin it. She had watched this done before with a stone knife less sharp than the one she now possessed, but she explained the cuts she made to Sky, who was amazed to see the hide come off practically in one piece. Though it was only a fair-sized buck, it was necessary to discard one section of the skin.

"We can't use the part where the bullet went in," she ex-plained. "Usually, this is done only for skins that are used in ceremonials, but your father never kept his arrow mark out of respect for the deer who is giving us meat and moccasins."

The meat had to be aged, but she did not want to leave it suspended from the tree as bait for the mountain lion. She low-ered it to the ground and dragged it into her hogan, her arms aching from the exertion. Certain that what she was doing must be taboo, she hoisted the carcass up to the rafters. They would have fresh meat and jerky after the meat had aged, but she had done all she could for one day. They could build the racks for the venison and cure the buckskin later. Thea's sensibilities were proper enough, she thought as she massaged the muscles in her arms and neck, but one person could not do everything.

Sky ran off to tell his cousins the details of the morning's work, and Elspeth pulled off her bloodstained dress with an effort. She wanted nothing more than to lie down on the in-viting blanket spread over fresh pine needles that was her bed, but she had been disciplined not to nap during the day. With great effort she made her way to the cabin. There were sparkles of light dancing before her eyes when she entered the kitchen.

"You look dreadful, dear," Thea said, assisting her to a chair. "What you need is a nice cup of tea."

The captain returned after the first snow, bearded and disappointed with his ore samples. A frown gathered between his brows as he surveyed the farm, but he unloaded his horses and gave them fodder before he walked heavily into the house.

"We got a deer, Father!" his son greeted him. "What we didn't eat, we dried, and Mama put some up in jars. We built a cellar to store our food. It'll keep all winter there."

"Your father's tired," Thea interjected quickly. "He's hungry. Go wash your hands. Dinner's almost ready, Robert."

They did not embrace; indeed, they hardly looked at each other. The captain took off his heavy jacket and sank down at the table without changing his shirt or washing. Elspeth observed that his beard was longer and less tidy than usual, and his dark eyes had a fanatical gleam. He seemed unaware of how bad he smelled. She tried to dismiss these things as due to the weather and the fact he had been gone so long, but his expression troubled her. She recalled what Thea had said about prospecting being a compulsion. He did not speak until he had cleaned his plate and wiped up the gravy with a thick slice of bread. He belched and leaned back in his chair.

"I feel like I'm on a goddamned reservation," he said. "It looks like an encampment of Indians is living here." Elspeth rose to collect the dishes, and he leveled his attention at her. "What the hell are you doing creeping around in moccasins, for God's sake? You weren't wearing moccasins when I collected you at Fort Wingate."

"They're good protection," she told him mildly. "The children were barefoot; I made us all moccasins. I wasn't wearing them at Fort Wingate, because they'd had to cut them off. They were frozen to my feet. If the Navajo walked all the way to Bosque Redondo, I imagine some of them lost their feet as well. To frostbite."

"If the children need shoes, I'll get them," he grumbled. "They're my responsibility, not yours."

"The crop was very good," Thea said to distract his attention. "There are shelves and shelves of jars in the pantry. Enough to last all winter if we're careful. The potatoes didn't do as well, but we had too much corn, so we dried it. Everything's turned out remarkably well . . ."

"For you, maybe," he muttered, pushing himself away from the table. "I'm dead tired. I'm going to bed."

When he was at home, Elspeth and Sky slept in the hogan, and the scent of cedar burning on the fire made memories crowd in upon her: she was peopled with phantoms. She lived every moment she had spent with Valerio over again in her mind, until their last parting and the sound of shots reverberating in the canyon. She recalled her first sight of him, tall and beautiful in the sunlight, and she tried desperately to retain the hope that he had not vanished forever. She thought so much about him and her Navajo family that she seemed to hear their voices on the wind outside, crying out to her from their exile. She was filled with despair, hopeless and helpless in her present situation. I don't know where I am, she thought, and recalled that Maria had spoken the same words at the hacienda before Valerio had come to free her. I must find out where we are in relation to where the captain goes for supplies. That was the key to everything, though she saw no possibility of joining the People on the reservation in the immediate future. She was needed here too much. She adjusted Sky's blanket and brushed his hair back from his forehead. He was a fine little boy. She sometimes forgot how young he really was. He was not yet six, but his sense of responsibility made him seem older. Sleeping, he became her baby again, and her chest tightened with love for him. Whatever she did, she must think of his welfare before anything else.

As she went about her tasks during the days that followed the captain's return, she was constantly watchful, even calculating the weather to see if it was propitious for him to go for supplies. If the sky was gray and heavy, it meant more snow; he would not leave the farm under such conditions. Though they needed staples like flour and sugar badly, he put off his trip as long as possible.

"The snow's too deep," Sky said as if he were reading her mind one morning when she was studying a break in the clouds. "He could be tracked too easily. He's waiting until there isn't so much snow on the ground."

He waited until shortly before Christmas, when he could delay the trip no longer. Elspeth's hope rose when he put on his heavy clothing and saddled his horse, but it was dashed when he bridled the other horses and took them along. His action served a double purpose. Their supplies were so depleted that he would need the packhorses, and taking them deprived her of the means to follow him in the snow. Some scraps of blue revealed themselves in the sky, and a feeble sun warmed the air slightly. It would probably remain clear during his ride, though it would take longer to reach his destination riding through the deep drifts. She would not be able to follow him very far. The bare trees offered no cover, and she and her son would be clearly visible on the white landscape, but it was an opportunity to see which direction he actually took.

They followed the furrows left by the horses' legs for several hours, breathing painfully from the exertion of trekking through the snow in heavy clothing with shawls wound around their heads and necks. He did not make the diversion of stopping at the stand of rocks as he had in the summer. He was conserving his horses. His trail led directly west, as far as the eye could see. They finally had to give up and rest before they returned to the farm.

"Why are we doing this?" Sky asked at last. "It's more fun to track animals in the snow."

"Yes," she agreed, putting her arm around him, "I know. But if we can find out where he goes, we can get a message to Kind Man. Perhaps we can learn something about our People." He had been away from the family for a year. "You remember Many Beads and your other mothers, don't you? And Oldest Boy and his sisters, and the baby who became your brother?"

"Yes, and my father, too. He went away and didn't come back. My grandmother said he went away forever."

Elspeth did not want to promise him something she was not confident about herself. "Perhaps. We must try to get news of our family, and they are very far away. We can't hope to get news if we don't know where *we* are."

"I can find the place where the captain goes when the snow leaves," he said boldly. "I can track the captain alone. I'm the man who does all the chores, now."

Elspeth smiled and kissed him. "I'm sure you could, but I couldn't allow you to do that. There must be a way. We have until spring to think about it."

"Maybe the braves in the hills would help," Sky suggested.

Elspeth was filled with apprehension. "You've seen braves in the hills?"

"Not since it snowed. But I saw them a few times before then."

"Near the cabin?"

"No," he admitted reluctantly. "Sometimes, when I'm chasing a rabbit, I leave the farm. I know you don't want me to, but—"

"How far did you go? I won't punish you this time. I want to know about the braves and what they were like."

"One day, I went pretty far up the side of the hill. I ran into one of them. He was tall and thin. His hair was not in a hair-bow. He was not Dineh."

"Did he speak?"

"No. He didn't seem to see me, but he did."

"Think carefully. Do you remember how he was dressed?"

"High moccasins," Sky recalled at once; at his height, he would notice that first. "No shirt. Buckskin trousers, naked in back except for a loincloth."

"Was his hair braided or loose?"

"Loose. He wore a headband. You look frightened, Mother."

"No," Elspeth assured him, rising to make the trek back to the cabin. "He was from another tribe, that's all. You said you saw the braves several times?"

"During the harvest. They were just watching."

Elspeth tried to visualize in her mind what they had seen: two women and three children working in the field. No man about. But, she realized with some relief, they also saw my hogan and the storage cellar. And the brave ignored Sky, did not look at him directly. She would not say anything about this, especially to the captain. Panic would be dangerous, any hostile action might prove fatal. She did not know how many Apache were in the hills, but she was certain they outnumbered the adults at the farm. She would build a loom in the spring, though she had no wool to weave. The captain had remarked that the farm looked like a Navajo encampment; she would increase that illusion. Even if they were not in Apache territory, Apache bands were known to wander great distances.

"He answers to George," the captain said when he came back. "He's a mangy old brute, but he may be some use to you. He understands a little English."

He might have been speaking of a dog instead of explaining the old Indian he brought back with him. The newcomer was clad in an amazing array of ragged blankets and cast-off European clothing, his hair so matted and filthy that it was impossible to distinguish a tribal hairstyle. Elspeth studied him. She felt it strange that he had been found alone and abandoned. The People looked after the elderly members of their tribe. If a person was cast out, it was for a good reason, which was almost always witchcraft. Other tribes might not follow the same customs, but the old man was a mystery; he made her uneasy.

Thea led the old man to the fire with her customary kindness and went to look for more appropriate clothing for him. He crouched near the warmth and devoured the bowl of food she had given him, shoving it ravenously into his mouth with his dirty hand. His teeth were broken, but he probably was not as old as Hosteen Yazzie. His small dark eyes, almost hidden by the folds of skin above them, were clear and bright, not covered with the cataracts that beset older Indians. If he really understood English, he did not react to the captain's subsequent remarks.

"Now, there's a noble savage," he said, without looking at Elspeth. "He's probably crawling with lice. You better get him out of here."

"What tribe is he from?" Elspeth asked, watching the old man closely to see if he responded to their words.

"No one seems to know. He isn't Yavapai, but that's probably just as well. They're mean. He came from somewhere in the Southwest, I understand. Served as a handyman until he got a taste for the bottle. Drinking makes him crazy, so keep him away from my supply of alcohol."

"Where will we put him?"

"In the stable with the horses. The hay should keep him warm. He isn't accustomed to first-class lodgings."

"That wouldn't be right," Thea objected as she returned with an armful of old clothing and blankets. "He's an old man, Robert."

"The children's hogan is pretty weatherproof," Elspeth suggested. "We could drape a tarpaulin over it if we leave a space for the smoke hole. It's small, but he can build a fire. He'd be warm and dry there."

"Whatever you like," the captain said, with a shrug. "He's all yours."

George observed the earthen-roofed hogan with suspicion. He had never seen anything like it, and even after Elspeth swept the snow from it and covered it with the tarpaulin, he would not approach it. Only after Sky encouraged him did the old man move to inspect his new home. Sky smiled and took his hand to accompany him inside, and the old man's fears fell away. Whatever his feeling toward the adults, he did not resist the Navajo child. He sat on his haunches and gazed upward at the smoke hole while Sky explained it in English, for he had already discovered that all Indians did not speak Navajo. By evening, a plume of smoke floated above the little hogan, and Elspeth and Sky returned to their own.

She had been a little nervous about the newcomer's proximity to her own sleeping place, but his goodwill toward her son reassured her. She lay awake wondering about the old man. Perhaps some Indians did cast out the old and useless members of their society, though it was a primitive practice. Or, perhaps he had wandered off to serve the white people after he had tasted their alcohol. The captain had provided more information than he had intended. He had found George in a town where someone had told him the little that was known about him. There was nothing to indicate that their new "handyman" was actually disturbed or believed himself to be a witch, though something about him troubled her. She would watch him carefully for a while, though she was not sure what signs a practitioner of witchcraft might reveal.

Part 4

Chapter 23

Sky's first Christmas was unlike those Elspeth remembered in Boston, but she and Thea managed to generate the mood of the season by decorating the tree George cut for them and making small gifts for the children. Their ornaments had been left in Santa Fe, but they strung red berries to garland the tree and placed the children's gifts on the branches. The captain shot several grouse for their dinner, and the feast approximated those to which they were accustomed in a more civilized setting. Elspeth carried a covered plate of hot food to George in his dwelling, after the captain disregarded their arguments about him joining them.

"It was more fun than a ceremonial," Sky assessed it later. "More food and less singing. I told my cousins not to eat the poison berries on the tree."

Elspeth smiled. "How did you like the candy Aunt Thea made?"

"It was good. Sweet like honey, but I wish you'd make corn cakes some time. I can find some honey for you."

"I'll make them next summer," she promised him. "I can only make them when the corn is young."

The summer seemed far away with the farm covered with snow and the time of the Big Crust still before them. At least they did not have sheep to care for during the winter, though they needed a few animals: a cow, perhaps, at least some goats for milk. Tinned milk was all right for cooking, but the children would not drink it.

He tried to make her sign the papers again before he left in the spring. Elspeth was determined not to sign them until she read them, but she let him place them on the table before her. The documents were written in the fine copperplate hand of a law clerk, but the legal firm's name on the letterhead was unfamiliar to her; though it was in Boston, it was not the firm her father had used.

"I didn't ask you to read them," he said, obscuring the letterhead with his hand. "Your signature's needed, that's all. Your sister signs papers all the time."

"Thea's your wife. She doesn't have a choice," Elspeth said equitably. "I won't sign anything unless I read it first. My father's instructions were clear."

He gathered the pages up quickly, before she could look at them again. "As long as I'm caring for your son, you'd do well to remember your place. No signature, no goats. It's as simple as that."

She could not believe what he had said. She glanced at Thea, who also appeared to be in a state of shock. Their gazes met and held, a clear message passing between them, and the captain was dumbfounded by the storm that broke over his head the next moment.

"You will provide milk for the children," Thea told him firmly. "You have no choice about the goats. We aren't indentured servants, or slaves, brought here to work your farm. As far as I'm concerned, the farm is mine, because I've worked it, not you. If you want the children to remain yours, you must provide them with milk."

Elspeth had been prepared to stand up to the captain, but Thea had done it so well that she did not want to ruin the effect of her demand. She stared at her sister with astonishment.

"It isn't that easy," he mumbled. "The goats, I mean. I don't know if I can buy any—"

"Steal them, then," Thea said, with blue fire in her eyes. "The Indians steal animals to provide for their families."

He was so surprised by her outburst that he backed away. "I'll try. I'll get them somehow."

* * *

"You were wonderful, Thea," Elspeth said as soon as they were alone. "I didn't think you had it in you."

"I'm surprised at how well it worked," Thea replied, sinking weakly into a chair. "I suppose it's true that bullies are actually cowards, and Robert is a bully."

"What you need is a nice cup of tea," Elspeth said, mimicking her sister's words after she had shot the deer, and they laughed as she went to prepare it. "What are those papers he wants me to sign?" she asked when she placed the teapot on the table to steep. "He said you've signed them in the past."

"I have no idea what they are," Thea admitted. "He calls it family business, but I don't know about such things. He'd never mentioned anything for you to sign until you came back."

"They're from a lawyer in Boston," Elspeth considered. "Do you suppose it has anything to do with our inheritance from Father?"

"I'm sure it must, though I don't imagine there's much left now. From what Robert's indicated, most of it went on the trip to the West. I'm sorry, Elspeth. I really don't know about such things."

"How long has it been since he asked you to sign anything?" Elspeth asked as she poured their tea.

"I don't recall, actually," Thea said, trying to remember. "It was after the war started, though. A few years ago. Why do you ask?"

Elspeth shrugged, uncertain why she had pursued the matter. "I don't know. I'm just trying to get a clearer picture of things, I guess. As a Navajo woman, I knew exactly what my position was, which goods were mine and which my husband's. It's important for a woman to understand such things, Thea. She has the children to think about."

The captain left one of the horses behind for the plowing, but Elspeth did not attempt to follow him. It would have been stupid to blunder into town while he was still there; besides, she was fully occupied with getting the crops planted. Old George provided more assistance than she expected. Wiry and agile for his age, he did much of the heavier work. He seemed to understand planting, but he was surprised when she turned the earth with the horse and plow. Regardless of what he was doing, he made Sky welcome, and the two became almost inseparable. They conversed in English, but more often by gestures. Though the old man did not use the sign language of the plains, he made himself understood with a minimum of effort.

"George wants to take me hunting!" Sky exclaimed at dinner one evening. "He's going to show me how to make a bow and some arrows."

"Can I go, too?" little Robert asked with interest, but Thea objected.

"We can't let them go off into the hills with the old man. We know very little about him, and anything could happen."

Elspeth could not resist the excitement in Sky's eyes. "He'd be learning such things if he were with his father," she decided. "I think it will be all right, if they don't go too far. George seems fond of Sky."

"I suppose you know what you're doing," Thea said, with a frown, "but I can't let my son go along. I'm sorry, dear," she added when he protested, "you aren't as accustomed to the woods as your cousin."

The captain did not notice the absence of the old man and the boy when he unloaded their supplies. He left two of the horses loaded with his own things, so intent on his prospecting that he made his first mistake. The bags of flour he had procured had hitherto borne the manufacturer's labels; they were the same product they had used in Santa Fe. This time, they were stenciled with the words U.S. ARMY. Elspeth put them away while the captain was occupied with the horses, plans forming so rapidly in her mind that she did not have time to approve or reject them. They must be within a day's ride to an army post, which should not be difficult to find, because soldiers would be out on patrol.

"Elspeth!" Thea called from outside. "Do you know how to handle goats? They have horns and they're butting at me."

Elspeth secured the three goats to the fence while Thea's children watched, interested in the animals but sobered by their mother's experience with them. Elspeth smiled at them and bent over to pull up a handful of grass.

"They're all right, now. They'll eat out of your hand," she said, holding the grass in front of the goats. "They're nice goats. They won't hurt you when they're tied up."

Little Robert and Elizabeth laughed delightedly when the animals devoured the grass from their hands. Elspeth watched them with amusement, but did not take her eyes off the goats. They were treacherous little animals, much more trouble than sheep, but she was glad to have them. The children would have to learn their idiosyncrasies before they were allowed to roam as freely as they did with the Navajo herds.

"Are they boys or girls?" Elizabeth asked, pulling her fingers away before they were nibbled along with the grass.

"Two are nannies. The larger one's a daddy goat. If we're lucky, there'll be some babies. You'll have all the milk you can drink."

The captain's activities diverted her attention. He was preparing to leave, and he was taking the horse they had used for the plowing. She wondered if he would ever be careless enough to leave a horse with them.

"I've done him a terrible injustice," Thea said after she was shown the flour sacks. "He wouldn't be trading with the army if he were a deserter. He wouldn't go near an army installation."

"Perhaps he wouldn't, but he looks like a prospector, now," Elspeth considered. "The important thing is that we know there's an army encampment within a day's ride. He knew where he could get supplies. Do you know the names of *any* of the forts in the western Territory?"

"I've only heard of Fort Whipple, but we couldn't be that far west. It's a large fort in Indian country, outside of a place called Prescott. The army wives who came from California stopped there en route to Santa Fe."

"The ones who came by boat?"

"Yes. The fort was quite a journey from where they debarked on the Colorado."

Elspeth tried to remember the details on the maps she had seen in the past. She decided that Fort Whipple was indeed an unlikely candidate for their army post, but she recalled that other forts had been built since the war began, as stopping points for the troops on their long marches in this wide land. It was logical to suppose that one had come into being between Fort Whipple and Fort Wingate.

"Did anyone mention the tribes Whipple was fortified against?" she asked.

"I don't recall that they did," Thea said apologetically. "You know the way they speak, Elspeth. They just refer to *Indians*, without mentioning tribes. I just assumed they were talking about Apache.'' She went silent for a moment. ''You don't think there are Apache here, do you?''

''There shouldn't be,'' Elspeth lied glibly. ''The only Apache to worry about—the Mimbrenos and Chiricahua—are close to the Mexican border, too far away for us to concern ourselves about. We mustn't make problems for ourselves that don't exist.''

She awaited Sky's return anxiously after the discussion about Apache, glancing toward the hills often while she went about her work. When she finally realized that she felt no menace from the hills, that they were alone, she turned her thoughts once again to the army post. If one of the purposes of the fortifications was the Indian threat, she wondered why the soldiers had not reached the farm on their patrols; surely, they must scout the area within a day's radius of their post. Standing in the middle of the field, she looked around on all sides, from the mountains to the river and the stands of trees and rocks on either side. The situation of the farm precluded its being sighted easily; indeed, unless a patrol followed the heavily shaded bank of the river itself, or descended directly down the hills by the incredibly rough road the captain had taken, it would be impossible to sight the farm. Only the Apache, riding in a less-ordered manner and stalking on foot, had seen it from the hills. The thought of the Apache unnerved her, and she knew better than to ignore her feelings.

Sky emerged from the hills like a proud warrior, a bow and quiver over his shoulder and a brace of quail in his hands. George followed closely behind him with a larger, sturdier weapon and more birds, disdaining the attention of the other children, who wanted to examine Sky's bow and to give him their own news.

''We have three goats of our very own,'' little Robert said. ''One for each of us. You should have been here when they came. They tried to butt Mother.''

Sky allowed Elspeth to examine his bow, a poor thing compared to Valerio's bows; she was surprised he had been able to shoot anything with it. She flexed it to feel its power and examined the arrows closely. They were unpainted and undecorated to reveal a tribe, and she noted that the fliches were of different feathers than those used by the Navajo. Sky would learn those things later, when he was with his people again.

"It's a fine bow," she said, with a smile. "We'll have some of the birds for dinner. You're a good hunter, my son."

He did not return her smile at once. He was the hunter, the provider, and everything about him indicated his new status. One of the goats bleated and caught his attention, and he stared at the animals with dismay.

"They're tied up!" he cried. And, without waiting to hear the reason, he dropped his bow and ran to free them. He had never seen a tethered goat before in his life.

Elspeth drew a picture of an upright loom to explain what she wanted to George, adding gestures to indicate the length and diameter of the poles. The old man puzzled over her drawing for several minutes, uncertain what the object was, and she explained it with further gestures, but she could see that he was totally unfamiliar with the loom, though she was never quite sure how much he understood. His face was so expressionless that she could read nothing in it, and there seemed to be a veil over his otherwise sharp eyes. He had brought stoicism to an art. The impression Elspeth received was that he did not care much for anyone in the family except her son. She was relieved when he walked away with the drawing, though not entirely certain she would get what she wanted.

She was determined to carry through the plan that had come to her earlier. If all Apache reacted in the way those she and Valerio had encountered, evidence of a Navajo encampment might discourage them more than fortified walls. Toward that end, she cajoled Thea into wearing her hair in the Navajo fashion as she did.

"It's a simple, uncomplicated style," she said, "practical for the sort of life we're leading. No fuss and no hairpins. Besides, I miss the grooming ritual. It was such a relaxed and pleasant time. I'll show you how to dress my hair, and then I'll do yours. Your hair's so dark, it will look wonderful."

"If you enjoy it, I'll be happy to do it," Thea said, with a smile. "Goodness knows, we don't spend enough time on ourselves. My hands are awful, my skin's dry, and it'll be sunburned again soon. I don't tan as you do. I've decided to make us some sunbonnets out of an old dress I have.''

Elspeth tried to see the sunbonnets through the eyes of the Apache. They would cover their Navajo hairstyle, but they would keep her hair, still dark from winter, from lightening in the sun. If the Apache appeared here, her hair should be as dark as possible. Sky assisted George in the construction of the loom, handing strips of deerskin when they were required to bind the poles together. Elspeth was pleased with the result. When they tied the loom to an overhanging branch near her hogan, it was workable as well as giving the impression that Navajo were living on the farm. Sky, who had been raised in the shadow of his mother's loom, smiled happily as he observed it. But he was as practical as his people.

"There aren't any sheep," he said at once. "You can't weave without wool."

"Aunt Thea is providing that. She's taking some things apart. There's enough wool in the shawls and lap coverings we made on our mother's loom to start a blanket. And I'm going to teach her how to weave on this one."

When she examined the pile of crimped wool, she was moved by the sacrifice of the beautiful articles they had woven in Boston. Thea had stayed up late into the night unraveling her last link to the past, but if she regretted it, she did not reveal it.

"There's such a hodgepodge of colors," she said. "Do you think we can really dye it to make it useable?"

"If the vegetable dyes are compatible with the commercial ones. Would you like to help me?

"I'd love to," Thea said enthusiastically. "This is fascinating, Elspeth."

They gathered plants to transform the pale blues and greens into the more natural colors used by the Navajo. The green turned deep brown when it was boiled with mountain mahogany, and they leached the blue into pale gray. They had separated the white wool to preserve it as it was. The tree limbs, garland with drying skeins, reminded Sky of his grandmother's hogan. In the evening, Elspeth spun warp string between her fingers, combining several strands of the commercial yarn together for strength, and Thea and the children watched until darkness fell.

"This place is like my grandmother's now," Sky said when they returned to their hogan. "It doesn't mean we aren't going back, does it?"

Elspeth put her arm around him comfortingly. "No. But there's no point in going if our family's still far away."

His sigh was too heavy for a little boy. "I wish we could find out about them. You aren't interested in finding the town anymore."

"I want to find it, but there's a lot of work to do right now. I've made a map showing where I think it is. I'll show it to you."

He studied the map carefully under the lamplight for a few minutes. "You aren't sure it's right," he said at last. "There may be a way to find out."

"How?" she asked, with surprise, expecting a suggestion that they follow it to confirm its accuracy.

"George came from that place, didn't he? He can find his way anywhere."

"Did he tell you he came from there?"

"No," he admitted, "but he was wearing some bluecoat clothes when he came here."

"He was in rags, dirty old rags. Was there part of a uniform among them?"

"Yes," Sky replied simply. "I know the weave of the cloth from when you were sick at the fort. Kind Man was the only one I liked. The others shot my father."

"*May* have shot him," Elspeth said, with a pang. "Does George understand enough English for me to question him?"

"Enough for me to understand him. He likes to listen without anyone knowing he understands them."

The old man was more crafty than Elspeth had thought, but she could not fault him for the dissimulation. She had done the same thing when she had to. George was not comfortable with them or he would not have resorted to eavesdropping. And, though she did not feel any more at ease with him, the obvious thing to do was ask him if he knew about the army post.

He was sitting in his hogan, clad only in his breechcloth, when he gave Sky permission for them to enter. They sat in close proximity with him, the only arrangement possible within his quarters, and Elspeth had to swallow her distaste.

He smelled like rank tallow. She had never seen him bathe, despite the proximity of the river. Her oil lamp revealed the disorder around them, but she tried to ignore it. George made no attempt to disguise his annoyance when he saw her and feigned little English in her presence. The feeling that there was something not quite right about the old man made her observe him more closely. As always, his face revealed nothing, but his filthy dwelling said something about the condition of his mind. He was a solitary; they were rare among the Navajo and always suspect.

"We want to find my father's people," Sky told him. "We are like you. We don't belong here. But we don't know where we are. We want to find the army place you came from."

There was a faint glimmer of interest in the old man's eyes, but Elspeth was uncertain about the reaction, which might have been self-serving; the captain had told them that George liked to drink.

"We want to find out where the captain gets his supplies," she hazarded, extending the paper on which she had drawn the map. "Our people have been put on a reservation. We want to get a message to them."

The folds over his eyes hooded their expression as he studied the map. They did not press him, but waited for him to speak. Among the Dineh, it was polite to wait. Nothing important was done in a hurry.

"I take you," he said at last, his voice confirming what Elspeth suspected. He would like nothing better than to get to the alcohol in town, and that would not do at all.

"We can't go without a horse," she said. "We don't know when we'll have a horse. We just want to know where that place is."

"Please, George," Sky entreated. "We have been here a long time. I don't know where my father is. The bluecoats might have shot him. You're my friend. You can help."

Though he did not look at the boy, George's attitude changed. He picked up a piece of charcoal from the ashes of his fire. Elspeth's heart quickened. He began to trace a meandering line southwest of the farm, well beyond the radius she had drawn, and tapped his finger over the spot where it ended.

"Camp Verde," he said. "Many bluecoats. He go there for things."

"Not *Fort* Verde?"

"No fort. Fort Whipple north, much bigger. Pretty far away. I worked there once. Camp Verde the place you want to go."

"I've never heard of it," Elspeth thought aloud.

"Not there long," the old man said. "Just since white man's war."

"He buys our supplies from the quartermaster there? The bluecoats know his name?"

"Morr'son, they call him. Not captain like you. Captain blue-coat name. He looks for gold like the other ones."

"He goes with someone else?"

George chuckled, revealing his broken teeth. "Those men go alone. Other men would steal from them."

"Does anyone know we're here?"

He shrugged his wiry shoulders. The matter was either un-important to him or he did not know. Elspeth was depressed by the confirmation that the captain had kept his army rank a secret; it confirmed the suspicion that he had deserted.

"If we rode parallel within sight of the river we would find Camp Verde?" she asked, studying the map.

He grunted his assent, but his small, crafty eyes were fixed on her. "I take you," he volunteered again.

"No. When we go, you must stay with Mrs. Morrison and her children. My son saw some tribesmen in the hills last sum-mer. What people were these?"

"Not Yavapai," the old man said. "If you go, you leave gun?"

"Yes," she agreed. She had already planned to leave them some defense. "Are you Yavapai, George?"

He spat on the earthen floor to indicate his regard for the tribe, but he did not reveal the identity of his own. Elspeth rose to leave, but Sky wished to remain with his old friend for a while, and she left the lamp with them.

She clasped the folded map against her heart in the dark-ness as she returned to her hogan, her spirits uplifted by the blank spaces the old man had filled in. The army camp did not seem as far away, now. She considered and dismissed the idea of trying to go on foot immediately. Thea was not capable of such an arduous trip, and Elspeth could not leave her and the children alone for so long with the possibility of Apache in the vicinity. She would write a letter to Stephen Cabot tomorrow to let him know their location and mail it as soon as the captain was careless enough to leave a horse on the farm.

Chapter 24

When the captain left a horse behind for the plowing the following spring, Elspeth did not hesitate. She and Thea had discussed what should be done during the winter. If he left the horse, she and Sky would ride to the army camp before they did the plowing. Making contact with the outside world was the most important thing on their minds. The year had been relatively uneventful, but the captain's personality was disintegrating rapidly. He spent more time alone in the hills, and when he remained at home during the winter, he behaved as if he were still alone. The only indication he gave that his family was still at the farm was the purchase of a bolt of dark cloth, which he threw on the table almost angrily, indicating that the women should make garments for themselves with it. He bought fewer supplies, and they had to make them stretch between longer intervals, since he was not there to go for them. Elspeth sensed that he might be running low on money; that, somehow, her refusal to sign any papers had made him more penurious. But he did not ask her to sign papers again. Aside from verbally abusing George when he was at home, the captain rarely spoke, and they were relieved when he left to prospect; his presence cast a dark cloud over the otherwise tranquil and productive farm.

"You'll be careful, won't you?" Thea said anxiously when Elspeth mounted the horse and pulled Sky up behind her. "I know you must go, but I don't know what we would do without you.''

"It's only a day's ride, Thea," Elspeth said, bending to clasp her hand. "I'll be back within three days. You have everything you need. George knows how to shoot the rifle. Just behave as if I were here. We'll be back before you know it."

Once she was on her way, she dismissed any lingering doubts about the farm from her mind. She concentrated on the map and the letter she wanted to post. She had waited for two and a half years for this moment. She wore the black dress she and Thea had made during the winter, a poor thing that wrinkled easily, but her appearance was the last thing on her mind. Thea had dressed her hair the evening before so it would be neat upon her arrival at the army camp. They had worn the chonga-knot for so long that they did not experiment with other styles. Valerio's silver ornament lay against her heart on its string of turquoise, as it had done for years; it gave her comfort, made him seem nearer. Her only concern was the length of the ride. She had not ridden since she left Dineyah and had to accustom herself to the feel of the unsaddled horse, to falling into motion with the animal. They stopped at noon to rest the horse and to eat dried jerky and peaches and sip some water, and she noted there were no bruises on her legs from exerting pressure on her mount. Riding was like walking, once learned one did not forget how to do it.

They reached Camp Verde by late afternoon. Within half a mile of it, soldiers were clearly visible maneuvering on foot and horseback. A small group looked up as they rode past. Someone barked an order, and a young soldier leaped into his saddle and galloped ahead of them toward the post. She was not surprised by the curious stares that greeted them when they entered the camp; the inhabitants had already been alerted that a woman and child were approaching on horseback.

The small garrison, cut off from the outside world as it was, had been built as sturdily as Fort Defiance, with the same complement of barracks and officers' quarters and an administrative building flying the American flag. Elspeth was aware of the pressure of Sky's arms around her, and she reassured him softly in Navajo. He had every right to feel uncomfortable among bluecoats after what he had witnessed in Tsegi. She, herself, felt wary. The suspicious soldiers slowly encircled them until she had to rein in her horse; she sensed the wall of hostility surrounding her.

"What're you doing here?" a barrel-chested sergeant with a sunburned face demanded, blocking her way. His abruptness struck Elspeth like a blow; this was not the greeting she had anticipated. Her silence emboldened the other enlisted men to speculate between themselves.

"She may be a diversion," a younger man said. "You ever seen an Indian like her before? Look at that chunk of silver around her neck. It's worth a pretty penny."

The sergeant reached for the necklace; she had to shy her horse to avoid him. "I wish to speak to your officer," she said coolly. "We've come to post a letter."

The sergeant took a step backward, and the other men considered her soberly, squinting against the sunlight. She returned their stare without realizing how incongruous her blue-green eyes were in her darkly tanned face.

"She's a white woman," the sergeant said at last. "Could have been captured by Indians, if the kid's hers. You ever see an Indian with hair and jewelry like hers?" When no one responded, he told one of the men, "You better tell Captain Hennessey we have a little problem here."

She endured their stares while she waited for the officer. Several women emerged from the living quarters to join the group staring up at her. Captain Hennessey joined them at last, as fair as the sergeant was tanned, with a set expression on his face. He conferred briefly with the sergeant and ordered the wives back to their dwellings.

"What can I do for you?" he asked, with bewilderment. "Who are you?"

"Mr. Morrison's sister-in-law. I've come to mail a letter. We've been out on the farm for several years without contact with anyone."

He accepted the letter without looking at the address. "There aren't any settlers around here. We've scouted the area thoroughly. We haven't seen any farm."

"If you had, we'd have been in contact," she reasoned. "Surely someone here knows Mr. Morrison. He comes for supplies."

"I know him," the quartermaster volunteered. "He's one of those prospectors who comes here. He buys a lot, but we thought he was hoarding caches in the mountains for himself. We didn't know he had Indian women and a child with him.''

''My sister isn't Indian,'' Elspeth explained, using the white man's term to communicate with them. ''She's awaiting my return with her two children and an old man named George, our handyman . . .''

''George?'' the sergeant said, with a smile. ''I wondered where he'd gone to. You remember George,'' he said to his comrades. ''The old Indian Captain Whittier's wife brought from Ehrenburg. Mrs. Whittier dumped him when they were transferred, because she couldn't abide drunks.''

There was a murmur of amusement, but Captain Hennessey remained grave. ''We didn't know there were women and children in the area,'' he said. ''There are hostiles out there.''

''Hostiles?'' Elspeth asked, hoping there might be some Navajo in the vicinity, but the response was disappointing.

''Yavapai, ma'am. They're trouble enough, but there have been some Apache sightings, too. It's a miracle your place hasn't been attacked.''

The officers' wives had retreated no farther than their doors, from which they were staring at her, and their faces did not surprise her as much as they should have. Their curiosity was mixed with a contempt born of fear. These people were terrified of Indians, perhaps with good reason, but she knew they would not speak to her in any case. Captain Morrison had made it clear that no one wanted anything to do with a woman who has lived with an Indian, borne him a child.

The women were certainly not ready to offer her tea. The officer surprised her by doing just that when he read the address on her letter.

''You must be hungry,'' he said. ''You and your son come to my office, ma'am. We should have a little talk. Hodges, bring a tray of food and a pot of coffee from the mess.''

The office was simple. The walnut desk must have been brought from the East; perhaps it had come here by way of the larger Fort Whipple, or was left behind by a higher-ranking officer in transit. Sky was uncomfortable, but too proud to clutch his mother's hand. He would have remained at the door if she had not motioned him to sit beside her.

''This is addressed to Bosque Redondo,'' the officer said,

turning the letter in his hands. "It's called Fort Sumner, now. General Carleton's unsuccessful solution to the Navajo problem. What's this medical officer to you?"

"An old friend," Elspeth replied. "Someone with whom I must get in touch."

Her reception at the camp had made her so nervous that she almost mentioned Santa Fe. It would not do for Captain Morrison's name to be connected with Santa Fe if he had deserted. Her answers became more guarded when she realized that Captain Hennessey was trying to determine her connection with the Navajo; irrationally, perhaps, she feared he could still send Sky away.

"Where are we?" she asked. "I know this is Camp Verde, sir, but where is it?"

He was shocked by the question. "You don't even know you're in the Arizona Territory?"

"I thought we might be in the part called Arizona," she replied. "I didn't know it was a separate Territory now."

"It has been since 1862," he said, gazing at her curiously. "Where were you that you didn't hear about it?"

"With my husband at Tsegi, I suppose. I've lost track of dates."

"At *de Chelly*?" he said, with mounting interest. "It's a miracle you weren't taken with the others. You must forgive me, ma'am, but there are questions—"

"The Navajo didn't kidnap me," she volunteered to save him the trouble. "I went with my husband willingly. I was with him for almost four years, until Carson came. They discovered who I was at Fort Wingate and sent me back to my family."

"Your brother-in-law and your sister. What sort of man is this Morrison fellow?"

"A prospector. A man who wanted to hide what he considered the shame of my actions." She dismissed her brother-in-law before there were more questions about him. "Are the North and South still at war?"

"The war ended last year," he said with disbelief. "We—the North—won. There must be some newspapers around here."

"I'd like to see them, perhaps take them back to my sister? May I look at your map?" She indicated the large map on the wall behind his desk.

He stood aside to allow her to stand in front of it. "We're

here," he said, placing his finger on the location of Camp Verde, "a little north of the center of the Territory."

Her gaze swept the map from Camp Verde to Fort Defiance near Tsegi, and across the New Mexico Territory to find Fort Sumner, where her people were. She was closer to Dineyah than she was to the reservation; she had suspected that. The distance was farther than she had imagined, though.

"I see," she murmured. "Thank you."

"You can't return to your farm this late," he said. "I'll find a place for you and your son to stay and provide you with an escort in the morning. If there's anything else I can do . . . Damn it, I can't understand that man—leaving women and children out there alone. It's very dangerous."

"There were a few Apache in the hills the first year we were there, but they didn't bother us," Elspeth reassured him. "I don't think they will. We've taken precautions, and we're armed, just in case. We haven't seen them since. Have you had trouble with the Yavapai? I know nothing of them."

"Not for a while. Their range is more to the northwest, but they're not to be dismissed. Their depredations have almost matched those of the Apache. It just isn't safe out there, ma'am."

"You *will* mail my letter?" Elspeth inquired as she moved toward the door. "If there's a reply, could you hold it for me? I don't know when I'll be able to come again."

He nodded and stared at her letter. " 'Williams,' " he read. "No other name?"

"Dr. Cabot will know who it's from. You've been very kind, sir."

"Wait," he said, realizing how little information he had obtained for his report. "Where are you and your sister from, ma'am? You're obviously educated."

Elspeth recognized that he was attempting to determine where they had lived before she went with the Navajo; she could not tell him that. "Boston," she replied as she and Sky slipped through the door, "but that was a long time ago."

"They'll try to find the farm," she told Thea when she returned. "They wanted to give me an escort, but I rejected it. Under the circumstances, it seemed best to keep them away as long as possible. Captain Hennessey was upset with your husband for not telling him we were here."

"You did the right thing," Thea said. "If the army discovers the farm on their own—and they surely will—Robert won't be able to complain. If we're lucky, he won't know you went there at all. And we know how to get to Camp Verde if we need help."

"I saw a map," Elspeth said, "and I brought newspapers. They're old, but we can find out what's happening in the world."

Elspeth told her about the end of the Civil War as they unfolded the newspapers on the table and began to pour over them. There were references to President Lincoln's assassination and the hanging of the conspirators in the plot, though the event that shook the nation had occurred during the previous year. Thea was as devastated by the news as if it had occurred yesterday, but Elspeth distanced herself from it as she searched for word about Fort Sumner. When she found an article, she understood Captain Hennessey's reference to "General Carleton's unsuccessful reservation."

The relocation was costing the government over a million dollars a year just to feed the Navajo. New Mexican politicians were clamoring for the removal of the general following an investigation into his expenditures. The Comanche Indians claimed the reservation was on their hunting grounds and were raiding the Navajo stock. The crops had consistently failed in the alkaline soil; the 7,400 Navajo were suffering terribly. The Bureau of Indian Affairs was trying to take control of the reservation from the War Department. There was no mention of the government abandoning the project, despite the plea of one Navajo headman to the superintendent of Indian Affairs:

I am thinking of my own country more than ever before, because there I could secure myself from my enemies; here, we have not a chance. We are all the time thinking of our old country, and we believe if the government will put us back, they could have us the same there as here. Poor as we are, we would rather go back to our country.

I think that in the world, the earth, and in the heavens we are all equal and we have all been born of the same mother. What we want is to be sent back to our own country. Even if we starve there, we will have no complaints.

Elspeth put her face in her hands. Sky came to her side and, uncharacteristically, lay his head against her hair. She responded by putting her arm around him tightly.

"What you read is not good," he said. "Does it say something about our family?"

"No, darling. Only Kind Man will be able to tell us about them."

"What did the map say? Are we farther away from Dineyah than we thought?"

"Yes," she said, with a sigh. "The red rocks and the cliff dwelling deceived us. We're much farther away, and there'd be no one to greet us. Don't fret. We'll find our people again."

"Maybe the bluecoats will send us to be with them," he said hopefully, and she kissed him on the forehead.

"I don't think they'd want to do that. They don't need more mouths to feed. The only thing we can do is wait. We must get some sleep. There's plowing to be done tomorrow."

"Elspeth," Thea said, looking up from the article on the reservation. "Elspeth, dear, I don't know what to . . ."

"There's nothing to say," Elspeth told her. "There's nothing we can do for them, Thea."

"But there is!" Thea exclaimed, standing up with the newspaper still grasped in her hands. "We can send mail, now. We'll write letters to Washington. We don't know who our congressmen are, if there are any from Arizona, but we can write to Congress anyway. We're citizens!"

Elspeth recalled the letters they had written on behalf of the Indians when they were in Boston and wondered if they had had any effect at all. She did not want to discourage Thea, whose blue eyes were bright with enthusiasm for a cause again.

"Yes," she said affectionately, "we'll do that. We'll write lots of letters to a lot of people. It can't hurt."

Sky's body tightened and his eyes narrowed as he listened to something she did not hear. She paused with the hoe in her hands, her gaze following the direction of his, and when she saw nothing, the anxiety about Apache that was always with her intensified. She glanced around to see where everyone was, planning their defense. George was cleaning the rifle he had adopted as his own near the cabin; Thea was inside preparing supper with Elizabeth. Young Robert was nowhere to be seen, though she had instructed him to remain in sight at all times. Torn between assessing the danger and searching for the child, she remained rooted to the ground for several moments, clasping the hoe like a weapon.

"Bluecoats," Sky said. "The hooves are shod. They've found us, Mother."

Elspeth closed her eyes with relief. She had expected the soldiers to find them sooner, and her gratitude that it was they instead of Apache was profound.

"It's all right," she said as the small patrol emerged from the bushes by the river. "Find your cousin. Tell him not to say anything about his father while they're here."

She took off her sunbonnet and wiped the perspiration from her face as she walked to meet the soldiers. Thea had noticed the activity from the window and overtook her, cleaning the flour off her hands with her apron. The riders came to a halt, and the officer leading them dismounted.

"Good afternoon, ladies," he said, studying them closely. "I'm Lieutenant Wills. Is everything all right here? Captain Hennessey was concerned when he heard Mr. Morrison hadn't come for supplies for a while."

"He's been gone longer than usual," Elspeth said. "We never know how long he'll be."

"Our scouts located your farm several weeks ago," the young lieutenant said. "We'll look in on you from time to time. We decided the easiest route was by the river." He surveyed the hills around the farm, his dark eyes squinted against the afternoon sun. "Pretty heavily wooded here. You haven't noticed anything?"

"Nothing," Elspeth said carefully. She had not mentioned the presence of the Apache in the vicinity to Thea two years ago, and she did not want to alarm her now. "It's been a good summer, Lieutenant. The crop's growing well."

She knew he had observed the Navajo structures, the half-woven blanket on the loom, but he was too polite to mention them and seemed at a loss for words until Thea invited the soldiers for supper.

"All I can offer is venison, but you're welcome to join us."

The prospect of eating home-cooked food was so appealing that he did not hesitate. "Yes, ma'am! Thank you. But are you sure you'll have enough? It isn't as if you were expecting us."

"The haunch I'm baking should suffice, Lieutenant," Thea

said, with a smile. "After you've taken care of your horses, please join us at the house."

Delighted to have company, Thea was behaving like an officer's wife, but Elspeth felt no need to caution her about what she said. She thought it ironical that they were in the position of protecting the captain, whom they now knew had deserted from the army. The real danger was that he might pull up stakes again if the visits of the soldiers became too frequent, a prospect that did not suit her at all. He might choose California the next time, if he could finance such a move.

The lieutenant volunteered to mail their letters to Congress at the army post and promised to deliver any letters that were received for them, relieving Elspeth's uneasiness that Dr. Cabot's reply might fall into the captain's hands when he went after supplies again.

Chapter 25

The captain sat at the table removing ticks from his arms with the lighted end of his cigar. He did not appear to be listening when they said the army had discovered the farm, an explanation that was necessary before he heard about it in Camp Verde. Thea looked away with disgust every time the cigar touched one of the bloated insects with an audible popping sound. Elspeth was glad she had removed the dishes from the table before the operation began. She wondered where he had slept the night before to acquire so many ticks and why he had not taken care of them before now, though it appeared he had attempted it. Swollen welts indicated that some had been pulled off, leaving the heads embedded in his skin. The remaining insects had probably secreted themselves in his clothing and attacked again when he was in the saddle.

"They were bound to find it sometime," he said at last, unaware of a blood-engorged tick on the side of his neck, which would be difficult to reach with his cigar. "Have they been around much?"

"Only once," Thea said quietly. "We haven't seen them since."

He made a derogatory noise in his throat. "Their patrols aren't what they used to be. This place can be seen pretty well from the hills. I suppose they asked questions?"

"Not really," Thea responded. "When I said my name was Morrison, one of the soldiers connected it with the prospector

353

who came to Camp Verde for supplies. Which reminds me, we're running very low . . .''

"Did you mention I'd been in the army?'' he asked, glancing at her warily. "I suppose you talked your head off.''

"No,'' Thea said, drawing a deep breath, "there didn't seem to be any point. They were only here for a short time.''

Thea had done very well, but Elspeth recognized she was feeling the strain. She moved to the captain's side and extracted his forgotten cigar from his hand. "There's one on your neck,'' she said. "I'll take care of it, and make a poultice to draw out the heads you missed. They get nasty if they aren't treated.''

She expected him to object to her "goddamned Indian'' medicine, to cause a scene that would take his attention off Thea. He disappointed her, but he changed the subject to pursue what occupied his mind more than anything else.

"I've hit it,'' he said to everyone in general, though he seemed almost to be speaking to himself. "A rich vein. I'm certain of it. I have to make a claim and get back there.''

Elspeth and Thea greeted the news without much conviction, trying to say something appropriate despite his inattention. The children were anxious to get outdoors now that the fascination of exploding ticks was at an end. Elspeth nodded her permission, considering the implications of what the captain said. In order to file his claim, he would have to go to Camp Verde; their food supplies were guaranteed, at least. In his excitement over the gold strike, he showed no indication of moving because of the army's discovery of the farm. They would not be whisked off to California as she feared, and this gave her some peace of mind. The deciding factor in their lives would be gold for some time in the future.

He came back from the army post rapidly, riding during the night. The horses were lathered and his face covered with dust from the ride. He did not unload the horses but strode directly into the field where the women were working.

"Indians,'' he said, wiping his face with his bandanna. "The fort's in an uproar. Damn them! A patrol found a prospector with an arrow in his back. Scalped. I can't go back to my claim until this subsides. They wanted me to bring you to town. That's what comes of letting them know you're here.''

He was so upset that his words came in a rush. Elspeth knew

the frustration and anger was mingled with fear, which communicated itself quickly to Thea.

"The hills are crawling with them," the captain said. "I saw a few myself about a month ago. That's why I stayed put so long. I didn't want to reveal myself. I might have wound up like the prospector they found. I've fought Apache. I know what they are."

"I think it's a small party," Elspeth said. "They wander in small groups. There wouldn't be any point in a large raiding party coming to such an unpopulated area."

"You think," he said. "You don't know a damned thing about them. They raised hell with General Carleton's troops all during the war, pinned down the Butterfield Stage until the route had to be changed. The army managed to lure Mangas Coloradas into a powwow so they could kill him, but his friend, Cochise, is still on the loose, plundering from his mountain hideaway in the south. The Chiricahua can be as fierce as Mangas's Mimbrenos, and they're on the move. They hate white men."

I wonder why? Elspeth thought after hearing the familiar story of a chief being murdered under a flag of truce. "There aren't any settlements here to raid," she repeated. "There's no need for hysteria . . ."

"The *army's* hysterical," the captain said, his voice rising. "It doesn't go into hysterics like a woman over nothing." He considered his own reaction and attempted to compose himself. "I hate the bastards. They're ruthless."

Thea trusted Elspeth's reasoning more than her husband's excited speculations. "I don't know what they're up to, but I can't believe they've come here just to murder us. I think Elspeth knows more than she's told us."

"I've encountered them before, and spoken about them with my husband. I've taken some precautions." She indicated the hogans and the partially woven rug on the loom. "There's a tribal prohibition about their having anything to do with Navajo. They're cousins, but not friendly. They didn't attack us when they were in the area before, though Thea and I were alone with the children. They saw the hogans and ran into Sky in the hills."

The captain stared at her. "You saw them before and didn't say anything?"

"There didn't seem to be any reason for alarm. They haven't

come back again." Elspeth did not mention her own terror of Apache, which had started with Concepcion's stories in Santa Fe. "If they come here, I think Sky and I can talk to them."

"You aren't alone, now," the captain said belligerently. "I won't hesitate to shoot your 'cousins' if they show up here. I bought more rifles; I'm going to put them in order right now. And don't say anything to the old Indian. He'd probably hightail it out of here if he heard about the Apache. We need everyone who can shoot."

He would not accept Elspeth's help when he took to his bed with a severe headache and high fever a few days later. He gave his opinion of her medicine through chattering teeth and continued to drink whiskey to combat his discomfort. When a rash appeared on his arms and neck, Elspeth and Thea thought he had the measles, a disease they had nursed before. But the rash grew darker and more papular; it spread over his body and coalesced into large hemorrhagic areas which alarmed them.

"He's burning up," Thea said. "We have to get some of your medicine into him to bring down the fever."

"He won't take it. You heard him."

"Mix it in a cup. I'll give it to him. He doesn't have to know what it is. We can mix it in his whiskey," Thea said, with sudden inspiration. "He won't taste it."

Elspeth hesitated. "I'm not sure. When medicines are combined, they can have curious effects. I don't know what the whiskey might do. But, if it's the only way we can get the herbs into him, I suppose we'll have to take that chance."

The fever and headache medicines, which Elspeth knew were safe in combination, made the captain more comfortable. He slept for long periods of time, waking only to sip some broth. He was so drowsy that he took the medicines without objection. Elspeth wondered about the depth of his drowsiness. He was so obtunded that she feared he might be going into a coma.

"He needs a doctor," she said. "He's very ill, Thea. I have no idea what it is. I'd better ride to Camp Verde."

"No! You might be attacked on the way," Thea told her. "If you go, we all go. He should have taken us into the camp as the soldiers suggested. Do you know how to hitch the horses to the wagon?"

Elspeth shook her head. "He always did that. The wagon wouldn't be a good idea, anyway. If there are more Apache than I think, they'd raid a wagon. We wouldn't have a chance. We're prepared for them here, as much as we can be. What will we do, Thea?"

"I don't know," Thea said, with a sigh, dark circles under her eyes from administering to her husband. "We have to think of the children. We'll have to stay here. We'll give him more of your medicine; maybe it will help. We'll just have to trust in Providence, Elspeth."

Elspeth realized that, though she was willing to ride for help, she could not leave Thea and the children here alone. If the Apache scare had any foundation, her presence on the farm was essential.

She increased the dosage of the fever medicine, giving him more than she had ever given, and the captain gradually improved. He was too weak to leave his bed, but his temperature was in remission for longer periods during the day, always falling in the morning for a reason unknown to her. She and Sky stayed in the cabin to help Thea, a situation that ran counter to her plan regarding the Apache. For short periods during the day, she attended to the usual outdoor chores, abandoning her sunbonnet so her hairstyle could be clearly seen as she worked. As she was tidying her hogan one afternoon, sweeping the hard earthen floor with a branch, her mind occupied by everything Hosteen Yazzie had taught her, a dim recollection stirred in her mind. She did not know why she had not remembered it sooner.

"It was the ticks," she told Thea when she returned to the cabin. "The Hosteen told me I would probably never see what he called Tick-Sickness. He said there was no medicine for it. The best that could be done was to keep the fever down."

The memory of the ticks made Thea shudder. "We seem to have done the right thing," she said. "Robert's feeling better. He tried to get up awhile ago, but he's too weak. He's going to be all right."

"The Hosteen said it was incurable," Elspeth said. "I forgot all about it until now. It's just as well, or I might have given up on him."

"You wouldn't have," Thea said, with a weary smile. "It

isn't like you. If you couldn't cure the disease, you'd treat the symptoms. Is everything all right out there?''

"George and Sky are keeping watch.'' She had disobeyed the captain by telling the old man about the Apache; instead of running away, he was taking his job as lookout seriously, anxious to use his rifle. "You're exhausted, Thea. Why don't you lie down for a while?''

"That would be lovely. I don't know how you do it, Elspeth. You never nap during the day. I wish I had your discipline.''

"It isn't discipline, it's habit,'' Elspeth said, with a smile.

The family was gathered at the table for the first time since the captain's illness. He was still weak, but his clarity of mind had returned. Accustomed to bringing in the harvest at their own speed, Elspeth and Thea ignored his orders. Thea had shaved his beard in the interest of hygiene, but the stubble that had grown since made even his clean, carefully ironed clothing look disreputable. He was particularly hard on old George, who was in no position to lend a deaf ear to his demands. Elspeth and Thea went out of their way to show their appreciation to the old man in order to counteract the captain's slights, but it was difficult to tell if their kindness had any effect. George kept his thoughts to himself.

The days were growing shorter, but it was still light outside when they had their supper. The captain's hands were not steady as he cut his meat, and Elspeth wondered if the fine tremor would ever completely leave them. The weakness had endured, and she knew how much it annoyed him, because he wanted to appear strong and capable. Suddenly, terrifying cries outdoors made them drop their cutlery. The sound penetrated Elspeth's soul; she knew what it was, and that she would never forget it, just as Concepcion had always remembered it. She and the captain rose at the same time and moved carefully to the window. She counted a dozen Apache in full view below the cornfield, ululating and waving their firearms. They must have come from the river, Elspeth thought, trying to suppress her panic. If they had come from the hills, they would have seen the hogans.

The captain pulled the shutters closed and, leaning against the wall, began to issue the well-oiled rifles to each of them, including the seven-year-old boys. Elspeth refused to take hers and placed Sky's against the table.

"We will talk to them," she said. "It's the only way. You know what a few burning arrows would do to this cabin."

"Talk!" he cried, his voice rising until it broke like an adolescent's. "You don't *talk* to Apache."

"Let me try," she said, more calmly than she felt. "If we fail, you can shoot. But, for God's sake, don't fire on them while we're out there. Bolt the door behind us and remain absolutely quiet."

The war cry ceased abruptly when she and Sky emerged, their appearance suggesting, if not entirely adhering, to that of Navajo. Elspeth's hair was in a chonga, the turquoise necklace Many Beads had given her, which carried the silver squash blossom, in sharp relief against her dark dress. Clad in buckskin, Sky was unmistakably Navajo as they walked from the cabin toward the circle of warriors.

She halted five feet away from them and did not look at them directly. To do so would not be Navajo; it would also reveal the color of her eyes.

"We are Dineh," she said in the language they understood. "If you need food, we will give it to you."

She indicated the hogans, and the brave leading the party could not help noticing the loom. He glanced suspiciously toward the cabin.

"You were in a man's house," he said, speaking faster than a Navajo. "You are a slave of the white man."

Elspeth maintained a placid expression, though her mouth was dry with fear. "That place was here when we came," she lied, as she would never have done to a Navajo. A Navajo had to repeat a lie three times to make it all right. "My older mother is in the hogan with a sickness. It will be *chindi* soon. We came here so we wouldn't have to go to Bosque Redondo. Maybe you know what happened to the white man who built the house. He never came back."

"Where is your husband?" the brave asked, obviously not wishing to meet him. "Is your husband here, too?"

"My father's hunting," Sky volunteered. "We are getting ready for winter."

"The harvest was good," Elspeth said quietly. "We have cornmeal, and some of the venison is drying. This place is good, but not as good as Tsegi."

She suddenly thought of George, who had shot the deer drying on the racks, and fear contracted her throat. Where was the old man and his rifle? Was he hidden in his hogan, or was the weapon aimed at them right now?

"We will accept cornmeal," the brave said. "We hunt for ourselves."

The leisurely walk to the storage cellar was the longest Elspeth had ever taken. The raiding party remained behind while she fetched the cornmeal, which she had placed in buckskin bags beforehand, conscious that the white man's flour sacks usually used for the purpose would arouse suspicion. If the captain became impatient and fired on the Apache now, she and Sky would die. And she did not know where George was. He had a clear shot at the Apache now, if he decided to take it. She trusted George's judgment no more than the captain's. Her nerves were so taut she could hardly breathe.

She steeled herself to walk in an equally relaxed manner when she and Sky carried the bags of cornmeal back to the raiding party. The bags exchanged hands without her looking directly at them, but a glance registered every detail in her mind. They sat their horses easily. They were straight and proud, almost arrogantly so, their black hair hanging over their shoulders and weapons in hand. Taller and more wiry than the Navajo, the infusion of Mexican blood obvious in their faces, they had lost all the gentleness of the Dineh since their separation from them many years ago. Their lips were thinner, their naked shoulders narrower. The decorations on their high moccasins, upon which she kept her gaze leveled, were composed of small beads and quills, like those of the plains tribes, from whom they had acquired their cruelty. In their own way, they were magnificent, as wild and ruthless and free as the land they wandered, but she appreciated the terror they instilled.

"Go in peace," she said softly. "May you walk in beauty."

She watched until they had ridden out of sight before she turned toward the cabin. Her knees were so weak that she could hardly put one foot in front of the other. Her whole body trembled in a belated reaction to the encounter, and she rested her hand on Sky's shoulder protectively. Unaware of the peril he had been in, Sky seemed untouched by the experience. Her heart went out to him.

* * *

The captain was sprawled on the cabin floor, and Thea stood over him with a rifle. For a moment, Elspeth thought her sister had shot him, but she knew a gun had not been fired.

"He was going to shoot," Thea explained, her blue eyes large in her pale face. "I struck him with the butt of my gun. Is he dead, Elspeth?"

Elspeth knelt to examine him, and released her tension with a laugh. "I think he will live," she said, "but you gave him a bad whack on the head."

"He was ready to pull the trigger. I had to stop him. They'd have killed you. You were walking toward the storage cellar. You don't think they'll return, do you?"

"No," Elspeth said as she sank into a chair, wiping the tears from her eyes and attempting to control her laughter. "Not that party at least. They know we're here. You were wonderful, Thea. I was afraid of that shot."

"How will I explain when he regains consciousness?" Thea asked. "I can't tell him what I did. He'd kill me."

Laughter welled up in Elspeth's throat again and she subdued it with an effort. She knew she was almost hysterical. "Tell him he fainted and struck his head," she said, staring at the Morrison children. "That's what happened, isn't it, children?"

"Yes," young Robert agreed quickly, nudging his little sister. "If Father had fired, you and Sky would be dead. The Apache would have killed you. We'd all be dead. Father fainted and hit his head, didn't he, Elizabeth?"

"I was watching the Indians," the little girl said.

An army patrol pursuing the Apache reached the farm the next morning. The soldiers did not dismount and were speaking to the children when the captain, followed by his wife and Elspeth, approached. The children went silent in the presence of their father, and Sky, uncomfortable around bluecoats, disappeared silently into the fields.

"The children said they were here," the lieutenant who had dined with them said. "It's a miracle you're alive. Some settlers west of the camp weren't as fortunate. We've been after them for two days."

"They were friends of my sister-in-law," the captain responded. "She gave them food. They left before I could get a shot at them."

"She *what*?" The lieutenant's blue eyes snapped with anger. "That was aiding the enemy, ma'am. I don't know what your association with those people is, but you shouldn't have helped them."

Elspeth remained silent, feeling that any explanation would be misconstrued, but Thea spoke up without reservation.

"My sister saved our lives, Lieutenant. She's as frightened of them as everyone else. Even if my husband had been well, we'd have been overpowered. There were at least a dozen of them. They were prepared to kill us. My sister knew they would leave if they saw Navajo here. They couldn't get out of here fast enough after she gave them the grain."

"They didn't really need it," Elspeth said. "They live off the land. Their acceptance of the cornmeal was almost ritualistic, a display of goodwill between two unfriendly tribes. They probably got rid of it before they rode very far. Have you ever tried to cook cornmeal over a campfire without a pot? They travel lightly, as you know."

"And they don't build fires," the lieutenant considered. "Not when they're being pursued. Well," he sighed, wiping his neck with his bandanna, "if they were here last evening, there's no point in continuing our pursuit. They've put too much distance between us. We'd hoped to overtake them by now."

"You still can," the captain said, with authority. "They can't have gotten that far. They don't ride at night. You should know that, young man."

"I do," the lieutenant said. "You talk like a military man, Mr. Morrison. With all respect, sir, we don't know where the hell they've gone. If they rode into the hills, we've lost them for sure. And I think they've gone into the hills. What is your opinion, sir?"

The captain was silent; the pallor still present from his illness increased. Elspeth observed him closely; he had nearly revealed himself.

"I don't really know much about it," he replied. "Everyone knows about Indians and the dark. I didn't think of them escaping into the hills."

Elspeth heard Thea let out her breath with a soft sigh. The lieutenant lost interest in him and prepared to go back to Camp Verde. The captain hunched his shoulders and, with his hands deep in his pockets, turned away and walked back to the cabin. Thea invited the men for coffee, at least a cool drink of water, but the lieutenant refused politely. They were still talking when Elspeth heard a hiss from one of the mounted men near her; he was trying to slip her a letter.

"Captain Hennessey told me to give you this," he whispered. "Didn't want that Morrison fellow to know about it. I've been carrying it in my tunic for quite a while. This Apache business delayed its delivery, ma'am."

Elspeth smiled and slipped the soiled, wrinkled envelope into the waistband of her skirt. She had begun to wonder if her letter had reached Stephen Cabot.

She sought a quiet place by the river, and her callused fingers trembled as she broke the seal. Drawing a deep breath, she withdrew the bulky pages of army stationery and read:

Fort Sumner,
15 July, 1867

My dearest Elspeth,

Your letter was awaiting me when I returned from Santa Fe today; despite the late hour, I'm replying at once. You can't know what your letter meant to me after losing contact with you for so long. Even on this recent trip, I continued to make inquiries of those who knew Captain Morrison, hoping for an encouraging word. I visited your old house and Don Diego's hacienda with the results I'll confide to you later, though I hardly dare put them on paper, because they might not mean what you want to hear. But, first things first. I'm very weary and must make some sort of order of what I have to tell you.

Conditions at Fort Sumner have been so appalling that I'm confident there will be a change. General Carleton has been removed from his post and further legislation is in process. I went to Santa Fe to testify before a committee and put more pressure on the congressman there, but the wheels of government proceed at their own creaking pace, and communication with Washington is slow, at best. Still, judging from the mood of the assembly, I felt more people were in favor of an alternate plan for the Navajo than were opposed to it. And the alternate plan, still in its infancy, will raise your spirits, my dear. If things go as I expect, they will be sent back to their homeland, which will be designated a reservation.

I regret to tell you that I've never been able to find the

family of Many Beads. I've been constantly alert during my work among the eight thousand Navajo here. The figure alone will tell you something about my workload. It is not a happy place; I won't distress you with that. Instead, I will relate an apocryphal story that circulated here over two years ago. I must stress that I have no firsthand confirmation. After the first crop failure, when we thought every able-bodied Navajo was in custody here, a brave on horseback presented himself to the guard at the gate asking to be taken to his family. The temptation of the commanding officer was to turn him away because of the food shortage; on consideration, he decided it better to have him here than roaming the territory "stealing." He was found capable enough to take training in the metal shop, one of the projects which has been established to prepare them to earn their keep. Without going into the food rationing, I'll tell you a little about it. Cardboard tickets were distributed to every man, woman, and child for their meager portions of food. Within a short time, the quartermaster was receiving back more tickets than had been issued. The Navajo are an artistic people; I admire them very much. When the counterfeit was verified, tin tags were issued by way of currency for the food, and this part of the story I can verify. The army was so confident about the tin tags that it took several months to recognize that those tags had been neatly counterfeited, too.

When the latest ploy was revealed, the brave who had surrendered at the gate and later worked in the metal shop, suddenly disappeared. He might not have been missed if he hadn't somehow managed to take a horse, too. Descriptions of him were rampant at the time, but the clearest one I managed to get was that he was tall, in his mid-twenties, and had a deep scar in his chest. I did not see this man, but those who did all remarked that he was as handsome as he was daring. The devil of it is that no one thought to identify the family he had come to join. The family as well as the man were idiotically given English or Spanish names like all the others, because so few in authority speak Navajo. They called him Miguel.

As I said, Elspeth, the story grew in the telling. I don't know how much of it is true, but something I heard at the hacienda made me think of it again.

Elspeth turned the pages of Stephen's letter, hardly daring to hope, unable to stem her excitement. The metalworker sounded so much like Valerio that she could hardly breathe. He had done exactly what she had expected when he surrendered to be with his family. He would have been looking for Sky and his wife. And, not finding them, he would have remained to help the People if he could. The timing of his arrival at the reservation was wrong. If he had been wounded, it was unlikely that it would take him over six months to recover and turn himself in at Fort Sumner. The brave had apparently spent some time at the reservation, as Valerio might have done if he had found his family, but only if his wife and child were with them. Did he escape again in an attempt to find them? Or did the brave disappear because he was sure to be implicated in the counterfeiting of the food tags? She wanted to believe it was Valerio, but the more she considered it, the more it sounded like some restless man who could not bear confinement. She continued reading:

It has occurred to me that I might be doing you a disservice by writing all I have learned at this time, Elspeth. If I can make the necessary arrangements, I will try to see you before the end of the year. Now that I know where you are, I can hardly restrain myself from escaping this wretched place like that young man did. In the meantime, please know that my thoughts are with you. Nothing has raised my spirits more than your letter during these dreary years.

Yours always,
Stephen

She folded the pages thoughtfully and stared at the river, which was running swiftly from the rains at a higher altitude, its roiling waters red with sediment. Her thoughts ranged from hope to despair; she wanted to hear what Stephen had withheld from her. She wanted to see him, too; he was the best friend she had made among the white people since she came West. The prospect of the meeting was covered with a dark cloud, though. The captain showed no indication of returning to his prospecting this year; indeed, his physical condition precluded it. That meant he would be with them much longer than usual and would, of course, remain during the winter. She glanced at the date on the letter again in an attempt to ascertain when Stephen might arrive. He had posted it in June, over three months ago; he might show up at any time.

She was not sure how the captain would respond to this guest from the past, who surely knew more about the circumstances under which he had left Santa Fe than he wanted revealed. She prayed that it would not be a signal for them to be taken to California, especially when it appeared that the People might be released to their homeland soon.

She did not have long to agonize over the captain's reaction. Stephen Cabot arrived two days later.

Chapter 26

The captain had resisted Elspeth's assistance as soon as he was out of bed. But, knowing that all was not well with him, he submitted meekly to Stephen's examination almost before the greetings were over. He did not seem to grudge the army physician's presence, though he studied him with narrowed eyes when he thought he was not being observed.

"You're a fortunate man," Stephen told him afterward. "I've never heard of anyone surviving spotted fever, which is surely what you've had. If the high temperature doesn't kill them, pneumonia or circulatory failure does. Whatever Elspeth gave you probably saved your life."

"Blind luck," the captain said. "If my constitution wasn't so strong, her Indian concoctions probably would have killed me. You don't look so well yourself, Cabot. You didn't catch anything from those Indians at Fort Sumner, did you?"

"It's been the other way around," Stephen replied. "They've contracted everything in the medical books from us. It wasn't an easy duty."

"Wasn't? You aren't going back there?"

"As a matter of fact, I'm going to be your neighbor, if you consider a day's ride that. I got myself transferred to Camp Verde."

Thea expressed her delight over the news, but Elspeth did not reveal any emotion. She had learned to compose her features like a Navajo in the captain's presence so he would not oppose

367

what she wanted. She observed and listened, and Stephen seemed to understand from the information she had imparted in her letter to him. His fine gray eyes were attentive to everything, and he knew that there could be a problem with the captain, too.

"I won't be mingling with the men much," he remarked to reassure the captain. "I'm not socially inclined right now, and I've nearly had enough of the army. If the soldiers come to me, I treat them to the best of my ability, of course. I just have no inclination to chat with them."

His lips were pale, and he was weary. Elspeth was concerned about him, and Thea studied him, too. They were aware of his history of consumption and wondered if the disease had been reactivated again by the long hours he had put in at the reservation.

"The soldiers won't keep you very busy," the captain remarked more comfortably. "Feel free to come out here whenever you have a few days off. We can get in some shooting before winter."

"I'd like that," Stephen replied casually. "I didn't have much recreation where I was. I'm looking to Camp Verde as a period of badly needed rest." Without changing his tone, he added casually, "You have a nice place here. Do you mind if I stroll around? I haven't spent a whole day in the saddle for some time. I need to stretch my legs."

The captain made an open gesture to indicate his permission. "I'd show you the place, but my legs aren't quite up to it. My sister-in-law will accompany you. She knows the farm fairly well and is responsible for its picturesque appearance."

He did not mention the Apache, and neither did Stephen, who appeared not to have heard of the incident. Elspeth and Stephen rose to leave without looking at one another or revealing how anxious they were to speak alone.

"If you see that damned Indian," the captain called after them, "tell him he'd better start chopping the wood he hauled. He's a lazy old bugger, and winter will be upon us before he gets it done."

"I don't know how you've put up with it," Stephen said when they were a safe distance from the house. "He's deliberately offensive."

"It doesn't matter, now," Elspeth said, able to smile at him for the first time. "I haven't paid much attention to him for a long time. I'm so glad you've come, Stephen. I only received your letter a few days ago. And their sending you to Camp Verde was the most wonderful luck."

"It wasn't luck, actually," he said, his gray eyes sparkling. "I had a devil of a time convincing the army that Camp Verde was the only place for my health. They wanted to dispatch me to Fort Whipple, because of the altitude and clear air there. As a physician, I'd have recommended the same. I told them that the workload would be too heavy at Whipple, which is a large place, and that there isn't much difference in altitude between there and Camp Verde. The only piece of luck was that the physician at Camp Verde hadn't had a long leave for some time."

They stopped to look at the goats, which had grown to six and were confined in a rough corral Elspeth had constructed at the edge of the field. Stephen leaned on the fence and watched the children running as freely as little animals in the field beyond.

"My God, how they've grown," he remarked. "You can measure time by the growth of children when you haven't seen them for a while. They look wonderfully healthy."

"They are," Elspeth said, studying his face. "You haven't done anything foolish regarding your own health? I'd never forgive myself if you jeopardized yourself to come here."

He turned to her with a smile. "I'm really just worn out, my dear. I'd been concerned it might be more than that for some time. I considered leaving the reservation if the old symptoms returned, because I'd have been a hazard to my patients there. Too many of them have contracted TB as it is. I was at a low ebb when I received your letter, but I'm feeling better already. You're responsible for nothing except giving me a reason to leave."

"You must rest, take care of yourself," she advised him seriously. "I wish you could stay here so we could look after you. The air at this altitude is fine. Thea hasn't had a relapse in spite of all the hard work she's done. She's as strong as a horse."

He laughed softly. "A very beautiful horse. You're both more beautiful than even I remembered. But," he added, taking her hand and turning it in his, "your hands shouldn't be callused like this. Doesn't he do anything around here?"

"Let's not speak of him," Elspeth said, withdrawing her hand. "I wrote you about it; nothing has changed. Except that he shows every indication of staying here instead of making his regular autumn foray into the hills. We usually don't have to put up with him so long. Of course, his health and the Apache . . ."

"I heard about that. Some of the officers are in awe of you; others are intensely suspicious. They don't know how closely the Dineh languages are connected. You took an awful chance."

"It was the *only* one," Elspeth said. "That narrows one's choices a bit. Frankly, I was terrified. I hope they never come again. I'd thought the 'picturesque appearance' of the farm the captain referred to would dissuade them, but they didn't come from the hills as I'd planned." She smiled at him. "Would you like to see my hogan?"

"I'd love to see it. In all the years I've spent with the People, I've never actually seen one of their dwellings."

When they entered the hogan, Stephen instinctively moved to the side where males sat and sank down beside the stones that marked the fireplace. Elspeth had not needed a fire yet and the place was devoid of ashes, swept as clean as the rest of the earthen floor. He smiled when she took her place across from him.

"I feel as if I've been here before," he said. "I've heard about their homes so much. Is this like the one you had in Dineyah?"

"As close as I could make it. There should be soft sheep skins on the floor instead of corn-husk mattresses and commercial blankets. There should be beautiful blankets here," she added nostalgically. "And it isn't as well built. Valerio built our hogan . . ."

Silence fell between them briefly, and Stephen studied her face, which revealed her emotions in his presence. "Yes," he said at last. "It's time we spoke of him. We might not have another chance during this visit. I told you I'd tell you everything I'd learned."

"What did you hear at the hacienda that you didn't want to write about?" she asked tightly, her eyes entreating. "I'm not at all convinced about the brave who came to the reservation only to escape again. I wanted to believe it was he, but if it were, he'd have come there sooner."

"That may be. I thought I was reaching when I heard that

story. I'm not so certain now. Perhaps I'd better relate my visit to the hacienda as it occurred. Bear with me for a moment. I went to your old house when I was in Santa Fe. I still didn't know where you were; I was drawn to the place. It was empty, of course. I suppose I'd hoped to find that you had returned. The house has fallen into neglect, the adobe walls have begun to crumble. There's nothing inside but your mother's loom, still covered with a quilt as you and your sister must have left it. I stood outside beside my horse, and two riders approached at a gallop. I loathe Don Diego, hadn't seen him since he collaborated with the Texans. He'd been returning home from a ride with Francisco when they spotted my bay horse. He seemed disappointed when he recognized me. They seemed very anxious to confront the rider at your house, but he and the boy dismounted and attempted to be gracious to me. Francisco's sixteen now. He bears little resemblance to his father, which I can only attribute to the care of the Brothers at the school. Anyway, after we'd exchanged somewhat stilted greetings, Don Diego remarked, 'I heard you've been working at the reservation. It's a pity you didn't manage to capture them all.' I thought he meant every Indian in the Territory and told him I didn't think Fort Sumner would hold them all. He said he was talking about the Navajo. 'We've had a visitor here several times. When we saw you, we thought he'd come back again. My men have never been able to overtake him, not once in three years. They told me he was a tall brave on a bay pony. He only comes here, to the Morrison place.' "

"He's alive," Elspeth said, drawing in a deep breath to accommodate the hope that swelled her heart. "He's been looking for us all this time . . ."

"I didn't want to tell you until I was reasonably certain," he said quietly. "I've argued against it every way I could so there'd be no mistake. I'd only just returned to the reservation the night I wrote to you. I was afraid to say anything. I didn't have time to inquire further there during the following weeks. I was occupied with my work and trying to get transferred. Before I left, I asked about the horse that was stolen when the brave escaped, expecting to hear it described as pinto, palomino, black or a gray, or that no one would remember. The army keeps a better record of its animals than its captured Navajo, though. I learned at once that it was an Indian pony named Santos, a bay."

Tears gushed from Elspeth's eyes and her hands went to her face. She was unable to speak for a moment. Valerio had done exactly what she had imagined he would do if he was alive, gone first to the reservation to find her, and after hearing Many Beads's story, escaped to search for her and his son. He had returned to the Morrison place time after time in an attempt to track the family.

"I must find him," she said, wiping the tears from her face. "I must find him at once."

Stephen reached across to her and put a hand firmly on her arm. "You don't know where he is," he said reasonably. "It's coming on winter. You and the boy would be riding around in circles as he has. You'd never connect. I understand your impulse, my dear, but you must think it through. I'm sure the Navajo will be relocated by spring, probably to their old homeland. He will hear about it, surely, and return there."

"He's in Dineyah now, I'm sure of it," she said. "I can't wait that long."

"You're sure of nothing," he said firmly, though his voice was understanding. "After several winters, there's nothing to sustain life there. It's much more likely that he's gone to the western part of Dineyah and sorties out when the weather permits it. My patients told me that many had fled to the western mountain area. San Francisco Peak is one of their sacred mountains. Do you know the area?"

She shook her head, still loathe to abandon her search. She knew he was right, but accepting his wisdom was bitter after her moment of elation. She and Sky could not brave the winter weather alone even in the Dineyah she knew. Tsegi was like an ice chamber without the comfort of a warm hogan, and the blizzards on the rim were too severe for a woman and child traveling without shelter. She had no conception about the Dineyah extending to San Francisco Peak. Such a quest would be madness.

The frustration made her weep again, and his hand tightened on her arm. "I'll take you to the canyon in the spring, I promise you. We should know more about the relocation then. But, even if a decision hasn't been made, I'll take you back to Dineyah, Elspeth. Trust me."

Winter did not announce itself gently with light snowfalls; it howled into the valley with strong winds that blanketed the ground with swathes of white before all the leaves had fallen from the trees. Elspeth was grateful that she had allowed Stephen to persuade her to wait until spring, though she was driven by the hope of finding Valerio. The most difficult part was not telling Sky that his father was alive and searching for them. She had behaved like an impetuous child when she first learned the news; she could not expect her son to respond with more maturity than she. He imagined himself immortal, as all children do, able to brave any difficulty, and he considered himself an expert tracker. At the least, he would have resented the delay; at the worst, he might have attempted the search on his own. She spoke to him often, and more optimistically, about his father, and told of the government's plan to relocate the People, perhaps on their own land, but she was careful not to give a time limit regarding the bureaucratic proceedings. Sky was well adjusted here and relatively disciplined. She wanted him to remain that way.

The early storms caught them by surprise and without adequate supplies, because the captain had been too weak to go to Camp Verde while the weather was still clear. He made no attempt to brave it now, though his strength had returned somewhat, and Elspeth could not fault him for that. She and Thea could make do, as they had often done in the past. When they chose to ignore his constant complaints, he turned his attention once again on the old man to bolster his self-esteem. He could not forgive himself for fainting during the Apache attack, and his dissatisfaction was compounded by Elspeth handling the situation so competently. George was an Indian, too, so he targeted him for persecution, ordering him about and abusing him verbally, as he no longer dared to order the women.

"Poor George will run away if he continues this," Thea said as she watched the men from the window. "I don't know what we'd do without him. He's making him shovel the snow from the path, now. He's an old man, Elspeth!"

"And there's no place he can run until the weather clears. The captain knows that," Elspeth said, joining her sister at the window. "He's always picked on the weakest member of the family. Now he's the weakest one, so he's turned to George."

"This is insufferable!" Thea exclaimed. She reached for her threadbare coat and shoved her arms through the sleeves. "I can't endure it."

Elspeth was taken by surprise by her reaction, and Thea was out of the door and down the path before she grabbed her own wrap to follow. The children had been playing on the floor near the fire, but stood in the doorway to watch, ignoring the cold. Elspeth paused only to herd them inside and close the door behind her. Before she was near enough to hear her sister's voice, she saw the steam of her breath as she reprimanded her husband, who had turned from George to receive the full force of Thea's reprimand.

". . . I won't put up with it anymore," Elspeth heard as she approached. "You've tormented us, and now you're tormenting an old man. George is our *friend*. He's helped us more than you have. You're being a bully, Robert. Perhaps you've always been a—"

The force of his gloved hand stopped her tirade and knocked her to the ground. Elspeth rushed forward and knelt beside her. Thea appeared dazed, but otherwise uninjured by the cushioned blow. The words that came to Elspeth's lips went unuttered when she observed the menace in George's hands as they tightened around the shovel and the sheer hatred in his dark eyes.

"No!" she commanded, more forcefully than she intended. "You've worked enough today, George. I'll bring some hot food to your hogan, shortly."

She wondered if he really would have done it. Unaware of what Elspeth had seen, the captain leaned down to help Thea to her feet. She pulled away from him and allowed Elspeth to assist her. As they moved toward the house, Elspeth's gaze followed the figure of the old man as he walked through the deep snow toward his dwelling. He had been provoked by the attack on Thea, who had been so kind to him, she thought. He really wouldn't have struck out with the shovel. He's taken a lot from the captain without rebellion, and he's always been kind with Sky.

But her arguments lacked conviction. She knew what she had seen in his eyes, and her initial distrust of the old man returned full force.

"Send him away?" Thea asked incredulously after the captain left for Camp Verde. "I can't believe I'm hearing this from you, Elspeth. Why should he be banished for something my husband did? I don't know what we'd do without George. I'm fond of him. We'd be alone without him when Robert's prospecting. I wouldn't welcome that."

"He's unpredictable, Thea. I've felt it from the first, but I'd begun to ignore it. Perhaps Stephen could find someone to help us out here. We should get rid of the old man."

"You sound like a white woman talking about Indians," Thea reproached her. "Not like yourself at all. He's been good with Sky, kind to all of the children. I think you're reading more into what you saw than you should. He was angry. We all were. He had every reason to be so. He's devoted to us."

"I've thought of all that. I don't want to be unfair. But I feel very strongly that he should go. The decision is yours, of course."

"There isn't any choice between decisions," Thea said almost crossly. "He stays. I respect your opinions, Elspeth, but you're being fanciful this time. George is like part of the family. His loyalty is a virtue, not a defect in his character. We'll just have to make certain that nothing provokes him. The winter won't last forever. We'll get through it somehow."

The captain was more cooperative in the weeks that followed. He did his share of the work and ceased abusing George. He and the old man were together a good deal, and there did not appear to be any animosity between them. When Elspeth observed them smoking a cigarette together and chatting amiably, she decided that Thea had been right. She had overreacted; there was nothing to worry about. In mid-November, a few sunny days melted most of the snow and Stephen rode out to see them for the first time in over a month.

The two men sat beside the fire, whiskey in hand, conversing easily while the women prepared their meal. Elspeth was relieved by the noticeable improvement in Stephen's health. The weariness was gone from his face, and he moved with purpose. He was again the Stephen Cabot she had known in Santa Fe. Thea noticed it, too.

"He's handsome," she said softly as they worked together at the stove. "He was very upset when you disappeared, Elspeth. He's in love with you." Elspeth leaned over to baste the roast he had brought with him. "He's fond of me, nothing more. He's a friend."

"That isn't the worst foundation for a marriage," Thea persisted gently. "I should know. One can fall in love with a man without really knowing him. The regret comes later. Stephen would be a fine husband for any woman."

Elspeth closed the iron oven more forcefully than necessary. "I know you want the best for me, Thea, but you should know by now there's only one man for me."

Elspeth had not shared the information Stephen had imparted, even to her sister, and she was anxious to have a word alone with him to find out if there were any new developments. She recognized that it was not going to be easy because of their confinement within the cabin and could think of no excuse for walking outside together in the cold.

The children fell upon the meat as if they were starved. Thea cautioned them to eat more slowly, partly because of manners, but more out of concern that one of them would choke.

"Let them enjoy it," the captain said, and turned to Stephen. "We haven't had any meat for a while, but now that the weather's cleared I'm going hunting. Would you like to join me? There's nothing like a good shoot."

"Not my sport, I'm afraid. I won't be able to stay long enough in any case," Stephen replied, his gaze meeting Elspeth's. "I suspected you'd been snowed in out here, so I brought the essentials: the meat, some tobacco, and the newspapers, which are more out of date than usual. Communication between the camp and Fort Whipple's been difficult, too. Drifts five feet high in the mountains. A rider finally got through during the thaw."

"I'm not interested in what's going on in the world," the captain said. "It's one of the advantages of living in isolation. But the meat and tobacco are more welcome than I can say. I'm going after venison, but I intend to shoot some fowl, too. Perhaps you can return for Thanksgiving, if you don't have other plans. We'll provide the meal next time."

"I'd be delighted to come," Stephen accepted promptly. "You know what a holiday meal is in the mess. The company and the cooking are far better here. I don't know what you ladies did with this roast. It's wonderful. And the first time I've eaten beef without chewing each bite for ten minutes at a time. Our cook would have incinerated it on the outside and caused muscular contraction within. I don't know how he manages it."

"By cooking it too fast," Thea volunteered. "I used to do

the same thing. Cooks learn gradually and at the expense of those who dine on their mistakes."

"You still have trouble with venison," the captain pointed out. "You should be able to taste the meat. It's smothered in spices and onions, and whatever else you use."

"It's gamey," she replied shortly. "What it really needs is a marinade of wine to tame it, but there isn't any wine so I use some of your whiskey."

Stephen choked with laughter and raised his napkin to his mouth, and the frown gathering on the captain's brow disappeared as if by magic. "I wondered what was happening to my whiskey," he said, joining into the merriment. "I thought one of you might be tippling silently, or that George had finally discovered where I'd hidden it."

The children left the table when Elspeth served the coffee, but Sky lingered, staring seriously at their guest. Stephen motioned the boy to his side and put a friendly hand on his shoulder. "You're looking very solemn, young man," he said. "I think you have something on your mind."

Sky leaned against him and addressed him in Navajo; "I need to know about my people. What is happening to them? Is my grandmother still at the reservation? When will they be going home?"

Ignoring the captain's consternation, Stephen responded in the same language, "Things are looking better all the time. Lieutenant McDonald of the Fifth Cavalry was sent to report on conditions at the reservation a short time ago. He said the People should be moved to a better place, where there is wood and water and grass. General William Tecumseh Sherman, a great warrior, wants the Dineh returned to their own country. He's going to the reservation in the spring to negotiate a new treaty with them. It is only a matter of time. You must be patient a while longer."

Sky's smile revealed his newly erupted front tooth and the gap beside it from his most recent loss. Stephen chuckled and ruffled the boy's hair. "You'll soon have a bite like a mountain lion," he said in English, and turned easily to the captain. "It amuses the boy to speak to me in Navajo," he explained, to avert any unpleasantness over the conversation. "He says I speak it like a baby, and I've just proven his point."

Elspeth appreciated the good-natured lie. Actually, Stephen

spoke the language rather well; he must have immersed himself in it at Bosque Redondo. He was an admirable man. Though they would not be able to speak privately during this visit, he had managed to convey the message he wanted to give her. The captain had confiscated the newspapers he had brought, and she was certain she would not see them before they were torn up and used to start the fires in hearth and stove.

If George appreciated the Thanksgiving dinner, he gave no indication. Elspeth wondered if he sensed the captain's opposition to his being in the cabin, or if he felt left out of the conversation at the table. Whatever went through his mind, he rose to leave as soon as he had cleaned his plate. When Sky excused himself before dessert to follow his friend, she cut two wedges of pumpkin pie for her son to take with him.

"George likes sweets," she commented, attempting to smile. "You can have your dessert together."

"It's my fault," Sky said as he balanced a dish in each hand. "I should have eaten by the fire."

She closed the door behind him and resumed her seat with a sigh. The captain had taken too much of the wine Stephen had brought and did not notice the incident, but she felt Stephen's gaze upon her and glanced at him.

He announced that he had to leave shortly after they had their coffee. "I've a patient in the infirmary I must look in on tonight," he explained to the disappointed Thea. "I felt guilty leaving him at all. The meal was wonderful as usual. Thank you. Perhaps I can stay longer the next time around."

Satiated and half-drunk, the captain made no move to accompany him to his horse, and Elspeth seized the opportunity to speak to Stephen alone.

"I don't know how you can endure it," he said when they were outside. "I wish I could take you away from here, all of you, but I'm in no position to do it yet. What was that business with the old Indian anyway?"

"The children wanted him to come. It didn't work out very well. Thea and I were afraid it wouldn't. At least, the captain didn't abuse him in your presence."

"He may have left because he wasn't given any liquor. I've heard about him. He's hardly a suitable choice to be here with women and children when Morrison's away."

"He's fond of Sky," she defended George halfheartedly. "He hasn't given us any trouble. We'll be all right, Stephen. I hope today won't discourage you from coming again soon."

"Of course not. I couldn't keep away if I wanted to, and I've no intention of being deprived of your company, if only for short periods, because of Morrison." They had reached his horse, and he stroked the animal's neck before saddling it. "When I think of you," he burst out suddenly, "all of you, out here with a drunken deserter and an unreliable old Indian, I can hardly bear it. Let me make arrangements for you to live at the camp. I can manage that at least. Morrison and the old man can look after themselves."

"It'll only be for a short time, now," she said, "just until spring. If we left, it would cause even more trouble, Stephen. And what would happen to Thea when Sky and I return to Dineyah? I can manage things here, but she's going to need a friend when I'm gone. That's what concerns me most. I can't abandon her and the children until some arrangement is made for them."

"But it's you I . . ." He checked himself before he spoke the word, but his expressive eyes betrayed him. "You can't be responsible for everyone," he said. "I don't want to add to your concerns. Rest assured that I'll help you find your husband, and don't trouble yourself about your sister and her children. I shall look after them. I could no more abandon Thea to this sort of life than you. I must confess something. It's gone through my mind more than once to turn Morrison over to the authorities so you'd be free of him. But when I weighed the consequences in my mind, I couldn't bring myself to hurt Thea. I suppose she must have some feeling left for him."

"I don't know," Elspeth said. "I honestly don't know."

Chapter 27

The captain had gone hunting with George several times during the winter, and he began to clean his rifle again in mid-February. Thea glanced hopefully at Elspeth. The tension in the cabin had grown almost unbearable, his presence permeating the very air they breathed. They found themselves walking more quietly and speaking in subdued voices in an effort to keep the peace. The children avoided the fire, playing outside in the biting cold to escape the mood in the house. Elspeth's fire burned in her hogan so they could warm themselves and make up little games when the weather was too inclement. She would have invited Thea's children to spend the night there, but that would have left Thea alone in the house with the man. Thea was showing the strain, her expression was set and there were faint smudges beneath her troubled eyes. Elspeth was ready to approach her sister with Stephen's suggestion about living in town when the captain stirred to clean his rifle.

"Tell George we're going out in the morning," the captain told Elspeth. "One more hunting trip while the weather holds. I don't want to get caught in a blizzard."

Thea gave an almost audible sigh of relief. "I'll collect the things for your pack," she volunteered. "I've mended your heavy socks and patched your jacket." She paused uncertainly. "What do you want to take with you? How long will you be gone?"

He shrugged. "Until we get a nice buck. How do I know how

long we'll be? Just pack the usual things and enough food so we won't have to shoot our dinner.''

George was at his fire, cradling his rifle, when Elspeth gave him the message. He stared at her for a long time without replying, so long that she thought he had not heard her. She wondered how old he really was, if perhaps he was losing his hearing. There was something eerie about the long, silent stare, his old fingers stroking the stalk of the weapon.

''Are you all right?'' she asked with concern. ''You mustn't go out in the cold if you don't feel well. I'll bring you some herbs if you need them.''

He shook his head and cleared his throat. He did not speak often. ''You good. Mrs. Morr'son good. George hunt tomorrow.'' The flickering fire exaggerated the planes of his face, his narrow smile. ''Get big buck for you.''

''Thank you,'' Elspeth said, reassured by his expression. ''You're a good hunter. I don't think Mr. Morrison could find a buck without you.''

The children lingered in the cabin the next morning, and Thea poured coffee for Elspeth and herself with relief.

''The coffee's almost gone, but I thought we should celebrate,'' she said below the babble of the children's voices.

Elspeth studied her over the rim of her cup. ''Stephen doesn't think we should be out here, Thea. He's suggested that he find a place for us at the camp. How do you feel about that?''

''I don't see how we could do it,'' Thea considered. ''We haven't any money. We couldn't allow him to keep us. He's a dear, considerate man, but it would only bring trouble. I'm quite happy here, really, except in the winter when . . .''

''I haven't asked, because I didn't want to interfere,'' Elspeth said cautiously. ''Do you still care for the captain? You don't have to answer if you'd rather not. I know it's an inappropriate question.''

''Between you and me?'' Thea said, smiling slightly. ''After all we've been through together? I thought you must have known. We haven't lived together as man and wife for over a year. I'd die if he touched me. He's angry and frustrated, and it's made him even worse. The situation's terrible, but he'll be off prospecting soon. The summers are lovely here.''

"What about next winter, and the one after that? You and the children can't go on like this. You'll get ill again. It'll kill you in the end."

A shadow passed through Thea's blue eyes. She was as beautiful as she had always been, and Elspeth's heart went out to her. "Let's not speak about it, now," she said. "Let's enjoy our freedom. I keep thinking that something will happen to change things. I don't know what, Elspeth. I'm not as practical as you are."

"Things don't happen out of the blue. You're too romantic. If you want things to change, you must help yourself. This isn't theater, Thea. It's life."

"Stephen's offer was very kind," Thea said wistfully. "He was ready to whisk us away. He's a wonderful man. I wish I'd met him . . ."

She did not have to finish her statement. Elspeth saw from her expression that Thea was in love with him. "Perhaps he'll visit while the captain's away," she said gently. "In the meantime, let's make the best of the time we have to ourselves. We can relax a bit and make up new games for the children."

They had only seen Stephen once in January, and Elspeth did not really think he would arrive during the captain's short absence. She was as surprised as the others when he rode in the following afternoon. She had made a sled, a plank of wood with a rope attached, and she and Thea were taking turns pulling it to the top of a snowdrift so the children could ride down, when Sky suddenly abandoned the activity.

"Kind Man!" he cried, running to meet the rider, who reached down and pulled him up behind him as he rode toward them.

"As pretty a picture as I've seen," Stephen said. "A New England Christmas card come to life. Pretty women and children with laughing eyes and rosy cheeks." He glanced toward the cabin as he swung out of the saddle. "Your horses are gone. Morrison and I didn't pass on the trail without seeing each other, did we?"

"He and George have gone hunting," Thea explained, with almost pathetic delight at his presence. "We were hoping you'd come. I made cinnamon rolls when I baked bread this morning. Come warm yourself.''

''Thank you. I've brought a few things; I thought you might be running low,'' he said, with his hand in little Elizabeth's curls. ''You made a sled.''

''It goes down hill all right, but it needs a team of horses to drag it up again. Thea and I have been playing horse.''

He laughed. ''I think we can do something about that. I'll make some runners for you. How long will he be away?'' he asked, lowering his voice.

She shrugged. ''Until he shoots the fabled great buck. They left yesterday. Do you know how to make sled runners?''

''No,'' he said, ''but I've had enough experience with them to try. It was my favorite winter sport as a boy. I think I can manage.''

He had brought some staple foods with him, including the much-needed coffee and some sweets for the children, who clustered around him while he drank his tea. Elspeth had not recognized how much the children needed a gentle, fatherly presence before, and she watched them silently. Things could have been so different. But she had long since given up thinking in terms of what might have been.

His thoughts were on the children, too. ''Where does your father keep his tools?'' he asked Robert. ''If we fix the sled now, you'll have it in the morning.''

''In the wagon,'' the boy said apprehensively, ''but we can't go in there. The floor is rotted. Father said he'd skin us alive if went near the wagon. Even Mother and Aunt Elspeth can't go there.''

''Well, he didn't tell me that, did he? I think I can manage to find a few tools without putting my foot through the wagon bed.''

They spent the morning watching the children play with their new sled. Stephen had not questioned the sleeping arrangements when he had been assigned the master bedroom the night before. Thea remarked that she frequently slept with her children.

Something Stephen had said the previous evening kept returning to Elspeth's mind as they watched the children tumble in the snow. He made a point of imparting the information to her alone before he went to his room.

"There's nothing wrong with the wagon bed," he said. "It's completely sound."

"Perhaps he thinks they might get hurt playing there," she said. "Sometimes it's difficult to know what he's thinking."

"There's no more chance of their hurting themselves there than in the house. Everything's stowed in an orderly manner, almost as if he'd made a private study out of the wagon. Maybe he just doesn't want his things disturbed. Why would he warn you and Thea away, too?"

Why? she thought. They had never questioned the captain's warning. They knew what the wagon contained and had no use for anything there. She had seen him go to the wagon only a few times during the year and always assumed it was to get a tool. She dismissed it from her mind when Thea clapped her hands and urged them to the cabin for lunch.

"General Sherman's one of the peace commissioners appointed to investigate conditions at Fort Sumner in April," Stephen remarked as they ate. "All agents were relieved from duty as of the first of this month, and all power regarding the Indians removed from the governor. There's talk of a treaty. If the Navajo agree to it, they'll be going home in the summer. Later than we thought, Elspeth, but things are moving in the right direction."

Thea stopped eating and stared at them. She had read the newspapers for the past six months without realizing the significance of what she read. "That means you'll be leaving, Elspeth," she said in a small voice.

"You've nothing to worry about," Stephen said gently. "I've promised your sister I'd look after you and your children, Thea. It will be my pleasure to do so."

"There's reason to believe that Valerio's been searching for us," Elspeth told her. "We've no idea how to find him, but he's sure to join the People in Dineyah if they're sent back."

"Of course," Thea said quietly, "you'd have to go. I know what he means to you."

Sky had been listening closely, but he turned away suddenly and cocked his head as if he heard something outside.

"Two horses, I think," he said. "George and the captain are back."

They could not have returned at a worse time, Elspeth thought, her gaze seeking her son's. She had not wanted for him to learn what they suspected about Valerio until they actually found him. "The whole thing is still months away," she said. "There's no need to speak of it now."

George entered silently and crouched by the fire to warm his hands. Thea rose to lay another place at the table for her husband, and Elspeth carried a plate of hot food to the old man, who ignored it, though he appeared frozen. They waited for some time, but the captain did not appear, and she went to the window to see what was delaying him. The horses were tethered outside in the snow, and the captain was nowhere in sight. A peculiar sensation tightened her scalp, and she turned to the old man.

"Where's Mr. Morrison?" she asked more sharply than she had intended, and added more softly, "I don't see him out there."

"Gun fired wrong," George said, as if his mind were somewhere else.

The words elicited total silence, and Elspeth had a sinking feeling in her chest even before Stephen jumped to his feet.

"Where did you leave him?" he cried. "Is he injured? He'll freeze, goddammit! Fetch my bag, Thea," he said, reaching for his cape and glowering at George. "Take me to him at once."

The old man did not move. "There is hungry spirit in that place," he said.

"What place? You're damned well going to take me there right now. Where the devil did you leave him?"

When George did not respond, Elspeth put a restraining hand on Stephen's arm. "George," she said as she knelt beside the old man, "you don't have to take us all the way if you don't wish, but you must guide us to where it happened. The spirit won't harm you. You know I'm a medicine woman."

The rheumy gaze that met hers made her uncomfortable, but she read the moment when he decided to trust her. He rose stiffly and shuffled toward the door. "Horses tired," he said. "Hungry. George feed them."

Elspeth put her arms around Thea and studied her taut face. "We'll return as soon as possible. Heaven knows where he left him, but we'll find him, I promise."

"You'll need . . ." Thea drew away, moved to the sideboard like a sleepwalker and stood there, undecided what to do next, staring at the cupboard.

"I'll get the food," Elspeth said gently. "See if you can find some warm blankets."

The snow that began to fall as they rode toward the hills almost obliterated George ahead of them, and Elspeth urged her horse forward so she would not lose sight of him. She had never distrusted him so strongly. If the snowfall became heavier, she was certain the old man would abandon them rather than return to the scene of the accident. She sensed his fear, though she could not completely explain it.

"Don't lose sight of him," she warned Stephen. "We'll never find the captain without him."

"What was that business about a bad spirit?" he asked, his voice muffled by his heavy cape. "Does he think the place caused the accident, or is he frightened of ghosts like the Navajo?"

"I don't know. If it's the latter, the captain's dead, or George thinks he is. The only thing I'm sure of is that he'll break and run if he has the chance."

"We'd better ride on either side of him so he doesn't have that chance."

The wide pine boughs gathered the snow, making visibility better when they ascended into the hills, but, by then, the light began to diminish into early dusk. Stephen paused to light their lantern, which illuminated the forest for only the few feet around them. Though Elspeth had often ridden in the winter, she had never experienced the total silence of the forest; its floor, blanketed by snow and pine needles, muffled even the fall of the horses' hooves. No birds or small animals stirred, and in the increasing darkness, even the call of the owl, the harbinger of death, was mute. At this distance from the cabin, the report of the captain's rifle could not have been heard as they had so often heard it when he was hunting; indeed, George had ridden a considerable distance to return to them. Elspeth's hands felt as if they were frozen into her mittens; she could not feel the reins between her fingers. Her face was warmed only by the breath trapped beneath the folds of her shawl.

"We'll have to light a fire soon," Stephen said. "The old man isn't riding in circles, is he?"

"No. We've been climbing steadily. I don't like it, though. If it hadn't snowed, we could have followed the tracks he made when he came down from the forest; they're gone, now." They had been riding single file again to wind their way through the trees, and she raised her voice to call, "How much farther is it, George? We want to make a fire."

"Not far," he replied. "George make fire soon."

Within fifteen minutes, he stopped and slid down from his horse. He pointed to a dark stand of trees that looked no different from the other trees to Elspeth.

"George stay here," he told them. "Build good fire. You ride in those trees."

"You'd better remain here, Elspeth," Stephen said. "You must be freezing."

"You may need me," she said, sensing that he was trying to protect her from whatever lay behind the trees. Something warned her that she should remain with the old man, but she wanted to help if the captain was still alive. "You'll be all right here, George. We'll be back soon," she assured him. "Nothing will bother you here. The fire will protect you. You mustn't leave the fire."

They pressed on at once; if there was a breath of life left in the captain, they could not waste time. They had not gone far when a clearing opened before them and they sighted the dark form, motionless, with a light dusting of snow covering it.

"This won't be pretty," Stephen warned her as he dismounted. "His gun must have backfired."

"I'll bring the lantern," she said.

The dark stain congealed in the snow did not look red in the lantern light, but she knew it was blood and that they were too late. The blast had forced him backward. He lay face-up, his features obliterated by the snow, which Stephen dusted away to examine the body. Elspeth had to look away. The explosion of the rifle had caught him full in the face. She had to steady the lantern in her hand. She finally placed it on the ground near

Stephen to avoid looking at the corpse, and she began to pick up the parts of the gun that lay around it.

"He died almost instantly," Stephen finally said. "The blast must have rendered him unconscious. A fragment lacerated the carotid artery. No one could have done anything, Elspeth. Why didn't George just say he was dead?"

"He did, in his way," she responded, securing the metal fragments in her shawl. "Thea mustn't see this, Stephen. Help me wrap him in the blankets."

The fire burned as promised, but George was nowhere to be found. He might have been whisked from the spot by the bad spirit he feared, if his horse and gun had not been missing, too. He had left them a little food and disappeared into the night.

"He may have returned to the farm," Stephen speculated. "It was clear he didn't want any contact with the body. We won't have any difficulty finding our way back."

Elspeth packed snow into the coffeepot and put it on the fire, conscious of the burden on the captain's horse. The rifle concerned her more than the old man's whereabouts. The captain's rifle had always been clean, well oiled; it was unlikely that it would have exploded in his face. She kept her suspicion to herself as she measured coffee into the boiling pot and sat staring into the flames as it brewed.

"I buried the dead when I was with the People," she said quietly. "I'll bury him. I should feel something, but I don't."

There was no smoke rising from George's hogan when Elspeth returned. She had not expected that he would be at the farm. The conviction growing in her mind had to be put to rest, and she left Stephen with Thea so she could do so. Thea had taken the confirmation of the captain's death calmly, perhaps too calmly. Her reaction worried Stephen, and he gave her a sedative so she could sleep.

"The reality won't strike her until later," he said. "I want her to be well rested tomorrow. The children will have to be told. It isn't going to be easy."

"You need rest, too," Elspeth said. "I'll return at dawn. I

thought Sky would remain in the cabin, but he must have gone to our hogan. He's never been alone before.''

Sky had built a fire and was sleeping soundly when she entered. The light from her lantern didn't rouse him. After she assured herself that he was all right, she knelt before the fire and placed the metal fragments on the floor to inspect them, beginning with the part of the barrel that had been closest to the firing mechanism. The edge was jagged, and when she tried to look through the barrel, no light penetrated from that end. She attempted to force the impediment out with a piece of the rod; after several attempts, she heard something fall. She searched the floor with her fingers, but when they closed around an object the right size it felt more like a stone than metal. She raised it to the light to examine it. The dried mud, as hard as adobe, was burned black but unmistakable. She used the rod again, more forcefully, and a core of the same material ejected in a cylinder conforming to the inside of the barrel. Her suspicion was confirmed, and she did not know what to do about it.

George hated the captain because of his mistreatment, but he had reacted violently only once, when Thea was struck by her husband. Elspeth wondered why the old man waited so long to take vengeance. The method he had chosen was clear to her now. The gun, in pieces on the floor, was not the captain's; he had cleaned his rifle before they went hunting. George had tampered with his own precious gun some time in advance so the clay would dry. Somehow, in the course of the hunt, he switched rifles. The determined premeditation of the act made her feel cold inside. She should have heeded her intuition about the strange old man. She could not change that now, though, and she had to make a decision before Stephen took the rifle fragments to Camp Verde.

She was surprised by the ambivalence of her feelings. She did not condone the murder, but she felt some sympathy for the old man who had suffered so many humiliations in silence. The rifle was clear testimony of what had happened. The army would pursue George for killing a white man if the metal fragments fell into their hands. Sky worshipped George, and the old man had been good to him, taught him the things his own father was unable to teach him.

The effect on her son if the truth were known influenced her decision. She worked for several hours cleaning all traces of adobe mud from the barrel and did not allow herself to think about her actions as she held it over the dying fire to recoat it with soot.

Chapter 28

"I want to stay on here," Thea said after the funeral. "It's a good life, Elspeth. A healthy one for all of us. I know you'll be leaving, but I think we can make it on our own. Aside from the few supplies that Robert paid for, we've been doing that anyway. Maybe we could sell part of our crops in Camp Verde. Perhaps there'd be a market there for the things I preserve."

"Who was Father's lawyer?" Elspeth asked. "We should have written to him a long time ago."

"There's nothing left of our inheritance. I'm sure we've been living on what Robert saved from his army pay. He said my inheritance barely got us out here."

"If that's the case, why were you signing papers? Why did he ask me to sign? I hardly saw the letterhead, but they had to be from the lawyer."

Thea shook her head helplessly. "I didn't see the name, either. But," she said, brightening, "I think I know where Robert hid his things. There had to be a reason for keeping us away from the wagon."

They found the captain's papers and maps, along with a metal cash box, after a thorough search of the wagon. While Elspeth pored over the papers, Thea counted the money from the box and carefully totaled it.

She leaned back with relief. "We're rich, Elspeth. There's

one hundred and ninety-five dollars here, not counting the Mexican coins. It'll last us for years. He kept a lot of cash on hand.''

Elspeth looked up from the document she was reading. ''Not much considering what he's had. There must be something in the bank in Santa Fe, either cash or something he couldn't cash after he left there.''

''You mean *deserted*,'' Thea said ''There was only two ways he could have left Santa Fe, Elspeth. He couldn't have bought his way out, because it was wartime. Stephen knows, doesn't he?''

Elspeth nodded. ''He's remained silent because of you. It doesn't matter, now. You must put it out of your mind along with everything else.''

''The children must never know. I'll make sure they don't. What have you found in the documents?''

''Robert didn't tell you the truth about your inheritance,'' Elspeth said. ''I haven't had time to read everything. Since I wasn't around when I reached my majority and didn't sign anything, there may be something left there, too. I'll write the lawyer, tonight.''

''He must have liked Mexican coins,'' Thea said, turning one under the light. ''They are pretty, aren't they? They shine so.''

''They're almost solid silver.'' Elspeth said. ''Valerio rode halfway across the Territory to barter for a few Mexican coins when he was trying to make jewelry.''

Thea put the stacks of silver coins into one of the buckskin bags from the box and handed it to Elspeth. ''You must have them,'' she said. ''You can take them with you when you go. Your husband can make beautiful things from them.''

The meadow was green and early wildflowers showing their colors when Stephen brought the reply to Elspeth's letter, along with the news that a treaty was being drafted to release the Navajo.

''They have to agree on compensation, so the People will be able to live there,'' he said. ''They're destitute. They had a quarter of a million sheep and sixty thousand horses before the Long Walk; they haven't a tenth of that, now. They'll never be able to raid again after this treaty. The government will have to grant an additional allotment. Sherman and Tappen won't allow them to return in such pitiful condition."

"Thea wants to remain here, Stephen, but it would be dangerous as well as impractical. The Apache aren't on a reservation."

"She'd be safer in Santa Fe. I intend to go back there. We can work something out. I still have my house, and I'll rebuild my practice. Physicians are needed there. Things have changed since the war. The hidalgos are no longer in control, and peonage isn't acceptable to a country that's abolished slavery. The things we didn't like in the Territory are changing."

He remained outside to play with the children as he always did when the weather was fair, and Elspeth hurried to Thea with the letter. They disregarded the enclosed checks to read the heavy pages. Their father's will had provided each of his daughters a yearly income, which was drawn on the interest from his estate. The principal was still intact. Mr. Townsend, the lawyer, had heard nothing from Captain Morrison in the past four years; he had been deeply concerned about the family. He had refused to send any more of Elspeth's money when the captain could not account for her whereabouts after she reached twenty-one. He had kept her allowance for her with diminishing hope of her ever claiming it. The young women had a comfortable income for life. He expressed his regret about the captain's death and enclosed additional papers for them to sign which would put them in control of their own finances.

"Father was cautious," Elspeth said.

"I had no idea." Thea sighed as she studied the checks. "I shouldn't have signed anything. If I'd retained control of our affairs, he couldn't have done any of this to us."

"You were young. You were ill. We both thought men should take care of such things."

"Well, he certainly didn't spend my yearly allowance on his family," Thea said bitterly. "He let us work like field hands."

"It's all in the past, Thea. You can make a new start and forget the bad times. Your property is still in Santa Fe if you want it. Stephen intends to return there. He'd like you to accompany him. You need the security of a town, a place to educate your children.''

''Yes,'' Thea agreed thoughtfully. ''But who knows when I might see you again?''

''We should be able to visit each other,'' Elspeth said, with a smile. ''I imagine I'll be able to leave Dineyah even if it is a reservation. And Stephen could bring you and the children to visit during the school holidays.''

''I don't want to be a burden to him. Did he really say he wanted to take us with him? You didn't suggest it, did you?''

''He was the one who said you should settle there. He wants to look after you,'' Elspeth reassured her. ''He's very fond of you, Thea.''

They planted as usual in the spring, though they were not sure if they would be on the farm at harvest. The negotiations regarding the Navajo drew on interminably. Stephen joined them when he left the army in late June.

''We should see you settled,'' he told Thea. ''Elspeth will want to leave at once when word comes. I think we should all leave for Santa Fe as soon as possible.''

''Whatever is the least trouble,'' Thea said. ''The wagon won't accommodate the load it brought here. I'll leave things behind. I want to start a new life.''

''An excellent idea,'' he encouraged her. ''Elspeth?''

''I'll remain here with Sky so we can harvest the corn and take it with us to Dineyah. I have medicines to gather, too, Stephen, and I need time alone with Sky to prepare him to rejoin his people. Santa Fe would confuse him. We'd be out of place there.''

''I didn't want any of you to be here alone,'' he considered. ''That was the purpose of leaving now. I understand, though. I'll arrange with Captain Hennessey to have patrols look in on you, and I'll return as soon as possible, hopefully with news of the treaty. You must promise to wait for me even if you hear something while I'm away.''

She tried to ignore the fondness in his gray eyes. She wished it were directed toward Thea, instead. *Once I'm out of the picture, he will become more aware of Thea's affection,* she thought. The trip to Santa Fe will give them time together. Thea is the woman for him.

She learned that the treaty had been signed when they rode to Camp Verde in mid-July. She purchased a buckboard and loaded it with items the People would need when they returned to their homeland. Sky was excited over the purchases; they assured him they were really going home.

"Captain Hennessey said the People will be leaving right away," he said. "We'll be going soon, won't we?"

"As soon as Kind Man comes," she told him. She had been speaking only Navajo to her son. "We'll harvest the corn early. We'll need time to dry it."

"They won't need our corn. The government's giving them money and sheep. Even horses!"

"They'll be lucky to get a crop. It'll be a difficult winter, and they'll share what we bring with their neighbors, as they should. There won't be many sheep for a while. What they'll be allotted isn't as many as it seems."

"They'll have money to buy more sheep. Everyone who plants a crop will get ten dollars a year! That's a lot of money."

Elspeth did not respond; she did not want to dim his elation. She wondered where the People were expected to spend their pittance, how they would get through the winter. The proud people—who once owned 250,000 sheep and 60,000 horses—were to be given only 15,000 sheep and goats and 500 head of cattle. There was not proper grazing for cattle in Dineyah; indeed, the Navajo were not accustomed to cattle. The two horses for each family the government had allotted were a deliberate attempt to limit the range of the braves. The animals could only be used to pull a buckboard when a family went to ceremonials and for assistance on the farm. She viewed the future of the tribe with trepidation. Her worst fear was that the allotment was equitable, that many of the People had lost their lives on the Long Walk and at Fort Sumner.

Stephen returned, dusty and weary, but smiling. "They're probably home by now," he said. "They crossed the Rio Grande two weeks ago. What a sight it was! A ten-mile column of Navajo with fifty wagons and several companies of soldiers. You could see their dust from miles away. Most of them were walking, to retrace their steps to their homeland."

Elspeth could not speak for a moment, her voice strangled by the fullness in her chest. "We're ready to leave when you've rested. Is Thea settled?"

"Indeed she is," he replied as he swung from his saddle. "She's staying in my house for the present. She was making curtains when I left, and it already seemed more like a home. She's the gentlest person I've ever known."

Elspeth smiled. "She's a natural homemaker," she said. "I know things will be better now. She needs someone to cherish her as she deserves."

He searched her face with disbelief. "Am I so transparent, Elspeth?"

"Nothing would make me happier than knowing you and Thea were together," she said gently. "The two people I love most in the world outside of my own family."

"You must think me inconstant," he said, his gray eyes earnest. "I've known for some time that my affection for you could never be returned. No one will ever displace your husband in your heart."

"I'll be content with the affection accorded a sister-in-law. You've made me very happy."

"The only thing that will really make you happy is finding Valerio," he said, smiling. "I wonder if he knows how fortunate he is."

When she drove the heavily laden buckboard away from the farm, she felt as if she were coming out of captivity, too. Her heart felt light for the first time in four years. Her eyes glowed with anticipation, and she could feel the color in her face. Riding beside her, Stephen and Sky were as exhilarated as she, and, the first day out, they traversed over ten miles with relative ease, despite the difficulty of the mountain road. They camped that evening among red sandstone rocks that made Sky think they were closer to their destination than they were. Elspeth had to show him on the map how far they still had to go. Stephen watched her by the fire with a mixture of pleasure and foreboding after Sky went to sleep.

"I have to say it," he remarked at last. "I don't want to be a spoiler, but it's only fair. You mustn't expect things to be as they were. Not as you remember them. I haven't wanted to describe what I saw at Fort Sumner, my dear, but some of your family may not be there, and those who are will have changed.''

"I realize that. But it feels so good to be doing something, at last. You must promise me something.''

"Anything, you know that.''

"If I choose to remain in Dineyah regardless of what I find''—she paused, trying not to imagine the ultimate disappointment—"you must not oppose my decision. I know I'll be needed there.''

"Let's cross that bridge when we come to it,'' he said. "We don't know what we'll find.''

They reached the flat, red country, with its multihued buttes and mesas extending to snowcapped mountains, within a week, pressing forward steadily. Stephen drew in his breath at the sight, and Elspeth pointed out the directions of the four sacred mountains to her son, though only one was faintly visible. They were essential to his understanding of his new life, and he regarded the land of his people seriously.

"I had no idea,'' Stephen said. "No wonder they've longed for this place. It's splendid.''

"We're still a great distance from Tsegi,'' she told him, "but this is Dineyah.''

They remained to watch the sun set in a blaze of crimson, which paled the rose-hued earth until it was enveloped in the purple tapestry of evening. She experienced a calm she had not known for many years, but her companions exclaimed over the sight.

"Does the sun do this every evening?'' Sky asked, with excitement. "I don't remember the sun doing this.''

"It's different every evening,'' she said softly. "Never the same. Nothing is ever quite the same, but is always beautiful. You shall see.''

They had to pause to repair a wheel on the buckboard the following day and noticed the first signs of habitation, crude brush shelters, which were more visible than hogans had been against the earth. The scattered families they encountered were worn by their long ordeal but retained a measure of their inherent peace, as if they drew strength from their sacred land. They distributed some of the corn to the most needy while Stephen assessed their health. The women no longer wore the familiar blanket dresses. Elspeth was astonished to observe them clad in long calico skirts and dark velvet blouses, which made them look like gypsies. She recalled how much Maria had treasured the full skirt she had worn at the hacienda; now, all the women wore them as if they were their native garb.

"They couldn't weave at the fort," Stephen explained. "The skirts came first from well-meaning white women who probably thought they were more modest. The fashion caught on rather quickly, and the Navajo women learned to sew their own."

"But velvet blouses, in this heat? The government must have supplied the fabric. What on earth were they thinking of?"

"Attractive, aren't they?" he said, with a smile. "Probably a supply mix-up. It happens often enough in the army. The women don't seem to mind them."

"Are many of them ill?"

"Some," he admitted. "Mostly TB. I anticipated it, of course. Nutrition was poor at the reservation. It won't be much better here for a while, either."

"They're just starting to plant. It's midsummer. I suppose I did imagine things differently. There are hardly any sheep. The flock used to be as plentiful as the clouds in the sky."

He put a sympathetic hand on her shoulder but did not remind her of his caution not expect too much.

The rosy sandstone walls loomed on either side of them as they made their way into Tsegi, crossing and recrossing the ever-changing banks of Chinle Wash. The small number of families that had made their way back began to alarm Elspeth. Many homesteads were still deserted, though the valiant peach trees had come back into leaf, with small fruit evident in the foliage.

"It's a long distance for them to travel on foot," she said, to reassure herself more than her companions. "One of the most distant places they have to reach. They probably haven't arrived yet. An entire clan held out on top of that anvil-shaped rock we passed when we entered. I wonder what became of them?"

Sky remained silent as they negotiated the boulder-strewn path of the Wash, pausing frequently to dislodge fallen branches to get the buckboard through. In midafternoon, he suddenly looked around him and said, "I know this place. We're near the cliff dwelling that is not *chindi*. We're home!"

But it is *chindi* now, Elspeth thought as she tried to orient herself without the usual landmarks: we left Hosteen Yazzie there. It is his burial place. The tamarisk trees still made a delicate screen between the Wash and where Many Beads's place had been. She skirted them with the buckboard, and they reached the remains of a hogan, its burned logs tumbled inward, its clay walls washed back into the earth. She recognized it as the spot where she once sat at her loom, where Maria had first appeared to her, and gave a soft cry.

"It's my hogan," she whispered. "I know where we are, now. We'll leave the wagon here and walk the rest of the way."

They moved forward pushing the lacy branches aside in front of them. A few sheep were grazing in a hastily built corral against the canyon wall, the same corral where they buried their children's umbilical cords, but she saw no horses. If Valerio had come, at least he would have a horse, she thought, her heart sinking. The family should have the two from the government. She brushed aside another branch and saw a brush shelter in the same place where they had spent so many long summer days.

"Someone's here," she said, her breath half suspended. "Someone's come back."

Two women rested in the shelter, and when she recognized Many Beads she nearly rushed to throw herself into her arms. Instead, she approached slowly, attempting to control her emotions. They had not seen each other for so long, so many things had changed, she did not know what to expect.

Many Beads rose to greet her in the same manner, almost as if she did not recognize her. There was another woman in the shelter with a young girl, but it took Elspeth a moment to recognize Big Woman. She had lost so much weight that she would have to be called by another name. Only two woman and a girl, she thought, and a boy with a pockmarked face. Where was Many Tears Woman? Where was Oldest Boy?

"We came as soon as we heard," she told Many Beads, studying her face, which seemed incredibly old. Her cheeks were sunken and her eyes were dull. She wore a calico skirt and a shapeless velvet blouse, held together in front by a neat row of safety pins. Her neck was devoid of turquoise necklaces, except for the one that matched Elspeth's, the silver blossom Valerio had made.

"I have thought of you," Many Beads said, reaching out to touch Sky's hair. "My grandson. I have another grandson." She spoke almost to herself. "He is fine. Come to your grandmother, my boy."

Sky rushed into her arms and tears brimmed in Many Beads's eyes. She made no attempt to hide them. "Your little brother is here," she said, motioning to the other boy, when she recovered herself. "This is Surviving Boy. He was only a baby when you saw him last." She looked at Elspeth. "You cared for him as your own, and once again he has survived."

Elspeth wanted to take the child into her arms, but he shied away from her. She understood, but it pained her deeply. No mention would be made of the dead. Information would be difficult to obtain about them. Remembering her manners, Elspeth introduced Stephen. "I would like you to meet Dr. Cabot, who has been very good to us."

"We know this man," Many Beads said, with an attempted smile. "He saved Surviving Boy in that place. He is welcome. We will make some coffee and cook for you."

She and her daughter kindled the fire and began to prepare food, slapping white-flour bread between their palms and frying it in an iron skillet. Elspeth felt as if she, too, were a guest, instead a member of the family.

"I recall treating the boy, now," Stephen said. "I was so busy during the smallpox epidemic I didn't ask names. I remember him, particularly, though. His mother gave him her food, and when she fell ill, she went very quickly."

Elspeth swallowed hard. "Many Tears Woman," she said, "my friend and my sister—the other mother of the boy. I don't know how to find out about the men. They never speak of the dead."

"I don't like the way the younger woman looks. They shouldn't share their precious food with us, Elspeth. Why didn't you offer what you brought?"

"They're being hospitable. We must allow them that. It's odd to see a coffeepot on the fire. I need a cup of coffee." She sighed. "Something's wrong, Stephen. There's a wall between us. I suppose it's because I wasn't part of their experience during the past four years."

"It'll pass," he said. "Give them a little time. It's understandable if they regard you as an outsider at first."

After they had eaten, Many Beads volunteered some additional information about the family. "The husbands of two of my daughters came to join us in that place. They have gone to get logs to build a hogan. We will have the Blessing Way ceremonial when it is built. Maybe it will make us safe until we can find someone to sing the Enemy Way, for we have been among our enemies."

Only her sons-in-law had turned themselves in at Fort Sumner, Elspeth thought painfully. The brave they had thought was Valerio must have been someone else. She wanted to speak his name, but she feared their reaction. Perhaps he had gone to the camp and been unable to find them; she had to believe that.

"We've brought some corn and some meat," she said quietly, "and some seed for you to plant."

They accepted the food gratefully when Stephen carried it from the buckboard.

"The *Interior* gave us some seed," Many Beads said, the English word sounding strange from her as she arranged the bags of meal in the shelter. "We've been trying to plow, but the earth has grown hard from going untilled."

Sky jumped up and ran to the wagon. He returned with some shovels and Many Beads nodded as she accepted them. "We had these where we were, but the land was bad there. Sour. Nothing grew. Our land will take care of us, though, if we care for it."

"I will help you plant," Sky said eagerly. "I know all about farming. We've lived on a farm for a long time. We must plant as soon as we can, or there won't be any corn for winter."

Many Beads drew him into her arms and smiled, revealing several missing teeth. "You are a good boy, and you are strong. If you help us, the corn will grow high," she said.

Elspeth wanted to be alone so she could weep. The wariness toward herself did not extend to Sky. Why should Many Beads be wary of me? she thought. Surely, I have not changed so much since we parted. Perhaps she thinks I've brought the necessities out of pride. I haven't been through what they have. She felt out of harmony with the family, a stranger. Nothing was as she had anticipated it would be. Big Woman had not spoken at all, and Stephen finally asked if he could examine her.

Many Beads agreed with complete trust in him. "She has not been herself for a long time. There is a grief in her that will not go away. Maybe you can do something until we find a Singer."

After a cursory examination, he turned to Elspeth. "It's what I thought. She'll have to be isolated from the others, especially the children. She told me her husband started coughing blood on the way home. He shouldn't be out there hauling logs in that condition. At least she won't be alone. She's very depressed already."

"Two of her children aren't here," Elspeth said. "Oldest Boy and her baby. She's grieving. I'll build another shelter. It won't take long. Explain the reason to her."

She was grateful for an activity that would divert her from her own depression. In the evening, she put her bedroll outside the new shelter to provide Big Woman with some company. Sky remained with his grandmother, and Stephen settled down a short distance away, as he had during their trip. She wanted to share her feelings with someone; they were too painful to keep inside, but she knew she could not even speak to him tonight. She wept quietly under the low-starred sky, softly at first, but finally had to muffle her sobs so the others would not hear. If Valerio were alive and Many Beads knew about it, she would have mentioned him. She did not know what she would do, now. That she was needed here, there was no question. With Big Woman and Limping Man ill, help was needed, both with their care and the work, but she was not certain she could endure it without Valerio.

Perhaps he just had not arrived yet, she tried to console herself. If it was he who had been at their house near Santa Fe, he still might come to join his family. She knew it was a narrow hope, but she clung to it. It was better than no hope at all.

She was grateful for the hard work in the cornfield the following morning. The perspiration pouring from her face prevented further tears. She and Many Beads worked in silence, helping

Stephen turn the earth, and the two boys deposited seed at proper intervals behind them. She was so engrossed in fighting the stubborn earth with her shovel that she didn't see Sky drop his seed bag and run from the field. She was unaware that he had left until she heard his cry.

"*Dine nééz!* Father! Father!"

Two riders were approaching, dragging logs with their horses, and Elspeth wiped her face to look at them. One of them might be Valerio, she thought, trying not to succumb to an illusion. Would Sky know his father at this distance after so much time? Only when one of the men dismounted nimbly and swept Sky up in his arms was she able to believe it. She picked up her skirt and ran toward him.

He was not as she remembered him. He was thin, as wiry as an Apache, and clad only in a loincloth, which revealed a large scar on his naked chest. He opened his free arm to her and held her closely against him.

"I didn't think I'd ever find you," he said, with tears staining his face. "I should laugh with joy and I weep, instead."

"With happiness," she whispered. "Oh, my darling, I thought you were . . ."

"I know. My mother told me at Fort Sumner. It made things worse," he said, with his cheek against her hair. "So many years, not knowing where you were. Searching always. You are beauty, *querida*. You are my life."

"You are beauty," she responded as she had at seventeen, "everything is beautiful again."

The coughing of his companion made him loosen his embrace to assist him. Elspeth led Limping Man's horse while Valerio supported him on its back. "He coughs blood," he said. "He has the same sickness many of the People have."

"We've made a place for him. Stephen said he and Big Woman should be separated from the others so they won't get it, too."

Stephen appeared to help them carry Limping Man to the shelter. He remained there to treat him.

"He's a doctor," Elspeth said. "He will help him."

"You came here with a white man?" Valerio asked, searching her face. "After what our people have been through, you brought a white man here?"

"They know him. He saved Surviving Boy in the camp. You must remember him."

"No," he replied grimly, withdrawing from her. "How did you come to know this man?"

She suddenly recognized the reason for Many Beads's distance, why her mother-in-law had been so wary about mentioning Valerio to her. She thought Stephen was her man; now, Valerio was struggling with the same suspicion.

"He is a friend," she assured him. "He has spent years trying to help the People. When he was at Fort Sumner, he tried to find my family for me. There are good white men, Valerio. I realize it must be difficult to believe."

He took her hand and smiled. "Forgive me, *querida*. I should have known better. You have a constant heart. There is only one woman in all the world for me."

"And only one man for me," she said.

Many Beads's attitude changed as soon as she saw them together. Without explaining her previous protection of her son, she began to display the affection that was more normal for her. Elspeth had forgotten how subtle the old woman could be. If Stephen had been Elspeth's man, her mother-in-law would have manipulated events to make them leave before Valerio returned, even if it meant the loss of her grandson. She had nearly succeeded the night before. Now, the mask slipped away, and there was only warmth and happiness in her face.

Neither of them mentioned the incident, though both recognized that the other understood.

They recounted their experiences after they finished the planting that evening. Sky sat in his father's lap and Elspeth held his hand openly. Many Beads did not consider the display of affection bad manners. Stephen listened with interest as they told their stories.

"The only happiness we had was when my sons-in-law turned themselves in," Many Beads said, "and my son followed them later. We were so happy to see them. You were right, my daughter. I was wrong. We should have searched for them."

"We were starving," Elspeth said, recognizing how little her mother-in-law had altered the true story to change its significance completely. "They had been away for so long. We would have perished from the cold if we'd tried to find them." She did not mention the Hosteen's death, which had deprived them of their only shelter. "If the shots had killed my husband, I'd have felt it."

"You've felt many things," Many Beads said. "You knew we must take shelter in the ruin when no else did, before the shots were fired. When you first came here, we were told you had this power."

The benign presence of Hosteen Yazzie could almost be felt around them. They were sitting around the fire with the ghosts of those they could not mention. She no longer sensed Maria's nearness, though. She seemed far away, now, and Elspeth missed her.

"I wouldn't be here," Valerio told Elspeth, "if my brothers-in-law had not found me. I was drawing my bow against the troops when the bullet struck. I'd have frozen in the snow if Slim Man hadn't carried me to a cave. There were still bluecoats in the area. I could not breathe." He indicated the ugly scar on his chest. "I was unconscious most of the time. I didn't even know he tried to cut the bullet out. He tried to get food to you, but you had gone. We tried to follow when I could travel and we met Limping Man, but the wound began to bleed again. They were concerned about their families, so they left me with my Pueblo friend. I was there a long time. Slim Man has now returned to his clan."

"He wouldn't have been so sick if they had sealed his wound with fire instead of cutting it," Many Beads said reasonably, and Stephen smiled. "My son came to the reservation when he was able to ride. He came alone. When we told him the soldiers had taken his wife and child at Fort Defiance, he bided his time until he could escape to find them. We didn't see him again until we came back to Dineyah. He was waiting for us." She paused to wipe her eyes, and her voice broke when she added, "It was the best thing that happened to us in four years."

"Your brother-in-law hid his trail well," Valerio told her. "My Pueblo friend found out that he'd left suddenly, deserted from the army. I knew you must be with him, but he didn't leave a trace. I began to wander without any idea where to look for you."

"You took a chance," Stephen interjected. "You would have been shot on sight if the army had spotted you."

"Without my wife and child, I had nothing to lose," Valerio said simply. Then, more cheerfully, "They put me in the metal shop at Fort Sumner. I learned a lot, and I took my tools with me. The Pueblos value silver ornaments. I can trade with them for more sheep."

Stephen smiled and glanced at Elspeth; he did not mention the duplication of the metal ration tickets.

Valerio turned to Elspeth and searched her face. "Where were you? We've spoken only of ourselves. You've said nothing, *querida*."

"It's late," she replied softly. "Sky has fallen asleep in your arms. We'll speak of it tomorrow."

"Will you walk with me?"

As he transferred his son to his mother, and they rose to leave the fire, Elspeth heard Many Beads ask Stephen, "What does that word, *querida*, mean? He has always called her that."

She smiled, wondering how he would explain the Spanish term of affection to her mother-in-law, whose language did not even contain a word for love, though the Navajo were the most affectionate people in the world.

The moon illuminated the canyon walls with silver and made dark lace of the tamarisk trees. She could no longer hear the voices on the wind that stirred the cottonwoods, the voices of those she would never see again. They walked in a loose embrace, speaking softly, and she knew they would live in harmony again. There would be no more raids; they would be poor, but they would live in peace. The Long Walk would leave a scar that would never heal completely; it would grow into a folk legend to be told by the fire on winter nights. But the Dineh drew strength from their land: they would walk in beauty again.

As if he heard her thoughts, Valerio said softly, "It will be all right. We will have hogans again soon. The water has gone underground for the summer, but the valley floor looks like a lake under the moon. We could almost swim in it as we did in that lake so long ago.''

She opened her arms to him. ''No one will see us but the stars. The People do not come out at night. If there are ghosts here, they are gentle spirits who would never harm us.''

A touch of romance... from Cordia Byers